BONDED LOVE

What Reviewers Say
About Renee Roman's Work

Where the Lies Hide

"I like the concept of the novel. The story idea is well thought out and well researched. I really connected with Cam's character..." —*Rainbow Reflections*

"[T]his book is just what I needed. There's plenty of romantic tension, intrigue, and mystery. I wanted Sarah to find her brother as much as she did, and I struggled right alongside Cam in her discoveries."—*Kissing Backwards*

"Overall, a really great novel. Well written incredible characters, an interesting investigation storyline and the perfect amount of sexy times."—*Books, Life and Everything Nice*

"This is a fire and ice romance wrapped up in an engaging crime plot that will keep you hooked."—*Istoria Lit*

Epicurean Delights

"[*Epicurean Delights*] is captivating, with delightful humor and well-placed banter taking place between the two characters. ...[T]he main characters are lovable and easily become friends we'd like to see succeed in life and in love."—*Lambda Literary Review*

Hard Body

"[T]he tenderness and heat make it a great read."—*reviewer@large*

"[A] short erotic story that has some beautiful emotional moments."—*Kitty Kat's Book Review Blog*

Visit us at www.boldstrokesbooks.com

By the Author

Epicurean Delights

Stroke of Fate

Where the Lies Hide

Bonded Love

BONDED LOVE

by

Renee Roman

2020

BONDED LOVE
© 2020 By Renee Roman. All Rights Reserved.

ISBN 13: 978-1-63555-530-1

This Trade Paperback Original Is Published By
Bold Strokes Books, Inc.
P.O. Box 249
Valley Falls, NY 12185

First Edition: June 2020

Credits
Editors: Victoria Villasenor and Cindy Cresap
Production Design: Susan Ramundo
Cover Concept By Tina Michele
Cover Design By Tammy Seidick

Acknowledgments

Many thanks to everyone who has read one of my previous books, and to those of you who are new to my works, thank you for spending time with me. Thank you all for sharing in my passion.

There aren't enough words to convey my heartfelt gratitude to my two editors, Victoria Villasenor and Cindy Cresap. Your patience and guidance are a gift beyond comparison. I look forward to every interaction with you. Thank you.

And to those who share their love with me, be certain in the knowledge it does not go unnoticed or unappreciated. I couldn't do this without you.

Dedication

To those who thought finding love was impossible…
think again.

CHAPTER ONE

"Hi, Marcus. I'll have everything set for delivery on Friday if you're ready for installation." Blaze Carter tuned out the background noise of hammers and a wet saw to hear her conversation, though they were both familiar and comforting. She circled the date on her calendar. "Great. See you then."

One more thing off her checklist of pending projects. She hadn't been this busy in a while, and she liked the constant demand to be working with her hands. It kept her mind from wandering in directions she didn't want to think about. The holidays were only a couple of months away. One more year of no one special in her life to share them with. The idea of dating wasn't all that appealing. She hadn't had a great track record in that department. Sure, she could find someone for sex, but no one she'd recently slept with sent shivers up her spine or gave her any other indication perhaps she wanted more than a casual dalliance.

Blaze ran her hand over the freshly sanded wood, pleased with the silky-smooth surface. The live edge countertop, with its natural finish and beautiful grain, wasn't the only modern touch she'd produced at the request of the interior designer her clients, Janice and Rich, had hired to turn their recent purchase into their dream home. She'd already built and whitewashed the oak cabinets, as well as the island that would be the focal point of the kitchen. The overhanging counter would accommodate four stools. With the open concept design of the main floor, entertaining would be easy. Everyone knew the kitchen was the most popular gathering place of any party, and Blaze believed it was the heart of a home. People who enjoyed cooking put their heart and soul on a plate, and nothing said home more than a family meal. Maybe that's why she'd become melancholy lately. She hadn't lived with her parents for years, and even though she saw them every now and again, she missed the warmth of those special times.

After vacuuming off the length and edges, she used a tack cloth to remove any remaining dust. The music playing in the background provided a steady rhythm as she brushed the first layer of varnish onto the contrasting surfaces in long, steady strokes. The motion was akin to how she made love to a woman. She paid attention to the details and the nuances of her lover's response to her touch. Blaze cherished seeing those beautiful moments. She liked to take her time, liked watching the results climaxing had on a woman's body. The flush of color, the moan deep in her throat, the arch of her back. Until they happened, the layers between them remained, but vanished during orgasm.

"Christ," she mumbled. It had been months since she'd sought company for a night. Obviously, she was overdue, and her body tingled in agreement. She concentrated on the wood. There'd be time later to indulge, but until then she was going to do what she did best. She'd love the wood beneath her fingertips.

Three hours later and satisfied with her work, she called it quits. During the renovations on the small warehouse she'd purchased for her business located on the outskirts of Lake George, Blaze had the foresight to include a full bathroom, anticipating there'd be times she'd be working late and not have time to go home to shower and change. The small closet held a couple of outfits and a spare pair of broken in boots.

Once the shop was locked up, she put her helmet on and righted the Harley. The vibration of the motor added to her already heightened state of arousal. She was ready. More than ready, really, but she wasn't sure what…or who…she was looking for tonight. There was only one way to find out.

❖

Trinity Greene hardly noticed the clamor around her. She scrolled through the screens of lab results on the three patients she'd been assigned. They were all in stable condition, and she was determined to make sure they stayed that way. The young man with the broken leg suffered trauma as a result of thinking he was a stunt double and was being prepped for surgery. Nothing in his pre-op bloods indicated a need to delay going to the OR. She made a note in his electronic chart, uploaded the labs, and signed off on the case. The older gentleman who'd come in complaining of chest pain would be headed to the radiology suite. With enzyme markers absent for a heart attack, the lead ED physician had decided on a preliminary diagnosis of either gallstones or an infected gall bladder. With an elevated white count, she tended to agree, though she wouldn't sign off until they were sure.

Her last patient was the most disturbing. The little girl arrived with her mother after claiming she'd climbed on a counter and fallen. The child had a mild concussion and bruises along one side of her body, which didn't contradict the explanation, but her behavior was suspicious. Whenever the mother was close, the child appeared afraid. Yet when the medical staff approached and the mother stood off to the side, the young girl seemed relieved.

A little while ago, she'd gone for X-rays and a CT scan, when the radiologist found evidence of old injuries, especially to her extremities. Trinity remained professional, but inside she seethed. She'd seen the same thing several times since she'd started working in the ED and it affected her the same way each time. She convinced the ED pediatrician to involve social services and the hospital social worker talked with the mother. Trinity hoped this time her gut was wrong. It rarely was.

Though her parents had never physically abused her or her siblings, she knew how stressed out a parent could become, especially under less than ideal circumstances. Yet another reason she'd never have children.

"Hey, what are you still doing here?" her roommate, Kelly, asked. She'd come on duty over an hour ago and was Trinity's shift replacement. After she'd given updates on the patients she was handing over, Kelly had disappeared into one of the rooms.

"Just finishing up with labs." She put a couple of comments in the system, then signed out.

"Don't you *ever* have *anywhere* else to be?"

Kelly hadn't meant to criticize, but that's what it felt like. As though Trinity didn't have a life outside of work. The sad part was, she was right. Maybe it was time she indulged in something just for her. Something that would take her away from the suffering of tonight's patients.

"I think maybe I do." She changed out of her scrubs and gathered her backpack from her locker before passing the nurses' station on the way out. "Thanks, Kell. I owe you one."

"Have some fun. Let those gorgeous red waves fly."

Trinity inhaled deeply. The night air had a hint of the coming fall. The light jacket she'd grabbed would come in handy. She slid onto the seat of her white Jeep Cherokee and willed herself to relax. She was off duty and there was nothing more to do except kick back for a little while. A beer or two sounded good after the busy twelve-hour shift. She'd pick up something to eat on the way home. Maybe she'd even run into an acquaintance and could talk about something besides work. At the very least, there'd be music and she could lose herself on the dance floor with total strangers.

CHAPTER TWO

B laze hesitated. Now that she was there, the feeling of not
wanting to settle for casual again assaulted her. Anxiety
had never been an emotion to stop her, and she shook it off. What
the hell. As long as she was there, she might as well go in. Moving
through the small gathering of women talking outside the club, she
smiled politely. Even though she knew a few by name, she didn't
feel like engaging.

She took her sunglasses off, allowing her eyes to adjust to the
darker interior, then tucked them inside her jacket and handed it and
her helmet to the coatroom clerk.

"Enjoy," said the woman in the tight T-shirt with an EroZone
logo on the front.

Blaze nodded and tucked the worn plastic number into her back
pocket, then headed for the bar, ready to chase away whatever had
her out of sorts.

The bartender, Jackie, leaned in her direction. "The usual?"
They'd done away with formalities a long time ago, saving their
energy for the women who wanted it.

"Sounds good. On ice."

Jackie quirked her head.

"I'm pacing myself."

She nodded. "Got the bike?"

Blaze laughed. "You know me too well."

"Everybody does." Jackie turned to fix her drink.

She tried not to be put off by the comment, convinced Jackie hadn't meant anything by it. Nonetheless, it stung. Did everyone think she was a superficial person without depth? Sure, she was known as a no-strings-attached woman who enjoyed another's company, but that didn't mean she lacked character. Did it? As the glass was placed in front of her, she glanced at Jackie, trying to decide if she wanted to know the truth.

"Jackie, is that how you see me?" Blaze glanced around. "How others see me?"

She leaned back. "*I* don't. It's not unusual to show up alone and not leave that way. I can't say how others see you." Jackie put her tab slip in a glass and moved on to the next customer.

The revelation did nothing to make her feel better, but she wasn't going to spend the night trying to pick it apart. It would keep for another day. She'd come here to unwind, let loose, and maybe hook up. Do exactly what was, apparently, expected of her. She leaned against a wall to watch the people dancing. The pounding rhythm traveled along her spine and settled in her pelvis, and she moved her legs to relieve the pressure that remained from earlier. Blaze sipped the smoky liquor, closed her eyes, and let the music take her away.

She took a deep breath, then another. Nothing felt right. Memories of previous encounters played in her mind. The last woman she'd been with had been on a bit of an alcohol buzz, and she questioned why she'd gone against her scruples when it came to sleeping with drunk women. The more she ruminated the more she considered maybe coming here had been a mistake. She could always take care of her own physical need. She willed her shoulders to relax and opened her eyes.

A tall blonde stood in front of her, one side of her mouth quirked into a smile. "Hi. You okay?"

"I will be."

She took a step closer. "I'm Mindy."

Mindy was a little older than Blaze, with small crow's feet that called attention to her expressive blue eyes. Definitely attractive.

Definitely looking to hook up. Her head screamed for her to politely walk away, but something in Mindy's eyes begged for understanding. She held out her hand.

"It's nice to meet you, Mindy. I'm Blaze." The long, tapered fingers ending with blunt, manicured nails slid into her hand. Mindy's grip was firm, and she held on long enough that Blaze couldn't miss the inference. Mindy let go and she finished her drink.

"Do you want another?"

Their gazes held, and her breath froze in her chest. "I'm not sure what I want." She spoke the truth. She'd never been hesitant about what she wanted, but from the moment she'd walked through the door, the evening hadn't started out in the usual way, so why should her interaction with Mindy be any different?

Mindy looked out over the crowd before facing her again. "Neither do I." Her smile wavered, appearing as tentative as Blaze felt. "But maybe I can give you what you need," Mindy said.

What she needed was to get out of there. The walls felt like they were closing in on her. She almost abandoned Mindy, but her silent plea moved Blaze into action. She reached for Mindy's hand. "Let's get out of here."

She didn't want to think about anyone noticing her departure with another woman on her arm. What difference would it make? All the single women were there for the same thing—entertainment of one type or another.

"I'd like nothing more," Mindy said.

Blaze led the way through the crowd, and they gathered their belongings. Once outside, she breathed easier in the night air.

"My apartment is just over there." Mindy pointed across the road.

She thought about her bike, but she'd be back before the bar closed. With Mindy on her right arm and her helmet hanging from her left hand, she walked toward the converted warehouse that bore a sign stating, "High-end, luxury apartments." Mindy kept up with her long strides, though how she could maneuver uneven pavement in stilettos amazed Blaze, and she laughed inwardly while wondering if Mindy would wear them to bed. She tried to envision the last person she'd lost herself with and was sobered when she couldn't remember her name. Maybe that was the reason she left without anyone most of the time over the last year. What had changed? Why was she finding it more and more difficult to enjoy the casual liaisons she once did? Mindy's voice jolted her back.

"Here we are." Mindy smiled as she unlocked the door, then led the way up to the third floor and keyed another door. Once they were inside, Mindy tossed her coat on a chair. "Can I get you anything to drink?"

"Water would be good." Blaze set her helmet on the floor and draped her jacket next to Mindy's. The fireplace was the focal point of the open floor plan, and she wished it was lit. There was a distinct chill in her bones she couldn't remember feeling earlier. Mindy must have noticed.

"Would you like me to turn on the fireplace? I wish it were real, but all the apartment buildings have gas or electric these days."

Blaze took the offered bottle. "Sure."

Mindy picked up a remote and the miniscule flame roared to life. The overhead lights dimmed as she gestured to the couch. "Everything is so convenient nowadays it's a wonder we even walk on our own anymore." Mindy stood still, looking a little lost. Maybe she was having second thoughts. She wasn't the only one.

Blaze set the unopened bottle down. "If you've changed your mind there's no hard feelings. My mood isn't the greatest tonight."

"No. It's not that." Mindy sat. "I haven't done this in a long time." She clasped her hands in her lap and looked down. "Not since my partner died four years ago."

Four years could seem like a lifetime. "Have you been intimate with anyone since?" Blaze asked.

Mindy shook her head. "No. At first, I felt guilty for even looking at another woman. Then…" Mindy's voice cracked.

Blaze took her hand and held it between hers. "Then?"

"I haven't felt very desirable. Dana made a point of telling me I was old and lucky to have her." Mindy looked up with unshed tears pooling in her eyes.

Her temper flared. *Why the hell do women do that to each other?* "I can assure you, you're very desirable." She could put aside her own feelings of angst but couldn't help wondering what had been different about tonight for Mindy, and why she'd chosen Blaze.

"You don't have to say that just to make me feel better." Mindy tried to pull away, but she held on.

"You're right. I don't." She brushed the tears away from Mindy's cheeks, then pulled her to her feet. "Show me your bedroom."

Mindy was about to protest, but Blaze silenced her with a finger to her lips. They looked into each other's eyes for a long beat before Mindy nodded and led the way down the hall. She glanced around at the neat space. Mindy must have prepared for company. Nothing looked out of place. Maybe she should find out more, but Mindy already suffered a lack of self-confidence. She didn't need to add to her insecurities by stopping to ask questions.

Blaze undressed to her sports bra and briefs, then slowly undressed Mindy with tenderness, letting her eyes roam over Mindy's body, hoping to dispel the trembling that had started the minute they'd entered her bedroom. She laid Mindy on the bed before joining her and then explored her body, kissed her gently, giving Mindy what she thought she needed. Though she knew nothing about her, she deserved to move on with her life. If a night of tenderness and connection could help, Blaze could oblige.

Late into the night, Mindy lay asleep beside her, her breathing deep and regular. Blaze slipped from beneath the covers and gathered her clothes, quietly shutting the bedroom door behind her. She found the bathroom to relieve herself, then washed up. After she was dressed, she went to the kitchen to find paper and pen and wrote a note.

Mindy,
Never doubt yourself. You're beautiful in every way. Thank you for a lovely time.
Blaze

She walked to her motorcycle as the last stragglers left the EroZone. Blaze was glad she didn't recognize any of the faces. She was done being some woman's idea of a notch on their post of conquests. Mindy certainly hadn't been a conquest. She'd been a lost soul who, perhaps, had recognized the same in Blaze, and she didn't want to be lost any longer.

The engine beneath her rumbled to life and she adjusted her clothing. She hadn't let Mindy touch her, wanting Mindy to be the focus of attention. Her own needs would have to wait a bit longer.

Chapter Three

B laze paced through the house. She'd been restless for days. "Meow."

Blaze chuckled when Baxter jumped beside her and rubbed her head against her hand. "Thought you'd come home for a late breakfast?" Baxter purred appreciatively as she scratched her head. Another cry confirmed food was what she wanted, not her absent human.

"Yeah, yeah. Let's go see what stinky meal is on the slate." Much as she loved the fur bag, she never understood why cat food had to smell so obnoxious.

Her duty with Baxter done, she made up her mind to do something other than pace. The rosebushes needed pruning and the bird feeders had been empty far too long. Once those tasks were done, Blaze glanced around at the expansive gardens and went to the shed for a shovel and pickaxe. She'd been having an ongoing conversation with herself about the lilac bush she'd been trying to save. The bush was obviously old, and there'd been one sparse bloom this spring. As much as she hated giving up on it, there was nothing more she could do. It had to go.

By the time she finished, the sun was setting and sweat streamed down her chest. The offensive bush lay in a heap of dry, rotted, twisted branches. They'd soon join the compost pile. The physical exertion felt good since she hadn't been to the gym in weeks. After storing her tools, she dragged away the limbs and stumps. Satisfied with the progress she'd made, she headed for the shower.

After she ruffled a towel over her hair and pulled on clean briefs and a bra, she stared at her reflection. "Now what?" she said out loud. There was no one to answer her. The tension she'd experienced earlier began to build again and she threw her hands up in defeat. "Fuck it."

She wore her favorite leather pants and a slate gray T-shirt. On the way out the door, she picked up her wallet and grabbed her leather jacket from the hook. The minute she stepped onto the porch, her shoulders relaxed a bit, and she took the time to clear her muddled mind. Blaze trotted down the steps, then headed for the garage. She slid a leg over her bike, sighing as she pulled on her helmet. The weather was perfect for an evening ride. It would help her let go of the doubt she'd been stressing over. It wasn't like her to feel sorry for herself, and she didn't understand why she was letting questions of her future take up so much mental space.

On autopilot, Blaze made her way onto the hard-packed dirt road that led away from her house and down to the paved county route. She took the familiar curves at her usual pace; emotional turmoil wasn't a reason for being careless. Without a clear destination, Blaze let the bike determine where she went. Before long, she found herself on the Northway, and nearing the town of Queensbury, known for its shopping outlets. Blaze wasn't in the mood for browsing, but a good cup of coffee and a slice of homemade pie might help sweeten her mood. With her target location less than two miles away, she signaled for the next exit, and decelerated as she took the curve to the stop light. She was feeling a little better, glad to have gotten out of her own head.

The light turned green, and she eased open the throttle to start her left-hand turn. The screech of nearby brakes made her look over her shoulder just in time to see the red muscle car almost on top of her. She gunned the motor to get out of the way, but the grind of metal and the jarring impact felt like she'd run into a brick wall, ending her hope of escaping a collision. She let go of the handlebars and tried to launch herself toward a grassy area on her right, but her trajectory was wrong. The sky filled her vision as she fought to remember the collision rules she'd learned a long time ago.

Something about going limp, rolling… She saw trees getting closer, then felt something snap when she slammed into a tree and then hit the ground, the air was stolen from her lungs before the darkness closed in.

❖

Through a murky haze, like being deep underwater, Blaze was aware of discomfort in her chest. She went to swat it away, but strong hands held her down.

"Hey, can you hear me?" A male voice came from above her head.

She fought to focus. Her helmet was on and her visor open. "Yeah." It was hardly more than a whisper and she tried again. "Yes."

"Good. That's good. What's your name?"

She looked to her left. Someone had cut open the sleeve of her jacket. An IV line ran to bags of fluid held by another person. She looked to her right. Something about her arm was wrong, but she couldn't figure out what. The guy above her tapped her sternum to get her attention. It worked.

"What's your name?" an EMT asked again.

"Blaze. Blaze Carter."

"Blaze, you've been in an accident. We're going to transport you to the hospital. Hang in there. We're going to give you something for the pain before we move you."

She wanted to tell him no drugs because she hated the way they made her feel, but it was too late as the cold medication ran up her arm and into her bloodstream. A cervical collar was put in place as her helmet was removed. It was as though she were watching everything happening from outside of her body. But when they slid a backboard under her and tightened the straps, she let out a groan.

"Almost done. You're doing great, Blaze." This time it was a female voice talking in her ear, reassuring her.

"Bike," Blaze said, needing to focus on something else.

"Why is it riders always think about their bike?"

Another male voice from somewhere near her legs responded. "You can't understand unless you ride."

The woman gently tapped her left shoulder. "It might be repairable."

She nodded and a hot poker of pain shot down her neck and through her right arm. She held her breath until it passed.

"Hey now. Not breathing isn't allowed on my watch."

Blaze took a breath. "Arm…right."

"It's the only injury we've found so far, but the hospital will do a thorough exam."

She needed to know more, but the drugs made her feel disconnected and unable to form a complete thought. An oxygen mask was placed over her nose and mouth.

"There could be internal damage. You were tossed a long way from the scene."

"Not tossed. Jumped," she said into the mask. One of the EMTs lifted it up and she repeated herself.

"Why?" the woman asked as she took her blood pressure. The guy at her head moved the mask up to expose her mouth.

"Didn't want to get trapped. Big bike." Her eyelids felt like lead. She fought against the meds, the discomfort, the pain. She would not surrender her control.

"Smart. It probably saved your life." Another guy snaked his hand inside her waistband. "I'm checking for a pulse in your legs. Sorry." He pressed his fingers against her groin, first one side then the other. "Positive on both sides." The sirens ended. "Okay. We're here." Machines were tossed onto the gurney with her as the back doors flew open.

"What have we got?"

She gave in to the fatigue, knowing soon enough she'd be handled by a whole medical team. *Damn.* They were going to cut off her leathers. Blaze tried to focus on the gurney moving down the hallway, but bright lights stabbed her eyes and she kept them closed. Curtains whisked along a track and the gurney stopped, and she was moved onto a stretcher. A person in scrubs and a mask leaned over her.

"Blaze, I'm Dr. Rhonda Gaines. There's going to be a lot happening around you while we assess your injuries."

"Mask off." Blaze struggled to get the words out.

The mask rose above her face a few inches. "Again?"

"Mask off. Don't need it." She wasn't sure, but she could have sworn the doctor pursed her lips.

"Somebody get her a cannula." She studied Blaze. "Humor me."

The mask didn't return. Short plastic tubes in her nostrils took its place and the ends wound behind her ears. At least she could talk.

"Did you lose consciousness?" someone asked.

"Yeah." She didn't know why she'd blacked out, but it would be foolish to lie. "Not sure how long."

A familiar voice from the ambulance spoke up. "Best estimate we have is less than five minutes. Witnesses said she was groaning shortly after she landed in the trees."

"Okay. CT of her head, chest, and abdomen. I want an MRI of that arm, with and without contrast. Let's keep her sedated while we work."

She grabbed for the doctor with her working hand. "No. Hate the feeling."

Dr. Gaines sighed. "Listen, tough guy, I run the show here. We're going to be moving you around a lot and your arm is severely injured." She patted Blaze's hand. "Let's work together. We'll go with light sedation, but if you need more you tell someone. Got it?"

Compromise was something she could work with, so she agreed. She felt the medication kick in, but not as much as the first time. She was moving again. The lights, the voices. Everything at once and none of it made sense. As much as she didn't want to, Blaze gave in. She was too exhausted to keep the bravado up. There was something in the words she'd heard that should have upset her, but she couldn't quite make sense of it. She drifted off, oblivious to the chaos around her.

❖

Annoying. That's the first thought that came into Blaze's head as she began to surface from her drug-induced sleep, hating not knowing how much time had passed and irritated by the rhythmic beeps too close to her ear. She tried to swat at whatever was poking her shoulder, but her arm was heavy and wouldn't move. When she tightened her right bicep, pain shot up her neck and she groaned. She no longer felt the collar.

"Try not to move around, Ms. Carter. Okay?"

She didn't recognize the soft, reassuring voice. She pushed through the thick layer of cotton in her head until she could open her eyes all the way. The first thing she noticed was wavy auburn hair, followed by expressive green eyes. The greenest she'd ever seen, and she was beautiful.

"Are you in pain?"

"Only when I move." She tried to smile, but even the small movement stole what little comfort she'd been in. The woman came closer, placing a hand on her arm.

"I'm Trinity, one of the ED nurses. I'm going to give you something to help you relax."

She started to protest.

"Ms. Carter, I know you don't like pain medication. The doctor ordered a sedative to take the edge off because your body is already traumatized. You need to stay still and relax, and the medication will help you do that. Okay?"

Blaze needed to ask about her injuries and when Trinity approached with a syringe, she found her voice. "Before you give me that tell me about the damage."

Trinity set the medication on the tray. "You've had blood work and scans. The orthopedic surgeon will be in to talk with you soon." She adjusted her IV line, pushed the medication, and straightened Blaze's pillow.

"I know my arm is broken, but why a surgeon? What's wrong with it?"

Gaze diverted, Trinity avoided the question and Blaze's unease grew. "I don't have that answer. I'm not the doctor. I can only tell you the surgeon needs to discuss options with you."

Blaze wanted to tell her she was well aware that nurses, especially those in emergency medicine, knew more than they were allowed to say, but when she tried to talk again she had no saliva, and she ended up licking at her lips with a dry tongue. "Water," she croaked.

Trinity finally met her gaze. "I'm sorry. You can't have anything, but I can wet your lips and tongue if you like."

Blaze nodded, knowing she didn't have much choice. She opened her mouth and Trinity gently swabbed her tongue, then her lips. The cool wet gave her a sense of being refreshed even if there hadn't been enough for her to swallow. She watched Trinity's face for some indication of what she wasn't saying, but her professional mask was firmly in place. What she didn't miss was the sorrow in her eyes and she understood whatever her injury, it wasn't good.

Just then, a figure whipped through the curtains, trailed by another person with a clipboard. He moved up next to her as Trinity stepped back. "Ms. Carter, I'm Dr. Jonas, with ortho. We have a decision to make."

"About my arm?"

"Yes." He looked slightly annoyed. "I take it no one's talked with you about the injury?"

"No, but I know it's broken." She'd guessed that the minute she came to, remembering the pain from a broken leg she had in high school when she'd been a bit too aggressive on the soccer field.

His features softened. "It's more than broken, though the break is clean, which is good. There's a compound fracture and the bone has come through your forearm. I'm hopeful there's not a lot of nerve damage, but we don't know how affected your movement will be."

Blaze felt her stomach lurch though it was empty. "No. It can't be." Her voice cracked.

"I know this must be upsetting, but from what the paramedics wrote, you landed with your arm under you, though we haven't found any other injuries. It could have been much worse." He gave her a small smile.

She didn't want to cry. Not in front of people she didn't know. "You don't understand. I'm a carpenter. My arms...my hands... they're my life."

"I see. Then you need to listen closely because this is a decision only you can make. I need to go in and realign the bones, repair tendons and muscles if necessary, and close the wound. What I want to know is do I aim for function or strength during surgery?"

"Both." She needed both. How was that a choice? She had to rely on her ability to be delicate with the wood when carving and the strength to mold it into any shape she desired. It would be the only acceptable outcome.

"That would be optimal, but when I get in there to assess the damage, I may have to choose one or the other, so I need to know your preference."

Preference? They weren't talking about a car color or a brand of running shoes. This was her fucking life. She gathered the inner fortitude she always relied on to get her through difficult times.

Blaze met his steady gaze, recognizing the intelligence in them, and she trusted what she saw there, knowing he'd do his best. "Function. If it's an either/or choice, I want full use. If you can't guarantee the strength part, I'll work on getting stronger on my own."

Dr. Jonas kept eye contact with her as she watched him weighing possible outcomes. "Right. So, this is my surgical nurse. She's got consent forms for you to sign. I take it you're right-handed?"

Blaze swallowed the bile that rose to burn her throat and she choked it away. "Yes."

"So, you'll scribble with your left and she'll witness it. A formality."

She turned away as she struggled to comprehend what her injury might mean, glad she was no longer in a fog.

"Ms. Carter..." Dr. Jonas said.

"It's Blaze. I'm trusting you to put me back together, so first-name basis."

He smiled at her then. "Rick. I'm going to do my very best."

She stared at him for a minute. "I don't suspect you'd ever do anything less."

He squeezed her uninjured shoulder. "Sign the forms. I'll meet you in the OR in a little while."

After she'd signed the required papers, Trinity came back in to ask if she was up to talking with the police. They told her the guy behind the wheel was drunk and facing a slew of charges. She was grateful for the witnesses who had come forward in her defense, giving their version of what happened. It helped knowing she remembered details with a degree of clarity, but it did nothing to make her feel better about heading into a surgery that could end her career. Then what would she do? What were her options if she couldn't do what she loved? What her father and grandfather had taught her with patience and understanding?

She wanted to hear her father's voice. He'd always given her the encouragement she needed to tackle the hardest challenges in her life, like when she came out at school and had been bullied by a few of the girls and some of the boys. He'd taught her how to be mentally tough, then he'd taught her a killer right hook. Blaze glanced around at the monitors and equipment surrounding her bed. She was trying hard not to move too much, but she was stubborn, and determined to find her cell phone. Unfortunately, she got caught.

"What do you think you're doing?"

Blaze froze in her half-raised position. Trinity stood near the foot of her bed, fists on her curvy hips. *Even pissed, she's sexy as hell...maybe more so.* "Oh, hi. You wouldn't happen to know if they found my cell phone, do you?" She forced a smile as she eased back against the stretcher.

"Your phone? Who do you want to call?"

She wasn't going to be belittled for wanting her parent. "My father."

Trinity's arms dropped to her sides; her features softened. "I'm so sorry. I never thought to ask if anyone had been notified about your accident. When the EMTs told me a motorcycle accident victim was heading in, I..." She pressed her lips together, though her face remained unreadable.

"You what?"

"My job was to make sure you were medically stable, and I didn't think beyond that." Trinity turned to the small table in the corner and opened the drawer. She pulled out a clear bag with a label on it and brought it to her. "This is everything the first responders found near the accident scene or on your person."

The label stated her name, date of birth, and admission date. On a separate line was a string of numbers she assumed stood for her medical record. The bag held her cell, wallet, money, and watch. Trinity opened the bag and set it on her lap. Blaze reached in and prayed her phone had survived. It had been in the front left pocket of her jacket. After she pressed a button and swiped the screen, the background lit up. There was a small crack in the corner of the glass cover, but otherwise it appeared to be fine. She sighed with relief.

"Thank you."

Trinity nodded. Her mouth opened, then shut. "I'll come back in a few and get you ready for surgery."

Blaze wanted to know why Trinity looked so concerned, but if she was going to be knocked out for a while, she had to make the call now. She took a breath, then pressed the contact. Her father's gravelly voice instantly comforted her.

"Hello?"

"Hi, Pop." She heard her mother then, and the sound of bedsprings. *Shit.* She pulled the phone away long enough to look at the time. It was almost midnight. Her parents would have been in bed for a while.

"What's wrong?"

She thought about making an excuse, but they'd pin her ears back if she did. "I'm all right. I had an accident earlier. On my bike."

"Where are you?"

Blaze checked her patient bracelet to be sure. "Glens Falls Hospital." Guilt overwhelmed her. Even though hearing her father's voice was just what she needed, her parents were older, and she didn't want them driving in a panic in the middle of the night to reach her. "Don't come till morning, Pop. I'm heading to surgery and…" The words were out before she could stop them, and she cringed. She really needed to censor herself in situations like this.

"We're leaving in a few minutes."

"Pop, slow down. You don't have to—"

"You're not trying to tell me what to do, are you?"

This was one battle she wasn't going to win. When her father set his mind to something it was a done deal. Just like her. "No."

"I didn't think so. Surgery on what?"

"My arm. It's pretty bad." She glanced at the oversized bandage. Part of her wished she could see it. The other part—the sensible one—was grateful she couldn't. Her father's voice roused her from wondering how bad her injury really was.

"Blaze, you'll be okay. You're made from tough stock."

"Thanks, Pop. You're the one person I can always count on to keep things in perspective." Trinity stepped into the curtained space and began pulling items from cabinets. "I have to go."

"We'll be there when you wake up. Josh came rolling home yesterday. I'll have him drive."

"Yeah, that's good."

"I love you, Blaze," her father said.

She closed her eyes against the sting. "I love you, too." After disconnecting, she tossed her phone back in the bag and zipped it the best she could. "Would you mind holding on to this until my folks arrive?"

Trinity glanced between her and the bag. "I'll make sure they get it." She took it and stuffed it into a pocket on the leg of her scrubs, then went to the hand sanitizer before putting on a pair of gloves. "I'm going to add another line to your arm for sedation and medication." She tore open an alcohol pad and placed it on a square of gauze, then palpated the top of her hand. "You have great veins, so I shouldn't have any problems."

Blaze watched Trinity efficiently place a second IV line.

"I'm sorry for the extra stick." Trinity cleaned up the trash around her and brought back two syringes. "These are fast acting sedatives. One will make you very groggy but coherent and the other will put you under. The anesthesiologist will administer them when she gets here."

A few minutes later, the anesthesiologist entered the room with a binder in her hand. "Time to review your medical history, Ms. Carter."

Blaze sighed. She wished everyone would stop calling her Ms. Carter. She wished for a lot of things. She didn't want anyone else in control of her life. The drunk driver had already interfered enough. All she could do was pray to the universe and trust that everything in her world would right itself again.

CHAPTER FOUR

Trinity sat at the nurses' station, catching up on notes and checking the monitors for any concerning readouts. She paused when she pulled up the electronic chart for the patient in trauma two, wondering why she looked so familiar. Then it hit her. She'd seen her at EroZone a few weeks ago.

Carter, Blaze. Female. 38-year-old. Compound fracture of right radius.

The summary went on to include other details, and while necessary, they hadn't been what caught her attention when she'd walked into the bay. Confused but conscious, the woman on the stretcher was covered in leather. Her tussled hair gave her a sexy appeal, and the slate gray eyes were bright with pain.

Nothing in her training had prepared her for seeing someone from the local lesbian club, lying exposed and vulnerable. As unprofessional as her thoughts were, she couldn't help wondering about her.

That night at the bar, the sexy butch she now knew as Blaze had been alone, her eyes closed as she leaned against the wall. She'd thought about approaching her, but the opportunity had been lost when she'd left with another woman, a motorcycle helmet in her hand. She wished she hadn't hesitated. Though if she had, treating her would have been awkward and she didn't want personal feelings to get in the way of doing her job. Especially if they'd hooked up and it hadn't gone well. Being a hunk didn't guarantee she'd be good in bed.

The anesthesiologist exited the treatment room and Trinity came to attention. "All set?"

"Yeah. I have the consents and I've given Ms. Carter her first injection. I want to make sure Dr. Jonas is ready for her before we take her down."

"Thanks." Trinity wanted to see Blaze one more time before she headed into surgery. After all, she was responsible for seeing the patient remained medically stable prior to going to the OR. She stood at the foot of her bed, watching the steady rise and fall of her chest, her eyes closed. For the first time since her arrival, Blaze's face was relaxed, without worry. The curtain was whisked back along the rail, setting her into action, and she began to unplug monitors.

"Okay. Let's get her moving." The anesthesiology nurse transferred IV bags to the pole affixed to the stretcher, then took off the brakes. Trinity did the same on the opposite side. "Hey, you okay?"

Trinity nodded.

"Do you know her?"

"Not really. I've seen her around, but we were never introduced." She wasn't sure how to explain her interest. "It's hard knowing she's here because of a drunk driver." The excuse was plausible, but her concern was deeper than usual.

"I know what you mean. We'll take good care of her."

She watched them move down the hall toward the elevator and couldn't help worrying about the outcome. She needed to disconnect. They'd barely interacted, and her behavior was out of character. When Blaze had made her phone call, Trinity could tell she was close to her family. A much closer relationship than she had with her own parents, certainly. Her fingertips brushed against her pocket, making contact with Blaze's belongings. With any luck, she'd get to meet Mr. and Mrs. Carter, and she looked forward to the prospect of learning more about Blaze. On a professional level, of course.

Trinity returned to the station, determined to focus. The screens revealed nothing remarkable for the patients still waiting to be admitted. She was about to fix a cup of coffee when she felt her pocket vibrate. Her own phone was sitting on the counter, so it had to be Blaze's cell. She hesitated. If it was Blaze's parents, she could at least let them know she was in surgery. She pulled the cell out of the bag and swiped the screen, hoping it wasn't locked.

"Hello?"

"Jesus. It's about time you answered, I've been trying all day..." The person on the other end paused. "Blaze?"

"No. This is Trinity. Can I ask who's calling?"

"It's DJ. Is Blaze there?"

"I'm sorry, she can't come to the phone right now." She didn't have the right to tell anyone outside family where Blaze was, or what had happened.

DJ sighed. "Can you tell her to call me when she's done doing whatever, or whoever, she's doing?"

"Okay."

"Thanks."

Trinity shook her head and slid the cell back in the bag. She needed coffee. Pronto.

❖

"Mr. and Mrs. Carter, I'm Trinity Greene, one of the trauma nurses." She held out her hand. *She has her father's eyes.* Mr. Carter shook her hand.

Mrs. Carter took her hand in both of hers. "I'm Millie. Do you know how she is?" she asked. She looked fragile and worried, as any loving mother would.

"Let's go to the family waiting room. We can talk there."

They hesitated. "Our son, Josh, went to park the car. We should wait for him."

Just then, a near carbon copy of Blaze Carter strode energetically toward them. He was younger than his sister, but he could almost have passed as Blaze's twin, though his eyes matched his mother's, the darkest blue she'd ever seen. They were a handsome family.

"Hi. What's the news?" He wrapped his arm protectively around his mother's shoulder.

"Josh, this is Trinity. She's been taking care of your sister."

She shook his hand. "I see the resemblance." She gestured for them to follow her to a small waiting area and sat away from others who were talking quietly. "I don't have any news about the outcome of her surgery because they're still in the OR."

The family exchanged concerned glances. "Isn't that a long time? It took us a few hours to get here. Shouldn't they be done by now?" Mr. Carter asked. The tone of his voice spoke volumes about how much he loved his daughter.

"What did she tell you about her injuries?" She didn't want to breach patient confidentiality laws, but if Blaze had told them even a little, she would be okay explaining more.

"Just that her arm was broken, and she needed surgery." He looked down for a minute. "And she thought it was pretty bad."

Trinity nodded. "She suffered a compound open fracture of her forearm. The radius." She pointed to the bone. "It was broken here and here and sticking though the skin here." Mrs. Carter visibly paled and she tried to reassure them. "I know it sounds horrible, but considering she was on a motorcycle, it's amazing that's her only injury, aside from some minor scrapes and bruises." She tried to think of a positive spin on the news. "Luckily, she was wearing a helmet and riding leathers."

Josh nodded. "She's constantly telling me to not be stupid and to wear the right gear. I always waved her off." A visible chill shook his body. "I'll make sure I do from now on." His mother patted his leg.

"Can I get you anything to eat or drink while you wait?" It was the only comfort she could offer without having more information.

Mr. Carter stood. "You've been more than kind. I'll go get us some things, if you show me where I can find them. I'm sure you're busy." He let her lead the way. Once they were out of hearing range of his wife and son, he asked her to wait. "I need to know if there's more to Blaze's injuries other than what you've told us. Just between you and me, without all the rules and regulations keeping you from saying."

"None that I'm aware of, Mr. Carter." Trinity wondered if she should share her personal opinion about the severity of the break. She'd seen a lot of compound fractures in the ED. Some had good outcomes. Others left the individual with a barely functioning appendage. She wasn't sure why she felt the way she did. Caring about her patients came naturally and always had. But in Blaze's case, her injury and the look of devastation in her eyes when she talked with the surgeon, brought out a higher level of empathy. If Trinity could no longer do nursing, she wondered if she'd handle the news with the same degree of courage Blaze had shown.

"Please call me Paul, and thank you. I know it's too soon to know how much use she'll regain, but we're all praying for the best."

"So am I." She went to shove her hands in her pockets and pulled out the bag. "Blaze wanted me to hold this until you arrived." Trinity handed it over. "I answered a call from someone named DJ. I thought it might be you or your wife. I didn't tell her where Blaze was, just that she couldn't come to the phone."

Paul took the bag and nodded. "She's Blaze's best friend. I'll call her as soon as we know more. Thank you for everything. Especially for looking after Blaze." He walked down the hall, caressing the bag, and she could only imagine he wished he could touch his daughter instead.

The nearby alarm on the nurses' station warned her of an incoming ambulance. *Shit.* Coffee would have to wait. She hurried back to the monitors and checked the readout for the arriving patient. While she did, she opened the small fridge under the counter and grabbed a caffeinated cold brew coffee. She downed half before heading to triage bay one to prep it. Staff began to appear, and every single member of the team did their part while waiting for the arrival of yet another emergency. In the back of her mind questions remained. How was Blaze doing and how well was surgery going?

Chapter Five

B laze coughed. Her throat was sore and her chest felt heavy. She was pretty comfortable, but for some reason she couldn't move. A familiar hand lightly gripped hers.

"Blaze, it's Pop."

She fought to open her eyes. The sight of her father was like a balm to her soul. She squeezed back. "Hi." It came out in a harsh rasp and she winced. Her throat felt like a raw piece of meat, but she wanted to talk to him, and needed to find out how her surgery went. She moved her hand to her throat and that's when she saw her arm in traction above her head.

"Let me get your nurse." He went out to the hallway and came back in with Trinity trailing behind.

"I'm glad to see you're awake." Her face revealed nothing. "Are you in pain?"

She shook her head, still not believing how an evening ride had gone so terribly wrong.

Trinity took her stethoscope and listened to her chest, then lightly pressed it to the top of the hand suspended in the air. She moved to the cuff around Blaze's left arm and took her blood pressure. Everything must have been okay because she hung the stethoscope back around her neck and offered a shy smile.

"I think she's thirsty."

Her father had stayed quiet through the exam, but he'd always been her champion and she loved him for his caring nature. Blaze nodded.

Trinity pulled her chart from the end of the bed. "Well, the good news is there's no PO restrictions, so you're in the clear. I'll be right back." Trinity turned to her father. "Would you like anything? We have juice, diet ginger ale, and chocolate milk."

"If you don't mind, ginger ale would be good."

It wasn't long before she returned. "Here you go." Trinity handed over the ginger ale, then pulled the hospital table to the side of her bed. "I brought water and juice for you until your stomach settles. Anesthesia is sneaky sometimes."

She wasn't about to argue. Trinity filled two cups halfway and she reached for the water.

"Small sips, okay?"

Blaze would do just about anything to get rid of the pain in her throat. It hurt when she swallowed, but it was cold and felt good at the same time. After she'd emptied the cup, she was ready to talk. "What time is it?"

Trinity checked her watch. "A little after eight a.m. Why?"

"Aren't you supposed to be off duty by now?" She wasn't sure, but she thought the overnight shift ended at seven.

"I'm not on the clock." Trinity looked at the floor, breaking their connection. She took a breath and glanced up. "I stayed to see how you're doing."

Her father cleared his throat. "I'm going to find your mom and Josh. Let them know you're awake." He winked at her. He was giving her and Trinity a few minutes of privacy.

"Okay, Pop." Once he was gone, she turned her attention back to Trinity. "It was nice of you to stay. I'm okay."

Trinity straightened as though offended. "It's my routine to check on patients who are admitted from the ED at the end of my shift."

Blaze's heart sank a little. She was disappointed the only reason Trinity was there was her sense of duty. There was something about her, something sweet and intriguing. But she wasn't about to cross a line. "I appreciate your concern, but there's a team here to do that. I want to talk with Dr. Jonas. Do you know—"

The door swung open and DJ stormed in. "For Christ's sake, this place is like Fort Knox. Do you know what I had to go through to get in? And not a minute before eight o'clock." It took her till then to realize Blaze wasn't alone in the room. DJ looked between her and Trinity. At least she had the wherewithal to stop ranting. "Are you her nurse?"

Trinity didn't hesitate to respond. "All the medical staff here are responsible for Ms. Carter's care. And yes, I'm a nurse."

DJ huffed. "Well, that's great but someone needs to fix the visitor policy."

"Are you family?"

DJ pursed her lips before she answered. "No, but I may as well be."

"You can lodge a complaint with the administration." Trinity turned back to face Blaze, effectively dismissing DJ altogether, though DJ wasn't someone who was easily dismissed.

"I found out from your father you've been here since last night. I tried to reach you for hours, then the person who answered told me you couldn't come to the phone."

"That was me."

DJ shot a hot glare in Trinity's direction. "Useful. Thanks."

Blaze focused on Trinity, whose eyes softened when they connected with her. "It happened after you gave me your phone. I thought it might be your parents. I'm sorry I couldn't tell her anything more. Hospital policy."

"It's okay. I appreciate you answering the call."

Always the drama queen, she knew DJ wouldn't let the subject drop and decided to play referee. "Would you mind giving us some time?"

"Of course," Trinity said, her tone curt but professional. "I'll see if Dr. Jonas is making rounds." She smiled sweetly at DJ, then refilled Blaze's cup, before quietly shutting the door behind her.

Blaze took another drink. Her throat was still scratchy but better. "Was that really necessary?"

DJ sat in the chair next to her bed. "I don't know what you mean. I don't think she should be answering your phone."

She didn't have the energy for DJ's antics today. "Enough. Either you're here to see me or to bitch about the staff. If it's the latter, you can leave. I have enough on my mind without playing mediator." This was DJ's way of showing her support. She was well aware DJ's demeanor could rub people the wrong way, but she was the one friend Blaze could always count on.

DJ had the decency to look chagrined. "You're right. How are you feeling?"

"Considering I was airborne last night, pretty good." She wanted her arm down, though she was grateful she still had one. She reached around on the bed, trying to find the call button. At least she could give DJ something to do. "Can you get me a nurse? I need to go to the restroom."

DJ reached beside her bed and held up a urine bag. "Go whenever you want. Instant bedpan." She reclipped the bag to her rail.

Maybe she didn't have to go at all. Maybe it was just the irritation of a catheter that made her think she did. The thought of anything unnatural in her body made her cringe. She wanted out of here as soon as possible. "Great." Her stomach growled, then she passed gas. Loudly.

"My, my. All your orifices are awake this morning."

Her face heated. Of all the situations she'd been in, her current one was the most humiliating. "Sorry."

DJ waved her off. "Let's do a recap. You had an accident, landed here, had surgery, and have someone willing to play secretary for you as well as a nursemaid. Does that sum it up?"

"Apart from the flying through the air with the greatest of ease, pretty much. Except Trinity isn't a floor nurse. She's an ED nurse. She took care of me last night and then stayed after her shift to check on my post-op condition."

DJ's expression softened. "That was nice of her, but I don't think it's standard policy. I just want to know you're getting the care you need." Her eyes glistened with tears, although she'd never let them fall in public.

Even though Blaze was still annoyed with her, she was glad to see her. "Can we get back to me for a minute? I could use your help with a few things." She didn't want to sound ungrateful, but there were times during their friendship when DJ pushed her buttons.

DJ pulled out her phone and stylus. "Ready."

"I need you to stop by my house and feed Baxter. I'm not sure what my folks have planned. If they're hanging around for a few days, they can stay at my place and see to her, but one less thing for me to worry about is a blessing right now."

"That I can do. What else?" She looked around. "I can bring food, or smuggle in something you're not supposed to have, so what will it be?"

"Nothing until I know the game plan. It's not like I can go anywhere. Put my porch light on and pick up some groceries for the fridge. Milk, bread, eggs. You know, the usual stuff." She loved DJ, but her tolerance level for sitting still was almost nonexistent, just like Blaze's recent love life. "You go ahead. Drop by the family room and say high to my folks. I know they'd love to see you."

Without protest, DJ kissed her cheek and left. The whirlwind of chaos that seemed to follow DJ went with her, and Blaze took a calming breath, wondering about her future and how fate had stepped in to derail any immediate plans.

A few hours later, Blaze picked at her food. It wasn't horrible, but her appetite had waned after talking with Dr. Jonas. While he was optimistic about the repairs and praised her for having strong bones and well-developed muscles, her recovery would be a waiting game. Over the next few days, he would assess when she would start physical therapy, followed by occupational therapy, if needed. He wouldn't give her odds on having a fully functional arm, professing it was just too soon and every person was different. She got that. It didn't make her feel any better.

The good news was she could have her arm lowered in twenty-four hours, giving her more mobility, then they would talk about her discharge. She was going to have a long road ahead of her and she had to get her head in the right frame of mind.

Blaze had sent her family to her place for the night. She'd professed exhaustion to get her parents to agree, and to stop her mother from doting on her. Josh had spent his time trying to keep her spirits up, joking about childhood antics with phrases like "Remember when…" She loved him, but his high energy grated on her nerves at times and today was one.

Blaze pushed the tray away. She wanted to be up and walking. She'd never been a person to be idle for long periods of time. The last twenty-four hours had been the longest day she'd ever lain in a bed for a stretch, including the times she had a woman beside her, and since there wasn't anyone to keep her company, Blaze was determined to be moving on her own. After studying the contraption that held her limb aloft, she was fairly confident she could unhook it and get up under her own power. *Shit.* She'd forgotten about the catheter still in place. The damn thing was irritating as hell, and just one more thing keeping her hostage. It needed to be gone. *Maybe if I pull really slow it won't hurt too bad.*

She flipped back her covers, tugged at the edge of the ridiculous hospital gown, and tried to see where the tube ran. She didn't want her pee shooting all over when she got the damn thing out. She glanced around the tray and nightstand, hoping someone had inadvertently left a clamp lying around.

"I would have thought you knew what you looked like down there by now." Trinity stood with her hip cocked, arms crossed, and a smirk on her face.

Her head snapped up at the same time she flicked the gown back down. She'd been caught…again, and it was going to be hard to talk her way out of this one, so she opted for the truth. "I want this out." She pointed to the rubber tubing running along the inside of her leg.

"And you were going to do what, exactly?" Trinity came to the side of her bed. When she spoke, her eyebrow rose as if she were trying to figure out the logistics.

"Pull it out very slowly?"

Trinity's eyes hardened. "Wrong. You need someone with experience to remove it so that you don't tear the urethra." She went to the supply cabinet and gathered items, then brought them to the bed, placing them between Blaze's knees on another pad. After yanking a pair of rubber gloves from the rack, she turned as she pulled them on. "Lucky for you I have a lot of experience." Trinity snapped the cuff of a glove and sashayed back to where she lay.

"Uh…" She glanced at her call button. Maybe she should get reinforcements. After all, DJ had been rude and Blaze imagined this would be the perfect opportunity to get back at her. Trinity could make the experience a lot more uncomfortable than it might be with someone neutral. She went for the less obvious reason for begging off. "Aren't you usually in the ED?"

"Yes, but I've got plenty of time." Trinity shared a knowing smile. She wasn't going to get rid of her that easily. "You want the catheter out, right?"

She swallowed, admitting if only to herself, nothing should stay inside her for that long. "Yeah." Her voice betrayed her lack of confidence.

"Ms. Carter—"

"It's Blaze." If this woman was going to be between her legs, she definitely didn't want to be thinking of her mother.

"Blaze, I'm not going to hurt you. It will be uncomfortable for a minute, but it will be over quick. Okay?"

Knowing she didn't have much choice, she nodded. If Trinity was offering, wouldn't it be better to show she trusted her? She didn't really have a good excuse not to, other than wishing the hot nurse was between her legs for a whole different reason. "Okay."

"Good. I'll let you know everything I'm doing. Try to relax." Trinity pulled the curtain around her bed before adjusting her gown.

She focused on breathing and keeping her body from tensing. After the bed was adjusted, Trinity emptied her urine bag and changed her gloves again. She unclipped the part attached to her leg, then attached an empty syringe to the extra branch.

"This is why you can't remove it on your own," Trinity said as she pulled back the plunger. "There's a balloon near the tip that's filled with saline to keep it in place. If you tried to pull it out without deflating it, you could rupture your urethra. That would have been extremely painful and a source for infection." She looked up. "I'm going to remove the catheter now. There shouldn't be any pain, only pressure, so tell me right away if it hurts. Try to relax your muscles and breathe deep. Ready?"

Blaze concentrated on Trinity's confident, soothing voice. She could do this. She closed her eyes when she felt gentle fingers spread her folds, then a little pressure.

"All done." Trinity removed the tape from her leg.

"Already?" She wasn't sure what she'd expected, but now that it was over, she couldn't wait to get out of bed.

Trinity wrapped the tubing and other items in the pad and tossed them in the trash. "I told you I had a lot of experience."

Blaze was unsure if her choice of words were meant to be an innuendo. More than likely it was wishful thinking on her part. "So, I can get up now. How do we do this?"

"You don't. Traction stays in place until tomorrow, so it's the bedpan until then."

Her groan was followed by Trinity's stern expression. Maybe she should have left the damn thing in. She would have to use charm to get her way. "Can't I just hold it up? I really want to move."

"No. Do you want the bedpan or not?" Trinity seemed to be losing her patience.

She'd damn well hold it and wait for another staff member. Trinity was acting like she'd done her a favor. "Thanks, but no. I wanted to get up, so I may as well stay put."

Trinity's face pinked. She was about to say something, but the whirling dervish blew into the room carrying a tray with two coffee cups. She stopped short.

"Do you sleep here?" DJ asked.

"DJ," she said, her tone a warning.

Trinity's color darkened. "I was just leaving." She stared hard at DJ before moving toward the door. "I'm glad you're feeling better," she said over her shoulder before disappearing.

"Doesn't Nurse Nightingale have other patients? Why is she always here?" DJ asked. She set the tray on her table and plopped into the chair, a canvas bag clutched on her lap. "Baxter screamed for twenty minutes yesterday. I stayed long enough to feed her and give her a few pets." She removed the cups and dropped the tray into the trash. She went to flip back the sip opening and paused. "Please tell me you can have coffee."

Blaze nodded. "Yes." Of course, if she had any more liquids, she was going to have to use the bedpan. The staff were used to helping people with their bodily needs. She'd get over any hesitation soon enough as long as she didn't need to have the pretty, self-assured nurse doing it. She could do without being in that position with Trinity.

"I brought you some things." DJ held up her brush, deodorant, floss, and a small stack of boxers, T-shirts, and shorts. "And I picked this up off your nightstand, knowing you're going stir crazy." She held up the novel she'd been reading.

As annoying as DJ could be, she had a heart of gold, and it was the main reason Blaze cherished her friendship. "Thanks, but I hope to hell I'm not here long enough to finish it." She was only halfway through the speculative fiction romance written by one of her favorite authors.

DJ perked up. "Oh, you getting sprung?" She glanced at the pulley system holding her arm aloft before noticing the missing urine bag. "Hey, they unhooked your pee bag," she said, excitement evident in her voice.

"That's what Trinity had just finished doing when you whipped in. You almost got a show."

"As much as I love you, I'm glad I didn't have to witness that. Wasn't it strange having a woman between your legs for reasons other than sex? Was she rough? I certainly wouldn't want her yanking anything from my insides." DJ sat back and sipped her flavored coffee, totally unaware of her lack of sensitivity. It was so DJ to just blurt things out uncensored, and likely one of many reasons for her failed relationships. She hated to admit it, but DJ could be high-maintenance.

She shrugged. "A little, but she was very professional, and it didn't hurt at all."

DJ harrumphed. "So, when *are* you going home?"

Blaze could tell she was becoming restless. Hospitals weren't her thing, and visiting anyone for longer than half an hour would make her antsy. That, on top of her dislike for Trinity and the fact she happened to be with Blaze whenever DJ came around, was proving too much. "The sooner the better, but I think I have to go to rehab first, so you don't have to come by again. My folks are staying until I'm out of here, and Josh is going to check on my bike and see what the damage is."

"Don't be silly. You can't drive left-handed. I'll take you wherever you need to go until you get the okay to get behind the wheel." She finished off her coffee and tossed the cup. "The sooner you get away from that nurse, the better. She's stalkerish." DJ picked at a thread on her pants, then checked her nails.

Blaze rolled her eyes. It was going to be a long morning if DJ insisted on staying and knowing Trinity likely wouldn't return while she was there left her sad. Blaze enjoyed her visits, even though they were only as a professional courtesy, and she hoped she got to see her again.

CHAPTER SIX

Trinity almost laughed out loud when she'd walked in on Blaze looking between her legs. Her confession of what she wanted to do and how she was going to do it, made her temper flare. Doing something as stupid as pulling out the Foley catheter would have resulted in pain Blaze couldn't have imagined. It was a good thing she'd shown up when she did, and it was part of the reason she felt the need to check on Blaze—she was headstrong, and that was never the good kind of patient.

She'd wondered if Blaze had a girlfriend, but if so, surely she would have been there already, and since Blaze called her parents first it probably meant there wasn't one. She'd wanted to find out more, but DJ had shown up and disrupted her plans. That, coupled with Blaze barely saying anything when DJ had been so rude, made Trinity decide to curb her curiosity. Just as well. She didn't have the time or desire for a situation that might turn out badly. Especially not with a woman she didn't even know.

"There you are." Kelly glanced at the clock. "Where have you been? I thought maybe you had car trouble. You left before I did."

Trinity sanitized her hands before reaching for her coffee mug. "I stopped to visit a couple of patients." She rinsed out the dregs from goodness knows when and dried it with a paper towel.

"Anyone in particular?" When Trinity didn't answer, Kelly went on. "How is Ms. Carter?"

She rolled her eyes, knowing Kelly wouldn't be convinced she hadn't seen Blaze.

"She's hot, isn't she? Is that why you've been staying late and coming in early?"

Kelly's voice was low enough that the conversation stayed private, but heat emanated from Trinity's ears, a telltale sign she'd been caught doing something she shouldn't, though that was silly because she hadn't done anything wrong. Ignoring Kelly's inquisition, she decided to feed her a partial truth.

"It's a good thing I did. She was trying to figure out how to remove her catheter."

"Oh my God. Seriously?"

"Uh-huh." She didn't want Kelly thinking it was a big deal. "I explained what could have happened, then I took it out."

Kelly stared at her for a long time.

"What?"

"Nothing."

"That's not the look of nothing, so give it up." She went to the Keurig machine and selected a dark roast with extra caffeine.

"You seem particularly interested in the well-being of Ms. Carter. You're walking a fine line and I've never known you to even come close, so I'm wondering why."

Once Blaze had left the ED, her medical treatment was no longer Trinity's concern. Of course, she could visit her and find out how she was doing, but performing professional duties was tricky territory, and she should have thought more about it before acting on impulse. She rationalized her actions. "I signed off on her chart. It was the change of shift. Besides, I was there." Worrying about Blaze doing damage to herself shouldn't have come into play. There were nurses on duty who could deal with her. At least she'd documented what she'd done and the reason before she left the orthopedic surgical unit. But the desire to see her again remained.

"Still," Kelly said. "It's unlike you. What's going on?"

Trinity shook her head. "I don't know. There's something about her I'm drawn to. You're right though, it won't happen again."

"But she's hot, right?" Kelly waggled her brows, making her laugh.

"Yes, she's hot." She turned to the monitors in front of her, hoping for a distraction. The last thing she needed were fantasies about a patient four floors above her with the most gorgeous bedroom eyes she'd ever seen.

❖

The next evening, Trinity reviewed the inpatient roster and smiled upon seeing Blaze's name. Kelly's words repeated in her head. The pull was undeniable. She'd never felt an emotional tie to anyone who'd come through the ED before, and even though she was handsome and the confident butch type Trinity was attracted to, hadn't she already decided there'd be no relationship on her radar for the foreseeable future?

The ED was exceptionally quiet with only one patient in trauma bay two. The teenager was sleeping off the residual effects of alcohol poisoning. The doctor had ordered ipecac, followed by IV fluids, and they'd monitor him for a few hours to ensure he was out of danger. The alcohol in his system would take a while to dissipate. He was lucky his friends had panicked when he'd become unresponsive and brought him here.

Trinity finished charting, checked in with the staff, and swiped out. She chewed her lower lip. It was seven thirty. Maybe she'd just say hi and then be on her way. There was no harm in being friendly. She gathered her things and took the stairs to the fourth floor. By the time she reached the door, her legs burned, and she was a little short of breath. She really needed to make time for the gym.

The door to Blaze's room was closed and Trinity wondered if she was sleeping. As she reached for the handle, DJ came sweeping out. They made eye contact and Trinity couldn't help being on guard.

"You," DJ hissed as she invaded Trinity's personal space. "Why the hell are you here again?"

Not usually at a loss for words, Trinity was shocked by her intensity and just stood there when she should have defended herself. DJ didn't give her a chance.

"What do you want from her?"

"I don't want anything." For the first time since meeting her, Trinity saw beneath the rough exterior, recognizing the pinched features as concern. "I'm sorry if you think I have ulterior motives. I was there when she spoke with the surgeon, and I'm as concerned about her injury as you are."

DJ swiped at her bangs with a visibly shaky hand. "I doubt that. You don't know her. Not like I do." DJ pushed off the wall and stared at her. "I think it best if you don't see her right now. She needs to concentrate on her recovery."

Without a valid argument, Trinity turned and walked away in a haze toward the stairwell. What had she been doing? True, Blaze had piqued a personal interest, but the hospital was no place to act on it. It would be best to wipe Blaze from her mind and ignore visions of the bottomless gray eyes that had captivated her. Even in pain, Blaze was strong-willed and determined. Undoubtedly, there were other admirable characteristics she possessed. But Blaze wasn't available, that much was clear. DJ had just pissed on her territory, marking Blaze as her own. Maybe they were more than friends and Blaze simply hadn't said as much. It wasn't her business, and the fact that it irked her suggested she needed to back off.

It was time she stopped her ludicrous infatuation with a stranger and concentrated on her own priorities. Ones that didn't include Blaze Carter.

CHAPTER SEVEN

From my assessment you're going to need therapy three times a week for at least two months. Maybe longer, unless you're devoted to your home regime." Cassie, the physical therapist, looked over her chart as she perched on the edge of Blaze's bed.

Blaze blinked hard, thinking she'd been mentally prepared for whatever the therapist would tell her. The news drove home the severity of her injury. *Two months.* And that was just the beginning, a best-case scenario. What if she never regained…no. She couldn't think like that. A defeatist attitude wouldn't do her any good. Therapy wouldn't be half as difficult as the death of her grandfather.

"When do we start?"

Cassie's mouth quirked into a smile. "I like your enthusiasm. If you can keep that attitude, you'll be amazed at the progress you can make. It's going to be painful and hard at first, but I know what I'm doing. Thirty plus years have taught me a thing or two about healing and possibilities. Having a strong will is a big part of recovery."

They set up a schedule to begin the day after her discharge. Blaze's insurance would cover home therapy for the first month since Cassie didn't want her driving yet. She was looking forward to going home tomorrow. As promised, Dr. Jonas made sure she'd been "unstrung" four times a day to stretch her muscles, and she wiggled her stiff fingers often. He'd finally taken away the traction this morning, satisfied there was minimal residual swelling. In her favor, the strong muscles in her forearm had helped hold most of the arm's anatomy in place when it broke, but he'd had to do a major repair on a muscle that had been torn. He wasn't sure how much strength she'd regain.

Alone with her thoughts, she craved the company of her parents and her pain in the ass brother, a home cooked meal, and a shower in her own bathroom. The perfect remedy to counteract her discontent. *Tomorrow.* She could have all of those tomorrow. It would also be the day she got to see her arm unbandaged for the first time. She stared down where it rested on a pillow draped over her thigh with another tucked under her elbow for support. Everything considered, she was fairly comfortable. Her pain level was tolerable most of the time and she'd asked to be switched to a non-narcotic medication. The highlight from yesterday was going to the restroom for the first time without assistance. Wiping with her left hand had been a bit of a challenge because everything was backward, but she'd figure out how to manage on her own in every way.

She wondered what was taking DJ so long. She'd left when Cassie came in to do her assessment, saying she needed real coffee from across the street. Knowing DJ, Blaze guessed she'd been bored. Blaze reviewed her restrictions list and her therapy schedule and made her own list of things for her parents to bring tomorrow so she would be comfortable on the drive home. Some of her shirts might have to be cut to accommodate her new bandage, depending on how big the final one was, so she included an oversized, faded flannel shirt, one of her old tank tops, and sweats. Her father was heading to her workshop to see what projects he could finish for her and to make calls to customers to explain the imminent delay in orders. She agreed with his suggestion of giving her remaining customers the option of voiding their contracts.

There was a knock on her door and her heart sped up. Trinity hadn't been by yesterday and had yet to show today. "Come in."

A petite PCA popped her head in. "Hi, I'm Pam. I heard you're going home tomorrow and thought you might like to freshen up a bit today."

Disappointment coursed through her. There wasn't any reason to expect Trinity to continue to drop in. She likely checked on her patients for a day or two, and once they were better, she wouldn't keep visiting.

"A shower sounds great." It had been four days since she'd been admitted, and she was beginning to feel skeevy. She had clean underwear and the shorts DJ had brought her, but warmer clothes wouldn't arrive till tomorrow.

"I'm sure it does, but not today. You'll have to wait until the bandages come off for that. A sponge bath is the best I can offer. If you don't mind my help, you can do what you can reach, and I can hold your arm."

Blaze didn't know why she would have preferred Trinity to be the one to help her, especially after the catheter thing, but she couldn't help it. Maybe she'd been off the last couple of days. Coming up with a plausible excuse eased the irrational feeling of abandonment but not the desire to let her know she was being discharged.

"I don't mind your help, but my only clean clothes are boxers and shorts."

"I think I have a solution. Be right back." Pam slipped out the door.

The least she could do was be ready when Pam returned. Blaze swung her leg over the side of the bed and lifted her injured arm with her other hand so it followed the rest of her body. She'd learned that little trick the hard way the first time she'd tried to move, leaving behind her broken arm and shoulder where it lay on pillows. Those muscles weren't working the way they normally did.

"What kind of a coffee shop runs out of stoppers?" DJ strode in with a tray and a bag precariously perched in the middle. She set them down and smiled. "Where are you going?"

"I'm getting ready for a bath."

"Really? That's great. I didn't want to tell you but you're getting a little ripe around the edges."

Blaze grabbed the closest object in her reach and threw the box of tissues, aiming for her head. DJ deflected it, then attempted to look shocked. "Gee, best friends aside, I thought you'd like to know." She sat back in the chair and peeled off the lid. The rich, sweet caramel aroma filled the space between them.

Blaze laughed. "You didn't happen to see Trinity in your travels, did you?"

DJ looked into her coffee and used a stirrer to whip up the foam. "Not today."

"Did she say anything to you the last time you saw her?"

"No. Why?" DJ finally made eye contact. "What difference does it make? If you need something, I'm sure one of the staff will get it. Most of the people seem nice."

Why indeed. That was the sixty-four thousand dollar question. She couldn't help the stirring she felt in her lower belly whenever Trinity was around. "I wanted to thank her for checking on me, that's all." What she didn't tell DJ was she'd been hoping to get Trinity's phone number.

Pam came into the room carrying a stack of scrubs, saving her from explaining her interest any further. Pam grinned. "They aren't the latest fashion statement, but they're loose and pretty comfortable."

"They'll be fine." Blaze stood, holding her arm. She nudged her chin toward the bathroom. "Shall we?" Getting naked in front of one more person wasn't top on her list, but getting clean was, so she'd endure.

DJ pulled out her phone. "I'll be here when you're done, but I can't promise the pastry will survive."

"And you call yourself my best friend," Blaze said over her shoulder.

Twenty minutes later, she came out wearing some of the most comfortable clothes she'd ever worn. The scrubs had been washed enough times that the material was smooth and soft, and the drawstring closure, while a bit challenging, could be loosely tied since Pam had brought a size she could work up and down on her own.

"Feel better?" DJ dropped her phone in her bag and got Blaze's coffee and Danish ready for her.

Blaze sat on the edge of the bed after thanking Pam for her help. Her disappointment lingered, but she shook it off. With no sign of Trinity, she focused on the cheese pastry, picking up half and taking a bite. The sweet, soft, gooey layers melted in her mouth and the cheese was just right. Not too tart and not too sweet. She chewed and swallowed, then washed it down with the lukewarm coffee. "That's really good."

"I know. I was tempted to buy the whole lot, but neither one of us can go to the gym at the moment so I settled on three. There's one for you for later." DJ shared a naughty smile.

"Oh, so it's okay for me to put on pounds."

"You never gain weight, and you know it. No matter what you shove in your face, it's like you're on a liquid diet." DJ wrinkled her nose. "Your dad messaged me while you were cleaning up. He has a few questions about orders."

"I'll call him in a bit. How's everything going in the real estate market?"

"It's steady. I've signed a few contracts for million-dollar homes. If they sell, I'll make enough for that European trip I've been gushing over."

"You'll get there." DJ excelled at selling and Blaze wondered, as she often did, why DJ's personal life contrasted her work one. She'd had a few live-in girlfriends, but none of the relationships had lasted. After each one ended, DJ spiraled into depression for months, and Blaze did her best to keep her spirits up. DJ could be charming, and funny. She was great at crunching numbers and was a definite fashionista, making her a great catch, though none of the women she dated stayed around for the long haul. Knowing her friend emotionally suffered from the fallout hurt her, too.

Blaze finished and tossed her trash in the can. She was getting good at left-handed baskets. "Thanks for the treat."

"Welcome." DJ stood up abruptly. "I've got a showing. What time do you want me to come back?"

She waved her off. The last thing she wanted was for DJ to be here more than she already was. Her heart was in the right place, bless her soul, but DJ could become overwhelming and Blaze's patience was at an all-time low. Aside from that, she was pretty sure DJ's presence was why Trinity hadn't returned. Maybe she'd stop by later.

"I'm good for tonight. Mom and Pop are picking up dinner and bringing me clothes to wear home. I'll text you when I'm sprung."

DJ looked skeptical. "You sure?"

"Yes. I'll be fine. Being up and moving is exhausting. I'm going to take a nap. Cassie will drop by this afternoon to show me some exercises and give me some devices I can use at home." She flexed her fingers and felt the tug up her arm. She was stiff and sore in a dozen places. The bruises spattered across her body reminded her how fortunate she'd been to escape with only one injury. The paramedics had been correct. It could have been a lot worse.

"Okay." DJ bent to kiss her cheek. "Text me if you think of anything." She slung her ever present bag over her shoulder. "Tootles."

Alone for the first time all morning, Blaze settled back on the bed. It took her a bit of fluffing and stuffing to get the pillows just right, but she managed. Her eyes closed, and her vision filled with flashes of Trinity. Blaze wanted to know what her real motives were for being around so much the first few days, followed by her sudden disappearance. As she drifted, Blaze tried to figure out what kind of person Trinity was when she wasn't wearing her professional mask.

CHAPTER EIGHT

Trinity was still seething over DJ's comments. DJ knew nothing about her, and regardless of her warning, she wanted to see Blaze again and hoped she hadn't gone home. She stowed her purse and jacket in her locker and held the small bakery box. Trinity worried if giving her the modest gift was too much of a personal gesture. *I'll probably never see her again so what does it matter?*

Trinity waved to the familiar staff and waited outside Blaze's door. The sound of the TV almost guaranteed Blaze was alone, and she took a breath before poking her head in. Blaze sat in the recliner with the remote control, pressing the channel button every few seconds. She tapped on the door. "There's nothing good on at this time of day." Blaze's disarming smile welcomed her, and her heartbeat kicked up a notch.

"Hi," Blaze said as she shut the TV off. "Thanks for rescuing me. I feared a slow death of boredom."

"I wasn't sure you'd still be here." For a second, she considered telling her why she hadn't come sooner, but it would serve no purpose. Hurting others wasn't in her nature, so she let it go.

"I get sprung tomorrow. I can't wait to go home."

She hoped Blaze couldn't see her disappointment. "Most people are more than ready after a couple of days at our luxury resort."

Blaze laughed. "I imagine so." A current in the air between them washed over her. It wasn't tension, but whatever it was it made her skin prickle and she presented the box. "I brought you a treat."

"You did?" Blaze looked surprised. "That was nice of you." She took the offering and struggled for a moment before she got the lid open. "Scones!" She grinned. "One of my all-time favorites."

She was going to respond when a shadow crossed Blaze's face, and she wondered what had caused it. "Everything okay?"

"Yeah. Grandma made them every Friday night when I'd go there after school." Blaze glanced up. "Good memories. Thank you."

Although Trinity still didn't know much about Blaze, she learned a little more every time they were together, and she liked everything so far. Even the stubbornness. "They're one of my favorites, too. They're from a little shop in downtown Queensbury. The baker makes a different flavor every day."

Blaze's face relaxed. "Then you'll have to have one with me."

She hesitated and glanced at the clock. "I'm not sure I have time."

"Please?"

Trinity couldn't refuse her. "I'll be right back." A couple of minutes later, she pushed open the door with her hip and set two cups of tea on Blaze's bed table. "The best I could do." She dropped packets of sugar next to the cups, then pulled the visitor chair over so they were facing. "No milk." She grimaced. "That's just wrong."

Blaze laughed a hearty, rich sound. "I agree."

As they nibbled, she asked about therapy, home care, and Blaze's family. Safe topics. Nothing too personal, and nothing to indicate she wanted to ask if she was single or interested in dating. Trinity hadn't dated in a long time and had no intentions of starting now, so there was no reason to ask that kind of thing anyway. She had to go before she said something she'd regret and stood. "I'm glad you're going home. The food here isn't great." She fought off the urge to giggle. Her nerves were making her giddy.

Blaze looked sad. "It's the company I'll miss the most."

Ignoring the warning bells screaming in her head, Trinity handed her phone to Blaze. "I'd like to check how therapy is going, if you don't mind me calling." The excuse was lame, and she refused to dwell on all the reasons she should have bitten her tongue. Hard.

Escaping without a way to contact Blaze would have been the smart thing to do. The ethical thing to do. But she couldn't.

"I'd like that."

They said their good-byes and she left, wondering when she'd given herself permission to act on her feelings.

❖

Trinity gripped the wheel and concentrated on the wet, dark road. Rain slashed across the windshield in sheets. Her twelve-hour shift had turned into fourteen. She was beyond tired. Emotionally drained and physically empty, all she wanted was a hot shower, food, and her bed. At least she didn't have to return to the hospital until the late shift day after next. By then she'd reenergize and be ready to face another onslaught of casualties and run-of-the-mill emergencies.

Tonight's cases had involved a weather-related collision. There were four people involved and none had escaped injury. One of the patients was in a coma and likely to have lasting damage due to traumatic brain injury. Their life would be forever changed because of a moment's poor judgment, which reminded her of the close call Blaze had.

Her eyes burned, so heavy with fatigue she had to consciously force them to stay open. Three blocks. *Focus.* She leaned forward, reduced her speed, and went through her ED protocol as a way to stay alert. By the time she finished reciting it, she was sitting in her driveway with a mixture of sweat and humidity clinging to her skin. *Maybe I'm coming down with something.* She gathered her backpack and keys while studying the onslaught outside, then made a dash to the door. She needn't have bothered as rain pooled in her shoes and whatever hadn't soaked into her hair trailed down her neck and inside her meager jacket.

Trinity unlocked the door and listened. Kelly was probably sound asleep by now. She hoped she'd missed getting drenched. The day had been challenging enough with news of Blaze's discharge and not having a chance to see her again before the onslaught of emergency vehicles. Once inside, she kicked off her shoes and peeled away the wet layers, dropping them on the rubber mat. Gooseflesh rose along her arms and legs as she stood there in only her bra and undies. The ensuing shiver ran from her head to her toes. A hot shower was the only thing she could think of in her immediate future. Pausing outside Kelly's door, she listened, then smiled. The gentle intermittent snore confirmed Marge made the right decision by letting her go while the getting was good. She moved quietly to the bathroom and cranked the water to hot.

Steam began to fill the bathroom and she stepped into the shower, letting the hot needles pelt her back and shoulders. Flashes of the night's blood, pain, and gore played on the inside of her eyelids. All she could do was let them run. She enjoyed having a few quiet moments with Blaze, and that had been the highlight of her day. With her discharge, she'd no longer have to make time to visit her. Not seeing DJ was a bonus.

With the chill finally receding, Trinity picked up her sponge, squeezed out a liberal amount of lavender soap, and worked up a lather. She rinsed the suds from her body, her skin tingling from the vigorous scrubbing, and finished her routine by washing her hair, knowing it would take hours to dry on its own. The last of the ED odors vanished down the drain and she turned off the water. Once she was dry, Trinity shrugged into an oversized T-shirt that had been washed so many times it was nearly threadbare. For a moment, she considered food but was too tired to cook, afraid she'd fall asleep in the process and burn the building to the ground. She drank a glass of water, then brushed her teeth. With no energy left, she crawled between the soft sheets and pulled the comforter up, snuggling deeper. The air conditioner was set on low in order to keep the humidity in the apartment at a minimum, and she gulped down several breaths of the chilled air, attempting to ease the last of the tightness from her chest.

Twenty minutes later, she was still awake. It wasn't often sleep evaded her, and her mood changed from bone tired to aggravated. *Maybe I should get up and work on my thesis.* She was almost done. Once she finished her conclusions and did a final read through, she'd hand it in. Trinity had been working toward her master's degree for a couple of years, taking classes when she could and doing a lot of online research. With her degree, she'd be able to apply for the position that would be opening soon. Marge was retiring as head trauma nurse and Trinity had coveted the job for the last year. Because they were friends, Marge had willingly agreed to wait until Trinity met the requirement of an advanced degree in nursing before giving her notice. Last week, she and Marge met for breakfast and had worked out the details. Marge was going to give the minimum requirement of four weeks' notice at the end of the following week, giving Trinity four days to finish. It would take another week before she heard if she'd passed. The waiting game would stress her to the max, but she'd get through it.

She flipped to her other side. Her eyes were leaden, but her mind was all over the place. She started counting the number of patients that had been under her care in the last week, which always worked better than sheep. That's when Blaze's face flashed before her.

Blaze. There was a long list of reasons why Trinity didn't want to think about her. No matter how hard she tried, Blaze's voice or smile or eyes—God, those eyes—filled her vision. In a last-ditch attempt to remain distanced, she reviewed her case in clinical terms, hoping once she focused on the familiar, she'd be able to let go of her annoying attraction.

Thirty-eight-year-old motorcycle accident victim. Five feet, ten inches. Blaze was one long drink of water. *No, no, no. Focus.* Compound fracture to the right radius. Multiple contusions along her thighs, arms, and back. A strong, broad back that rippled with taut muscles. *Jesus. Stop that.* Radiology studies revealed no other broken bones. Negative for concussion. Blood work unremarkable. Blood pressure upon arrival was 155 over 90. Nothing of note. Except for the muscular forearms and similarly strong thighs. *Ugh.* Unable to deny she hadn't stopped thinking about Blaze since she arrived by ambulance, Trinity gave in to seeing her in a less than professional light.

Her first impression had been what had sealed the deal. Though Blaze was clearly concerned about her injuries, she trusted the staff to take care of her and had been nothing but polite. And even in the face of devastating news regarding her arm, she'd remained calm—a testament to her character. The only time Trinity had seen fear was when Blaze was talking to the surgeon. After surgery, she'd proved her resilience by doing everything she could to move along her recovery. She chuckled in the dark. Well, that wasn't entirely true. Blaze had looked pretty scared before she removed the catheter. Despite all she was going through, Blaze treated everyone around her with respect, even when she was likely in a lot of pain.

It wasn't difficult to understand her attraction. But honestly, she didn't have the energy to pursue Blaze, and ethically, she shouldn't be considering dating a patient. Certainly not one she'd met under such dire circumstances. Besides, she already had too much on her plate. Maybe DJ and her overprotective tigress routine had done her a favor. Trinity hated being talked down to, and no matter what DJ's feelings were, she had no right to be so rude. As sleep finally crept in, she pushed away thoughts of DJ and returned instead to beautiful slate gray eyes, like liquid smoke, and strong, hard shoulders.

CHAPTER NINE

I can't." Blaze swiped at the sweat running from her hairline with her left hand. She'd been exercising her arm for thirty minutes and her muscles were shaking, pain coursing along her nerves. When the bandages first came off, she tried not to be shocked by the eight-inch scar on the inside of her forearm. It looked like something from a Frankenstein movie, though the stitches were smaller and the incision line narrow and clean. Once the stitches were gone, she could start applying an ointment to help reduce scarring and smooth the skin. She wasn't vain. The scar wouldn't faze her, but if she didn't fully regain use, that would devastate her.

The first week had been gentle manipulations while the bandages were still on. Trinity had texted, asking how her therapy was going. Blaze considered calling her, but she wasn't sure when Trinity was at work, and settled for a few friendly exchanges. Even those limited communications made her smile and took the edge off what she was going through. The following week, therapy had become a bit more aggressive. Dr. Jonas had been impressed by how quickly her bones were knitting and he said she could manage wearing a forearm brace with Velcro straps. She'd been pleased by the freedom since it allowed her to shower more comfortably. Into her third week, Cassie wasn't letting her off easy.

"You're doing great," Cassie said. She replaced the tennis ball in her hand with a stress ball. Cassie had her working with a variety of items, some providing more resistance than others. "Let's give this a try. Squeeze and hold for five."

Blaze laughed when she looked at the object in her hand. The Pillsbury Dough Boy stared back at her, his eyes bulging when she squeezed. "You expect me to be able to concentrate looking at this?" She squeezed and counted. It was hard to maintain her grip, but she managed.

"Nice. Now give me five more." Cassie sat next to her on a stool, marking her progress in the notes.

"Five!"

Cassie smiled. "You're right. Give me seven."

Blaze should have known better. They'd been working together long enough for her to know whenever she complained Cassie pushed her harder, telling her she could do it if she wanted it bad enough. She did. With every fiber of her being, she would do whatever she had to in order to work again. In the meantime, she'd try her damnedest to not become annoyed by the delay.

Ten minutes later, Blaze sat with a towel draped over her neck while Cassie worked her magic with a heat rub that was followed by an ice bath to keep the swelling down.

"You're awfully quiet today. Is your arm hurting that much?" Cassie continued to massage her arm and fingers. They'd become friends of sorts, talking about all kinds of things while Blaze went through her paces. Cassie had enjoyed the change of scenery so much she'd asked Blaze if they could continue their therapy sessions at her house.

She shook her head. Cassie wasn't going to let it go and fixed her with an intense stare until she caved. "Women."

Cassie didn't miss a beat. "Ah, yes. We're a fickle bunch."

She laughed. "True enough." Blaze wanted to drop the subject altogether, unlike she'd been able to do herself. She slowly flexed her wrist as much as her tight tendons allowed, then stretched her fingers. "I can still only lift a coffee mug," she said, impatient with the progress. She wanted to be back at work. Her father had completed the special-order cabinets she'd started since it was her only time-sensitive project. She'd called her other customers who'd ordered commissioned pieces, telling them it might be months before she could work again. They'd all expressed a willingness to wait, and it was a testament to their belief she'd be returning to her craft. Blaze prayed they were right.

"I told you at the beginning healing would take time. If you weren't so physically fit, you'd still be in a cast."

Cassie submerged her arm in the ice-filled water, taking her breath away. Even though she'd done it dozens of times, her body reacted to the shock the same. "I know…" She hesitated and looked out the window to the forest of trees beyond her yard. "I wish I could go back in time."

"Before the accident?" Cassie must have sensed she wasn't really talking about her injury then.

She sighed. "No. I don't know. The last few months I've felt like something big is going to happen in my life, but I can't pinpoint it. It's confusing and…" She shook her head.

Cassie took her other hand and held it. "Listen to me. I'm older and wiser." They both laughed. "Trust that whatever's ahead of you is meant to be." She patted her hand. "And if it's a woman that's got you questioning things, don't be so proud that you can't make the first move."

"I don't know if I want to." Blaze had been thinking about going to the hospital to find Trinity, but what would she say? *"I thought we hit it off when you brought the scones and I'd like to get together socially?"* Talk about being a stalker. She sighed. Maybe she'd been wrong about Trinity's interest. It wasn't like there was any obligation on Trinity's part to keep in contact, even though she'd been doing so. Blaze had other things to worry about right now.

"So, what's next?" She nodded to her arm. Cassie had taken away the ice, dried her off, and was pulling on a light compression sleeve before replacing the brace.

"Tomorrow you have a follow-up X-ray and scan. We'll have your usual therapy on Wednesday and should know the results by then. Based on what Dr. Jonas says, we'll adjust your sessions accordingly for the next month."

Blaze had already asked Cassie a dozen times how long she thought therapy would last and when she'd be able to resume working. Cassie had remained vague. It wasn't up to her. Blaze knew she couldn't guarantee an end result. She stretched her fingers.

"Don't overdue the exercises. If you reinjure the tendons and muscles now, you might lose any progress you've made. Got it?" Cassie warned her as she packed up her goods. "I'll see you Wednesday. Take care."

Blaze sighed. All she could do was wait.

❖

By the next morning, she was going insane. Without the use of her arm, even small household chores were a pain in the ass, and she still couldn't drive. Josh and DJ had been lifesavers, but being dependent was making her crazy.

"I've got a few errands to run and I'll pick up your groceries," Josh said as they idled in front of the hospital entrance.

"I can get them on my own."

"Stop being such a pain in the ass. You can cook me dinner tonight while I sous chef for you."

Blaze forced a smile. She'd never been good at letting people help her, and now it seemed like that's all she did. "Yeah. Okay. I'll call you when I'm done." She got out and took the elevator down to radiology. The room was packed, and she dreaded having to wait, being short on patience these days. After checking in, she sat in the quietest corner she could find and scrolled through old text messages. There were days she didn't bother looking at them, and she had to be more vigilant. It was hard to remember the world was still functioning at its normal pace, even if she wasn't.

Maybe she should think about a night out. As much as she was a familiar fixture at EroZone, she kept her private life private, and this was one time when she was glad she did. Blaze didn't need anyone else doting on her, and she definitely didn't want anyone feeling sorry for her. She didn't even have a personal Facebook account, only one for her business, Hand and Chisel Woodworking. She advertised on Twitter, but she never answered personal messages when she received them. Blaze groaned when she saw there were eighty-seven text messages that she'd either read without deleting, needed to answer, or never opened. The only ones she consistently paid attention to were the occasional ones from Trinity. They were quick check-ins, but they always lightened her mood. She could use one now. *Get your shit together, Carter.* When her name was called, she shoved her cell back in her pocket, glad she could delay dealing with things she had no interest in.

The technician verified her date of birth and name. Plain X-rays took a few minutes and then she was prepped for the MRI. Once the IV was placed she lay down on the narrow table and went into the tube. Music played in the headset, but Blaze wasn't paying attention. Midway through, dye was injected, and the warmth spread through her.

The table slid out of the MRI machine, and she waited the few tense minutes it took the tech to come inside.

"Okay, Ms. Carter. The pictures are nice and clear, so I'll remove the IV and you can be on your way." She flushed saline through the line, then removed the needle and put a small compression wrap around her arm. "Two hours and you can remove the bandage." She helped Blaze sit up.

The room spun for a minute before righting itself, and she took a couple of deep breaths. She understood how people could become claustrophobic inside the narrow space.

"Are you okay?"

Blaze stood and smiled. "Yes. It gets me every time."

The tech laughed. "You aren't the only one. If you're dizzy I can walk you to the waiting room and get you something to drink."

"No, no. I'm fine. I have a ride home, so no worries." What she needed was fresh air. She'd been in the basement of the hospital more in the last month than she'd been in her shop, and she wanted out. Every time she was there, she relived unpleasant memories. Her pulse raced as she walked through the corridors trying to find the way out. She took another left and somehow ended up inside the emergency department. Blaze swore under her breath. She began backtracking, reassuring herself she'd find the elevator soon. Instead, she took the corner too tight and ran into someone who had been moving quickly. They grabbed on to each other to keep from falling, then the air left her lungs.

"Blaze?" Trinity asked, then looked around. "What are you doing here?"

Her stomach dropped and she hoped her voice didn't betray how glad she was to see her again. "I was here for a scan and got turned around." She breathed a little easier with Trinity's nearness.

Trinity's hand slid down her arm. "Hey, are you okay?"

Blaze liked the physical contact. "A little lost is all." She didn't mean location alone. Blaze was lost in emotions and feelings she'd sworn off after a relationship had gone south a few years ago. Lost in all things regarding Trinity.

"I can help." Trinity took a step back, breaking their connection.

Even wearing scrubs, Trinity was beautiful. As she led her through the maze of corridors, Blaze got to admire her profile, noting the fine contours of her cheekbones and the perfectly shaped nose, and lips begging to be kissed.

"Here we are." Trinity gave her a sweet, small smile. "Take this elevator to the first floor, then turn left." She waited as though wrestling with internal thoughts.

Trinity might have wanted to say more, but since she didn't, Blaze did. "Thank you. And thanks for texting to check on me. It's meant a lot."

Trinity's smile was wider this time. "You're welcome. I hope your scan results are good." She turned to leave after quickly squeezing Blaze's arm.

Blaze caught her hand. "Can I see you? Outside of work?" Blood rushed through her veins as she watched Trinity's facial expression change.

"What do you mean?"

Trinity glanced at their entwined fingers and Blaze was afraid to let go, that the fragile connection would end before she got an answer. "Do you like to hike? Outside?" Good Lord, she was a hot mess. But what did she have to lose?

CHAPTER TEN

Trinity laughed. When she'd said yes, Blaze's surprise had been priceless. She didn't know if she was excited or terrified by the invitation. On the one hand, she enjoyed the tingling sensation when they touched. On the other, the one that ruled her practical side, she was terrified of the implications. *Is hiking considered a date?* No. She wanted to get to know Blaze and this was a perfect opportunity. There was nothing intimate about being sweaty and out of breath. She could fantasize about Blaze all she wanted, but that's where it stopped, even if they did get together socially. Her career meant everything to her, and though she'd never had one, she was convinced relationships got in the way of chasing your dreams. Since Blaze wasn't a patient anymore and she'd made the first move, ethics weren't involved. But that didn't mean Trinity would give in and lose sight of the big prize.

Still, it was as though she were meant to see Blaze. Was this a stroke of fate intervening to reassure her she hadn't been mistaken about Blaze wanting to get to know her better, too? Trinity was at a loss and having second thoughts. Should she send a text saying it wasn't a good idea after all, or should she forge ahead? Either way, she needed to clear the air between them. They could be friends, but nothing more.

She headed to her locker. There were a half-dozen errands she needed to run, and if she continued to ignore them, she'd have a lot of explaining to do. Not that Kelly lacked understanding. With their schedules as all over the place as they were, everyday chores like laundry and grocery shopping tended to fall by the wayside, but they'd worked out a system of taking turns and ready or not, it was hers.

The midmorning sunlight greeted her, and she turned to face the sun, enjoying the warmth. Fall was beginning to show its colors, and she was grateful for each warm day. And each new day brought her closer to her plans. Her latest goal had been obtained—she'd earned her degree. Now she had a new one. She'd turned in her application for the promotion on the first day Marge's job had posted. If…no… *when* she got it, she'd have to come up with more goals. They kept her motivated. They also gave her an excuse to avoid relationships, which in her opinion only caused trouble.

If only she knew where her focus should be next. Something that would carry her through not only the not-so-distant future, but further. That's where she was stumbling. Every decision up to this point had been directly related to work, and while she loved what she did, she was also aware there had to be more.

Kelly was her best friend and shared in all her highs and lows, but she couldn't take the place of a partner. She wondered what real intimacy felt like, though that was just a pipe dream because she hadn't been in anything she could even call an intimate relationship. Ever. As a child, she'd watched her parents' interactions and saw the dismal complexities of being with someone long-term, especially when the odds hadn't been in their favor from the start. It was hard to tell if they liked each other, let alone loved one another. So, rather than fail the way they had, Trinity had shied away from letting anyone close, but it had come at a price. Moments that should have been spent in celebration with her partner she'd spent formulating her next goal, never enjoying the success in the moment.

She walked across the parking lot and the smell of warm tar assaulted her. As she slid onto the upholstered seat, she admitted her life was busy but simple. She'd given herself plenty of opportunities to be intellectually stimulated. However, when it came to emotional stimulation there hadn't been any. Inertia kept her from starting the car, and Trinity stared out the windshield. The future was out there, she just needed an idea of what it looked like, and no matter how much she fought against it, she kept coming back to Blaze. And that's where things became complicated.

❖

Trinity folded the last towel and stowed the stack in the linen closet. The clock on the kitchen wall got her moving. She'd planned on making a casserole and a salad for dinner. Kelly would be too exhausted to care if she ate, but they both needed food to survive the demand of long hours. She checked the calendar where they wrote their shifts, a routine they'd adopted shortly after moving in together. Kelly was off for the next thirty-six hours, part of which would be spent in a sleep coma following the twelve hours she was finishing. Their jobs were demanding, but rewarding, too.

She piled the counter with ingredients and got to work chopping the vegetables and pulling apart the roasted chicken, cutting and shredding it into bite-sized pieces. A drizzle of olive oil in a hot pan would ensure the shallots and garlic burst with flavor, and once they began to turn translucent, she added the veggies. Trinity had even splurged by buying fresh pasta and quickly cooked the tender noodles in boiling water. Everything went into a huge bowl and she mixed the ingredients with a jar of alfredo sauce before filling a casserole dish and sprinkling grated cheese over the top. The casserole needed thirty minutes in a hot oven which gave her enough time to make a tossed salad. She stored the remainder from the bowl in zippered baggies and stowed them in the freezer for quick meals. Neither of them ate well when working, so they tried to prepare food ahead of time.

She texted Kelly to let her know she'd taken care of dinner and hoped she made it home for a hot meal. While she washed and spun the lettuce, her mind wandered back to her encounter with Blaze. Her phone vibrated and she swiped the screen with her pinkie.

"Hi."

"I'm leaving the hospital now, so wait for me. I know it will be delicious."

She giggled. Kelly loved when she cooked and begged her to do it more. "Okay. I'm going to open a bottle of wine."

"What happened?"

"Nothing." She tried to keep her voice even.

"We'll talk over dinner. See you in twenty."

Sliced cucumbers, radishes, red onions, and grape tomatoes tumbled on top of the greens. The nice bottle of Chianti she'd bought a few weeks ago was a bit of a splurge, but she didn't treat herself often and pushed away the guilt. While she pulled the cork, she thought about one of the recent conversations she and Kelly had about needing to be good to herself more often, and that included letting herself love and be loved.

She nearly dropped the plates. *Love?* The word wasn't often a part of her vocabulary, and she needed to ruminate why. Sure, if she was thinking about becoming involved with someone, her goal should include love.

"Huh." There she was again. Making one more part of her life goal oriented. How silly was that? Wasn't it?

"God, that smells good." Kelly bowled through the door and dropped her backpack with a loud thud. She went to the fridge and grabbed a bottle of water, downing half before sitting in her usual seat at the table.

Trinity took the casserole out of the oven and placed it on the hot pads, then shook off her gloves, but didn't move. If she sat, she'd have to have the conversation she was suddenly dreading. Kelly must have sensed her hesitancy and poured wine into her goblet, then waved for her to join her.

"Unless someone you know and love died, admit you want to talk about whatever's bothering you." Kelly began scooping food. "But I'm starved, so I'm not waiting for you to decide."

She laughed. Leave it to Kelly to break the ice and get her talking. "Fine." She scooped a small portion onto her plate and added some salad. Somewhere along the way she'd lost her appetite. She took a sip of wine and a deep breath. "I saw Blaze today."

Kelly chewed a mouthful of salad, then sipped more wine. "Oh. How is she?"

"She was upset when I found her. She'd gotten turned around in radiology and I brought her to the elevator."

"Do you think she's having memory issues?"

Remembering the look on Blaze's face, Trinity grinned. "No. I think she felt like a rat in a maze."

Kelly nodded. "Understandable," she said as she studied her. "What else did she say?"

Trinity sighed. "She asked if I wanted to go hiking."

"Like on a date?"

She pushed her food around, not looking up. "No." She tried to ignore the feeling of being watched, but it didn't work. "Yes?" She dropped her fork. "Christ, I don't know. She was sweet and nervous, too. I'm not sure what to make of it."

"Ah," Kelly said, holding up the wine bottle. "The real reason for this."

She nodded. "I've never gone out with a patient socially, and…" Trinity was having a hard time explaining her feelings. "Her life seems so together. How could I ever be her equal? I've had to fight every step of the way for what I want. Could she even understand nothing's come easy for me?"

"Slow down. You've had, what? One actual conversation with her over a scone? Unless you've been pouring your heart out in those quick little texts you've sent, you have no idea what baggage she has. You're making assumptions based on how you see yourself. So what if you've come from different backgrounds? That doesn't mean you can't find common ground. You'll figure it out, if you want to."

"I suppose you're right." She needed to remember to not make a rash decision when it came to Blaze. "There's something else, though."

"Like?" Kelly sipped her wine, giving her time to identify what else was bothering her.

"There's this whole other issue with her friend."

Kelly shoved another forkful of food in her mouth. "You won't know what that's about unless you ask her."

Trinity remained quiet.

"Now what?" Kelly rolled her eyes.

"What if I'm wrong about Blaze's interest?"

"For once, will you not worry? Go have a good time and see what happens. Stop trying to plan everything. Sometimes you just have to fly by the seat of your pants," Kelly said.

Trinity smiled and shook her head. "You're right." She stood, needing to let Kelly's words sink in. "I'll get these. You go take a shower."

"You sure?"

Trinity gave her a gentle shove. "Go." She brought the casserole dish to the counter. "But I get to pick what we watch tonight," she said over her shoulder. Kelly would likely pass out after a short time anyway.

"Deal," Kelly yelled from the hallway, making her smile.

"I'm so glad you're in my life." It was good to have someone to focus on other than Blaze. There may not ever be anything between her and Blaze, but at the very least she could enjoy whatever time they spent together.

CHAPTER ELEVEN

H i." Blaze leaned against her vehicle, not wanting to appear desperate to close the distance between them.

Trinity smiled shyly, then glanced up at the expansive blue sky. "You've picked a perfect day for an outing."

Occasional puffy white clouds floated on the breeze. She glanced at Trinity. "It's definitely perfect now." She hadn't meant to say the words out loud. Blaze cleared her throat and hefted her backpack. "Ready?" she asked after Trinity put on hers.

"Lead the way." Trinity's green eyes rivaled the still lush grass beneath their feet, though it wouldn't be long before the first frost came to the mountains.

She took in the familiar surroundings and ruminated about safe topics, a hard task to accomplish since she was already feeling the effects of having Trinity by her side. "This is one of my favorite trails. It's less than five miles long and loops around a pond." She thought of the wildlife she'd seen the last time she was there and hoped there would be some today. Dappled sunlight soon gave way to full exposure as they made it to the edge of a meadow and Blaze stopped long enough to shed her windbreaker.

"How does your arm feel?" Trinity drew closer.

"Today's a good day." She'd been downgraded to twice a week PT for a month and had been given the okay to drive, as long as she wore the sleeve. Cassie told her she wasn't going to promise she wouldn't need her soon, but when that day came she'd be both happy and sad. She enjoyed their conversations.

"That's good. Are you back to work?" Trinity stumbled and Blaze caught her.

"Soon. Before the holidays." Trinity was so close. Close enough to lean in for a kiss. A kiss that shouldn't happen anytime soon. Blaze backed away. "I forgot to warn you about the rocks. Sorry."

Trinity waved her off. "I should pay attention to where I'm stepping, but just in case, how are your first aid skills?" She winked, and the air left Blaze's lungs.

"I'd manage to save you, if that's what you're asking."

"Good to know."

A while later, they made it to the edge of the pond, and Blaze picked out a spot before pulling a small blanket from her pack and spreading it on the ground. "M'lady." She made a grand gesture, making Trinity giggle. She began removing several small containers, a baguette, and a thermos. She poured iced tea into one of the paper cups. "I was going to bring wine but decided against it." She displayed the cheese, meats, and olives.

"That would have been nice," Trinity said. "But it's a tad early for me."

"Yeah," she said, grinning. "That's what I thought, too." She crossed her legs and handed an eco-friendly paper plate to Trinity.

"So," Trinity said. "Is this a date?"

"Uh…"

Trinity laughed. "I didn't mean to put you on the spot. It's just…"

She tipped her head. "Just what?"

"I was wondering why you didn't have more visitors at the hospital."

"You mean a partner?" Blaze didn't want to seem like she hadn't had a serious relationship, and she tried to remember the last time she'd been interested in a woman enough to date. It had been years.

"Yes. A partner."

Blaze shrugged. "Not in a while."

"Tell me more." Trinity took a chunk of bread and a wedge of cheese.

"There's been several women over the last decade. I thought we'd hit it off well and we'd make a good couple, but something always happened to end the relationship before it got very serious." She'd never bothered to analyze why they'd ended.

Trinity was paying close attention. "Please tell me you had a first love."

Blaze laughed. "I'm not going to tell you about my high school crush. That was embarrassing." Trinity smiled and she went on. "Chloe was my first partner as an adult. A friend gave her my name. She wanted someone to build a curio cabinet for her parents' anniversary. We had several meetings to go over details and agreed on a design." Blaze took a breath before continuing. "Chloe's parents fell in love with it, and Chloe was so happy with the end result, she insisted on taking me to dinner as a thank you. We dated for six months before Chloe moved in and we settled into a comfortable relationship. A little less than two years later, we decided our lives were taking divergent paths. The split was amicable, and we'd kept in touch until Chloe moved out west to follow her dream of making it big as an actress. Last I knew, she'd managed to land a few minor parts and was contemplating surgery to make her 'stand out' from the field of wannabes." Blaze shook her head. "Like I thought—our lives were on different paths."

"It sounds like it worked out for the best."

"I think so. I hope Chloe got to follow her dream." Blaze watched Trinity delicately chew, fascinated by the movement of her mouth. She caught Trinity staring at her when the movement stopped. "What about you? Any past loves you want to share with me?"

"None."

Blaze gave her an incredulous look. "Really?"

Trinity nodded. "I was an A student through school, then pulled a 3.9 in college. I didn't have time for romance, and then when I did, I took the first job I was offered and started working even harder to move up the ladder."

"And your family?"

Trinity winced and played with a bit of cheese. "Not much to say."

She sensed Trinity's discomfort and decided to change the subject. They were just getting to know one another, and with any luck, she'd have lots of time to learn more. "So, I take it hiking isn't a regular activity for you?"

Trinity laughed and the tension of the moment broke.

"Hardly. I barely find time for the gym, and then only rarely. What about you?"

"What do you want to know?"

"No offense, but I pictured you more of a weightlifter than a hiker."

Blaze cocked her head, not connecting the dots, and Trinity pointed to her forearm.

"Your arms are...big."

Heat rose in her cheeks. Some women didn't go for muscular partners. "Yeah, they are. I blame years of sawing and splitting wood. And carving takes a lot of precise muscle use. More than you would think." She'd taken up hiking when she couldn't work out and found it was more to her liking than watching egos on stage at the gym. The ones who were there to show off their physiques rather than to keep in shape.

"They suit you," Trinity said. She held up her much thinner but toned arm. "I couldn't pull off the look."

Blaze laughed. "You've got curves and..." Shit. Admitting she'd noticed meant she'd checked Trinity out. She waited for the fallout.

"Do I now?" Trinity's eyes sparkled with mischief.

She glanced from her eyes, to her mouth, to the column of her neck. Trinity's breathing sped up. God, Blaze wanted to kiss her. "Uh-huh." She had to get moving before she did something stupid. Something that could possibly push Trinity away. "Now that we've replenished a bit, are you ready to keep going?"

Trinity's expression closed for an instant, then she helped pack up. "I'm ready if you are."

Their hands brushed as she reached for the bread and she regretted how quickly Trinity pulled away. Once they were back on the trail, Trinity seemed to relax. Along the way, Blaze pointed out an eagle, a red fox and her pups, and a few interesting birds.

"Nature at its finest," Blaze said. "Too bad some people see them as a nuisance."

"Do you live close to all of this?" Trinity waved at the vista in front of them.

"Yes. It's a big part of why I returned after college. I can't imagine living in the city again. There's nothing quite like watching the woods come alive with creatures. I try to be respectful of all life, great and small."

An hour and a half later, they returned to their cars. There hadn't been much more conversation, but the silence had been comfortable.

"Thank you so much for the invitation. I had a great time and I learned so much about the wildlife, you should be a guide."

Blaze toed the dirt. "After the accident, I had to find a way to keep in shape and fill the empty hours, and there are so many places in the area for hiking I decided to give it a try. I love it." She heard a bird singing a serenade and tried to locate the cardinal.

"I can see why." Trinity tossed her pack on the passenger seat, then closed the distance until they were almost toe to toe. "I enjoyed talking with you, too. I don't socialize a lot, and this was a nice break."

"You're welcome. Anytime you want to get away from the stress, let me know. I'd be happy to play tour guide for you." Before she could stop, she reached for Trinity's hand and gave a gentle squeeze.

Trinity squeezed back. "I may just take you up on the offer."

As Trinity drove away, Blaze glanced at her arm. She still wore the sleeve. The scar was sensitive and the heat of the sun could burn the newly healed skin. The rest of her burned, too. But it wasn't the sun causing it. Trinity caused desire to flare hot inside of her. She had it bad, and she wasn't sure if it was good for either of them.

❖

"We should celebrate," DJ said.

"It's not like I won an award or something." As a result of her latest scan, Carrie had reduced her therapy sessions. During that time, she'd show her how to build up her strength, and maybe after that she could start working again.

"No, it's better. You could be making no progress at all."

Blaze had to admit she was more than ready to return to her shop. She was going stir-crazy and was more than a little needy for physical closeness. It was another part of her life that had been put on hold, but no-strings sex didn't have the same allure it once had. Trinity had called, letting her know she was working split shifts and doing mandatory overtime for the next few days. Her need to tell Blaze provided a glint of hope that Trinity might be interested in getting together again. Blaze had a gut feeling it was best to take things slowly. She didn't want to give Trinity any reason to disappear again. "What do you suggest?" With Trinity unavailable, she may as well do something.

"Want to go barhopping?" DJ asked.

Inwardly, Blaze groaned. In so many ways her best friend had never grown up. She hadn't been barhopping in more than a decade and she had no intention of starting now. "No."

"Gee, okay. What the hell is wrong?"

"I'm sorry. I just…I want to do something, but not that." She cradled the phone between her ear and shoulder. DJ was only trying to help get her out of the funk she'd been in for the last few weeks. It started when she read her hometown paper online and found out two of her classmates had died. One of cancer, and the other of a heart attack. Although she was almost forty, she'd believed she had her whole life ahead of her. Finding out that might not be the case was sobering at best. Depressing was more like it. Even though DJ would entertain her, Blaze couldn't stomach the thought of going from place to place only to wake up hungover. Hiking with Trinity had been way better than going to a bar.

DJ preferred to get into relationships that eventually ended for one reason or another, rather than wait for someone who complemented her. Blaze wasn't interested in a messy relationship or one destined to end, just so she could be with someone. If that's what having one meant, she needed to reconsider where her future was headed because she didn't think she could handle the drama. "What about a movie?" Blaze suggested.

"We aren't that old."

She blew out a breath. "Then you decide."

"Okay, but I can only come up with one more idea, so you have to say yes." DJ huffed.

She wasn't quite begging, but Blaze knew the tone, and she didn't have the heart to disappoint her. Since her accident she'd promised to help DJ get over her last relationship, and so far, she wasn't doing such a great job. "Okay. You win."

"Yeeesss."

Blaze could almost picture DJ fist-pumping. She laughed. "So, what are we doing?

"Dancing!"

She dragged her hand over her face. She had two days to mentally psych herself up for the impending outing, and she would do her damnedest to make sure DJ had a good time.

"Great." She knew she sounded less than enthusiastic.

"If you get any more excited, you'll strain something," DJ said. "It's just what you need, and it will be good for me, too."

Blaze swallowed her pride. She hated being a downer. That wasn't who she was, and she needed to figure out what to do to move forward. "I'm sorry I've been a bit off of late."

"Hey, you know I'm just giving you a hard time. Anything I can help with?" Concern laced DJ's tone.

She didn't need DJ to take on any more than she already had on her plate. DJ could be a pain in the ass, but her heart was always in the right place. Unfortunately, DJ rarely let anyone else see that side of her, including love interests, and it was likely a reason her relationships failed. "I'll be fine. Just a cycle. Maybe it's PMS." *If only.* Based on her mom's history, she would be approaching menopause in the next few years. Something else to look forward to.

"We both know you don't PMS. You never have. Whatever it is, there's nothing a night of dancing can't cure." DJ loved to dance.

"True enough." Blaze stared at the stack of invoices. She needed to get back to her normal life. "I've gotta go. What time do you want me to pick you up Friday?"

"I'm not riding on that beast between your legs." DJ giggled, and Blaze couldn't help joining her.

"I'll drive the Wrangler."

"Good. Let's go for a quick bite first. How about seven?"

"Seven it is. Later."

They made kissy face noises and Blaze ended the call. She tapped her pen on the stack of papers and contemplated her upcoming trip to EroZone. For the past few years, going had been almost a weekly occurrence. Her frequency had greatly decreased recently, and she hadn't been back since the night she'd met Mindy.

Having accepted her fate, Blaze had to admit she was looking forward to going out with nothing on her agenda but having some laughs and hitting the dance floor, though she wished she'd be going with Trinity. But DJ was a great dance partner, and inviting Trinity would be stepping on DJ's toes. They'd been dancing together for years. Friends ribbed them, saying they might as well be a couple, but she couldn't go there. They'd tumbled into bed together at college, but it had been a byproduct of the loneliness they'd both been feeling, nothing more. Blaze wasn't into DJ that way, and had she not been homesick, it never would have happened. They'd agreed it had been a mistake and, luckily, had been able to keep their friendship intact. In fact, they'd grown closer, and she'd always been grateful for DJ's friendship.

Yet, here they were. Blaze had no prospects for a long-term relationship—though she wished she had a chance to prove the theory wrong, and maybe she needed to start thinking about that more seriously. Conversely, DJ kept jumping into them, only to be disappointed. Maybe she was beginning to understand DJ's constant need for more than casual. DJ was honest in saying she didn't want to grow old alone. Blaze had to admit she'd been thinking the same thing of late.

She flexed her fingers, staring at the scar that would be a constant reminder of how fragile life was. One minute she was enjoying her comfortable routine, the next she was waking to pain and confusion. The one good thing had been meeting Trinity. The hike had been great, and the quick texts here and there made Blaze smile, but none of it felt like they were dating.

Maybe Trinity was only interested in friendship. There wasn't any denying Blaze's magnetism to her spring green eyes and a body shape that commanded attention. It was also possible Trinity was straight and what she thought was mutual attraction was only sexual curiosity. Blaze was used to women, straight and gay, who liked the side of masculine she played on, and the size of her bike attested to her physical strength.

The stiffness in her hand and the uncooperative muscles in her arm were finally starting to recede. Cassie said she might never be one hundred percent, but she could live with ninety, if she got there. The thing she needed to focus on was getting clearance from Dr. Jonas so she could return to doing what she'd loved her entire life— carpentry. Then she'd concentrate on figuring out where the rest of her life was headed. The problem was, she wasn't entirely sure what she wanted yet, and whether Trinity was meant to be a part of it.

CHAPTER TWELVE

Trinity hopped up on a stool and looked around the crowded club. She'd given in after Kelly's badgering and let the crew drag her along for a night of dancing. She'd almost contacted Blaze, but she wasn't sure if she wanted to expose her to the antics of their group. They could get a little out there when they all got together. She still felt a bit guilty.

"Hey, want to dance?" Kelly shouted across the small table.

She shook her head. "Go ahead. I'm gonna chill for a bit. Have fun."

Kelly looked like she was about to protest, then her eyes softened as though she understood what Trinity was feeling. "Okay. Join us when you're ready."

Swinging her legs on the high barstool reminded Trinity of sitting on the wall of the playground when she was much younger. She sipped her beer and slowly took in the crowd of women gathered in groups surrounding the huge dance floor. The variety of sizes, shapes, and ages was a wake-up call. There were days she felt like she was too old to waste time on frivolous activities like dancing, yet here she was, and she wasn't the only one. She would bet money many of the women were doing the same thing she was—unwinding after a hectic day.

Trinity stopped cold when she saw a familiar face. *Blaze.* She was smiling and laughing at the woman across from her. When the woman turned her head, Trinity's heart sank, and she dreaded the thought of DJ and Blaze out together. She'd been doing so much overtime the only contact they'd had since their hike were a few random texts. Now she regretted not having found the time. Unable to look away, Trinity studied Blaze, knowing she hadn't noticed her and likely wouldn't, not in this crowded space. Blaze's form fitting jeans showed off her muscular thighs and a tight rear she hadn't had the pleasure of noticing before since she'd worn loose hiking shorts. The sleeves of her white oxford were rolled up to reveal her impressive forearms. Trinity's imagination ran a bit wild as she pictured the many ways Blaze used those muscles to have them so well developed. The right one bore the compression sleeve, but no brace. A good sign, from a medical standpoint. But Trinity's thoughts were anything but professional right now.

Kelly and a couple of the other nurses plopped into seats, out of breath and laughing.

"Wow, I must be getting old. Two songs and I need a break." Kelly swallowed half her drink and smacked her lips.

She dragged her gaze away long enough to comment. "We are not old. We simply expend all our energy saving lives. We just need to work on our cardio."

"Ha. I thought we did that horizontally." Kelly bumped shoulders with her.

"You are so bad." Trinity finished off her beer. "Anybody want another?" She took their orders and conveniently headed to the bar the same time Blaze did, wanting to get closer to see if she noticed her. She found a spot at the bar with an empty stool between them.

"Another round, Blaze?" the bartender asked between opening beers and juggling dirty glasses.

"Might as well." Blaze glanced in her direction while she waited. Her expression changed from bored to surprised.

"Hi," Trinity said.

"Hey. Did you get the night off?" Blaze asked.

Blaze looked unsettled and she wondered why. "Yes. The first one not following a twelve-hour shift in a while."

Blaze nodded, then tossed money on the bar and picked up the drinks. "I need to get back to DJ. Enjoy your evening."

The response felt cold. Nothing at all like their previous interactions. "Are you upset with me?" The statement got her attention and Blaze turned, her eyes traveling over Trinity's body like a seductive caress.

"I'm not."

"Sure sounds it."

"You're right, I'm sorry. My mood hasn't been the best lately." Her tone held regret, but there was something else revealed in her expression that Trinity couldn't decipher. Blaze leaned close to her ear. "You're very beautiful and I'm glad you're having fun."

She hadn't expected the compliment, but her body reacted, and she was able to get out a "Thank you," before Blaze walked away. She hoped the heat in her face hadn't been visible. Still, though, she didn't have a clue what might have soured Blaze's usual upbeat mood. She pushed her credit card forward to pay for the drinks.

Trinity signed the paper, then slid her card into her back pocket. On her way to the group, she couldn't help glancing over her shoulder. Blaze stood alone at the table looking lost in thought. Trinity glanced around until she found DJ on the dance floor rubbing up against a tall brunette. Her gaze returned to Blaze and Blaze smiled, tipping her bottle in Trinity's direction. Maybe she was working through whatever was bothering her and Trinity couldn't resist smiling back. She got to the table and Kelly helped keep the bottles upright.

"Why are you flushed?" she asked.

"No reason." Trinity took a long drink. She could feel Blaze's eyes on her, and a flash of heat shot to her core.

"Oh. I know that look. Who is she? Where is she?" Kelly looked around like an eagle scanning her surroundings for prey.

"Stop it." Trinity sighed. "You promise not to make it obvious?"

"Cross my heart."

She sighed. Kelly would be relentless if she didn't tell her. "The gorgeous hunk in the white shirt and jeans at eleven o'clock."

After a few long seconds, Kelly's hand moved to her hip as though sizing her up. "You mean the one with her arm around the waist of a willowy blonde?"

Her head snapped around. Sure enough, DJ stood next to her, her arm waving in the air as she talked. "The one in jeans is Blaze Carter and the woman waving her hands around is DJ."

"Really?" Kelly continued to stare, and she was about to nudge her when three more of the group came from the dance floor to grab their drinks.

"Hey, what are you two up to?"

Kelly tipped her head. "Watching the hot butch across the way in the white shirt."

"That's Blaze, and she's definitely hot." One of her colleagues gave a knowing smile.

Trinity wasn't sure if she should be jealous or use the opportunity to pump her for information. Blaze was the type of woman she'd like to get to know better.

"Are they together?" Trinity asked.

"Nah. That's her best friend. Last I knew she was as single as ever, but she doesn't mind casual."

The knot that had formed in her gut loosened a tad. She wasn't interested in anything more than casual either. At least, that's what she kept telling herself.

Her friends headed back to the floor and Kelly turned to her.

"So, what's going on?" Kelly asked.

"I enjoy her company, that's all."

Kelly nodded and walked away as though knowing there was more she wasn't saying. Blaze stood alone again. Trinity glanced at the writhing masses, and when she didn't see DJ in view, she took a breath and made her way over. This time the smile from Blaze was knee-weakening.

"Hi again," Blaze said. "I apologize for before. Can we start over?"

Trinity nodded, happy to give that a try.

She raised her wrapped arm and extended her hand. "I'm Blaze."

Trinity couldn't help laughing as her smaller hand slid into Blaze's, and she liked how it fit. "It's nice to meet you, Blaze. I'm

Trinity." Checking one more time for DJ, she gathered her courage. "Would you care to dance?"

Blaze set her drink down. "It would be my pleasure." She gestured for Trinity to lead the way and lightly placed her hand at the small of her back.

The intimate gesture wasn't unwelcome, and the heat generated by the simple touch had her head swimming. They found a small opening on the edge of the dance floor and gyrated to the beat of one of her favorite songs. She couldn't help but notice Blaze's excellent rhythm and how well she commanded her body. The fast song ended and a slow one started as the DJ announced, "This one's for all you lovers." She froze in place as couples around her engaged in embraces.

Blaze stepped close and held out her arms. "Another dance?"

She knew she shouldn't, but she moved forward anyway. Trinity was glad she'd worn three-inch heels. While she was still shorter, at least she wouldn't be staring at Blaze's chest. Trinity became sidetracked by thoughts of what her breasts looked like and she stumbled. Blaze easily kept her upright. She blushed. "Sorry."

"A misstep isn't a reason to be sorry." Blaze pulled her closer. "Save apologies for the big stuff." Blaze's lips brushed against the curve of her ear and a streak of pure heat shot through her. "Do we have big stuff to discuss?"

Trinity relaxed against her. "Maybe, but this isn't the place. Let's just dance." When the song ended, they remained in an embrace that felt too intimate. She didn't have a chance to back away.

"There you are." DJ looked Trinity up and down, clearly noticing Blaze's arm around Trinity's waist. DJ turned back to Blaze. "I've been looking for you. I think I've had enough of this." She glanced in Trinity's direction and Trinity's anger bristled.

Blaze's features hardened. "DJ, meet Trinity. Trinity, this is my rude friend, DJ."

DJ pursed her lips, like she'd just tasted something bitter. "Sorry," she said.

At least she had the decency to rein in her sarcasm, though Blaze's jaw clenched anyway, and Trinity was relieved when DJ headed back to the table. Blaze sighed.

"I apologize. She's been through a recent breakup and I haven't been much of a friend lately." Blaze watched as DJ downed her drink and yanked on her jacket. "Perhaps we could talk more when I'm not babysitting?"

She wanted to be pissed, but she couldn't be. Not with Blaze. "Sure. I look forward to it." Blaze kissed her cheek, then paused next to Trinity's ear. "You really are beautiful."

Trinity watched them leave and didn't miss the glare DJ threw over her shoulder. Once they were gone, she went to find Kelly, knowing she'd never leave without letting her know. She was just returning from the bar with fresh beers.

"That was quite the show." Kelly sat on a stool and tossed a peanut in her mouth.

"We were just dancing." Not that she hadn't thought about doing more, but she wasn't about to admit that little detail.

"Not you and Blaze dancing, though it looked pretty hot. DJ."

"Oh. Yeah."

"For a minute I thought she was going to scratch your eyes out." Kelly grinned. "What did she say to you? You didn't look very happy."

"Not much, but I don't think she liked the fact that Blaze was dancing with me instead of her." Honestly though, if DJ hadn't walked away, she'd be checking for dagger marks in her back.

"And what did dreamy stud say?"

"Her name is Blaze," she said, laughing. "She called her out for being rude and that's when DJ stalked off."

"Huh."

Huh exactly. She wasn't sure she'd go anywhere near Blaze if her bulldog was around, but she did want to see her again. And another slow dance wouldn't hurt. She glanced at Kelly. "You about done here?"

Kelly finished her bottle, burped, and got to her feet. "Yep. Nothing more to see here." She laughed.

Trinity had to agree. The hottest woman in the club had left with someone else. She pushed away the surge of jealousy. It was ridiculous to be upset over Blaze leaving with DJ instead of her. But if she had her choice, it certainly wouldn't be the last she saw of Blaze. *Time to go home to my empty bed.* At least the apartment wouldn't be empty. Kelly would be banging around for the next hour pretending she was picking up, when really, it just took her a while to settle down. And Trinity would lie in bed pretending to read, all the while speculating how far away Blaze lived and if she was sleeping alone.

❖

"Still at it?" Kelly leaned against the counter and held her mug in both hands.

Kelly had been dead to the world after pulling a double, but the smell of fresh coffee likely roused her. Trinity had applied for the head trauma nurse position and Kelly was her biggest cheerleader. She'd been dreaming of the day she'd be given the responsibility of keeping the staff on their toes and patients alive, and she was studying for the test all applicants had to take if she made it to that stage of the interview process. "You know it." She glanced at the clock above the sink, surprised she'd been studying for more than four hours. "You hungry?"

Kelly laughed. "When am I not?"

She pushed her pile to the far end of the table. "Cop a squat. I'll make breakfast."

"Don't you ever run out of energy?" Kelly ran her finger down the nearest open book. "Are you trying to memorize all this stuff?"

Trinity pulled a bowl from the lower cupboard, then a pan from the side cabinet. "Not really. I just want to have a handle on the urgent-care medications and what they're used for. I mean, I'm familiar with some of them, but there's quite a few I'm not." She cracked open eggs, letting them slowly tumble into the bowl. It was how she approached all situations. Methodical. Logical. Rushing meant mistakes, in her career and life in general, and she didn't like making mistakes.

"True. Every doc has their favorites and no two are alike." Kelly leaned back. "So, when are we going back to EroZone to find hot and handsome?"

She laughed. Trinity had briefly talked with Blaze earlier in the week, but three nurses had the flu and she was filling in a lot. With her interview and practical in the near future, she hadn't wanted to commit to getting together when she might not make it, so she'd told Blaze to expect a last-minute text if she was suddenly free. Blaze had been gracious and understanding. Unlike some of the women she'd tried to explain how difficult her schedule was, Blaze hadn't given her a hard time.

"We? I thought you were pretty serious about Linda." She stirred the eggs and dropped the bread in the toaster.

"Doesn't mean I can't appreciate other women. You have to admit Blaze is a hunk."

"A hunk, huh?" Trinity tamped down the flare of jealousy.

"Bet I wasn't the only one she got tingling. She's got those amazing bedroom eyes and a body I could certainly spend some time getting up close and personal with."

Trinity rolled her eyes. "I didn't know you were such a pig." She was kidding, of course, but she prickled at the thought of Kelly having the hots for Blaze.

"Maybe I never had a reason to be." Kelly wiggled her eyebrows, then stopped. She reached out to touch her hand. "You know I'm just kidding, right? I'd never move in on someone you're interested in. Lord knows, how you sustain yourself on what little sex you have is beyond me." Kelly spread butter on the toast and plopped pieces on their plates. "This looks great. Thanks for cooking."

She was being childish. Maybe she *did* need to see a little more action. Work was stressful enough, but with studying and surviving on minimal sleep, sooner or later something was going to give, and she'd just as soon keep everything functioning. "Are you off Sunday?"

Kelly nodded. "Yes. You?"

Trinity swallowed a mouthful of eggs along with her pride. She hated to admit her attraction, but there wasn't any reason to deny it, especially when it was so obvious to Kelly. Still, she didn't want to come across as a woman desperately looking for a hookup, and even though she'd gone out alone on plenty of occasions, she preferred to go with someone. "Want to go dancing?"

Kelly grinned. "Any particular reason?"

She bumped Kelly's shoulder with her own. "Why would you think there's a reason?" They stared at each other for a minute before bursting into fits of laughter. It felt good. She hadn't laughed in a while. She'd been taking life way too seriously lately. And if Blaze was free to meet her, even better.

CHAPTER THIRTEEN

Days were ticking by. This was the season Blaze loved most—fall. Summer flowers had died, and the beds needed work. Standing in the middle of the driveway, she closed her eyes, letting the cold air caress her like a lover's touch. She was grateful to come home every day to the house she'd built and the peaceful acres teeming with life that surrounded her. She'd stocked up on birdseed, peanuts, and ears of corn to provide food for her forest friends when the ground was covered in snow and ice. She couldn't become complacent about all she had. Still, she recognized the gnawing need inside her. Soon another year would be over, and she continued to return to an empty house with no one to greet her, though if Baxter could talk, Blaze was sure she would take offense. She shrugged off the melancholy along with her jacket and hung it on the peg.

"What did you do today? Catch any mice?"

The orange tabby snaked around her legs and cried loudly, letting her know she was none too happy with dinner being late. Again.

"One of us has to work and it's obviously not you."

Baxter didn't seem to care what her opinion was, as long as food was in her near future. She sat by her dish mat looking up expectantly.

"At least you're one female I can always rely on." She shook dry food into a dish with cartoon drawings of fish and mice, gave Baxter a pat on the head, and set it down. "Bon appétit."

Blaze thought about her own dinner, but she wasn't in the mood to cook, and eating alone wasn't the same since her picnic with Trinity. By now she'd hoped for more meals together, but Trinity's profession demanded she work long shifts and overtime. Days off were an infrequent luxury lately. She grabbed a bottle of fruit juice and headed for the bedroom. Her clothes smelled of wood shavings, a scent she'd grown up loving, but she wasn't sure it would be welcome at a restaurant. Not everyone shared her appreciation of woodsy scents. She stripped, then tossed everything in the hamper before stopping in front of her full-length cheval mirror. The figure in the reflection was in good physical shape. Her stomach was flat, her arms and legs were muscled. Her forearm bore a thin red line, and Cassie assured her it would fade more with time. Blaze turned sideways. Her ass was a bit too round for her liking though no one had complained, so she was okay with it. Maybe she'd let her hair grow. She needed a change, but she knew she'd regret anything but a subtle difference in style.

The shower spray hit her chest, the warmth comforting. A good meal might help her feel more content. *Content.* Somehow the word didn't hold the same conviction it once had. Maybe that was what had been gnawing at her insides. Was she ready to take that step into the next phase of her life? What did that even mean? Blaze shook her head and concentrated on what she was doing. In less than five minutes, she was standing with a towel wrapped around her. She was going through the motions, bits and pieces just seemed to…happen. She was living on autopilot. She needed to touch base with her family. When they were together, she was happy. Not so long ago she'd been relaxed and unfazed by being on her own. At least, she thought so. She didn't want to be like some high school acquaintances she ran into every so often. Nothing in their lives had changed since graduation, and it would be easy to wake up one day and find out her life was a mirror image of a decade ago. She needed to grow emotionally. Take a risk. Make a move. All she had to do was figure out what her next step should be. *Easy.*

Baxter stood at the door watching her.

"Do you think you get an opinion?"

A loud meow and a swish of the cat's tail was her answer. "Think again. But I do need a second opinion." Baxter's head tipped. There was only one person she could rely on for guidance. She smiled at the icon of her father and pressed the number.

❖

A couple of hours later, Blaze sat at a table for two and ordered a bottle of Chianti. She'd never known DJ to turn down a decent glass of wine. Her call home had been productive, and even if her father hadn't provided the answer, he'd told her where to find it. She was confident he was right.

She also wanted to share her epiphany with DJ, though she wasn't sure what her reaction would be. With her arm in better shape, she'd been back to work as much as possible, and when she wasn't…well, that was the part she was dreading telling her. Then, magically, as if a tornado had blown through the door, DJ was there.

"Oh my God. Traffic is ridiculous. What the hell. I had a distress call from my BFF, and no one was going to get in my way." She gulped down water. "Okay, I'm ready." DJ sat with her hands folded near her plate with a look of expectation on her face.

Blaze shook her head. "You *can* take a breath you know. It's not life or death." Blaze leaned back while the waiter opened the bottle, then poured a tasting into her glass. She'd always thought the ritual was unnecessary until she'd been served a bottle that had turned to vinegar. After she took a swish and a swallow, she nodded and he poured more for them both, then went away.

"Well, it could be. Are you sure it's not? You sounded pretty intense." DJ took a drink, set it down, and gave a thumbs-up, signaling her stamp of approval.

She hated when she hesitated to address an issue, but she wasn't keen on rushing into explaining *why* she had the feelings she did. "Let's take time to settle in, then I'll tell you."

DJ stared for a moment. "Okay, but this could be a two-bottle session." She added more to their glasses before they ordered food.

"Good thing we can Uber home. How's work going?" Blaze asked. It was an unnecessary question since she and DJ talked regularly, but she was using the opportunity to start to open up the flow of conversation until she was ready to focus on herself. DJ graciously chatted about her latest successful showing and how much she was looking forward to the big commission. DJ wanted to be known as the Realtor who closed the most houses in a month, enabling her to ask for a larger commission percentage.

"Do you ever get tired of working so much? You should take a vacation." Blaze knew she wasn't afraid of hard work and putting in the hours required to accomplish her goals. Unlike her personal life, real estate was something she excelled at. Relationships, however, she failed at miserably. DJ had redeeming qualities, but she could be difficult at times. Blaze was the only one she let see her vulnerable side, and that didn't make for solid relationships.

Blaze wondered if the reason DJ's relationships continued to fall apart was her lack of taking time off. Even weekends belonged to her job, and Blaze knew she hadn't been away in a few years.

"I take time off. I'm not working now, am I?" DJ shoved a piece of calamari in her mouth and chewed. She wrinkled her nose. "I'm done for the day."

"It's a little difficult to show houses in the dark, and you know perfectly well what I mean."

"Sometimes I show houses at night. My clients work crazy hours too, and I have to be flexible. My life is fine just the way it is, thank you." DJ blinked a couple of times before sitting back. "Why do I get the feeling we aren't really talking about my life? Spill it."

At least DJ hadn't lost the ability to read her mood. Like now. "Don't you ever want more out of life?" Blaze sighed. "I've been thinking about mine a lot lately."

DJ smiled. "Thinking's important."

"Funny." She took a breath. "I'm content with where my life is." She held DJ's gaze. "But I don't think it's enough any longer. I want...more." There. She'd said it and she was still breathing.

"More what?" DJ set her fork down and leaned forward.

"I want someone to come home to. I want someone to share my day with. My joys, my sorrows. All of it." She stared into the contents of her glass. "I'm tired of living alone. I want a partner."

DJ's eyes widened, then she cleared her throat. "Baxter will be none too happy to hear the alone part."

DJ was trying to make a joke, but Blaze sensed there was something else beneath the surface that she wasn't sharing. "Can't you be serious for once? I thought you'd understand."

She nodded. "I do, but where is this coming from? Why the sudden change of heart? I thought you were happy."

Blaze looked up. "I thought I was happy, too, but I've been restless, and I can't seem to focus. My thoughts are all over the place."

DJ's hand covered hers. "Honey, we all have moments of questioning. I'm not sure that means you aren't happy. What's the one thought that keeps coming to mind? The one thing you can't shake?"

It didn't take her long to come up with an answer. "Trinity." She didn't know why there was a lump in her throat. She should be glad she'd finally been able to say her name out loud, even if she hadn't been able to put it into words until now.

DJ slid her hand away. "I should have known."

Blaze couldn't tell if DJ was upset or angry by the news, and she didn't know how to respond. DJ had never been overly crazy about the women she'd dated before, but Blaze always thought she could rely on her support. "Thanks for being here for me."

"That's not what I meant, and you know it." DJ flushed in what Blaze assumed was embarrassment. "It's just…shouldn't you be focused on your recovery for a while? I remember at one time you imagined spending time with your wood was probably like marriage. Being committed, but never knowing if you needed to step back and observe from a distance."

She chuckled. "That was like, twenty years ago, and I wasn't the one who said the word marriage." That would be getting a bit ahead of herself. "Finding a partner for more than sex would be a good start. I'm nowhere near thinking about marriage."

The waiter cleared their appetizer plates and set down their entrees. She'd opted for linguini with clam sauce, while DJ settled for shrimp scampi.

"Could we have a bottle of Riesling? Something that goes well with these." DJ gestured to their plates. The waiter took the empty wine bottle and glasses. Once they were alone again, DJ avoided eye contact. She played with her food.

"Hey. What's wrong?" Blaze never had to prod DJ into talking.

DJ shrugged, still moving food around her plate. "I just thought we'd have some time to hang out since I'm single again." She finally glanced up. "It's selfish of me. So, what got you thinking about a relationship?"

"I've been tossing it around for a while. Especially since the accident." Blaze hoped DJ would give her feedback. She had more experience in the relationship circuit than Blaze did and was open to hearing her take on it. "I'm not sure. I was in the shower and thinking about how routine my life was. That led to having a one-on-one conversation with myself. The next thing I knew, the word 'content' popped into my head." She waited while the bottle of wine was opened and poured into clean glasses. "Then I called my father and it all tumbled out. I realized I'd never wanted routine to be part of my life, it just sort of happened. Then I thought about how many nights I went to a diner or the club just for the company. I don't want to spend the rest of my life alone and wishing 'if only' like so many people I know."

DJ's fork stopped midway to her mouth. "Like me?"

"God dammit, DJ. For once the conversation isn't about *you*." She pushed her plate away. The evening wasn't going at all like she'd thought. Maybe that was part of the problem. She'd always been a planner and that left little room for spontaneity, something that was going to change, starting now.

DJ's gaze traveled around the room. "Okay, okay. I get it. Could we please not include the entire restaurant in our conversation?"

She glanced up to find several nearby patrons staring at her. "Sorry," she said, loud enough for them to hear. Thankfully, they went back to their own conversations. Blaze zeroed in on DJ. "I was hoping for some support. Was I wrong to count on my best friend to understand what I'm going through?"

"No. Of course not. I'm still stinging from Ryan leaving. I'm lonely, too. I understand perfectly."

Blaze had turned all of her attention inward, which wasn't a bad thing because it wasn't something she tended to do. That didn't excuse her from not realizing DJ had her own issues to overcome. She gave her a half grin. "Look at us. We're both having women troubles from different angles." She reached for DJ. "I really am sorry you two didn't work. If it's any consolation, I think she was the best one so far. I liked her."

DJ rolled her eyes and chuckled. "Great. I let a good one get away." She finished her glass of wine. "So, what do you think we should do about it?"

"Social networks, dating sites, lesbian groups?" Blaze raised her glass and drained the contents. "Have another bottle of wine and call for that Uber."

"Ha. That's the best idea you've had all night."

Blaze motioned to their waiter and ordered another bottle. She didn't believe it was the best idea. She wasn't even sure if coming here tonight and telling DJ what she'd been thinking had been any better. But *she* felt better for having gotten it out in the open, and if push came to shove, she knew she could depend on DJ. She always had and saw no reason for their relationship to change. After all, they were best friends, and that meant they were there for each other, especially in trying times and mutual woes.

Chapter Fourteen

The week dragged by and Trinity dealt with one tragedy after another. For the briefest instant she again wondered if she'd made a mistake in choosing the trauma unit, especially knowing she could work anywhere with her newest degree. Then she remembered the times she'd seen miracles happen.

The woman who'd been in full-blown cardiac arrest before the team worked tirelessly for forty-five adrenaline-filled minutes. She'd smiled when she regained consciousness and told Trinity, "I wasn't ready to go." The little girl who'd fallen from her swing and landed on her arm. The break had been clean, and the doctor ordered a mild sedative while they'd reset the bone, then wrapped it in a hot pink fiberglass cast. The child had taken the incident in stride, as had her parents, and asked Trinity to be the first to sign it.

Those were the patients she was there for. The ones she could help heal. The ones who were grateful in the chaos of the ED for being made to feel like they mattered…because they did. Maybe her kindness was the first time that individual felt cared for. Those were the ones who needed her skills the most, and she tried to remember not everyone had the opportunity to make better choices about their own lives. She should know. She'd been one of the ones who'd almost become a statistic of poverty.

An alarm sounded in triage room four. Kelly sprinted by with a crash cart, focused on getting in the room with the team. Trinity stayed back. There were plenty of people responding, and sometimes one more body just made the job more difficult. Part of her abilities included knowing when she'd be more of a hindrance than a help, and she was okay with not always being in the foreground. In fact, she didn't mind being behind the scenes on occasion. The rush still hit her.

She quickly assessed the remaining patients' monitors and reviewed charts. Room three was ready for discharge. Room two was being observed for the next few hours before the doctor decided if more tests were needed. Room one was waiting for a bed. Satisfied for the moment, she pulled up labs and checked levels again, making sure she hadn't missed anything. A little later Kelly came around the desk with her cheeks flushed and her eyes wide.

"Can we not have any more of those tonight?" Kelly said. "I'm exhausted."

Trinity knew the feeling. After the adrenaline rush, they all suffered the crash, leaving them feeling drained. She reached under the counter and grabbed a bottle of juice. "Here. Sit down for a few minutes. I've got this." She indicated the monitor that showed real-time vital signs for the patients in their area. Everyone was stable. *One more hour.* Then they could both head home for some much-needed sleep.

"Thanks." Kelly cracked the seal and downed half the contents. "This was the best idea the administration ever had."

She had to agree. When supervisors had asked about ways to make improvements and meet staff needs, someone had suggested keeping a stock of beverages available at each workstation for when the chaos kept them from getting a break to rehydrate and replenish.

"I can't wait to get home. My feet are screaming today." Kelly slipped one foot out of her Crocs and rubbed it. "Calgon, take me away."

Trinity laughed at the outdated commercial reference. "You're showing your age." She made a few notes in charts and let out a long breath. "A hot soak sounds really good though."

"What can I say? I like retro stuff." Kelly tossed her bottle into the recycle bin. "If you won't get all fidgety, we can take one together and have a glass of wine."

It was all she could do not to laugh. "I'm not fidgety." Trinity remembered the time they'd gone to a concert and had stayed at a hotel for the night. It had a huge whirlpool tub that they'd gotten into after a few drinks, but she'd felt funny about it. She hadn't known Kelly long, and when she'd slid in wearing nothing but a skimpy bra and even skimpier panties, she'd tried to look anywhere but at the almost naked woman in the bubbling water.

"You did the last time. You turned fifty shades of red."

"Okay. Maybe I did feel a little uncomfortable, but in my defense, I barely knew you then." Her excuse sounded lame.

"True, but it's not like I tried to hit on you, though later I wished I had." Kelly raised an eyebrow.

Trinity wasn't sure if she was kidding or not. Sometimes she still didn't know when Kelly was being serious or just messing with her head. "If you expect me to get into the tub with you, you need to cut that out. It's creepy." She laughed when Kelly stuck her tongue out, reassuring her it had been a joke.

"Okay, weirdo, let's go."

Forty-five minutes later, Trinity sank below the bubbles while holding her glass above the water. "This was a really good idea."

Kelly nodded. "I know, and you're not even being fidgety."

"Ass." Trinity laughed. The hot water soothed her tired legs. "I'm just happy we have a garden tub and I don't have to touch you."

Kelly's hand flew to her chest. "I'm crushed." She finished her wine. "But seriously, one lesbian to another, that's like…not something either of us needs to hear."

"You're right, but it would still be weird to be intimate with a friend." She couldn't help thinking about Blaze and DJ and whether they'd ever been friends with benefits.

"What are you thinking?"

She shook her head, unwilling to say out loud what she feared the most when it came to Blaze.

Kelly sat up, nearly exposing her breasts. "Come on. Sooner or later you're going to tell me."

Trinity pointed in a downward motion. Kelly rolled her eyes and slid deeper.

"You really need to get over your fixation with my tits."

She gasped and Kelly broke out in a fit of laughter. "You're a real comedian." Kelly was right. Sooner or later she told her everything important. Blaze was becoming important. She bit her lip. "Whenever I hear her voice or see her, my pulse kicks up, then I pull back."

"Why? Is she not as charismatic as you thought?"

"No. That's not it. I want to get to know her better, but I'm not sure I want her to know about me." She poked at the bubbles. Kelly would know her hesitancy came from her childhood and her less than nurturing parents. She needed to remember she wasn't a child anymore.

"I know nothing personal about Blaze, but from everything you've said, I don't imagine she'd hold your past against you. Do you?"

"I don't think so." She pushed around the bubbles. "What if she can't handle my work schedule? Women don't seem to understand how demanding it can be."

"You're just making excuses now. If Blaze wasn't interested I don't think she'd respond to your messages. Didn't you tell me she said she'd miss you when you saw her at the hospital?"

Trinity nodded.

"Then she asked to see you socially. I could be wrong, but I'm pretty sure that means she likes you."

"Maybe. What if she wants me to go places with her and do things together?"

"You mean date?"

She swallowed hard. She'd been so afraid of being pulled away from her career goals, Trinity couldn't even fathom what dating would be like. However, when it came to Blaze, she'd begun to reconsider a lot of things. "What if she does? And what if it fucks up everything I've ever wanted, and she breaks my heart?"

Kelly sat up, revealing more than before. "Eyes up, perv."

Trinity wished she had more wine.

"First, you haven't even talked to her about dating. Second, you have no idea if she'll rock your world in the sack."

Trinity was about to say she hadn't thought about sex with Blaze, but that would have been a lie. "Go on."

"Third, if, and it's a big if, you actually make it to a relationship and manage to get over yourself, isn't it time you see if you can have something real with someone you're attracted to?"

All of what Kelly was saying made sense. There was one thing she wasn't sure she was ready to deal with emotionally. "What if she breaks my heart?"

Kelly took her hand. "And what if you break hers? If she's willing to give that much of herself I think you should be, too."

Trinity chewed on her lip. Kelly gave her a lot to think on. If she was going to take a chance at making her life have more meaning than how many hours she could work in a week, Blaze seemed like the perfect person for the role.

CHAPTER FIFTEEN

H ello," Blaze said.
"Hey, stranger. I haven't heard from you since our little heart-to-heart. How's it going?"

"Sorry. I've been swamped with contacting clients and new orders. I got the okay to start working full time again, as long as I don't overdo it, and I've been falling into bed exhausted. Even Baxter is pissed at me for lack of attention." Blaze moved around the shop, taking inventory.

"Do you want to go out tonight?" DJ asked.

"I don't think so. I'll be here for a while longer and I doubt there'll be any energy left when I'm done. My stamina isn't where it was yet."

"Oh," DJ said.

Blaze heard the disappointment in her voice. "Want to get together tomorrow? I'm going to sleep in, but I know how much you enjoy a late brunch at Phyllo's." DJ had a habit of guilting her into doing things without even trying.

"Sure. That sounds great. I'll pick you up at one, unless that's too early."

"No, that should give me time to get a cup of coffee and a shower."

"Okay. I'll let you go then. Have a good day."

"You, too. Later." Blaze disconnected.

She sighed. Between work and trying to squeeze in the occasional cup of coffee or a quick bite to eat from a takeout joint with Trinity, there was little time left for entertaining DJ. Though when DJ was busy selling and listing, the same could be said for her. Blaze wished she'd slow down and find a woman who would not only be good to DJ, but good *for* her. Someone who would complement DJ's innate ability to say it like it was, but who could show her how to soften her approach. DJ offended people without even trying, and with Trinity it seemed as if she'd thrown her miniscule filtering ability out the window. Blaze continued to wonder why, but any worry about it disappeared when she got to spend precious moments with Trinity. Whether it was five minutes or forty-five, her heart always raced the moment she caught sight of her. She still hadn't shared much about her family and Blaze had a feeling it was a sore spot, so she tried not to push even though she was curious. She'd never taken it so slowly with another woman, and she was really enjoying the building anticipation and gentle flirting they'd fallen into.

She pulled her datebook closer, forcing herself to focus. Three more new clients had left messages, and the sooner she got them on the schedule, the better. She had a life to live, too, and she was determined to make the most of it.

Later that night, Blaze ruffled her hair and watched the wood dust fall like snow onto the floor. She loved working with fresh cut wood and cherry was her favorite, and she saved the wood chips for her outdoor fire pit. After the last remnants had been swept up and the floor vacuumed to remove any remaining dust, she surveyed the fruits of the past week's labors. She was slowly getting back into the swing of working longer hours. Her arm would stiffen a bit when she overdid it, but with Cassie's guidance, she was able to recover in a day or two. Since the accident, she'd learned to do a number of routine tasks left-handed and she did the same in the shop when she could.

The kitchen island she'd crafted had a chevron pattern of shiplap on the front and the sides were stained a matching shade of gray. The quartz countertop would be installed once she delivered the piece, and Blaze helped the owner pick a white background with accenting threads of gray marbled throughout, highlighting her handiwork. The company she hired to deliver large pieces would be there with reinforcements on Monday morning and she'd supervise the installation later that day.

The live edge dining room table needed another sanding and multiple coats of polyurethane before she could schedule delivery. The variegated acacia wood had beautiful shades of light and dark running its length and would fit any decor. When she'd met with the soon-to-be owners, she'd been in awe of the flawless, eclectic mix of modern and antique that was the signature style of the home. They'd given her carte blanche as to the wood choices and asked her to find chairs that would showcase the beauty of the table, the focal point of the dining area.

The last piece she'd finished was her favorite. A lesbian couple had commissioned her to create a headboard with shelves, as well as a hidden compartment that she hadn't needed to ask what it would hold. She had also incorporated reading lamps that could be angled and dimmed according to each woman's preference. Blaze had chosen ash for what she considered one of her best pieces in recent years since she'd hand carved an intricate detail pattern into the facing edge. She'd been inspired by the couple's obvious love and passion. The long, narrow mirror set in the lower section concealed the requested space and opened from the top, similar to a transom. It would be virtually invisible to the casual observer, which was good because they planned on having children in the next year or two.

Blaze glanced at the clock on the corner of her massive oak desk. It was almost eight o'clock and her stomach rumbled. She'd barely eaten the last two days, opting for yogurt, apples, and vitamin drinks. Now she was ready for real food. She quickly showered and put on clean clothes, then headed to Maxi's for one of her favorite meals, a black and blue burger with hand cut seasoned fries. Her mouth watered just thinking about it.

With the doctor's okay, she was back on her bike, after promising she'd wear the brace when she drove. She'd been relieved to find out the Harley hadn't needed any major repairs. It had jumped the curb and landed in six-foot-tall hedges. The small dents and dings had taken a month to fix, but her mechanic assured her the machine was sound.

She hadn't expected the sudden anxiety when she'd first gotten on, and it had shaken her. That's when she called one of her Harley buddies who'd crashed and totaled her bike. Blaze asked how she'd gotten back on after that. Twenty minutes later, she'd driven it up and down the driveway until she was certain she could handle the machine again. Being at ease in traffic had taken her a bit longer, but she'd been determined not to give in to the fear.

The motorcycle purred beneath her as she took the familiar curves before cruising into the city of Lake George. It had been the hub of everyday life since returning from college. Even though she lived only four miles from town, the house she'd built was set near the side of the mountains she now spent time hiking in, and Blaze scoured the landscape for pieces for her craft. She'd had to ask the Park Commission for permission to remove fallen trees in the Adirondacks. The six-million-acre protected forest relied on Mother Nature to give back to the earth, and its decomposing foliage fed the wildlife in a multitude of ways. The commission had agreed to let her remove two hundred pounds a year, and she was required to catalog the location and weight of each of her finds. She gladly complied with the strict regulations as they made for the lush landscape she'd decided long ago she never wanted to leave.

Maxi's lot was half-empty when she pulled into a space along the side of the building. She strapped down her helmet and finger-combed her hair. The late October evening was brisk; the colder temperatures came early in the mountains, and she loved how alive it made her feel. She always wore a leather jacket and she welcomed the temperature change. She strode in and glanced around the familiar space. With Thanksgiving still a few weeks away, Maxi hadn't decorated for Christmas, and Blaze appreciated slowing down and not rushing into the holidays even though she loved them.

"Blaze." Maxi's enthusiasm traveled through the dining room as it always did when she was greeted by her longtime friend and owner of the restaurant. She gave Blaze a bear hug, making her laugh. For a tiny little thing, she still gave the best hugs ever.

"Maxi. How are you, darling?"

"Still kicking." Maxi's smile lit up the room. "To what do I owe the honor of a visit?"

Blaze remembered when the restaurant had opened back when she was in high school. She'd saved her allowance for a month and brought her then sweetheart to Maxi's for her first "official" date. It was a night she'd never forgotten. The food had been great, and way better than her date. Unfortunately, the girl she'd been crushing on for more than a year told her she appreciated Blaze and her good manners, but she saw her as a friend—not someone she'd date. Blaze had been crushed, but she got over it, and they remained friends until college separated them.

"I was craving one of your burgers." Blaze sat at her usual table near the cozy fireplace that had a small fire burning to chase away the chill. She loved the atmosphere, though she wished she had someone to share it with. Maybe she'd bring Trinity there. Maxi's voice jarred her back.

"Black and blue and a draft?" Maxi stood—all five feet of her—next to the table with her hands on her hips.

Blaze nodded. "Sharp as ever."

Maxi snapped the kitchen towel that was ever present at her hip. "Such a sweet talker." Maxi disappeared behind the swinging doors, and one of the waitresses who'd been there since Blaze had returned to town brought her a stein of her favorite Belgian wheat beer. It was ice cold with just the right amount of foam. Not knowing what else to do while she waited, she pulled out her phone and checked her email. She scrolled through and glanced at a notice from her supplier about a two-day delay in a shipment and sighed. There was a newsletter from her carpentry group that she marked to read later when she could concentrate.

Blaze took in her surroundings, wondering what she was doing there. Alone again on a Saturday night without a clue what to do next. DJ would always be up for getting together, but after her last show of possessiveness, she wasn't in the mood to go down that road tonight. She needed to find out what else was bugging DJ and decided to ask her point-blank the next day.

"Here you go, sugar." Maxi slid a heaping platter in front of her and smiled.

Blaze kissed her cheek, making her blush. "You always know how to brighten my…" Blaze glanced out the window. "Night."

Maxi lightly slapped her arm. "Save some room. I made raspberry pies this morning."

Blaze groaned. "You should have told me before I ordered all this food."

"You can always take it home."

She thanked Maxi and made her way through most of the burger and some of the fries before stopping. She was nearly full and hated feeling stuffed. As much as she didn't want to waste it, she pushed the plate away. She'd have the kitchen bag it up to feed some of the strays that frequented her warehouse. Once her beer was gone and her leftovers wrapped, she went to the register to pay her bill. Maxi rounded the corner.

"You weren't going to sneak off without saying good-bye, were you?"

Blaze admitted to being a bit distracted and promised to try not to let it happen again.

Maxi placed a large container inside her bag. "Let me know how you like it. I expect to see you again sooner rather than later."

"Yes, ma'am."

She stowed her package inside a reusable market bag and strapped it to the back of her bike. Blaze slipped her helmet on, but instead of turning the key she sat. Lost and unsure, she had no desire to go home to sit alone. Her phone dinged. Convinced it was probably DJ, she almost ignored it before checking the screen. Trinity had sent a text.

I know it's late and not sure what you're up to, but we're heading to EroZone if you want to join in.

It was as though wishing had actually worked.

Her father had told her to trust her gut, and her gut told her she wanted to spend time with Trinity wherever she might be. She revved the engine and roared out of the parking lot.

Thirty minutes later, Blaze kicked down her stand and inhaled deeply. She zeroed in on the only reason she was there. Somewhere inside these walls Trinity waited for her. Her earlier ambiguity over what to do next had been replaced by the anticipation of seeing her again.

The familiar thrum of the music's bass comforted her, and her shoulders dropped. She hadn't realized how much tension she'd been holding. She checked her jacket and helmet and surveyed the bar, then checked out the dance floor, not seeing Trinity anywhere. Maybe she wasn't there yet. She tipped her head and caught the bartender's eye. "Neat." The drink slid to a stop in front of her and she tossed money into the tab glass.

She took a minute to settle in. This place didn't fit her the way it used to. Or maybe she didn't fit it anymore. Blaze realized her days of casual sex and forgettable women had come to an end, and she was okay with the knowledge. She wanted to be done with her membership in the "Lonely Hearts Club." There was still the question of Trinity's level of interest and she briefly thought she might have to resort to fucking her worries away by letting her body take over for a while. Blaze shook her head. That wasn't going to make her feel better.

She sipped her drink and glanced at the person beside her.

"Blaze?"

It took her a minute to remember the name of the woman with the intense blue eyes. "Mindy," Blaze said. "How are you?"

Mindy smiled. "Much better, thanks to you."

She set her drink down. "How so?" Blaze followed Mindy's gaze to a handsome butch a few barstools away who nodded and smiled in their direction.

"Kyle is thoughtful and sweet and kind." Mindy blushed. It suited her.

"I'm happy for you. You deserve a good person in your life."

"I never had a chance to thank you for—"

"You don't have to thank me. I meant it when I said being with you was my pleasure."

At least their night together hadn't been meaningless sex for Mindy. That was something.

Mindy kissed her cheek, then stepped back. "I hope you're happy as well."

She gazed around the familiar space again, then stopped when she caught a flash of red hair. *Trinity.*

"I'm working on it. Take care, Mindy." Blaze watched Trinity as she leaned on a table and laughed with the friend she'd been with the last time. Her gaze met Blaze's, as though she'd called her name out loud. Her lips moved into a slow, seductive smile. Blaze's pulse raced, and she knew she'd found her release for the night. All she had to do was find out if Trinity was interested in taking the next step.

CHAPTER SIXTEEN

Trinity had argued with herself throughout the day as to whether she should text Blaze or let the chips fall where they may. Perhaps she'd stalled to see if Blaze would be there with DJ again. Maybe her lack of action had more to do with her own fears of involvement rather than whether there was something going on between the two of them. In the end she'd given in, and ten minutes before they left the apartment, she texted Blaze about her plans.

As she drank her beer something drew her attention to the bar, and there she was. Blaze had been invading her dreams for weeks. Now she was standing on the other side of a sea of bodies tossing back their heads and shaking their asses. The primordial mating dance. Blaze smiled. She didn't miss the haze in her eyes, and Trinity's pulse galloped in response as she made her way across the room. She stayed planted in her seat, unable to move. The black 501s Blaze wore had no right to look that good, and the black and gray pinstriped shirt accentuated her eyes.

"Good evening." Blaze waited a beat. "I'm glad you messaged me. I've been thinking about you."

Trinity forced herself to remain calm, but she wanted Blaze to kiss her. Touch her. Squelch the fire smoldering inside of her. It was there whenever she thought of her, and all she did was think of her. She had to remember whatever happened from this moment on, Blaze's intentions were still unknown. There was no reason to be nervous. "Hmm...why is that?" A slow song came on and Blaze leaned in.

"Dance with me."

Trinity nodded, unable to form words since her mouth had gone dry with desire.

Blaze turned to Kelly. "We haven't been formally introduced. I'm Blaze."

"Kelly."

"You'll excuse us while we share a dance?" Blaze cut her gaze to Trinity.

Kelly stared at them and Trinity fought an urge to stomp her foot to get her attention while Blaze patiently waited.

"Sure," Kelly finally said. She laughed and grinned at Trinity before giving her a wink and taking a sip of her drink.

Blaze took her hand. "Shall we?"

Maybe it was Trinity's imagination, but it appeared as though the throng parted, and a spot meant just for them opened in the center of the floor. Heat wafted from Blaze, scorching her skin. When their bodies touched, the flame inside her flared. The seductive sway of Blaze's hips against hers made her yearn for more. She backed away enough to relieve the pressure and found her hypnotic eyes.

"Are you here alone?" Trinity asked.

Blaze's irises darkened. "I definitely am," she said before pressing her thigh between Trinity's again, making it clear they shared similar thoughts. "I'd never be that rude after getting your invitation."

Trinity contained a groan and pressed closer, imagining herself as the match that set Blaze's body on fire. She sucked in a breath and held it.

Blaze's lips brushed her ear. "I have you." She spun them in another slow turn. "I know we haven't seen much of each other, but I'll take care of you if you'll let me." Even though the music hadn't stopped, Blaze did.

Trinity drank in the smoky depths of her gaze. Did she mean on the dance floor, or had they moved on to a more intimate meaning? *God, I want to say yes.* The room dipped, and she fought the feeling of vertigo. Had she ever been this attracted to another person? In the next moment they stood embracing as the dance floor emptied. Trinity bit her lip. Desire, hot and deep, coursed through every cell in her body. She had to move. "Let's finish our drinks." She took Blaze's hand and led her back to the table. She liked the sudden feeling of power as Blaze willingly followed.

Kelly stared at her. "Glad to see you two got reacquainted."

Trinity grinned. "We did." She picked up her beer and pretended to be pacing herself, but she really wanted to down it and leave. Blaze stood next to her sipping a dark brown liquor. "What are you drinking?"

"Scotch. Neat. I prefer the feel of a slow burn. I enjoy when the heat hits my stomach and explodes to the ends of my fingers and toes." Blaze's eyes reflected her words and she finished it off.

She watched Blaze swallow, and her throat contracted with the motion. And those lips. Dear Lord, her mouth was made for kissing. "Would you like another?"

"Thank you, but no. I'm driving."

"Will you have more when you get home?" She was stalling to give her time to calm down, but she didn't want her time with Blaze to end.

"That depends," Blaze said, her voice throaty and deep, and her gaze questioning what she was really asking.

"On?"

Blaze lifted her hand to her lips and kissed her knuckles. "If I'm otherwise occupied."

She turned to Kelly, who was staring unabashedly. "If you're okay, we're heading out." Kelly would understand her leaving, and she was glad they'd decided to take separate cars.

"Okay." Kelly appeared to have recovered. "Blaze, it was nice to meet you." Kelly turned to her. "I'll see you at home."

Blaze's eyebrow rose but she didn't say anything and followed her through the crowd. Once they were outside, she felt a need to clarify. "Kelly and I are housemates."

"Glad to know I'm not encroaching. I guessed as much since she didn't mind us leaving together." Blaze took her hand and led her down a row of cars until they stood beside a big Harley. "My ride. Want to join me?"

The thought of riding snugged up against Blaze with the rumble of the engine between her legs was tempting, but for practical reasons, she needed to have her car. "Another time?"

Blaze nodded.

"I'm parked over there." She pointed to her Jeep Liberty. "I can follow you."

"Let me have your phone so I can put in my address in case we get separated." She made quick work of updating her contact info, then straddled the machine like she'd done it a million times. She probably had. "I'm a few miles away on the side of a mountain. It's secluded and a little tricky to find. Stay close if you can." Blaze pulled her helmet on and revved the engine. The roar of the powerful motor filled the night.

Trinity got in her car and took a deep breath, then pulled around to where Blaze waited. She nodded at Trinity and she tipped her head in return. Blaze slowed the bike to the stop sign and Trinity concentrated on the motorcycle in front of her, not the person driving it. All her focus was on the drive, which was good, since she couldn't think about what she was about to do. A couple of miles later, they took a right turn and began a steep climb with switchbacks. Blaze was making an effort to keep her close, but it couldn't have been easy. She didn't know much about motorcycles, but she knew speed helped to keep the machine upright, and she watched her gun through some tight sections. The single headlight on the otherwise empty road let her zero in on the bike's location, but she was relieved when Blaze pulled onto a long, single lane road. Trinity followed her for what seemed like an eternity, but the odometer displayed she'd traveled less than a mile before they turned into a wide, paved driveway then up to a double garage. A motion light above the building came on to dispel the darkness. Blaze dismounted and met her at her car. Of all the times she'd pictured being alone with Blaze, now that the moment had arrived, she stood immobilized. She wasn't afraid of being in the middle of nowhere with her. Trinity feared intimacy. Kelly had pointed out her lack of experience when it came to sex, and she doubted the same could be said for Blaze. What if she couldn't satisfy her? What if she fumbled as though this was her first time having sex with someone older than she was? What if... Blaze's voice chased the "what-ifs" away.

"Glad you were able to keep up." Blaze held out her hand until they were standing together. "I really want to kiss you." Blaze pulled her closer when she didn't protest.

Trinity held her breath before their lips met. *Please don't make me regret this.*

Chapter Seventeen

B laze took her time, enjoying Trinity's soft lips and the sweet taste of her mouth. She could have kissed her for an eternity. Blaze pulled away first and hoped she'd enjoyed it, too. She moved her hand down Trinity's arm and laced their fingers. "Let's go inside." They walked up the short set of steps to the door. She entered her code and waited for the chirp, then a click, and guided the way. The lights came on automatically, bathing the open space in soft illumination.

"Wow." Trinity slowly turned, taking in the open floor plan. "It's beautiful."

"Thank you. When I decided I wanted a log cabin, I had a certain style in mind." Blaze originally thought she'd sell it when she started the project but had fallen in love with the house and the landscape.

The decor was a mix of rustic and modern. It suited her. At times she was modern in her way of thinking, old-fashioned in others. Like when she asked a woman for permission before kissing or touching her. It was something she'd taken a lot of ribbing for because it wasn't in keeping with being what others considered as "butch" behavior. She despised labels. Nothing bothered her more than a lack of respect, in or out of the bedroom.

"I'm glad you like it because it's definitely me." She took Trinity's jacket. "Look around. I'm going to feed Baxter before she swats at me." The feline wound around her legs, then stilled, watching Trinity from a safe distance. It wasn't often she had company.

Trinity bent down and she cautiously went to her. "Baxter, aren't you a beautiful boy." Baxter meowed loudly.

She chuckled at the common mistake. "Actually, it's she." Trinity sat back on her heels. "It was a case of mistaken identity. I was told the kitten was a male, only to find out a short time later *he* was definitely a *she*, but by then the cat knew her name, so I left it." She shrugged and continued mixing Baxter's dinner. Trinity came closer.

"I think *her* name is perfect. It's androgynous, like her owner's."

Just like when they'd danced, Trinity's nearness stirred her. Not just her body. Trinity's presence touched her deep inside, and the connection they shared was more than physical. It wasn't logical, and it didn't make sense. But it was true, nonetheless.

"Now that I've taken care of my demanding wench, can I get you something to drink?" She met Trinity's steamy gaze and fell into the swirling shades of green, dark as the forest.

"Whatever you're having is fine." Trinity smiled and stepped back.

Blaze tamped down the need racing to her lower extremities. She didn't want to dull her senses. Not with Trinity, and not now that they were finally alone. She also didn't want to rush things. She grabbed a couple of beers and handed one to Trinity. Blaze opened the double doors that led onto a wide covered porch running the entire length of the house. It was her favorite place to contemplate life, work out mathematical problems, and find her peace. But peace had eluded her lately.

"This is breathtaking." Trinity gazed out over the lush gardens lit by moonlight.

"I think so, too." She gestured to the wicker couch padded with luxurious cushions. "Let's sit for a bit."

Trinity sat close and took a drink. "How long have you lived here?"

Blaze took in the expanse of stars. Without city lights, they were thousands of twinkling pinpoints. "I finished about five years ago. It was a triumphant moment." The feeling of accomplishment she'd experienced would likely be her "once-in-a-lifetime," professionally. She'd love to build another, but she would never give up this house. It would be her family's home when the time came. *Family?* She mentally tucked the word away for another time.

"You built this?" Trinity's amazement was apparent. "By yourself?"

She felt a bit of the Carter pride rise to the top, though she tried to keep it in check. "My father and grandfather were both master carpenters. I followed in their footsteps. It's why I was devastated by the news that my arm…" She trailed off, swallowing around the lump in her throat.

"But you've healed. You're back working, aren't you?" Trinity touched her arm reassuringly.

Blaze took a steadying breath. "Yes. I couldn't imagine not doing what I love. Someday…" She didn't finish her thought. The future didn't need to be a topic of conversation tonight. "Anyway, I decided to push what I knew, and building this house was a learning experience like no other. My father taught me a lot during construction." She shrugged. "Some was trial and error, but I got there."

"Tell me more."

She loved how sincerely interested Trinity sounded. "The house took more than two years to build. I lived in the garage during most of that time, making do with the basics, like a toilet and laundry sink. I'd do it again if the opportunity presented."

Trinity turned in her seat. "You'd sell your home?"

Blaze smiled. "Never." Trinity looked relieved. "This is my love. I don't plan on ever leaving unless there's no alternative."

Trinity went to the railing. Blaze liked the way the darkness silhouetted her figure. She stood behind her and wrapped an arm around her waist. She felt Trinity's sharp inhale. "Is this okay?"

"Yes. It's nice to be touched." Trinity shook her head. "That sounded weird and not what I meant."

"I'm a tactile person. Comes with the job."

Trinity laughed. "I imagine it does."

"I want to show you the front view." They stayed close as she led the way along the porch and around the side of the house. Two steps led to the front porch and she leaned against the rail and pulled Trinity closer, pointing in the distance to a shimmering body of water that glistened with moonlight. "That's Lake Champlain. My grandparents had a seasonal home there and I spent summers with them." She was quiet for a moment. Her grandmother had died over a decade ago and her grandpa a few years later. Blaze was sure he'd died of a broken heart. She knew how that felt.

"I like hearing about your family." Trinity turned in her arms. "I'd like to hear more about you, too."

Her center became heavy as she stared into Trinity's expressive eyes. "I don't want tonight to be all about me." She stroked Trinity's thick, wavy hair, brushing it from her face before raking her fingers through the incredibly soft strands.

"What do you want tonight to be?" Trinity caught her hand and pressed her lips to her palm.

"About us and getting to know each other on an intimate level. If that's okay?" If Trinity wasn't ready, she wouldn't continue, though what she wanted to do was to use everything in her power to convince her she could go slow. Right now, all Blaze could think of was tasting every part of Trinity.

"I'd like that."

She let out a breath. "Are you sure?"

"I am." Trinity swallowed. "Take me to bed."

Blaze groaned. She hadn't been sure where the night was heading, though she'd hoped. "Gladly." She picked up their bottles and placed them on the counter. After closing the doors, she pointed up the wide planked stairs. "I hope you don't mind the loft. If you prefer, we can go to the guest bedroom down here."

"The loft is perfect."

Once they were upstairs, the air was warm. She stood at the foot of her bed and tipped her chin at the expansive wall of windows. "I have the sun to wake me every morning. It's why I chose this piece of land and positioned the house the way I did."

Blaze pulled Trinity into her arms, her mouth over her waiting lips. They were as soft as the first time and readily yielded to her. She took advantage of having a layer of clothes as a barrier between them, knowing once they were naked her restraint would dissolve. The tangy taste of beer lingered and she pressed her tongue inside, wanting to explore, wanting Trinity with a passion she'd withheld from others. They broke away and her chest heaved as her pulse quickened. Trinity's arms circled her neck and pulled her down for another scorching kiss. Following the hunger that drove her need to satisfy not only Trinity, but her own growing desire to be touched, Blaze picked her up and moved her to the bed, then lay down beside her.

Blaze ran her hand down the center of Trinity's chest, lifting the edge of her shirt, and smoothing her hand over the silky flesh. "I want to touch you."

"Please."

Blaze snaked her hand between them, rubbing the seam of Trinity's jeans against her center. Trinity whimpered and Blaze's clitoris throbbed in response.

She'd always been able to control her sexual urges and take her time, but Trinity made her unable to restrain herself. She straddled Trinity's hips and sat up, bringing Trinity with her. She inched Trinity's shirt up and over her head to reveal a black lace bra, the cups overflowing. She held her breasts and ran her thumbs over the firm nipples, making Trinity moan.

"I want to hear more. Do you moan when you come?" She kissed her mouth, then trailed her way down her chin and over her throat to Trinity's earlobe, pulling gently with her teeth. She unhooked Trinity's bra and kissed the skin beside the straps before moving them down her arms. She tossed the bra aside and pressed her lips to the dark pink areolas without touching the prominent nipples that tightened when she blew across them.

"Blaze..." Trinity said, her hands on her shoulders.

Blaze laid her down. "I am going to devour you." She pulled Trinity's jeans down her slender legs, worshipping every inch of revealed skin. She wanted to know every place on Trinity's body that made her squirm or moan or hold her breath. Blaze was going to take her, and for reasons she couldn't name, she was going to make Trinity hers. The shape of her…full breasts, womanly hips, and the slight rise of her lower belly…was female perfection.

"Naked. Now." Trinity tugged at Blaze's top.

Her steamy gaze made Blaze's nipples harden and Trinity licked her lips. She leaned over to capture her mouth and shivered when Trinity's tongue pressed inside, searching. Moisture pooled between her thighs.

Trinity yanked at Blaze's shirt, quickly working the buttons. Her breasts remained captured beneath her sports bra.

"A little help here would be appreciated," Trinity said in frustration, even though a smile played on her lips. She ran her fingers down Blaze's abdomen and her muscles twitched.

She stood and removed the rest of her clothes, wanting to be done with the layers between them. She wanted to hear Trinity moan in pleasure, scream in ecstasy, but a flash of doubt seized her. Unexpectedly, Blaze questioned if she'd know how to please her. Tonight wasn't about sex, even when Trinity accepted the invitation, and she'd hoped they would end up in her bed. Her emotions were engaged just as much as her body when it came to Trinity. Finally, she stood naked with Trinity watching her intently. She'd gotten up on her elbows for a better view.

"Come here." She moved closer and Trinity brushed her fingers through her wet heat.

Blaze gritted her teeth. She was frantic with longing, driven to feel more than just a fleeting touch. It was almost painful. She grabbed Trinity's moisture-covered hand and climbed into bed until she was over her. She nuzzled along the tender flesh of her neck, nipping some spots and licking others. Blaze worked her way down Trinity's flushed body, sucking on her nipples and trailing her mouth along her stomach before dipping into her belly button. Heat, electric and all-consuming, coursed through her. She was a hot ball of energy and the lightning show hadn't even started yet. She stopped at the apex of Trinity's thighs, taking her in. Her mound was covered in dark red tight curls trimmed back from her slit. Blaze settled between her legs and spread them wider, exposing her glistening center. When she inhaled, Trinity's scent filled Blaze. She slid her index finger along the soaked folds before her tongue followed the path. Trinity tasted like clover honey. The sweetest she'd ever had.

Trinity gasped. "Oh God." She arched into her, but Blaze held her down.

She had every intention of going slow. Of setting the pace and holding off Trinity's orgasm as long as she could. No matter how much she wanted to see Trinity come and knowing she was responsible for her pleasure, she would take her time. And God, did she hope it wouldn't be the last chance she got to do so.

CHAPTER EIGHTEEN

The views from every angle of the home were breathtaking, though they couldn't compare to Blaze when she'd stood next to the bed a few minutes ago. Her wide shoulders, well-developed arms, and trimmed waist were how she'd pictured her, and when she'd come closer so she could run her fingers through her soaked folds, she couldn't stop from groaning as desire coursed through her.

Now Blaze was licking her, making her crazy, and she wanted to do the same to Blaze. She focused on Blaze's tongue as it stroked along her length, snaking inside her every now and again. She ran her fingers through Blaze's thick hair and massaged the scalp beneath them, pressing Blaze closer. Her body jerked when Blaze swiped past her sensitive center.

"I need to come. Please."

She brought her to the brink, then slowed again. "I like hearing you ask for what you need." Blaze licked her again. "But you never have to beg." Blaze followed her words by entering her with two fingers.

Trinity raised her hips, driving Blaze's fingers deeper while her tongue focused on her clit. Heat radiated outward from her center and her entire body tightened in anticipation of the orgasm that was so close she whimpered. Blaze kissed her inner thigh as she pulled out.

"Come for me, baby."

Blaze drove inside again, filling her. Trinity's body shook with the intensity of her orgasm. She felt a gush escape and Blaze greedily lapped at her while she called out her name again and again, making her throat raw. Blaze climbed beside her once she'd quieted and pulled her into her arms, cradling her and kissing her tenderly.

"You are even more beautiful when you come." Blaze stroked her arm and kept her close.

"That was amazing."

Blaze kissed her again then pulled her on top. "I love how your body tells me what to do, even if you don't."

She kissed her back as she gently pulled and tugged at one nipple, pressing her thigh between Blaze's and rocking against her. Blaze grabbed her hips, pushing her up and down along her center. She raised up on her arms and watched Blaze's face, her eyes hooded, knowing she was close and wanting to please her. "What do you need me to do?"

Blaze's unfocused gaze found her. "Hang on." Blaze flipped them over and rode her thigh, using her elbows to support her weight. "You made me so ready, I'm going to come quick."

She moved her hand between them and held her fingers so when Blaze moved, Trinity stroked her hard clit. "Come in my hand."

Blaze groaned and dropped her head against her chest and ground harder. She felt the moment Blaze's orgasm began and slid inside her. Trinity relished the tightness that held her captive. Blaze bit her nipple. She cried out in surprise as Blaze shook against her, moaning. After a few minutes, she stilled completely.

"So good." Blaze kissed her fully, bruising her swollen lips.

Blaze moved to her side, resting her head in her hand, and ran her fingers through her tangled strands. They lay against each other and Blaze tenderly stroked her skin. The slightly rough pads of her fingertips were strangely soothing.

"Can you stay the night?" Blaze asked.

She hoped Blaze didn't notice her stiffen. Trinity rarely stayed overnight; a rule she didn't plan on breaking any time soon. She didn't regret her decision to sleep with Blaze, but one night might turn into two, then another. She had to think about her promotion, and the demands it would entail if…no, when…she got it. She hardly had any time now, and when she got the new job, she'd likely have even less. As tempting as Blaze was, she couldn't lose focus on her career, and it wouldn't be fair to Blaze to pretend otherwise. Besides, they still hadn't talked about dating or commitment, and she wasn't about to be a U-Haul lesbian or one who lived with lesbian drama.

"I shouldn't. I have a lot to do tomorrow and it's my only day for chores." She knew it sounded lame, and she hated when women used mundane excuses to leave. She'd rather they told the truth. She looked up at Blaze's questioning eyes. Eyes that already knew the truth. Honesty was always better. "What I said is true, but I also don't do overnights." She tried to sound nonchalant. "It's not my thing."

Blaze brushed her fingers against Trinity's cheek. "That's a shame, but I understand. I normally don't either." She found her mouth again. The kiss was slow burning and passionate, and Trinity almost changed her mind. Thankfully, Blaze was the more rational one.

"Let me get dressed and lead you back down the mountain."

"You don't have to. I'll find my way."

"I know, but I need to know you're okay." Blaze shrugged. "Old-fashioned chivalry isn't dead yet."

She cupped the back of Blaze's head and pulled her down, wanting to feel her warmth and the passion she'd experienced between them. She made the kiss languid and hoped Blaze could tell how much she'd enjoyed their time together. Even though she wasn't ready for their night to end, she was resolute in her decision to leave. Second-guessing reasons to stay would make her crazy.

"Thank you for keeping my dream of a knight in shining armor alive."

Blaze's face darkened for an instant, but it was gone so quickly she wasn't sure it had even happened.

"That's just me." Blaze sounded as though she were attempting to shrug off the compliment as she reached for her clothes, leaving her underwear and bra behind, and pushed her feet into her low boots.

Blaze waited until she was dressed, then took her hand, and they walked down the stairs together. They stopped at the bottom, and she took the opportunity to tell Blaze what she needed to know. "I'm so glad I didn't listen to DJ."

"What do you mean? When?" Blaze's expression froze in confusion.

"While you were at the hospital. I think it was the second day after your surgery."

Blaze's jaw bunched. "What did she say?"

Now that she'd mentioned the encounter, Blaze's reaction confirmed what she'd suspected all along—that Blaze knew nothing of DJ trying to keep them apart. "First, she asked what I wanted from you, then she said it was best if I stayed away so you could concentrate on your recovery. And she hasn't been particularly warm to me since."

Blaze's face fell. "I assure you I never asked her to intervene." She brought their joined hands to her chest. "I enjoy our visits." Blaze kissed her knuckles. "Every single time we've been together has been wonderful."

Maybe she should have waited to say something instead of bringing it up after they'd been intimate. Had she ruined the moment? Trinity needed to break the tension. "Even the time I caught you trying to remove your catheter?"

Blaze groaned and looked up at the ceiling. "It's not on the top of my list, but you rescued me from disaster, so...yes, even then." She smiled.

"Good." Trinity giggled.

"Would you like something to eat or drink before you go?" Blaze seemed to want to delay her departure.

If she stayed any longer, she wouldn't be able to leave. "I really do have to go. Maybe next time?" Everything inside of her revolted against giving Blaze hope of another encounter, or date, or whatever their times together constituted. She had no expectations when she'd made up her mind to follow Blaze home, but there was no question Blaze was special, and because of that reason, spending more time with her was dangerous. Yet, she couldn't draw the line in the sand.

Blaze hesitated, then met her gaze. "I'd like that." She sounded sincere, but her features were tight, and Trinity wondered what was going on in her head. She didn't have to wait long.

"I'll talk with DJ. Despite her rough exterior, she really is a good person, though she's always been a tad overprotective."

"I don't want to cause a problem between you two. I can see how close you are."

"Don't worry about us. We've been through hard times before. Its par for the course in our friendship." Blaze leaned in to whisper, as though to tell her a secret. "I've been known to be a bit stubborn sometimes, and we've had to battle it out to clear the air."

She felt the tug of a smile. "You don't say? I would have never guessed."

"Hard to believe, I know." Blaze smiled that knee-weakening smile of hers. Trinity let out the breath she'd been holding, glad to see Blaze wasn't upset with her for the revelation.

They walked together to the door. She turned and placed her hand on Blaze's chest. "Thank you for tonight. I really enjoyed spending time with you." She could have elaborated, but the connection between them had turned tentative. When she looked into Blaze's eyes, they were so communicative and filled with emotion, she knew there was more there than she was sharing.

Blaze cupped her cheek. "As did I." Her mouth opened as though she wanted to say more but she quickly glanced away before speaking again. "Do you have far to go once you're on the main road?"

"Not too far. I'm near the hospital." She put her hand on Blaze's arm. "I really can find my way."

Blaze's brow creased. "Let me do this." Concern etched her face and tiny worry lines appeared around her mouth.

Trinity was touched. "Okay."

Blaze grabbed her keys and helmet and walked her to her car. "Watch for animals." She kissed her tenderly.

"I will."

❖

The intersection was empty of traffic. Trinity reluctantly waved good-bye in response to Blaze's raised hand before turning onto the main road. She glanced at the clock on the dash. Three thirty. She and Blaze had been together for almost four hours, a lot longer than a quick hookup. Blaze had shared enough about herself that Trinity had a better sense of why she'd been drawn to her. Not to mention how much she'd enjoyed their time together in bed. Sex with Blaze had been spectacular. Her only regret was that she hadn't done everything to Blaze she'd wanted. The urge to taste her still lingered, but she'd get over it. They'd left the door open for getting together again, but she wasn't banking on it. Words didn't always reflect reality, and she didn't want to feed her obsession with Blaze. No matter how hot she was. Blaze wasn't in her life plan and neither was commitment.

She walked into the house and tossed her things on a chair. She went to the refrigerator and pulled out the jug of iced tea. She poured a glass and drank it down, the taste of Blaze's mouth mingling with the cold liquid. She touched her swollen lips while visions of the passion they'd shared filled her mind.

"Did you enjoy your evening?" Kelly asked, startling her from recalling the night.

"I did." She refilled her glass. "Want some?"

Kelly shook her head. "Is she as hot in bed as she looks?" She cocked an eyebrow.

Trinity smiled. "And then some." She laughed. "What time did you get home?" She stifled a yawn.

"A little while after you left."

"I'm sorry I woke you."

"You didn't. I had a bad dream." Kelly glanced at her feet. "You know the kind." She wiped her brow and attempted to smile but didn't quite make it.

She put her arms around Kelly to let her know she did, and it was always horrible. Seeing people die in front of you time and again wasn't for everyone, and those who chose the medical field bore witness to the atrocities of life, finding it impossible to always remain distant. They were human, after all. "Are you okay?"

Kelly hugged her and stepped away. This time she met her gaze. "I will be now that I have you to distract me with tales of lust." She sat at the kitchen table. "Please tell me there was lust."

Trinity grabbed a bag of popcorn and sat across from her. "It was better than that. There was steamy passion." She thought about her choice of words and she couldn't remember ever using the word passion for a one-night stand. She forced herself not to go there. The last thing she wanted was to be confused about her feelings for Blaze. She liked her and wouldn't mind seeing her again, but that's where it ended.

"Are you okay?" Kelly asked. "I've never seen you this way after sleeping with someone."

She bristled. "What way?" There wasn't any reason to be defensive. She'd had sex. Very hot sex. That was all there was to it.

Kelly thought for a minute. "Like…starry-eyed or something."

"Oh, please. I had great sex, which isn't a word I'd use to describe any of my past encounters. Give me a break." She grabbed a handful of popcorn and sat back, feigning nonchalance.

Kelly studied her. "Huh," she said, then sat back after reaching into the bag, too. "That good?"

Trinity let out a breath, happy they'd moved onto another subject. "Epic." Blaze had fulfilled her sexual fantasy of being with a confident butch woman. At least she'd enjoyed their encounter, since it likely wouldn't happen again.

CHAPTER NINETEEN

Blaze had a hard time sleeping and wondered if Trinity turning down staying the night meant she'd only been interested in sex. She shook off the disturbing thought, but it niggled at her throughout the morning until she was distracted by brunch with DJ.

DJ sipped her mimosa. "What did you end up doing last night?"

Blaze cut her ham with precise movements. "I had a late dinner at Maxi's, then went for a drink at Ero." She chewed thoughtfully, lost in memories.

"Just one?" DJ teased her.

Blaze laughed. "Only one."

"Sounds pretty sedate to me. I'm surprised we didn't see each other, but maybe I wasn't there yet. Jax and I went to a movie before we dropped in for a nightcap."

"Hmm. I thought you said we weren't that old?"

"We aren't, but when the woman I plan on hooking up with asks, I go with the flow."

"I see. Is that how it goes?" Blaze grinned. "Anyway, I wasn't there long. I met up with Trinity and we ended up leaving at the same time." Blaze smiled at the memory of Trinity's skin under her hands.

"From the look on your face, I'd say the night didn't end there." DJ smiled, but there was something beneath the smile that

Blaze assumed had to do with her issues around Trinity, whatever they were.

"No, it didn't. We had a good time together."

"Come on. 'Good,'" she said with air quotes, "isn't normally in your vocabulary."

Based on what Trinity told her, she had no intention of giving DJ any details. It was time she found out the reason behind her actions. "Why did you tell Trinity to stop visiting me?"

The color left DJ's face. "I'm not sure—"

Blaze held up her hand. "No excuses. I want to hear the real reason."

DJ sat back as she pushed her plate away. "Fine. I did it because you had enough on your plate and I didn't want her to be a distraction from your recovery."

"Maybe a distraction was just what I needed." Blaze leaned forward as her temper flared. "Her absence made me think her visits were based solely on her duty as a nurse."

"So I was right. She did have ulterior motives for seeing you."

The smug look was more than Blaze could take. "Whether she did or didn't really doesn't concern you. My life, my choice." She resisted slamming her hand on the table. "I would think you'd be happy I'm finally showing a real interest in someone since you never liked the fact that I'd resigned myself to casual, unemotional sex."

DJ couldn't hide the hurt, and Blaze regretted lashing out. Maybe Trinity's rejection had left her stinging more than she thought.

"I never meant to do anything to hurt you. You have to know I had good intensions. I'm sorry."

She thought about how things had turned out between her and Trinity. Did she really need to make a big deal out of the situation? DJ's actions had always been in defense of Blaze, even if she'd gone about it in an odd way. That was DJ, and this was just another example of her concern for Blaze's well-being. Blaze sighed and signaled for coffee. "I know. Just please remember when it comes to the women in my life, what happens is up to me, for good or bad. Got it?"

DJ nodded. "Yes, ma'am." She saluted and Blaze laughed. "So, now tell me. Your night was better than most?"

Blaze's smile grew. "It was exceptional." She paused for a long minute. "I'd like to see Trinity again."

"So, you've decided she's someone you want to date, even though you're not into dating?"

"I know. She's different." Blaze looked up. "It's hard to explain. I asked her to stay the night."

DJ didn't seem fazed. "Did she?"

"No. She had things to do because today's her only day off and she's working tomorrow." Blaze stared into her mug. "Enough about me. What's going on with you? Anyone new in your love life?"

"Nah. I don't know if I can keep doing this." She fiddled with her napkin.

"You were out with Jax last night. What about her? No possibility of long-term?"

DJ shook her head. "I invest so much energy into a relationship, and I get very little in return. Maybe there's something wrong with me."

Blaze covered DJ's hand. "There's nothing wrong with you, honey. You're a beautiful, intelligent woman. You just haven't found the right person yet, but I know you will." She wanted to sound reassuring, but Blaze had her doubts.

DJ let out an exasperated sigh. "After the last failed relationship, I've questioned everything, and wonder what I have to offer. At this rate, I'll be a wrinkled old lady by the time I find someone else. I don't think I have it in me to try to find love again."

"When it's right, you know it will happen. Stop grasping at straws. None of your previous partners were good enough for you anyway." Blaze snagged a raspberry off her cheesecake.

DJ slapped at her hand. "If you're my *friend*, why didn't you tell me?"

"Would you have listened?"

She looked like she was going to protest but didn't. "Of course not."

"Besides, they weren't bad people, they just weren't *the one*."
Blaze lifted her mug. "And that's something you have to decide for
yourself. My assessment might have been wrong, and I wouldn't
want it to come between us."

"You mean like what I did with Trinity."

Blaze couldn't argue with that, but DJ already looked dejected.
"Your heart was in the right place."

"As long as you know it always is." DJ drained her cup. "You'll
keep me updated with the Trinity situation, right?"

Blaze grinned. "Yeah. Thanks for the heart-to-heart. It might
not turn into anything, but at least I have an idea what I want in my
life." She shrugged. "I'll figure it out."

DJ stood after tossing money on the table. "I know you will.
This is on me."

"I invited you, remember?" she said while following DJ to the
exit, reaching to open the door for her. "Why do you get to pay?"

"Because sometimes I'm a jerk and you still love me." DJ
kissed her cheek. "Don't work too hard this week."

"You do the same." Blaze hugged her.

DJ slid behind the wheel. As she drove, DJ remained quiet and
Blaze imagined she was contemplating everything they'd talked
about. She wished DJ would find her forever person. She understood
what failed relationships could do to a person's self-esteem. She'd
had a few herself. Trinity had made her reassess her situation. Blaze
no longer wanted casual sex, knowing the situation was already
beyond that for her. She hoped Trinity felt the same way.

CHAPTER TWENTY

Blaze opened the garage. Since she wasn't staining or varnishing anything today, she planned on taking advantage of the opportunity to let the sunshine and fresh air inside. She emptied the grocery bags, stowing the beverages and snacks she'd bought in the refrigerator. A second trip to the SUV produced hangers of clean dress clothes along with a short stack of folded ones on top of her towels. Now that she was back to work full-time, she had to restock the essentials. The process of gathering the items brought a sense of order to her world.

She sat with a cooling coffee behind her massive desk and surveyed everything in her line of sight. The tools she'd acquired over the years were instruments worthy of her craft. Tables and jigs held pieces for her to work on. A huge partitioned room located in the far corner was used for staining, painting, and drying in a dust-free environment, and had its own ventilation system. She'd done well for herself, and she needed to remember that.

Blaze picked up the sketch of a new project and selected a piece of wood. Work refocused her. It was her best salve and had been able to calm her when nothing else could. Her phone rang and she glanced at the screen, then smiled.

"Hi, Pop," she said. "How are you and Momma?" She tacked the drawing on her board and set it in front of her while she listened.

"We're good. Missing our only daughter is all."

Her father's voice was still strong, but it sounded less so than the last time they'd talked just a few weeks ago, and the change concerned her.

"Work busy?"

She glanced at the stack of papers on the spindle. Orders had piled up while she was in PT, but she was beginning to tackle some of the bigger projects. "I'm staying out of trouble for sure. Have you been hiking lately?"

He laughed. "Whenever I can drag your mother away from the sewing machine. You know she's already started on Christmas presents. Hope you put your order in early."

Her mother shared her love of creating handmade items and gave them as gifts to family and friends in their circle. Blaze requested a dining room set including tablecloth, napkins, and a runner. Her mom had beamed at the request. Her father had made the table and chairs a couple of years ago, and she thought it fitting. "I did. Are Aunt Ellen and Uncle Bob coming for the Thanksgiving gathering?" They weren't her only relatives, but they were her favorite, especially since her uncle's disposition was so much like her grandfather's. They had accepted her announcement of her sexuality by pulling her into a tight hug and letting her know they loved her for who she was. It had been too long since she'd seen them, too.

"Oh, yeah. They're coming. Staying a couple of weeks, I think. I don't know why Bob keeps working. He should have retired last year before his side business took off, but you know him, he loves being busy."

"Must be in our blood." She smiled and her father laughed. "How's Momma feeling?" Her mother had been diagnosed with rheumatoid arthritis a while ago. She had good days and bad. The doctor told her it would be better to live in a warmer climate, but she wouldn't hear of it. She loved the seasons even more than Blaze did, and she couldn't picture her mother anywhere but in the family home.

"She has her days. Lately more good than not. She's in the garden. I know she'd love to talk with you if you have time."

Blaze flinched. There was nothing she would like better than to see her parents more. The accident had been a blessing in many ways. Having her family together, even if they did drive her a little crazy at times, was one she was grateful for. It also reminded her life was short and family was important. Though there wasn't any direct route to Old Forge, she needed to make more time for the two most important people in her life. "I always have time for you and Momma, even when I don't seem to."

"Good. That'll make her happy. Hold on."

The old screen door creaked. "Millie, our daughter's on the phone."

"Lord, it's been ages," her mother said in the background.

"Oh, now, don't go making a fuss. She's been busy in her shop and that's a good thing."

"Blaze, honey, you there?" her mother asked.

"Hi, Momma. How are you feeling? And don't blow smoke, okay?" Her mother never wanted to admit she wasn't one hundred percent, though Blaze could always see when she was in pain. The small crow's feet at the corner of her eyes deepened, and her otherwise smooth forehead became lined.

"Better now that I hear your voice. Today is a good day. The new med seems to be working. And your father...well, he's my Nurse Ratched." She laughed heartily and Blaze was warmed by the sound. Her mother had always been the rock of the family, finding ways to turn situations around and eke out the good in them. Blaze hoped she was following in her mother's footsteps, though there were times when she questioned that skill.

"He loves you, Momma."

"I know, dear," her mother said, her voice softening. "It's the only reason I put up with him. How's your arm?" She became somber, her voice carrying the concern of a loving mother.

She heard the screen door again, and her father mumbling about squirrels. "It's good. Getting better all the time."

"When are you coming home?"

Blaze glanced at the work orders again. "I'll be home for Thanksgiving, so don't give my room away."

"Oh, not till then?"

Her stomach twisted. How was it that her parents knew how to make her feel guilty? "I'll try to come up before then and help Pop with whatever needs fixing." Her father wasn't getting any younger, and there were times when he wasn't strong enough to do household repairs, though she always told him she needed his know how and the only way she could learn was by doing. They both knew the real reason, but neither mentioned the words "getting old."

"I'd like that. Are you bringing anyone to the feast?"

Her mother asked the same question before every visit, but this time the vision of Trinity flashed in her mind. "I'm not sure yet, Momma. I'll let you know if I am." She surprised herself by mentioning the possibility of bringing a date. Trinity had left the door open to seeing her again, but that didn't mean she wanted to spend time with Blaze's family, though she'd met them already. The holiday was still a month away. Maybe she'd call or make a surprise visit to the hospital. *Nothing stalkerish about that.* A text. She'd send a text.

"No pressure. I'd just like to see you spend some time with an actual person rather than wood."

"So would I, Momma." There was that melancholy feeling again.

"You okay, baby girl?"

Was she okay? Physically, she was almost as good as ever. Emotionally, she was fighting to right herself from being off kilter and out of sorts. "I will be. I have to get back to work, Momma. I'll call you soon about a visit."

"I love you, Blaze, and it's time you found a love of your own."

Blaze knew her mother was right, but she couldn't talk about her loneliness over the phone. She'd have that conversation when she got home. "I love you, too. Tell Pop I love him."

Tears pooled in her eyes as she hung up. Her parents' love had been the cornerstone of her youth and she relied on that strength now to push through the emotions that threatened to overwhelm her. *Time to get serious about building my own future.* All she had to do was find the right person, and her heart said Trinity was the right one for her. Her head argued it was *way* too soon. But maybe they could start spending more time together. That's how it worked, right? Dating, getting to know someone. That sounded right.

❖

"So, what are you doing right now?" Trinity asked.

Blaze glanced around. "Working in my shop."

"Have you had lunch?"

She laughed. "I tend to forget meals when I'm working."

"You could be a nurse. We forget to eat, too, and when we do its usually junk. I need to get back in the gym."

"I could never do your job. There's too much stress, and I like to eat too much." Blaze could hear Trinity open a beverage can and take a slurp.

"Can I come see where you do what you do?"

"If you'd like. I'll be here the rest of the day." She glanced at the clock, surprised she'd been there for five hours. Blaze sent Trinity the address and she said she would find it. Blaze had wanted physical space between her home and her shop, needing to keep the two parts of her life separate.

"What kind of food do you want?"

"You don't have to do that." This was one of the reasons Trinity's profession suited her. Caring about others seemed to come naturally.

"I'm going to eat, too."

The silence on the other end meant she was expected to come up with an answer. "Burgers." If only she could answer her own questions with that much confidence.

Blaze went back to working on the sink cabinet she was making. She felt the smile move her cheeks as she replayed the last time she and Trinity were together.

A little while later, she heard a car door and looked up as she set down the planer and wiped her hands on a damp towel. "Aren't you starting to feel like a delivery service?"

Trinity laughed. "What can I say? I have to eat whenever I can."

She leaned in and kissed Trinity lightly on the mouth. "Lucky me. So do I." The innuendo wasn't lost. Trinity's face flushed.

"Yes, well, it's burgers today."

"A close second," she said as she led her inside.

"This is quite the space. How long have you been here?"

Blaze tore off sheets of white paper from a big roll and made placemats for the desk, then picked up a framed one-hundred-dollar bill and handed it to Trinity. "About eight years. That was from my first order."

Trinity set it back down reverently and went to the large worktable, where she slid her hand over it like a caress. "And what happens here?" she asked, one brow raised.

Heat rose up her neck. "I lay out projects, make measurements, fit pieces together." She stood across from Trinity. "This is a child's bed frame. I just finished the dovetail joints and glued them together. Once it's dry, I'll sand everything smooth."

"Dovetail. That's interesting. Why is it called that?"

"It's one of the strongest joints because there are tails and pins that fit snug together. I can also use nails for additional support, but I prefer to glue them."

Trinity tossed her jacket on a hook. "Can you show me?"

"Sure." She squared off a couple of small boards, then made measurements and marked the wood. Once she set the depth on the router, she handed Trinity a vise grip. "This is a Keller jig." She held up a long, narrow board with insets. "It's a template for making dovetails. I line up the center mark on the jig with the center mark on the board. Then we clamp it in place." She demonstrated on one side.

"Like this?"

Blaze nodded. Then she took a scrap of wood and clamped it tight to the first piece. "This will help hold the wood in place." She handed a pair of safety glasses to Trinity and put on a pair, too. "Want to help guide the cut?"

Trinity nodded, and she moved her into place and stood behind her. "The router is loud." She placed a pair of noise canceling headphones over Trinity's ears. She looked adorable and sexy at the same time. Blaze tapped her on the shoulder. "Ready?" she mouthed. Trinity gave her a thumbs-up. She flicked the switch and the machine roared to life. She pressed close to Trinity with her hands over Trinity's smaller ones and guided her movements. Once the first set of cuts were made, they cut the pins, then removed the protective gear.

"This is how the two fit perfectly together." Blaze dry fit the joints.

"It's like they were made for each other."

"Yes. Once they're glued, they'll be bonded for life. A marriage of the two." She'd often thought of the joint that way. Strong together, weaker when apart. Trinity appeared deep in thought and she would have liked to know what she was thinking. "We'd better eat before the burgers get cold."

"Yes, we should." Trinity smiled.

Blaze led her to the desk, wishing they could work on projects together more. Though concentrating on work would be difficult when Trinity was around.

Two days later, Josh rode up on his sleek black Harley-Davidson. There was six years between them. Growing up, he'd mimicked everything she did, and the behavior had followed him into adulthood. She'd been a typical unashamed tomboy and her parents had encouraged her to be whoever she wanted to be. Another reason she was grateful to have the love of her family when so many in the LGBTQ community didn't.

"Well, if it isn't my wanderlust brother." She hugged him tightly. Blaze hadn't seen him since she could start doing stuff on her own, and she had sorely missed his presence in her life. "Were you missing me?"

Josh shrugged. "Just passing through and hoping to crash for a night or two. We need to catch up."

Though he was younger he was two inches taller, a fact he never let her forget, and he ruffled her hair the same way he had when he finally shot past her own impressive height as a youngster. "Glad you found the time. Of course, you can stay. You're always welcome here. You know that." She loved having him around. Though he didn't have the same passion she had for woodwork, he always told her how beautiful her pieces were, and she appreciated his eye for detail.

"I don't want to crowd your scene. You could be holed up with a woman." He winked.

"Not tonight." She had wanted Trinity to stay with her yesterday, but she was scheduled for a night shift, so she didn't ask. Blaze couldn't help wondering if Trinity was making excuses or there was more to it. Maybe it really had been a one-night stand and nothing more, and they'd end up firmly in a friends only arrangement. They'd already gone way beyond that, and the thought made her ache. Josh must have noticed her mood shift and he wrapped an arm around her shoulder.

"Hey. You okay?"

"Yeah." After a minute she shook her head. "No."

"Good thing I'm here then. Let's go grab steaks for the grill and some beer, then you can tell me what has my big sister down in the dumps." Worry creased his forehead.

She had never been one to complain about her life because there was rarely anything to complain about. This was different. This wasn't something happening *to* her. Loneliness was a feeling she'd never experienced before.

❖

Blaze enjoyed her buzz as she sank into the cool sheets, feeling relaxed for the first time in weeks. Josh's arrival had been what she needed. They'd talked for hours, hashing out the whys and wherefores of her feelings. He'd tried to talk her into making the three-hour trip home—the next pit stop on his trek—but she'd told him the timing wasn't good.

"When will the timing ever be good?" he'd asked.

It was true. She'd gone home only twice in the last year, both for family gatherings. It had been the usual hectic, raucous chaos that she loved, but she hadn't had time to talk with her parents alone. Now she longed to do just that, and she was done making excuses.

When morning came, she was going to tell him she'd changed her mind. Her projects could wait another couple of days. She needed her parents' wisdom. She needed their hugs and their unwavering love. She needed to know she wasn't crazy for feeling so unsettled, and that she had to trust her gut when it came to affairs of the heart. Even though she knew all this was true, Blaze had to hear it. The trip would do her good.

As sleep began to overtake her, a familiar vision appeared. Trinity's smile. Trinity's concern while she'd been in the ED. Trinity's lush body and warm gaze. They all brought her a sense of peace. Her last thought was the one she'd asked herself a hundred times since they'd first met. *Why do I feel so different around her?* It was a thought that would follow her into slumber.

CHAPTER TWENTY-ONE

W e should go shopping. Treat ourselves to something new," Kelly said as she licked her fingers clean of the powdered sugar from her donut. A grateful patient had dropped off two dozen treats from a local bakery to show her appreciation for the staff taking care of her elderly mother after a fall that resulted in a broken wrist.

Trinity pulled a piece of pastry from the Danish she was working on and popped it in her mouth. "Shopping is a luxury."

Kelly groaned. "One we both deserve. Have you done anything to celebrate earning your degree? Like buy new lingerie?" Her eyebrows rose.

Her wardrobe was serviceable but dated. Spending money on herself had never been a priority. Maybe the time had come to think otherwise. Besides, she was planning on going to a fundraiser in a couple of weeks and it would be nice to have something new to wear. Something sleek and sexy, but professional.

"Fine, but don't try to talk me into anything outrageous. You know how I feel about wasting money." Trinity drank the last of her coffee and made a note in the chart of her only patient, then pulled her study guide from her bag. She was going to take advantage of the rare quiet in the ED while she could. She hadn't heard anything about her application for the promotion, which wasn't unusual considering how HR worked, but she'd be ready when she did.

"Deal. Let's start at the outlets. We can always go to the mall if we need to." Kelly tossed her napkin and cup in the trash. "I'm going to gain a pound from that damn donut, but it was totally worth it."

Trinity watched her disappear into the restroom. She hadn't really thought much about the fundraiser for the Capital Pride Center where she'd volunteered while attending SUNY Albany for her bachelor's degree. The annual event was one she hadn't been able to go to the last few years due to her work schedule, but she loved the Fall Gala, which was rich with camaraderie and run by those in the community who cared about people who struggled to have their voices heard. Maybe she would ask Blaze to go. She felt bad for not making more time to see her, but she simply hadn't had a breath to herself, and when she did, she'd been barely functional before falling into bed exhausted.

"I need sleep," Kelly said when she returned.

Their shift was scheduled to end in two hours, but that was always subject to change. If an emergency hit the door, she'd automatically kick into high gear and any fatigue she might have felt would dissipate until the crisis was over.

"You sound like you're eighty years old. Maybe you need vitamins."

"Maybe I like getting my beauty rest."

"I should be worried then. I rarely sleep more than six hours."

Kelly guffawed. "You're beautiful. Whatever sleep you're getting is plenty. *I'm* the one who needs all I can get."

Trinity felt the heat in her face. She wasn't beautiful. If anything, she might lean to the pretty side, but she disliked some of her features. Her eyes were too big, her lips were rather thin, and her cheekbones were hidden under the layer of baby fat she'd never outgrown. "If you think complimenting me will get you out of the housework this week think again." She laughed when Kelly stuck her chin out.

"You're such a taskmaster."

"Hard-ass me isn't buying it. You should—" She started to give Kelly the reason she'd been lucky to have the nickname, but the dispatch radio crackled to life and they both jumped to attention.

"Go ahead," Trinity said and jotted notes as the paramedic talked.

A forty-two-year-old male in cardiac distress. She glanced at his vitals and headed to triage room one to prep for his arrival. Her shift would officially go into overtime, and she might be looking at a long morning ahead.

"Get your roller skates on, girl," Kelly said while prepping the crash tray.

"On and oiled."

The EMTs arrived with the patient and she ushered them into the room. "Mr. Harris, there's going to be a lot happening in the next few minutes, but I want you to keep calm. We're all here to help. Okay?" The man shook his head, though his eyes were wide with fear. The oxygen mask over his mouth kept him from asking questions she probably didn't have answers to, but that was okay. She'd make sure the physician on duty set his mind at ease.

Three hours later, she and Kelly dropped onto the couch with a stack of pancakes and a carton of milk between them. She slid a forkful of syrup-soaked goodness into her mouth and moaned. Maybe she'd regret the sugar intake, but she'd spent all her reserves on their last patient, and she desperately needed a shower before hitting her bed.

"These are sinful." Kelly crammed half of a blueberry pancake in her mouth and chewed. "It's a good thing we burned enough calories tonight for a double portion."

Trinity washed down the last of her midmorning breakfast with a couple of swallows of milk. "It's times like these I wish I took more vacations." When was the last time she took a real vacation? It had to have been at least two years ago, when she and Kelly had splurged and taken a cruise to the Bahamas.

"Linda wants to go to Aruba. Maybe we should join her."

She sat back and put her feet up on the worn coffee table to think about it. She'd squirreled away every extra penny for the last five years and her savings account bore witness to the overtime she'd endured. Would it matter if she took a few hundred for a much-needed break? Or would she be better off spending it on something more practical? Maybe she could cuddle up with Blaze for a few days instead. Her wondering was interrupted.

"What *are* you thinking about?" Kelly asked.

"Nothing."

Kelly backed her into the corner of the couch and stared her down. "I know you too well to believe that. Come on. Tell me."

Trinity sighed. There was no way around it. Kelly would see right through her. "I was thinking about a woman." Perhaps that would be enough.

"Oh, it's getting good now. Not just any woman, though, is it?"

She wasn't sure why she was reluctant to admit it was Blaze she'd been thinking of, and not just because she was great in bed. There was a noble quality to her that drew Trinity in, making her head swim and her heart beat a little faster. She was the type of woman Trinity often dreamt of though rarely thought herself worthy of having in real life. It was also why she was married to her career. Trinity had no time to mourn what she would never have.

"It doesn't matter," she said. "I don't have time for anyone." At least that was the truth.

Kelly took her hand and squeezed. "You could make time for the right person. Why do you insist on thinking you can't have it all?"

"Because I don't *want* it all. I've had to scrape my way along all my life, and when I finally get the position I've wanted, I'm not going to squander it by trying to juggle my time between work and a partner. It never turns out the way you think it will." Trinity had seen her parents struggle for decades. They loved each other—at least she thought they did, but the years hadn't been kind to either of them. They looked much older than they were. And she and her siblings hadn't helped. One had been missing for years. She'd finally managed to track him down through a high school acquaintance. Rumor had it, he was living in a trailer up north with a woman twice his age. All she could think of was his being destined to repeat the misfortune of their parents. Her next oldest sister had died of an overdose. Her younger sister was fighting the trappings of her circumstances, but Trinity had hope.

She took their empty plates and went to the kitchen, not wanting to discuss the haves and have nots of life. Kelly would find the perfect woman, marry, have kids, and settle down. Trinity had no intention of following her lead. Not when she had a secure, successful career in her grasp. All she had to do was stay focused, and if that meant having the occasional sexual encounter and nothing more, so be it.

After Kelly went to bed, Trinity stayed up. The TV was on, but she wasn't paying attention. Every time she thought of Blaze, her mind became jumbled. Blaze wasn't a woman to be played with. She deserved more than simple sex, because the sex they'd shared had been anything but simple. The emotions she experienced had gone much deeper, leaving her feeling as though she was missing something important. *I should tell Blaze I can't get involved.* But then, Blaze might not want more, right? She seemed happy with flirting and friendship though she sensed there might be something deeper. Maybe telling Blaze she didn't want to be involved was jumping the gun and being presumptuous.

Trinity rubbed her eyes as fatigue set in. No matter how much she weighed the pros and cons of seeing Blaze more, she couldn't let her emotions win over practicality. Bottom line, her job came first, because without the security of income she could easily fall into the abyss of becoming a statistic in a relationship torn apart by financial misery. That was one thing she would never allow herself to do.

CHAPTER TWENTY-TWO

W ell, look who the tomcat dragged in."
"It's good to see you too, Pop." After a fierce hug, Blaze sank into the chair next to his. He'd know something was eating at her and would gravitate to the one he always occupied whenever he was in the living room. "Momma around, or did you finally have enough and bury her in the yard?" Her father laughed. It was a standing joke between them, and one she never grew tired of.

"She's out back, puttering with that damn rose bush." Her father blew out a heated breath, but she knew his love-hate relationship with the rose bush was just a farce. He'd given it to her mother on their fifth anniversary and she had insisted it be planted beside the back stairs so she could smell it every time she walked out on the porch. She'd nurtured it until it was a monstrosity and the trellis she cajoled him into building had done little to keep the spreading vines from tearing at the clothes of anyone who wasn't paying attention and got too close. He'd tried to cut it back, but her mother had nearly beheaded him with his own pruning shears when she saw what he was going to do.

"Aww. Glad to see you still love it as much as she does." Blaze got up and went to find her. Josh had made a stop at the grocer, planning to cook on the old Weber their parents still owned. When she saw it sitting in the same spot it always had, she smiled. Memories continued to rush in with the simple times of family barbeques and laughter. *Family*. Her heart seized in her chest. She hadn't thought much about how she'd grown up until recently. At one time she thought she'd never want children of her own, but when she thought of her grandfather and all she'd learned from him, she couldn't imagine not having a role model like him in her life. She'd been with him in the end when he'd slipped quietly away while she held his hand. She missed him terribly.

"I think you love that bush more than you love Pop." Blaze walked down the middle of the stairs. She reached out and touched her mother's weathered face, amazed at how soft her skin felt even though she never lost her tan. Her mother was frailer than she remembered, too. Or maybe her eyes were more open.

"Only because it doesn't sass me back like your father." Her mother kissed her cheek and Blaze gave her a tender hug. "To what do we owe the honor? I didn't think we'd see you until Thanksgiving." She turned back to her beloved bloom-covered vines. Despite the late season, they remained until the first snow. In all the years Blaze had watched her tend to it, she'd never seen her bleed from a thorn.

"Josh came by and talked some sense into me. Told me to stop being a jerk."

Her mother faced her. "He said that to you?" Shock laced her voice.

Blaze laughed. "Not those exact words, but it's what he meant when we had a heart-to-heart."

"Good. For a minute there I thought I was going to have to look for his body." She giggled, then looked through the screen door. "So, where is he?"

She was just about to tell her when the distinctive Harley roared up the road. "You can rest easy, Momma. Your little boy is home."

"I hear. I wish he wouldn't drive that damn thing." They exchanged a knowing look. "At least not so fast."

Blaze's own bike was just as big and just as powerful, and she was certain her mother was thinking about her accident. Unlike her brother, she'd always respected the machine and its power, learning a long time ago that showing off and taking chances weren't worth the possibility of dying. Josh hadn't had a close call yet, although he seemed more aware of riding safely since she'd been hit by the drunk driver. Either way, he was an adult and how he chose to ride was up to him. Not that she hadn't had the "You know..." conversation. She made sure they were on the same page the week he bought it. But he'd been young and headstrong. Blaze couldn't control him any more than their parents could, and she refused to live in the "What-if" world for the rest of her days. Josh, to be sure, likely felt the same.

"He'll be okay, Momma. He's still young. He'll learn he doesn't need speed to prove his manhood." Her mother nodded. Blaze knew she wasn't in total agreement, but a prolonged conversation wouldn't change her brother's behavior.

Josh came bounding out of the house with his usual enthusiasm. "Mom, I'm home."

"So I heard." She hugged him hard, like her father had her.

"Did you hear I'm cooking dinner, too?" Josh held her at arm's length, wearing a huge grin.

"No. Do I have to worry about you burning the house down?"

"Only if I move that old grill inside," he said. Josh pecked her mother's cheek and she swatted his ass. They all laughed.

Blaze left them alone and went to find her father. He was still in his chair, the newspaper spread between his sinewy arms. He looked up at her, then folded the paper when she resumed her seat.

"As much as I love seeing you, you're not one for social visits." His words made her wince. His eyes softened. "You *are* my daughter. For good or bad, you take after me."

She blew out a breath. She'd always been able to tell her father everything that was going on in her life. Today should be no different. "I'm lonely, Pop." There. She'd said it.

"Okay." Her father leaned forward, intently watching her, listening with more than just his ears. "So what does that mean?

She thought about her choice of words. "It means," she said, "I'm ready to get serious about...dating." Her father stared for a minute and she endured his scrutiny. It wasn't uncomfortable because she could see the love in his eyes. "And maybe start a family of my own."

"Is this your way of telling me you're pregnant?"

Blaze laughed. A full and hearty sound that felt good, too. Her shoulders relaxed. She needed this. Needed her father's words of wisdom and her family's love to reassure her all was right with her world. Or at least it would be.

"That would be a resounding no." She took a breath. What did it mean? She'd been contemplating the question for months. "I can't see myself as the birthing type." Her father smiled. He knew her so well. "It means I'm ready to look for a long-term partner. One who wants a family, too. With me, one day."

"Family is a blessing, Blaze. I know firsthand how much mine means to me." His eyes misted for a few minutes before he reached for her. "You'll be a wonderful parent." He squeezed her hand. "I was wondering if you'd ever get the bug."

Blaze squeezed his weathered, rough hand in return. Years of working with wood and the tools of the trade had taken its toll on them. "Thanks, Pop. You and Momma showed me how it's done. I hope I do half as well with my children."

"I have no doubt they'll know how much they're loved. That's the key."

She nodded, knowing how true his words resonated with her. "How did you know Momma was 'the one.' Your forever person?"

His mouth quirked in a half-smile. "That was easy. She told me."

She pictured her mother doing just that, not leaving any room for him to question the wisdom of her declaration.

"Is there someone special who's caught your eye?"

Blaze took time to consider her answer. Finally, she met his hopeful gaze. "Maybe, Pop. Only time will tell."

Trinity had immediately come to mind when he'd asked. Granted she was beautiful and sexy, and they'd been spectacular in bed together. They still didn't know much about each other, but that was what dating was all about, yet she wondered if she was chasing shadows. Blaze understood there had to be a meaning behind the visions she kept having whenever she thought of Trinity. The only problem? She didn't have a clue if it was just wishful thinking on her part.

She started to say so when the screen door banged closed as Josh and her mother came in.

"Uh-oh. I think we're interrupting a moment." Josh shared a small smile. He'd had a few of his own moments with their parents, but usually with her mother. She'd always gone to her father for advice or when something was bothering her.

"Lucky for you we're done." Blaze slid her hand from her father's and stood. "Now, about that dinner you promised."

"I've got the grill, sis. You can make the salad and fix the potatoes. I know how much you love being in the kitchen."

Cooking was one of her favorite activities. She loved puttering in her mother's quaint kitchen, so unlike her own gourmet one. Sometimes the intimate space was more to her liking. This was one of those times.

"Lucky for you." She picked up a kitchen towel and chucked it at him, laughing. He'd shown up at the perfect time. It was good to be around family.

CHAPTER TWENTY-THREE

I hope you don't mind me dropping by." Blaze leaned on the counter of the station.

Trinity closed the distance between them. "Not at all. Are you okay?" Blaze didn't look distressed, but she wasn't sure.

"I'm fine. I was wondering," Blaze said, then glanced around. Several staff milled about. "Do you have time for lunch?"

She couldn't help but smile as Blaze's confident demeanor turned nervous. "I don't usually have time for a real lunch." Blaze's face fell. "But you're in luck. It's quiet for now. I think I can be away for a bit."

"Great." Blaze appeared relieved. "Where would you like to go?"

"I can't leave the building, but the cafeteria food isn't as horrible as people think."

"Right. I should have figured that out. The cafeteria is fine. I really just want to spend time with you." A light blush traveled up her neck.

"Let me get some money and..." Trinity said.

"My treat. Isn't that the way it works?" Blaze grinned, her confidence back.

"True. I'll tell the staff I'm grabbing a meal, then we can go."

They walked in silence. It felt as though something big was about to happen, but she had no idea what it could be. They picked a few dishes that appeared innocuous and settled at a small table tucked off to the side. She blew across her spoonful of soup.

"Were you here for your arm?"

Blaze took a breath. "No. I came to see you."

Trinity's own breathing sped up and she was unsure where to lead the conversation.

"I thought it would be nice to just…talk."

But that's where Blaze stopped and she was determined to keep her talking. "Tell me about your work. How you came to be a carpenter."

Blaze snagged a chip from her bag and slowly chewed. "I grew up with the scent of fresh cut wood. Pine, cedar, teak. You name it. My father built with all types of natural wood, depending on the project. As soon as I was old enough to realize he was out in the barn, I went to be with him and Grandpa. They were both patient and explained everything they were doing. I kept asking if I could do it too, but my father shook his head and said, 'Someday.' My someday came when I was seven. A scrap of wood and a small carving blade. They made me promise to be careful and not tell my mother, but she knew. It took me a long time to carve a heart from that scrap of wood, but I did it. I gave it to her as a birthday present. She cried." Her eyes glistened.

"Sounds like a beautiful present." Trinity wanted her to go on telling stories and reliving fond memories forever. The worry lines around her mouth smoothed, and the crow's feet all but disappeared. What Trinity really wanted was more time with Blaze. Endless days and nights.

"She still has it on the stand next to her chair. Josh gives me a hard time about it when we're both home, but I think it's a bit of envy. He never had the intuitive nature to work wood."

Trinity knew about envy. She experienced the same thing whenever she witnessed the kind of love she'd never felt between her family members. She'd seen the love Blaze's family had for each other the night of the accident. "Sounds like you're all close."

"We are." Blaze finished her sandwich and wiped her mouth, then looked up. "What are you doing for Thanksgiving?"

The question surprised her and caught her off guard. "Probably working. I'm scheduled off because I have seniority, but if someone asks me to cover for them I will."

"Is your family far from here?"

Blaze had no way of knowing she preferred to stay away. Holidays were just another excuse to get drunk. She hadn't spent a holiday with her parents in years. "No." When she didn't elaborate, Blaze tilted her head in acknowledgement and picked up the conversation.

"What about Kelly? Is she working, too?" Blaze asked.

She nodded. "She has the early shift, then she'll head to her brother's in Massachusetts."

"You don't go with her?"

"No. She asks every year, but Kelly rarely sees her family." What she really wanted to say was she would be uncomfortable as a third wheel. Kelly often asked the person she was dating at the time.

"Come home with me."

The thought of being around such a warm, loving environment was tempting, but she couldn't impose. "Oh, Blaze. It's kind of you to ask, but I couldn't."

"Why not? I know they'd love to see you again. I have to warn you though, the Carters are a boisterous group when we all get together." Blaze reached for her hand. "At least consider coming with me. Please?"

Trinity bit the inside of her cheek to keep the emotions welling inside at bay. The look in Blaze's eyes was genuine, and she knew she'd likely have a wonderful time, yet she hesitated. Spending a holiday with someone's family spoke of commitment, and she wasn't sure, despite her feelings for Blaze, if she wanted to get in that deep.

"I'll think about it." It would likely be the only thing she would think about.

CHAPTER TWENTY-FOUR

K elly had disappeared into the club fashion section while Trinity went to the nightlife and formal occasions section, not sure if she'd have any better luck than the last four stores they'd been in. Whether she deserved a little extravagance or not wasn't the question. She refused to spend more than a week's salary on a dress she would likely only wear a few times over the next couple of years, if that.

The good news was she had completed the second part of her application for head trauma nurse—her practical. The questions revolved around protocols, common practices, prioritization, multitasking, and a demonstration of remaining cool under pressure with a mock scenario of multiple patients arriving in the ED at the same time. She'd had to triage and assign staff while taking care of the most critical patient herself. She thought she'd done well, only stumbling once when she hesitated a minute in deciding between a heart attack patient and someone who'd been involved in a shooting. Her examiners had assured her the mock setting was harder than real life. In an actual emergency she'd have multiple staff to help make those decisions. It hadn't made her feel any better, but at least it was over, and all her studying had paid off.

She'd originally thought a black dress would be her best choice, but with the selection in front of her she might have to reconsider. She wanted a dress that roared *notice me*. One that would have people turn their heads to take a second look—and then a third. She ran her fingers over the edge of the hangers like she was going through a recipe card box. Navy blue, burgundy, purple, green. She stopped and held out the emerald green dress, taking in the intricate pattern of tiny sparkling stones along one sleeve and over the shoulder, before spreading down its length into a shower of sparks not unlike fireworks at night. It was stunning. It was also over her self-imposed budget.

"Try it on," Kelly said from the next rack. "It will really highlight your hair and eyes."

"It's too expensive." Trinity chewed her lip. It *was* expensive, but she couldn't let go of the soft, shimmering material.

Kelly lifted the hanger from the rack and turned her in the direction of the dressing rooms. "If it looks like shit then there's no harm, no foul."

"And if not?"

Her eyes twinkled. "Then I get to talk you into buying it."

"Not when it's out of my budget, so why would I want to try it on?" Though as she said the words, Trinity longed to feel the fabric against her skin. It was velvety soft and, even on the cheap plastic hanger, it flowed like a waterfall. *That doesn't mean it will look good on me.* "I'm not buying it even if it's beautiful." *Nope.* There wasn't any need to spend an outrageous amount on something as frivolous as a gown. Trinity stepped into one of the small changing rooms while she continued to argue with herself over the practicality of an article of clothing that would likely just rot away from lack of use. That was right before she looked at her reflection.

"Oh my God," Kelly gasped. She walked around her, looking her up and down and making appreciative sounds. "Girl, you have no right to look that fucking hot with clothes on."

Trinity felt heat rise to her cheeks. "I'm not that hot." She turned sideways in the full-length mirror while she checked herself out from all angles. She had to admit, she loved how the fabric clung to her curves before falling away in soft folds that touched the floor. When she wore stilettos, it would be the perfect length. She needn't worry about that little detail because it was going back on the rack. Besides, she wasn't sure about the open back. She'd had to remove her bra and pull down her panties a bit though the band was still peeking above the deep sweeping cut. Even without underwear, the fabric would come just above the top of her crack and she didn't know if she could be daring enough to pull off the look while knowing she wore nothing underneath.

"Are you kidding me?" Kelly smoothed a hand down the unadorned sleeve. "You go pay for this right now. Don't even bother to put your clothes back on. You should live in this from now on."

Trinity giggled. As much as she didn't want to admit it, she was killing it in the damn thing, and just as happy she'd made a point of getting to the gym a few times the last couple of weeks. Her stomach was flat except for the slight rise below her navel, and the material fell away from her body at the flare of her hips, concealing any flaws. Her cleavage rose just enough above the pooling fabric at the scoop neck to entice, and she was grateful her breasts were still high and firm. Now she wished she had a date for the fundraiser. Smokey eyes filled with desire flashed in front of her, causing her to shiver. She headed back to the dressing room.

"Hey. What are you doing?" Kelly's voice held a bit of panic.

She smiled over her shoulder. "I'm changing. Then I'm going to take this extravagance to the register."

Kelly fist pumped. "Yes!"

"Can you look for a silver clutch to match those stilettos I have? I'll be right out."

Buyer's remorse is real. Trinity had taken on the mantra for the last hour. Between the gown, wrap, clutch, imitation earrings, and matching necklace that Kelly insisted she had to have to "complete the look," she'd spent just over five hundred and seventy-five dollars. She couldn't think about it anymore. If she did, she'd take it all back. That wasn't what she wanted to do and she refused to give in to the inner voice that was turning into a huge pain in the ass. It's not like she bought herself things on a regular basis, evidenced by the new purchase being the first addition to her closet in more than a year.

Needing a distraction while Kelly went for pizza, she picked up her phone and scrolled through her Facebook page. She laughed at a cat antics video and snorted at a GIF one of her online friends had posted. Then she got the bright idea to see if Blaze had a page. *How many people could there be with her name?* It was worth a try. She typed in Blaze and clicked on the little magnifying glass. The results included a pizza business, a media station, and a carpenter. After reading the short description, she clicked on the carpenter link and Blaze's enigmatic smile and androgynous likeness filled her screen. Trinity held her breath, the fluttering, topsy-turvy feeling in her stomach hitting her like it always did when she looked at Blaze.

The page on her screen wasn't a personal profile. Instead, it boasted Blaze Carter as a master carpenter who crafted commissioned works, custom cabinets, and special requests. It didn't state her age or where she lived, but she already knew those. Her cover photo showed her beautiful log home in the background. She flicked back to Blaze's image, and their night together came roaring back in a rush so strong, so vivid, Trinity felt the pulse between her legs. Damn. She didn't want her body to betray her. Even while she tried to find reasons not to, she considered what excuse she could use for calling. *Hi, Blaze. I need some work done on my body and since you're a master*…Good Lord, could she be any more pathetic?

She ran her fingertip over the photo. Blaze wore a dark tan shirt with the sleeves rolled up to reveal her bulging forearms as she leaned on her jean-clad leg. Her smile was sincere and alluring, just like in person. Blaze was as hot blooded as they came. And God have mercy, she'd had the pleasure of watching her buck and moan to prove it.

"This better be the best damn pizza we've ever had." Kelly's abrupt entrance kicked her off the fantasy train and back to reality in a heartbeat. She tossed her phone down and jumped up like her ass was on fire.

Kelly set the pizza on the table and looked at her like she had three heads. "What the hell's wrong with you?"

Trinity fought the urge to glance at her phone, knowing Blaze's picture was still on the screen. "Nothing. I'm hungry is all."

Kelly tossed her jacket on the couch. "Why don't I believe you?"

Trinity bit her lip, refusing to give in. "Want a beer?" She stuck her head in the fridge. It was more an attempt to cool the heat in her ears, evidence she'd been caught red-handed doing something she probably shouldn't have been doing. Which was insane. She was a grown woman. She could check out someone's Facebook account if she wanted to. It didn't mean anything. She was just curious. When she didn't get an answer, she straightened to find Kelly watching her.

"Spill it, Greene, or I'm going to grab your cell to see what you've been trying so hard to ignore."

After opening a bottle, she dropped onto a chair and waved her hand. "Fine. Go ahead." She sighed.

Kelly snatched her cell and raised her brows. "Ooh-la-la. She's even more handsome in full light. It was kind of dark at the Zone." Kelly zoomed in and out. "No wonder you were all flushed when I came in."

"I was not. It's warm in here." Kelly rolled her eyes. "Okay. Yes, I was…reminiscing." God, this was embarrassing. She and Kelly had talked about dates and sex more times than she could count, but with Blaze it felt—disrespectful.

Kelly took a swig and flipped open the pizza box before grabbing a slice loaded with toppings. She chewed and moaned, then flopped it on her plate. "Is that what you're calling it now?"

"What would you call it?" She didn't really want to know, but she had to ask anyway. She snagged a piece for herself and took a small bite. It was really good.

"A curl your toes fantasy, if she was involved." Kelly tipped her chin.

Trinity couldn't agree more, but she wasn't quite ready to admit that she could do with a lot more than a fantasy about Blaze. "I'm thinking about asking her to the fundraiser." *Holy hell.* What made her decide to drop that nugget of info?

"Wow." Kelly choked on her drink. It all but shot out her nose.

She was glad Kelly didn't need the Heimlich maneuver. Last week she'd had to do the lifesaving technique in the cafeteria and the person had puked all over her arms. Nurse or not, puke freaked her out.

"She must have been exceptional. You usually prefer to go stag and check out your options, but I can't say I blame you for wanting her on your arm. The other women will be drooling and shooting envious looks at you the entire evening."

She should have been ashamed for thinking the same thing and hoping…knowing, they would make a striking couple. They'd both been treading lightly and taking things slow. Neither had mentioned the word dating, but the calls and texts and meals together had certainly felt that way. All of it scared the shit out of her. "I wish you were going."

"You know that's not my thing. I hate having to play nice with complete jerks."

"They aren't all jerks." Trinity tried to picture the attendees the last time she'd gone. There had been several stuffed suits, and those were the ones who contributed the most, so she'd swallowed her sharp-tongued retorts and done just that—played nice. "Just a choice few."

Kelly emptied her bottle and burped unceremoniously. "A few too many for my liking."

Trinity wrapped the leftover pizza and tossed the box in the trash can by the back door while Kelly rinsed their empties and put them in the bin. The bottle deposit money went to the cat adoption center. She thought of Baxter and smiled. They did what they could, when they could. She picked up her cell and dropped onto the couch. Kelly staked out her spot and put her feet on the old coffee table. Neither had any intention of replacing it since it was the perfect height for lounging. She was about to swap her cell for the remote when it buzzed in her hand. The screen flashed the name of the one person she'd been thinking about incessantly for weeks. Blaze.

"It's her." The words rushed out of her mouth.

Kelly glanced over. "Her who?"

She turned the screen so Kelly could see it. That got her attention.

"Well, Christ. Answer the damn thing."

Right. Easy. "Hello?" Her voice was barely above a whisper.

"Trinity? It's Blaze."

Like I wouldn't know. "Hey. How are you?" To her credit, her tone was casual and her voice calmer than the rest of her body. Blaze's voice was smooth and smoky, like aged whiskey.

"I'm good." Blaze hesitated. "I hope I'm not interrupting anything."

"Nope. Just kicking back on the couch, watching TV." She glanced at Kelly who was mouthing something about "boring." She covered the mouthpiece. "Shut up."

"Trinity?"

"I'm here."

"I won't keep you. The reason I'm calling is to ask you out to a dinner party at DJ's next Friday night."

She could hear her breathing over the phone. It reminded her of how hot Blaze's breath had been on her neck and her brain shut down. For the next thirty seconds she couldn't think until a throw pillow bounced off her head. "Ow."

"Uh…you okay?"

"Just my roomie thinking she's the social director tonight." She stuck her tongue out at Kelly and threw it back.

"I'm sorry. It was a silly idea. Don't feel obligated."

Trinity sat up. Her heart was hammering a little too hard, too fast. She was having palpitations. That wasn't good. "No. I mean, it's not silly at all. I'm sorry, but I have to work a twelve-hour shift on Friday."

"Oh."

Blaze sounded as disappointed as she felt. She wasn't too keen on anything that involved DJ, but a chance to spend time with Blaze was almost worth being annoyed. Maybe she could salvage the situation. "How do you feel about fundraisers?"

"I'm sorry?"

"I have a fundraiser to attend on Saturday night for the Pride Center in Albany, and I was wondering if you'd like to go with me. I know it's kind of last minute, but—"

"I'd love to."

She felt her eyes get big. "You would?"

"I'd be a fool not to go. I'll have the most beautiful woman there on my arm."

Blaze's tone had dropped into a deep, rich baritone that sent a bolt of live current through her, landing between her thighs. Her insides turned to jelly. "You don't have to say that just to be nice."

"I'm not."

"You're not nice?" Trinity felt an upward tug at the corner of her mouth. *This back and forth is fun.*

"Ha, ha. Very funny." She could hear Blaze's smile in her voice. "I'm assuming this is a formal event."

Shit. Trinity hadn't even considered Blaze might not have appropriate clothing for such an event. "Well, it is, but..."

"Trinity, I have a tux or two that I can brush the dust from. No problem."

She let out a sigh of relief. "That's good. For a minute there I thought..." God. What was wrong with her? She didn't normally have such a hard time with social etiquette.

"That I was just some lesbian sex object who only wore tight jeans and button-downs?"

"No!" Good grief. She panicked until she heard Blaze's hearty laughter. "Damn you, Blaze," she said before her own laughter kicked in.

"Oh my, how unladylike."

"I'll give you unladylike." The words were out before she could censor them, and her mind went into instant recall mode, picturing some of the very unladylike things they'd done together.

"Will you? I can't wait." Blaze's sexy voice pulled her back. "What time shall I pick you up?"

"I'll pick you up. After all, I asked you."

"I know, but I really don't mind. That way you can relax and have a couple of drinks."

Trinity chewed on her lip. She glanced at Kelly, having all but forgotten she was there. She stared at Trinity and, deciding to get away from her scrutiny, Trinity got up and went to the kitchen. "Only if you're sure."

"I'm sure."

"Okay. How about six? That will give us plenty of time to get to Albany."

"Perfect. One more question, then I'll let you get back to chilling."

"Sure." Her heart was doing that little trip-hammer thing again.

"What color are you wearing?" Blaze asked.

"Emerald green." She briefly thought about giving her more details, but she wanted Blaze to be surprised when she picked her up.

"That will be a fabulous color with your hair. See you then."

"Good night, Blaze." She disconnected, suddenly feeling like a schoolgirl on a first date. Only this schoolgirl was having deliciously naughty thoughts about her date. *I'm not going to sleep with her.* It's just a date. She grabbed a couple of beers and sauntered back into the living room.

Kelly hit the mute button on the remote and patted the space next to her. "Tell me all about Steamy Hunk and your upcoming date." Kelly took the offered bottle, all the while smiling as if she were the one who'd made plans.

"She asked me to go to a dinner party on Friday, but I've got a long shift scheduled." Trinity could probably get someone to cover for her since the long shifts paid better and were in high demand. But she didn't intend to start making herself available just because Blaze asked. That was how you sidetracked your career.

"I would have auctioned it off to the highest bidder." Kelly fanned herself with a magazine and laughed.

"Besides, it was at DJ's."

"Oh." Kelly was quiet for a bit. "So, you asked her to the fundraiser?"

All she could do was nod, still in disbelief that she'd had the courage to ask and even more amazed by Blaze accepting.

Kelly tossed the magazine down and shook her head. "Man, oh man, if I didn't think I'd come off as a total geek I'd hang around and take pictures."

Trinity lobbed the pillow that had landed in her face earlier. "It's not our high school prom." *Even though it kinda feels like it.* She tried to imagine what Blaze had been thinking throughout their conversation. Her gallant offer to drive was touching. She liked the thought of Blaze coming to pick her up, making her feel special. In return, she wanted to look her absolute best. Brushing a strand of hair out of her face, Trinity sat up quickly, nearly spilling her beer.

"Jesus, you're jumpy tonight. Now what?" Kelly asked.

"I have to do something with my hair." It was long, thick, and wavy. She usually wore it down or pulled back in a loose ponytail, but that wouldn't due for this occasion, especially since she wanted to show off the cut of the dress.

"I know exactly how you should wear it." Kelly took her hand and led her to the big bathroom.

It was the one they shared, because it was located between their bedrooms and had a double sink. There was a second guest bathroom that was smaller, with a counter that would never hold all their necessities. After she rummaged in the drawer for items, she motioned for her to sit backward on the toilet seat.

"It won't be perfect. You're going to need to make an appointment at the salon, but it will give you an idea of what I'm thinking." She proceeded to brush and tug, pin and primp, standing back several times to look at her work. "There," she said. "It's a little rough because, well…I'm not a stylist, but it's close."

Trinity stood transfixed by her reflection. Her mass of curls was swept up at the back in a neat, yet slightly messy do. Several slender tendrils of hair framed her face, softening the severity of an otherwise formal style. She imagined herself in the gown, but she couldn't quite picture it. She looked at Kelly.

"Help me put on the rest?"

Kelly's expression showed her excitement and they headed for Trinity's closet. After she had the gown on, along with the jewelry she'd bought to go with the outfit, they returned to the mirror, and she gasped. The woman staring back at her was beautiful.

"It's perfect."

Kelly came up behind her and held her shoulders. "You're perfect. And you're going to make Blaze weak-kneed when she sees you." Kelly tucked a loose strand just so and stood back with her hands on her hips. "Damn. I hate that I'm going to miss seeing her seeing you."

Trinity didn't want to hurt her feelings by telling her she was glad it would be a moment just between the two of them. Somehow, she knew it would be special. And intimate. Something only lovers should share. Wow. One time didn't make them lovers, but after Saturday night, maybe that would change. Her anticipation morphed into trepidation.

"Help me out of this." She pushed past Kelly and beelined for her closet.

"What the fuck is wrong with you?"

How could Trinity explain how her thoughts bounced between wanting to knock Blaze off her feet and not wanting anyone distracting her from professional success? Relationships demanded time and energy, two things she wasn't willing to give if it meant sacrificing her goals. She practically ripped the dress from her body, close to tears and treading in waters she'd never had to navigate before. She didn't fall for women, she just slept with them. Trinity was no longer sure she liked the person she'd become—all for the sake of pride. In herself, her work, and her ability to boast to her family that, despite the odds against her, she'd risen above the squalor she'd been raised in.

"I just didn't want it on anymore."

Kelly stood dumbfounded. She didn't look angry or hurt. Just confused. Trinity was confused, too. But she wasn't ready to admit, even to her closest friend, that she felt like she was on uneven ground these days and wasn't sure who she wanted to be anymore. She pulled on her clothes and turned.

"I'm sorry. I don't know what's wrong with me. You did a fabulous job with my hair. Maybe I'm getting sick." She forced a smile she didn't feel. "Would you take some pictures of the style with my phone so I can show the hairdresser exactly how I want it?"

Kelly took a tentative step forward. "You don't have to do this if you don't want to."

Her heart squeezed when she realized she'd been acting like a jerk. It was only a date. And not even that. A fundraiser. Nothing intimate and no reason to be so crazy over it.

"I really do love it." Trinity glanced in the mirror. Her hair *was* perfect for the gown. She glanced at Kelly in the mirror and smiled. This time she meant it. Kelly nodded and went to get her phone. She really needed to get her shit together and stop letting her imagination conjure up baseless thoughts about Blaze. She was just another woman and there was no reason to think there was anything between them except sex. She'd never let it go any further.

Chapter Twenty-five

H ello." The word came out sharper than Blaze had meant. She'd been high-strung ever since asking Trinity to join her for Thanksgiving.

"So, you are still alive," DJ said.

"Yeah. Sorry. There's been a lot going on. What's up?" Blaze asked.

"I'm calling to make sure you're still coming to the dinner party."

She groaned. "You know I'm not into stuffy hobnobbing, but I'll be there."

DJ chuckled. "Again with the enthusiasm."

"Be happy I said yes."

"I am. Are you bringing a date?"

"No." Blaze didn't want to get into it. Maybe it was a good thing Trinity wasn't joining her since there was still friction between her and DJ. She promised to show up a little early, even though DJ wouldn't be involved in the cooking aspect of entertaining. She'd hire a caterer to prepare all the food. She wondered who else would be invited. DJ moved in affluent circles, surrounding herself with upper class individuals who could advance her career and drop her name as someone who could sell even the worst real estate properties. Some were nice enough, but none of them could hold a candle to Trinity in terms of appeal, and she wasn't talking just sexually. Her attractiveness went without saying. It was a shame she was working again, but at least Blaze's invitation had received a counteroffer, one she was excited about taking her up on.

"So, I'll see you Friday at six?" DJ asked.

The things you did for friends. She sighed. "I'll be there."

❖

"Hope I'm not too early." Blaze brushed her lips over DJ's cheek and stepped into the lush apartment. One DJ could afford, and the type Blaze would never consider living in. It was too modern and too minimalist, even if it was well decorated.

"You're never too early, but you're the first to arrive."

She set the bottle of wine on the bar and headed for the kitchen, not that she needed to bother, knowing the food would likely be delivered soon. "Need help with anything?" She didn't plan on staying late, wanting to save her energy for her evening with Trinity tomorrow.

"Not really. I'm sorry your date couldn't make it."

Blaze slid two wine glasses from the ready supply and opened the bottle she'd brought, then poured a healthy dose. "Her name is Trinity, and I doubt it."

"That's rather crude. What did I do?"

She shook her head. "Nothing. Sorry." Blaze wasn't about to admit she would have canceled if she didn't think DJ would have been pissed. Having to be solo for the night didn't suit her mood. She never used to mind. In fact, before Trinity she often preferred it, because she hated feeling like she was expected to perform, but that wasn't who she was. She no longer cared what others thought. Her foul mood likely had more to do with the event. She wasn't fond of DJ's gatherings. They were attended by pretentious people whose only interest was spreading the latest gossip or talking about a recent conquest. She never understood why DJ surrounded herself with the likes of them, but then, ever since college, they'd moved in different social circles. She tipped the bottle toward her. "Want some?"

"No, thanks." The doorbell rang and she went to answer it in full DJ fashion, swaying her hips while balancing on stilettos with heels long enough to be considered lethal weapons.

Blaze didn't want to sour everyone's mood. She took another swig and went to greet the arriving guests. Her stomach dropped when she saw two of the women she'd slept with in the past. *Why the hell would DJ invite them?* She pushed her annoyance away.

"Blaze," Grace said. "It's good to see you after so long." She leaned in.

She hugged Grace tenderly. They'd dated for a while several years ago after meeting at the gym where Blaze and DJ had memberships. Both knew it wasn't going to last, but she'd enjoyed their time together and wasn't about to make Grace feel like she didn't matter just because they were no longer together. "It's wonderful seeing you, too. Are you still at the gym?" Blaze asked and took her coat. She hadn't gone back after her surgery and had no immediate plans to return.

"Yes, but it's not the same without you there."

When Grace moved away, Fagan sidled up next to her. She'd made the mistake of sleeping with her after she and Grace ended their relationship, and she was the main reason Blaze never slept with the same woman twice. Fagan had left a sour taste in her mouth.

"Blaze, darling. Where *have* you been hiding?" Fagan swept in for a full-on kiss, but Blaze offered her cheek and backed away. She was going to escape this den of iniquity as soon as possible. She tossed DJ a severe stare before DJ turned back to the rest of her arriving guests.

Two hours later, Blaze stormed through the front door of her cabin. It hadn't taken her long to figure out DJ had invited most of the eligible women she knew in hopes one of them would connect with Blaze, even though she wasn't alone by choice. She'd left pissed off and without a word to DJ.

Baxter blinked, stretched her long body, and looked up expectantly, likely hoping Blaze had forgotten she'd already been fed.

"Nice try, fur bag, but you're out of luck."

The cat turned and strutted away to check out her bowls. One was always full of dry food, but she gave one last meow to show her displeasure.

Upstairs, Blaze hung up her pants and tossed her shirt in the laundry, then grabbed her robe. She longed to hear Trinity's voice, but she didn't want to disturb her, and sent a text instead.

Hope your shift is going well. Looking forward to tomorrow.

She stared at the phone and waited as though she expected an immediate answer, which was crazy. Trinity was probably inundated with emergencies. Blaze sighed. Coffee would make her feel better. She slipped the phone in her pocket, prepped the Keurig, then pushed the start button. That's when her phone pinged and displayed Trinity's icon, along with a brief message telling her it was going okay for a Friday and she was looking forward to tomorrow too before she had to go.

She smiled. Whenever she thought about Trinity, that's what happened. It had to mean something. The text had been the highlight of her evening. She planned to have a sit-down with DJ and ask point-blank what the hell she had been up to tonight, though she had a pretty good idea.

While her coffee cooled, Blaze went for a shower and stepped into the steam-filled enclosure. The hot water sluiced over her tense muscles and eased her into a better frame of mind, though her irritation persisted. DJ always played matchmaker, so she shouldn't be surprised. She'd expressed wanting a relationship, so maybe DJ had stepped up. Why DJ hadn't told her the party was for Blaze's benefit was what really annoyed her. She would have declined before she'd been paraded out like a stud on the auction block. She shook her head and decided to let it go. For now. She was too tired to try to decipher DJ's reasons. A good night's sleep was what she needed to enjoy her first official date with Trinity.

She slid into the cool sheets and pulled up the blanket, snuggling into the softness. Even though she'd changed the sheets, Trinity's scent lingered in her bed. Baxter jumped up, circled a spot several times, then lowered herself on the corner. She blinked twice and began to purr, letting her know she was settled for the night.

Closing her eyes, Blaze envisioned red hair flowing over her in soft waves, and green eyes hazed by lust. She flexed her inner muscles as the blood surged through her. Her body and mind craved more of Trinity, and it was a craving she had finally begun to understand.

❖

Blaze held the stem of an ivory rose and lifted the bloom to her nose, inhaling. She hadn't thought twice about the color or the variety of flower, though she wanted to arrive with something that simply stated she was looking forward to spending the evening with Trinity. She smoothed her hand over her Armani tux and the emerald green pocket square she'd made it her mission to find. She rang the doorbell, looking down one last time at the rose before the door opened and she lifted her gaze. Any witty words she might have said stayed on her lips as she stared at the most beautiful woman she'd ever seen.

"You're a goddess."

Trinity's face turned a pale shade of pink. "Thank you for saying so, but I'm not. Come in."

Blaze somehow managed to make her feet move though it felt more like gliding than walking. Once inside, she turned in time to see the open back of Trinity's flowing gown. There was nothing she could do to stop her mouth from dropping open in total awe.

Trinity grinned. "You might catch something you don't want in there," she said as she lifted Blaze's chin with a manicured fingernail and smiled seductively.

What could she possibly say when nothing above her neck was functioning?

"Is that for me?" Trinity asked. A knowing smile lifted the corners of her mouth just enough to let Blaze know she was aware of the effect her attire was having.

"Yes," she said. "But it's not nearly as beautiful as you." She ran the soft petals down Trinity's cheek and along her neck, then stepped behind her and followed the path of her spine. The resulting gooseflesh was exactly what she hoped for. They were back on even ground. At least for the time being. Blaze slowly spun her until their eyes met and she took a deep breath to steady herself.

"Let me put this in water, then we can go."

Trinity went toward the kitchen and Blaze followed. She didn't want to miss any of this night, not one single chance to look at Trinity.

When she turned, Trinity moved closer. She looked deep into Blaze's eyes, as if wanting to know all her most intimate thoughts. "You're very handsome in everyday clothes, but you're magnificent in this tux." Trinity fingered the lapel and her hand brushed over Blaze's breast. Her nipples tightened at the light touch, one she remembered well.

Blaze swallowed hard. "I have no way of telling you how gorgeous you are. And this gown..." Blaze slid her hands over the sleeves then took Trinity's hands in hers. "It's stunning and perfect on you." She didn't want to want Trinity as much as she did in that moment, but she couldn't deny the need to touch her. To make love to her in, and out, of the gown. She had to rein in her desire. Blaze had no idea if Trinity was interested in dating, but since she'd been the one to ask Blaze to join her tonight, she was encouraged. Against her better judgment, she leaned in and covered Trinity's mouth with hers, gently tasting her. It stoked the fire already burning, and after Trinity moaned, it was all she could do to pull away. She shuddered in her arms before her eyes slowly opened.

"God, you need to stop kissing me like that."

"Why? Didn't you like it?" Blaze asked.

Trinity took a step back. "Oh, I did, but I paid a lot of money for these tickets and we need to leave now, before..." Her eyes never left Blaze's.

"Before?"

"Before we end up being late." Trinity smiled and she laughed, breaking the sexual tension thick in the air around them.

Blaze couldn't keep from touching her again, and she placed her hand on the curve of Trinity's hip. "Well, we wouldn't want to miss the festivities, would we?" Her insides felt like molten lava that flowed throughout her lower body, filling her with its heat.

"I just need to get my purse and wrap."

Reluctantly, she let her hand slide away. Her breath froze when she was once again given a view of Trinity's exposed flesh from her neck to below the small of her back. *I'm going to need to remember we aren't a couple.* Otherwise she might become possessive of what wasn't hers.

Trinity folded the matching pashmina over her arm and picked up a sparkling silver clutch before glancing up. Excitement twinkled in her eyes.

Blaze opened the door, afraid if they lingered, she'd lose what little resolve she had left. She would make tonight's attendance at the event one Trinity would remember for a long time. "Shall we?" She held out her hand and Trinity's smaller one slid into it.

"Yes." Trinity turned, then glanced back and forth between the car and Blaze. "Is this your car?"

"No. I didn't think a motorcycle or an SUV were appropriate transportation for this evening, so I rented it." She opened the passenger door of the Audi and Trinity slid onto the heated leather seat. Blaze took a breath as she rounded the front of the car. Somehow, she knew how much going to the fundraiser meant to Trinity, and she'd wanted her to feel as special as Blaze would with Trinity on her arm.

Trinity's eyes widened. "You rented an Audi just for tonight?" she asked. Her tone relayed her incredulity.

Blaze reached for her hand. "Not for tonight. For you, Trinity. You deserve to be treated well, and I'm honored you asked me to escort you. I'd never want to do anything to embarrass you." She squeezed her hand and let go, though letting go was the last thing she wanted to do. She pushed the button and the engine purred in response. "Besides, I didn't think a Harley would be quite the ride you had in mind tonight." She smiled and Trinity laughed again.

"No, it wasn't. I don't think this dress would let me spread my legs that far." Trinity's cheeks pinked.

All kinds of erotic visions bombarded her. Trinity had a knack for making her lose control. Blaze rested her head on the steering wheel and closed her eyes.

"That's not quite what I meant. Climbing on the back of that beast would require me to hike up my gown..." Trinity stopped talking, then groaned. "Well, I'm going to stop right there."

She chuckled. The GPS got her started on their journey, announcing they should reach their destination at 7:02 p.m. Blaze didn't want to be the first to arrive because she wanted the other attendees to ogle when they walked in together. They made a striking couple and she would like nothing more than to convince Trinity to share her view—even if it was only for one night.

CHAPTER TWENTY-SIX

Trinity glanced at Blaze's profile. The strong jaw and full lips added to her androgynous looks. Along with her almond shaped eyes and a regal nose, Blaze was cover model material. To look at her tonight in her well-cut tux and designer pique shirt, she appeared gender-neutral, though she did little to hide her breasts. Her looks suited Trinity's taste to perfection. Even with three-inch stilettos, she was shorter than Blaze, and she could only imagine how they looked standing next to each other. She'd been too preoccupied to glance in the hallway mirror before they left.

Butterflies batted her insides as she tried to relax and listen to the music softly playing. She remembered how formal the gala was and was happy she'd be there with Blaze.

"You know what I do for a living, but we've never talked more about your job." Blaze looked over at her and smiled as she easily handled the sedan. It was likely a kitten compared to the beast of a motorcycle she seemed to maneuver without any difficulty.

"What do you want to know?" She was proud of what she did.

"Have you been there long?"

"Five years in the ED. I was on surgical floors for a year before that. It wasn't for me." In-patients faced a different type of tragedy. Many times overwhelming, but she didn't want to go into that right now.

"Wow. You must have graduated young." Blaze took the exit ramp and glanced at the GPS.

"Not really. It took me a while to save up enough that I wouldn't be in debt for the next decade. I still had to get a student loan, but I didn't live on campus and I went to a state university, so it wasn't outrageous." She chewed her lip before going on. "I actually got my master's degree a couple of weeks ago, and I've applied for the trauma head nurse position. I should know soon if I've gotten it."

Blaze gave her a warm smile. "Congratulations. I can't believe you didn't say anything so we could celebrate. And I'm sure you'll get the position you want. From everything I've witnessed, you're excellent at what you do, and you're determined. I don't see what could possibly hold you back."

Her words warmed Trinity. Praise wasn't something she took for granted since she hadn't gotten much growing up. "Thanks."

The gala wasn't being held at the Pride Center because it wasn't large enough, but there was a beautiful former bank next door that had been converted into an events venue and that's where they were going. Valet parking was part of the package, but she wasn't sure if Blaze wanted to trust the car jockeys with her rental. "If you want to park the car yourself, I don't mind walking."

"Nonsense." Blaze put the car in park. "That's what they have insurance for." A valet approached her door and she got out, meeting Blaze on the sidewalk where she offered her arm.

"You are absolutely stunning, and I am very grateful you chose to have me on your arm tonight."

Trinity wasn't sure how to feel. The doorperson was waiting, there'd be photographers inside, and she had the hottest butch she'd ever been with next to her. She decided for this night, if only for tonight, she would just enjoy every moment of being with Blaze and try her best not to bring the night down by mentioning anything to do with her career goals. Tonight was a night for celebration and fun, and with Blaze beside her, she could easily do that.

"Then let's go show them all how proud we are to be part of the community," Trinity said.

Blaze walked beside her; the soft soles of her Italian shoes soundless on the concrete walkway. Trinity's dress moved with her, gently swaying around her legs and brushing the tops of her feet.

The more she was beside Blaze, the less she noticed their height difference, likely due to Blaze never looking down at her. Her gaze met Blaze's on what felt like even ground in a way she'd never felt before. The door opened and they stepped through into the growing throng of attendees. She took her invitation from her bag and handed it to the man at the podium. He nodded and pressed the microphone button.

"Trinity Greene and Blaze Carter, patron sponsors." There was mild applause as they were ushered to the photo area. That's when she became aware of the hushed voices and low whispers gathering around them. She tilted her face to Blaze who smiled at her with such adoration it made her breathless.

"No worries, love. They can't believe how beautiful you are. Neither can I." She raised their hands between them and brushed her lips over Trinity's. "Shall we give them what they're waiting for?"

She swallowed her initial trepidation about people staring at them and tried not to focus on Blaze using the word love. "Absolutely." She turned to the photographer and smiled as Blaze wrapped her arm around her, her fingers resting lightly on her bare back. After several flashes and a few poses, they moved into the crowd. Those nearest greeted them with words like, "beautiful," and "simply gorgeous." Her favorite was "stunning couple." She thought so too, though she still hadn't seen their reflection. She was about to guide Blaze toward the bar when she heard a familiar voice call to her.

"Trinity." Carol Templeton rushed to greet her with a fierce hug. "I'm so happy you were able to attend this year's event. It's so good to see you." Carol was the first person who'd introduced her to the vibrant queer community in the area where she attended college. She'd never had such a big support group, and she'd been grateful to be welcomed with open arms. Carol stepped back to face Blaze, then extended her hand. "I don't think I've had the pleasure. Carol Templeton, director of Capital Pride Center."

"Blaze Carter. It's a pleasure to meet you." She looked around at the venue. "This is a beautiful setting for a wonderful event. Thank you for all you do."

"How kind of you to say." Carol turned to Trinity. "Handsome and well-mannered is my kind of woman. You'd better keep her close." She leaned in and whispered. "There's a number of single women here. Someone's going to snatch her up if you don't." She winked and stepped back. "Have fun."

She wrapped her arm around Blaze's, and they headed for the bar. Little did Carol know she had every intention of keeping Blaze close. Just because she wasn't planning on falling into bed with her at the end of the evening didn't mean she was going to act as though they were just friends.

"That was interesting," Blaze said as they stood in line to give their order. "What would you like?"

She winced, not sure if Blaze had been offended by Carol's inference that Blaze was rather like a prize that others would be interested in winning. "A bag to hide in?"

Blaze's hearty laughter was a welcome sound. "Don't worry about Ms. Templeton's comments. I've certainly heard worse."

They stepped up to the bar together, and Blaze tipped her head as she pulled a money clip from her pocket. Trinity ordered a whiskey on the rocks, while Blaze ordered a club soda with a twist, keeping to her promise of being the designated driver. She placed a twenty on the bar before heading to one of the cocktail tables.

Blaze stirred her drink before removing the stick, then held up her glass. "To women who can shoot whiskey, among other things." Her eyes twinkled with mischief.

She laughed. "And to women who aren't afraid to be who they are." She lifted her glass and touched Blaze's. The band began to play a slow waltz and people started to move toward the dance floor.

"Shall we show them how it's done?" Blaze asked and held out her hand.

"It's been ages since I've even tried." The last time she'd waltzed was at a friend's wedding. The man who'd led her around the dance floor was okay, but she'd felt uncomfortable in his grasp and faltered several times.

"Just follow my lead and you'll do fine." When Trinity hesitated, she stepped closer. "Trust me."

She hadn't thought about the need to trust anyone other than herself since she was a teenager. People didn't keep their promises and when they did, there was often an ulterior motive. That was a long time ago, though, and Blaze wasn't anyone she'd known back then. It was time she let go of her childish fears and enjoy the moment. She nodded and took Blaze's hand. Blaze led her to an open space on the large dance floor, wrapped her arm around her waist, and held out her hand. She took a breath, knowing people were watching. She didn't want to embarrass Blaze...or herself. They began to move in a square, the basic waltz pattern, but she lost track when she glanced down and stumbled. Blaze held her tighter.

"Look at me, baby. Just me. Trust me with your body like you did before."

Their night in bed together came rushing to the foreground. She remembered letting go. Letting Blaze follow where *she* led, and then Blaze taking over, paying attention to every nuance of her. When she sighed. When she moaned. When she needed more, and where, and how. Trinity needed her to take the lead now.

Blaze started them off again, but this time she curled their joined hands into her chest, keeping Trinity closer. She slipped into the gray haze of Blaze's eyes, into the world of possibility she saw there. The crowd fell away and her body followed Blaze's. Soon they were moving in big sweeping arcs across a vast space, but she didn't look away, not trusting her own ability to not focus on the faces she might see in the crowd.

"Breathe, darling. I don't want you passing out."

She wasn't aware she'd been holding her breath, but after she sucked in much needed air, she moved easier, and listened to Blaze's voice in her ear.

"Breathe, two, three, four."

She found the rhythm intoxicating. Then she found herself in a deep dip and for a second, she panicked, but Blaze had her, holding her as though she were no more than a feather. She looked into her eyes, watching them darken as she leaned closer still. For a brief instant, she thought Blaze was going to kiss her before she brought her upright again and they circled the dance floor once more before the music ended. Her heart pounded in her chest. Blood rushed through her veins. Blaze held her hand and ended their dance with a slight bow. The room erupted into applause. Trinity glanced around in surprise. The dance floor was empty except for her and Blaze.

"You danced beautifully. I think you owe them a bow."

So, she did. The heat in her face remained long after they retrieved their drinks. If the last half hour was any indication, she was going to have the best time of her life, and Blaze was going to be responsible. Trinity couldn't have been happier with her decision to invite her.

Chapter Twenty-seven

B laze took a breath. Then another. She'd fought with every ounce of strength she had in her to remember Trinity wasn't her girlfriend. Hell, she wasn't even sure if this was an actual date, though it certainly felt like one. She had enjoyed meeting more of the community and those who supported it, but without a doubt the highlight of her entire evening were the moments Trinity had been in her arms.

They'd taken a break from dancing and had mingled during the remainder of the cocktail hour. A few women commented on Trinity's gown, envy in their eyes. After the short speeches and award presentations, they'd been served a delicious meal of filet mignon and sea bass, two of her favorites. The band continued to softly play in the background while they ate. Plates were being cleared and a dessert table appeared on the side of the room, but she was too full to eat anything else. All she wanted to do was glide across the floor with Trinity for the remainder of the evening. She loved dancing. Loved live music, and even more so when she had someone she cared about to dance with. She stood the moment Trinity slid her chair back and offered her hand.

"Thank you," Trinity said.

"Would you like another drink?" Trinity had only drunk water at dinner, while she'd stuck to seltzer.

"I think I would. I've been pacing myself." Trinity smiled.

Blaze lightly rested her hand on Trinity's back, still not sure how she was managing not to ravish her. "I promised I'd refrain so you could enjoy yourself." She ordered and slid another twenty onto the bar.

"I know, and I *am* enjoying myself. I don't want to lose control and become an embarrassment to either of us."

"You would never do that." Blaze handed off the drink and gestured to one of the many small tables surrounding the dance floor.

"How do you know I wouldn't?" Trinity sipped her cocktail.

"Because you're too sophisticated, and this isn't the place to go wild."

"Where would be the place to go wild?" Trinity asked.

The blood left the rest of her body and rushed between her thighs, settling there and making her center heavy. She glanced at Trinity's lips, then her full breasts resting in perfect position on her chest beneath the shimmering material. She'd lost the ability to think, but she hoped her mouth still worked. "I could think of a few places."

Trinity's eyes hazed over, her hand at her throat, as though she was lost in her own fantasies, and Blaze desperately wanted to know what they were. A familiar tune started to play, and Trinity rose. "Dance with me."

She managed to get her feet under her, praying her suit was dark enough to hide the moisture that had collected. "Gladly." She found an opening and wrapped Trinity in her arms, holding her close, but not quite touching. Blaze was unsure if she could refrain from pressing herself against Trinity's body if it came in contact with hers. They moved as though they'd been dancing together for years instead of hours.

"Are you afraid of me?"

Blaze smiled at the strange question. "I'm only afraid of what you do to me."

"And what do I do to you, my handsome escort?" Trinity's mouth twitched at the corners.

"You are so stunningly beautiful. I want you," she whispered in her ear. Trinity gasped. "But I also want to take you slow. Worship you. Show you how much you've affected every single person here tonight." She pulled back enough to see Trinity's eyes, to watch their rapidly changing color. To see the desire in them that clearly matched her own. She'd promised Trinity she would take care of her for the evening, and she had. Now she wanted what she had no right to want. Blaze wanted all of her. Her body...without question. But she also wanted her heart, and she was afraid it was the one thing she couldn't have. "I want to show you how much your inner and outer beauty has me mesmerized."

Trinity seemed to be warring with herself. Her eyes spoke volumes and mirrored Blaze's longing, yet her body had stiffened as though she were battling some inner force. She didn't want to find out if she'd be on the losing side, so she did the only thing she could. Blaze pulled Trinity closer until their bodies melded together, and they danced.

For the next hour, she luxuriated in the privilege of being the one Trinity was with. The one she lavished her attention on. The couple people saw unquestionably as together, leaving no room for another to step in her place. When she returned from a much-needed trip to the restroom, Trinity turned and found her with unerring accuracy. She said a few words to the couple she was talking to and made her way to Blaze.

"If you don't mind calling it a night, I'm ready to be out of these shoes."

Blaze had wondered for at least the sixth time how any woman could stand on her toes for an entire evening and look so at ease doing it. "Of course. Is there anyone you want to see before we go?"

Trinity shook her head. "I already thanked Carol, so I'm good."

She led the way through the revelers who were still going strong and handed her claim ticket to one of the female valets. The evening had turned crisp. Trinity gathered her wrap around her shoulders, and Blaze put her arm around her.

"Cold?"

Trinity laid her head on her chest, and Blaze inhaled her perfume. It reminded her of the fresh scent of spring. "Not now." Trinity snuggled in tighter.

There were so many thoughts swirling through her head, she didn't know what to say or where to begin. She felt a deep connection with Trinity and though neither had mentioned being exclusive, she wanted to talk about seeing her more. The rental car pulled to a stop in front of them and she held the door open while Trinity slid in. Blaze knelt and removed her shoes, rubbing each foot in turn. Trinity's hand rested on her arm for a moment and she smiled before straightening in her seat. Blaze rounded the front and handed the valet a tip, then unbuttoned her jacket and got in. She turned the heat on low while the GPS calculated their route home. Blaze glanced at Trinity who appeared lost in thought.

"Everything okay?"

Trinity's gaze met hers. "Thank you for being such a wonderful..." Her lips pursed, as though she were trying to find the right words.

"Dancer? Butch? Date?" she asked, not quite sure where Trinity was going with her comment.

Laughter filled the car. "Well, you're certainly all of those, but that's not what I wanted to tell you."

"What did you want to tell me?" She was trying to pay attention to the Saturday night traffic and to Trinity, whose solemn demeanor made her anxious.

Trinity shook her head. "It's not important." She glanced out the side window and Blaze knew there was more than Trinity was willing to share.

She laid her hand on Trinity's thigh and felt the muscle tighten. "The gala was fun. And my dance partner was not only beautiful but accomplished." Blaze gave a small squeeze before reluctantly moving her hand away. "Whatever's bothering you, I wish you'd talk to me."

Trinity looked down at her hands folded in her lap on top of the clutch. "It's been a long time since I've enjoyed an evening out like this. All dressed up, and not thinking about...other things."

"That's good. Right?" Blaze maneuvered off the highway and into town, moving more confidently now that she was in familiar territory. At least geography-wise.

"It is." Trinity nodded. When she raised her head, her eyes shimmered. "But I don't want…can't…get used to it. My career comes first. I have my eye on that promotion and it will mean everything I've worked so hard for was worth the sacrifices."

Blaze's heart sank with a resounding thud. If she understood what she was hearing, Trinity was picking her career over a relationship, meaning she would come in second on the list of priorities. That's not what she wanted for her future. She wanted a partner who would put as much into the relationship as Blaze would.

"So, there's no chance of anyone getting close?" Blaze pulled into the driveway and turned off the car. She moved so she could look directly at Trinity, knowing this moment would define if there was any possibility of taking their relationship to the next level.

Trinity took a breath. "Not in the foreseeable future." She looked away again. "I feel like I've misled you and that was never my intention. Being with you tonight…I found myself wanting more. More time with you. More of the way you treat me as though I'm special and—"

"That's because you are special. Whatever may make you think otherwise, everything you felt from me was real." She brought Trinity's hand to her lips and kissed it. "Still is."

Trinity gave her a sad smile. "I know, and that's why I have to tell you I can't make promises about tomorrow or the future. I've worked too hard, for too long, to rise above where I came from to throw it away. My career comes first. *I* come first."

She didn't want to count out a future with Trinity, but she also wasn't willing to sacrifice her heart for a woman she was just getting to know. "I understand, but I wish there was room for both your career and me."

"So do I. But all I have to offer right now is casual and occasional. Nothing more." Trinity leaned forward and brushed her lips over Blaze's. She glanced at the apartment, then back. "If you'd like to come inside, knowing that…"

As much as she had envisioned taking Trinity into her arms to make love to her, Blaze didn't want to invest her heart in someone who might never be able to give the same in return. It would be too painful to find out she would always take second place. Blaze steeled herself for whatever would happen in the next few minutes. She got out of the car and opened Trinity's door, and Trinity slid her shoes on. Once they were standing face-to-face, she ran her fingertips along Trinity's cheek, her emotions raging for dominance while her mind was in turmoil and her body was on fire.

"This has been a wonderful evening. I got to spend it with the most beautiful woman at the gala." She gathered Trinity to her, then kissed her slowly, passionately, hoping she could feel how much Blaze was enamored by her. How much she'd wished they could invest in something more together. But she couldn't be part of a one-sided relationship. *She* deserved more. And Trinity deserved her time in the sun. Blaze pulled back and ended the kiss. Trinity's chest heaved, her eyes never leaving Blaze's. She took Trinity's hand and walked her to the door. "Thank you again for the invitation. I'll never forget tonight." She brushed her thumb over Trinity's bottom lip and Trinity trembled under her touch.

"I take it this is where we say good-bye." Trinity's voice wavered, and Blaze almost lost her resolve.

"As much as I would like it to be otherwise…yes, it is. I'm looking for something serious these days, and I completely respect your honesty. Thank you for telling me where you stand."

Trinity closed her eyes for a minute as though to hold back her tears. "Thank you isn't nearly enough for how wonderful you've made me feel."

Every cell in her brain screamed a warning against what she was about to do. Blaze lifted Trinity's chin with her fingertips. "The pleasure truly was mine. I haven't felt this handsome or appreciated in a long time either. I'll never forget the times we've spent together. I wish I'd gotten to know you better. It's a shame you're not ready to let anyone in, but I understand." And she did. It wasn't that long ago she'd felt the same way. This time when their lips met, she held nothing back. She poured herself into the one simple act she would allow herself to indulge in without regret or remorse. Trinity's hand came to rest on her chest, and she took it as a sign to stop before she couldn't. Blaze stepped back. "Good night, Trinity."

Tears pooled in Trinity's eyes. "I'm so sorry I can't give you more."

She let her hand fall away. "So am I. Perhaps in another place and time." Blaze turned away, unwilling to show her pain. It wasn't Trinity's fault she'd gotten ahead of herself. She should have known better. She didn't want to look back, afraid Trinity wouldn't be there, while praying she was. She started the car and began to back out of the driveway. Her resolve broke and she turned to look. Trinity stood in the open doorway, beautiful as ever, with tracks of tears staining her cheeks. She took a breath and faced away. Trinity had made her choice, and it didn't include Blaze.

CHAPTER TWENTY-EIGHT

Trinity dropped her wrap and clutch on the closest surface and kicked off her shoes. She swiped at the wet tracks on her face, then sat in the recliner she often fell asleep in. The scenario from the evening played out in her head. If she were to ever consider a serious relationship, Blaze would certainly be at the top of the list.

When she and Blaze danced, she'd been transported to another place, as though she was Cinderella, and Prince Charming had found her at last. But the fantasy had ended when one of the center's board members had asked if she and Blaze had been together long. She hadn't been prepared for having to explain her relationship with Blaze, so she'd been as honest as possible, admitting it was their first date. The woman had looked at her incredulously, saying it appeared as though they'd been dancing together for years. Trinity had felt that way, too.

Blaze had been the quintessential escort. Never once had she acted possessive or done anything for her to regret extending the invitation, yet Trinity felt as though Blaze wanted their time together to continue well past tonight. Not that she hadn't imagined how wonderful it might be to come home to a woman who not only made Trinity feel as though she was the only woman in the world, but one who would complement her life in ways she never dreamed of. And that was what she feared most—losing her identity in Blaze's shadow because she had a commanding presence without even trying. Granted, it was wonderful to be doted on for an entire evening, but how long would it last? Did she even want to be cared for when all she'd known her entire life was looking out for herself and making her own way in the world? It was irrational to think there was more between them. She couldn't...*wouldn't* sacrifice her own goals for an unsure, unguaranteed future. No matter who it involved.

When Blaze made it clear that she had no intention of sleeping with her if there was no future for them, then kissed her as though her life depended on it, she'd almost wished she'd given in. Instead, she'd pushed Blaze away, and when she drove off, Trinity knew she'd made a mistake, and it was already too late to fix it. Blaze was gone.

"Hey. What are you doing home so early?" Kelly took one look at her and ran over. "Did she hurt you? I'll kill her."

Trinity shook her head. She was grateful she hadn't come home to an empty house. At least she could tell Kelly what a jerk she was for turning away the one person who might understand her compulsion for success. "Blaze was gallant and an absolutely perfect date."

"Then why are you crying?" Kelly led her to the sofa.

She sighed. "I told her there wasn't a future between us." Trinity chewed her lower lip. "Then she turned down my offer to have sex with me." It sounded worse when she said it out loud, like she was doing them both a favor.

"Gee. You said that?"

"Not in so many words, but I definitely implied if she came inside, we would."

"Huh." Kelly's eyebrow wrinkled. It meant she was contemplating how to tell her something that might hurt her feelings.

"Go ahead and tell me. I already know I really fucked up a chance at a great relationship."

"It's just...you won't always be under the gun at work. Someday, and probably sooner than later, you're going to realize there's more to life than your career, and, well...maybe you should have left the door open. You know, for down the road." Kelly squeezed her hand.

"I know. You're right. I didn't, but I think Blaze may have."

"Really? What did she say?"

Trinity closed her eyes and tried to recall the conversation. She'd been so lost in the depths of Blaze's dejected eyes, she couldn't be sure. "I think she said, 'In another place and time,' or something like that."

"Oh, honey, I'm so sorry you felt like you needed to put the brakes on. It sounds as though you two could have made a commitment."

The tears came unimpeded. Kelly had voiced exactly how she'd felt when Blaze turned from her and left her standing there. The last thing she remembered was Blaze's face as she pulled away. The saddest part was the lack of hope she saw.

❖

"I said I was sorry. What more do you want?" DJ was just shy of pleading.

Blaze hadn't wanted to deal with another confrontation. It seemed like that was all she was doing lately, but she didn't want to let it slide.

"What made you think inviting an ex-lover and a regrettable fling was a good idea? Or all the other single lesbians that were there?"

DJ shrugged. "We used to have fun with Grace, but you're right. Inviting Fagan was poor judgment on my part."

"The whole matchmaker thing was poor judgment, especially when you knew I was interested in Trinity." She wasn't sure why, but Blaze felt the need to drive home the point.

"You said you wanted a relationship. I thought I'd try to help. Sue me for being a friend."

Blaze dropped into the old leather desk chair she'd had forever. She should have replaced it by now, but sometimes worn and comfortable was the best option. Like a good friend. She shook off her anger, knowing staying mad never resolved anything. "Thanks for this. I was dying for a decent cup of brew." She had to remember DJ did things Blaze would never think of doing, and maybe that's how they'd remained close. In many ways they were polar opposites, but they seemed to balance each other out.

"Aside from pointing out my poor judgment, what else is going on?" DJ sipped and sat forward, waiting.

"I'm not sure. Despite how things ended between us, I can't help wanting to see her." She'd already told DJ about Trinity's decision that her career was more important than anything else right now, and she hadn't bothered to hide how much that hurt.

"After what she did? She tossed you away like a used bone."

"DJ, that's not fair and you know it. We slept together, then we had a date that might not have even been a date. Sure, we spent some time together, but it's not like we were heading down the aisle."

"I knew I didn't like her for a reason." She wrinkled her nose. "She should have shown you more respect than she did."

Hearing someone else talk in a derogatory way about Trinity felt wrong. "Drop it, okay? You have your own issues with respect at times."

DJ's face fell. "Okay. I deserved that."

Blaze probably shouldn't be sharing her latest internal battle, but DJ was the one person she thought would understand. "Whether or not I see Trinity again isn't my decision to make." She tilted her cup at DJ. "And I don't want you trying to help. I'll figure this out on my own, okay?"

"You know I worry about you." DJ touched her hand. "I can't help if I get carried away sometimes." Blaze nodded. "What do you plan to do about the situation?"

Blaze stood and circled her desk, leaning against the front. "I don't know." She stared into the distance, not at all convinced she'd seen the last of Trinity. Blaze squeezed DJ's hand, then let go. "I'll figure it out."

Chapter Twenty-nine

Trinity sat at the kitchen table with the envelope in her shaking hands. It had only been two days since her date with Blaze, and though she'd tried to keep focused, she couldn't help the gnawing in her gut that told her she would continue to miss her for a long time.

The reason she'd let her go was in the envelope.

She ripped open the letter and read the exam score sheet. She'd done well on the written part with an overall rating in the 90th percentile. She'd hoped for higher, but she'd take it. The next sheet was a summary of her practical performance under the watchful eye of her superiors, including the head of the ED. He'd stood back with a clipboard, watching her every move and the instructions she'd given staff. She had no idea what he was thinking as he leaned against the wall and made notes, though she tried not to look in his direction. The thirty-minute practical drill had left her pumped with adrenaline but emotionally drained. His summary detailed her performance strong points, noted a few "minor deficiencies," and included an overall comment of "an exemplary candidate who will likely excel under the guidance of a talented and well-seasoned team."

We're happy to offer you the position of Head Trauma Nurse in the Emergency Department. She read it a second time before jumping up and down. Trinity looked around the empty apartment. She felt like celebrating. She picked up her phone and texted Kelly.

She didn't get a response and it could be hours, but she needed to share the news with someone right away. She thought about her parents, but they'd be passed out by now or too drunk to understand her. And she didn't want to throw her success in her siblings' faces. After scrolling through the As, she stopped midway through the Bs. *Blaze.* She didn't know why, but something told her to go ahead.

Hi, Blaze. How are you? Wanted to let you know I got the promotion for head nurse of the ED.

She stared at the screen for five minutes before she went on down the alphabet. There wasn't anyone else in her contacts list who would be as excited as she was. More than half the people there wouldn't have a clue what she was even talking about. The limited number of people close to her dampened her spirit. She went to the fridge and eyed the bottle of pinot grigio. After checking a goblet for residual lipstick, she pulled the cork and heard it hiss. Satisfied it was still fresh, she poured a good amount. *What the hell. I don't have work until tomorrow.*

Trinity lifted the glass to her lips before taking a healthy gulp. Her phone pinged and she nearly lost the mouthful, forgetting she'd put the volume all the way up while doing the laundry.

Kelly: *I knew you would! We'll celebrate when I get home.*
Trinity: *When's that?*
Kelly: *About an hour or so.*
Trinity: *I'm starting without you!*
Kelly: *No doubt.*

Her smile widened and her jubilation returned. Kelly always made her feel like she belonged, no matter where they were or what they were doing. Her phone pinged again. She picked it up, thinking it was Kelly again. Trinity froze at the balloon that appeared, along with Blaze's photo and a brief note saying she was well and happy for her, along with encouraging her to celebrate, but that's where it ended.

She blinked at the short message. No terms of endearment. No "I miss you" or "I'd like to see you again." What did she expect? She'd sent Blaze away with the idea that she was agreeable to having sex with her, but she was otherwise expendable. Regret sat like a stone in her gut. Why had she been such an ass? Blaze had made her feel like she wasn't that kid from skid row who would never do anything of significance with her life. Like she wasn't a nobody. Not giving in to her attraction for Blaze was likely going to be one of the worst decisions she'd made in her adult life, but she'd never know for sure.

Her phone pinged again. Kelly would be delayed by a new trauma patient and told her to go celebrate. Trinity glanced at the clock. Kelly wouldn't be home for hours, and Blaze's lukewarm response confirmed she'd chosen a life of solitude and work over one that could be a literal dream come true. In a moment of supposed clarity, she'd fooled herself into believing she didn't need a fairy tale romance. Blaze forced her to see how very wrong she'd been. She did want it all. And she wanted someone to share in the ups and downs that came with a full, rich life. *Why didn't I let her in?* Trinity wasn't talking about a physical place, for once she was talking about her heart. The one place no one had ever been allowed in before.

The thought of celebrating alone lost its appeal. Blaze was the one she wanted to celebrate with, and she imagined a wonderful dinner followed by a night of lovemaking. One where she would bask in the glow of being adored. Cared for. Loved.

She stared at Blaze's name, wishing she could conjure her into existence, throwing all her inhibitions and self-preservation tendencies out the window for a chance at being immersed in happiness. Trinity realized she no longer cared about having goals if they didn't include Blaze being at her side to share in them. She settled on the couch with her glass of wine. Maybe she deserved to be alone if she couldn't be honest with herself.

CHAPTER THIRTY

B laze walked through her workshop. Even doing what she loved hadn't improved her sour mood. She ran her left hand over the rack of chisels, then picked up a handful of wood shavings from the bin and let them drift through her fingers. Trinity had drifted through her life, too. Maybe a random task would get her mind off missing her so much. Ever since her text, Blaze had speculated about the real reason Trinity contacted her. Not that she hadn't been happy for her, because she was. But she'd been let down when there'd been no further text. More confused than ever, Blaze had waited. After thirty minutes, she knew she'd lost her opportunity. Trinity had made their situation clear, and yet, Blaze couldn't help wanting to see if she'd come to Thanksgiving anyway.

She glanced at her scar. The tingling that skittered along her nerves still occasionally happened. Dr. Jonas had assured her it was a good sign, letting her know the nerves were healing, and the sensation would eventually disappear. Unlike the scar that would be a constant reminder of the night she could have died. All of that was in the past. She couldn't change it and she certainly didn't want to go back in time. She might have never met Trinity if it weren't for the accident. Her chest seized. Tears threatened. It was stupidity on her part. How had she been so enamored with Trinity that she'd let herself tumble headfirst down the rabbit hole? It wasn't like there weren't other women out there. Why was she so obsessed with this one? After the talk with her father, she was confident it was because she'd fallen for Trinity. Hard and fast. She thought about Grace, her last romantic interest, and compared what was different between them, but she couldn't put her finger on anything specific.

DJ had suggested alternate ways to meet women. The local lesbian group she'd joined a few years ago listed activities and she'd signed up for a hiking trip. Maybe this week she'd check out the local Harley-Davidson riders event. She needed to do something before she went stir-crazy.

Her phone vibrated across her desk and she rolled her eyes at DJ's icon, unsure if she was in the mood, but knowing she'd keep calling until Blaze answered. "Hey. Did you sell that million-dollar house yet?"

DJ blew out a breath. "I wish, but I will. How did the hike go?"

"The hike was fine. The women were…not my type." It was the kindest description she could use. Blaze was all for women being comfortable *au naturel*, but hairy armpits and unshaved legs wasn't for her.

"I'm sorry to hear that. What's next on your quest for dating perspectives?"

"It will take me weeks to get over this one."

DJ laughed. "That bad?"

Blaze had to laugh, too. "You have no idea."

"Seriously though," DJ said. "What about an actual dating service?"

She groaned. "No. Definitely no." Whenever she thought of exclusive dating, there was only one woman she could imagine being with. "Maybe I'll just go blind and call it a day."

"Blind?" DJ sounded panicked. "Dear God, what have you done now?"

"Calm down. I only meant I'll go blind from masturbating from now on."

"Oh. Has it really come to that?"

"I can still see."

"That's a relief. I think."

A few minutes later, they hung up after she promised to keep DJ informed regarding her dating prospects. Laughing had been cathartic, but a temporary solution to her situation.

She went to the table saw and stared at it. The smell of fresh cut wood would center her. She pulled on her compression sleeve, then picked out a board and carried it to the saw. The familiar noise from the whirling blade brought a comfort only a carpenter could identify with. She set the blade for the correct depth, then began to feed the wood lengthwise against the rail. Once there was enough wood sticking past the blade, she guided the end with her left hand, smiling as the scent of warm wood filled her with the familiar joy of doing what she'd been doing for decades. Her right hand moved the wood along until there were only a few inches left.

That's when it kicked back, whacking her just above the wrist. Stars filled her vision as she hit the emergency kill switch and crumpled to the floor cradling her arm. *Stupid, stupid.* Pain brought tears to her eyes. Blaze cradled her throbbing arm against her, sure that whatever lay beneath the compression sleeve she wore would be horrible. Once she was able to breathe and her vision cleared, she got to her feet and, cradling her arm against her, went for her phone.

She knew she had to call someone, but who? DJ would overreact and only add to her mounting anxiety. Her brother was out of town and in no way qualified to give sound medical advice. Her parents were usually home, but she didn't want to worry them, and she didn't want to wait three hours for them to get to her. There was only one person she could trust to know what she needed to do. Cassie, her physical therapist, was her best option. Trinity would have been a good option too, but with Cassie there were no emotions at play, and she definitely didn't want to deal with more emotions right now.

As fate would have it, Dr. Jonas was on call and had met them in the ED.

"I didn't expect to see you anytime soon."

Blaze figured she looked as embarrassed as she felt. "Neither did I, Dr. Jonas."

He removed her sleeve and sighed. He palpated the freshly formed angry bruise and Blaze hissed. "Kelly, let's get some fresh ice on this and set her up for X-rays and a possible MRI."

Kelly went to a cabinet and pulled out an ice bag, breaking the inner sac before shaking it to mix the contents. She placed a washcloth over Blaze's arm. "An X-ray tech will be in soon. Just keep this in place till then." She gave her a quick smile before leaving the room.

She wanted to ask Kelly about Trinity. As much as she wished she didn't, Blaze cared. She didn't have the full story as to why Trinity was so adamant about the promotion and how nothing and no one was going to become a distraction. That's what had hurt the most—being considered a distraction. Trinity's obvious summation that Blaze wasn't worth the risk of letting her into her life should have warned her off, but it hadn't.

The fate of her arm was a top priority at the moment. Trinity wasn't going anywhere. To their credit, neither her doctor nor Cassie had given her the riot act for reinjuring her still healing arm, though she obviously needed a reminder to pay better attention to what she was doing.

Cassie patted her thigh. "Stop feeling like you deserved this. It was an accident, just like the first one."

She pursed her lips. "I had no control over the first one, but this…" She nudged her chin at her arm as it lay on a small table with a new ice bag over it. "This could have been avoided."

"True, but I'm sure you had no intention of hurting yourself."

Blaze considered what she'd been feeling prior to everything going sideways. "No, but I was preoccupied, and I know better." Her father had cautioned her to always be aware of what she was doing when working around the tools of the trade because they were unforgiving if she wasn't paying attention. "What if there's no way to fix it this time?"

Cassie shrugged. "We won't know that until we hear from the doctor. Until then, all you can do is wait. And if you're a believer, pray." Cassie checked her pockets and pulled out some money. "I need coffee. You want to brave a cup?"

She smiled at her attempt at levity. And really, what else could she do but wait? "That would be great. Cream and a packet of brown sugar." Alone again, she hung her head and wiped at her forehead.

She was sick of all the waiting; waiting to hear about surgery, then waiting to get back to work. More recently, waiting to see if her heart was beyond repair. That hurt, too, had been her own doing. She wished she'd never met…Blaze sucked in a breath. It would be a lie to say she wished she'd never met Trinity. The times they'd been together she'd been on cloud nine. The feeling of meeting someone she wanted in her life for more than a few hours was one she'd hold on to even if there was no reason to hope.

The curtain shifted and she looked up to find Trinity standing there, and the look of worry tugged at her heart.

"Kelly told me you were here. What happened?" Her voice was soft and gentle.

Blaze held her breath. Trinity was the last person she thought she'd want to see, but she was wrong. She wanted to hug her. Hold her. Convince Trinity to give them a try. That's what she wanted to do. Instead, she stared at her arm.

"I lost concentration and…" What could she say? *I was thinking of you, not what I was doing? I was wondering why you'd texted me.* The words stuck in her throat.

"Do you need anything? Are you in pain?" Trinity's concern touched her more than she could say. A bit of hope snaked through her.

"Blaze?" The technician stood in the doorway.

She got up and the forgotten icepack fell from her arm. She raised her unaffected hand to touch Trinity's cheek. At the last second, she let it fall away. "I have to go."

As she started to walk away, Trinity reached for her. "I'll come back if I can."

"It's okay. I understand. Your job…" She was about to say comes first, but she wasn't the type of person who gave cheap shots, and she didn't want to become one.

Trinity's eyes glistened. "I'll be here when you're done."

She followed the technician through the swinging door and swallowed the lump in her throat. Her heart still ached. Still hoped. There were things in life she couldn't control and Trinity's feelings for her were one, though she wished otherwise.

CHAPTER THIRTY-ONE

Y ou're no sooner back to work and what do you do?" DJ glared at her from the driver's seat. "You…" DJ stabbed a quick finger at her before continuing. "Are so grounded."

Blaze sat stoically. The pain in her arm had subsided to a dull throb. Her doctor said to ice it twenty minutes every hour until tomorrow and call him if anything changed.

"Hey, is it bad? Because if it's bad, I totally understand your mummy impersonation but, really, you're freaking me out."

She glanced at her, then let her head drop to the headrest. "No. It's only a deep bruise. I didn't reinjure or rebreak it."

"Then why the long face, aside from the fact that you're grounded? Doctor's orders and all."

"I saw Trinity."

"Oh."

"Kelly was in the ED when I showed, and she must have told her. She came to radiology and waited while I had a scan."

"What did she say?"

"That she was glad my arm would be okay and she offered to give me a ride home, but then she had to go, so I called you." Blaze remembered every word they exchanged. "She also said she wanted to explain about the text she'd sent, so I guess that means we'll see each other again." She didn't think Trinity had changed her mind about seeing more of each other. Honestly, Blaze didn't care what excuse she used if she got to spend time with Trinity.

She'd battle with the disappointment she was sure to feel later when it came to that.

"I think she's just jerking you around. Maybe I wasn't so far off base after all." DJ pulled the car around and parked in front of the house.

Blaze faced her. "What is it about Trinity that has you acting like a mother hen?"

DJ hesitated. "You know how I sometimes get very emotional when I think someone is fucking with you?"

"Go on." Blaze focused on keeping her temper under control. DJ had always been able to push her buttons when no one else could.

"It started when she answered your phone and didn't tell me you were hurt. Then she kept coming around at the hospital after surgery and I got the distinct feeling she had ulterior motives."

"Like what? She's a nurse for Christ's sake. She's *supposed* to care. So what if she dropped in a few times to check on me?"

DJ eye rolled. "I don't know. Every time I came to see you she was there, and I got pissed, like we didn't have any time alone."

"That's a bit melodramatic, even for you," Blaze said. "What ulterior motive?"

"I thought she was looking for an opportunity to hit on you."

Blaze couldn't believe what she was hearing. "And what if she had? Wouldn't it have been up to *me* to tell her I wasn't interested?"

"Yes. Of course, but you only see the good in people and I wasn't sure her motives were altruistic." DJ rushed on. "You were already dealing with so much, and I didn't want her fucking with your head like all the other women who only want one thing."

Blaze's jaw bunched. "What do they want?"

"Sex. Everyone wants a night with the infamous Blaze Carter. But no one sticks around, right? And it's not like you want them to. Trinity seemed like just another hungry woman who wanted to feed on you. And I was right. She used you and threw you away, just like all the others have."

She was beyond angry. Blaze was hurt. "Is that the only thing women want from me? Is that what drives you to interfere even when I haven't asked for your help?"

"No...I—" DJ turned off the car.

"Let me spell it out for you. She was there when I talked to the surgeon. When she found out what I did for a living, she was worried I wouldn't..." Her voice caught and she turned away. She couldn't say out loud what she'd feared most in those first few hours, that her livelihood could go up in smoke.

"I'm sorry. I didn't mean to upset you."

After running her hand over her face, Blaze turned back to her. "Maybe your sticking your nose in my business is why she couldn't consider anything more. I could imagine her wondering if we hit a rough patch that she'd have you to contend with." She looked across the space between them. "I need to see her."

"That's a bad idea. She's not right for you—"

DJ reached out, but Blaze stopped her.

"No. This time you've gone too far. We're best friends, DJ. That's not going to change, but you have no right to decide who I'm interested in or who I date. If you can't understand that, then I'm the one who's sorry." She got out and quietly closed the passenger door.

DJ ran around the front of the car. "Blaze. Please." Tears streaked her face. "Tell me how to fix this. I'll do whatever you tell me to do. Please."

Blaze shook her head. "Go home." So many words were on her lips, but she refused to say anything when she was this angry. She went inside without another word.

After fixing herself a drink, she went and sat on the porch. Was it true? Did everyone see her as a conquest, someone to say they'd been under? Was she seen as a sex toy, an urban bar legend? Granted, she'd always kept things casual and had no problem with a night of role-play, but she'd never considered how that made her look in other people's eyes.

The one thing she did know was that Trinity was different. There was no denying the worry in her eyes when they'd talked at the hospital. The way Blaze's heart ached and her breath caught the moment she saw her spoke volumes. DJ was wrong, at least in that area. Trinity had her reasons, and Blaze knew what it was like to worry about getting hurt. She was convinced something in Trinity's past was in play, things Trinity hadn't shared with her. Things keeping her from giving her heart away. But there was always a way to fix things, all she had to do was find a way beneath the armor Trinity had surrounded herself with. Because there was no question Trinity was the one Blaze wanted. She just had to figure out how to show her she wasn't going away.

CHAPTER THIRTY-TWO

Trinity's heart had pounded in her chest when she'd raced down the hall to find Blaze. When she didn't see blood there was a sense of relief, but the worry on Blaze's face wasn't as easily dismissed. At least she had a few minutes to talk to her before and after her scan. Once reassured the new injury was superficial, she'd taken the opportunity to mention they had a few things to clear up before she'd had to rush off to meet an ambulance.

Thankfully, Blaze had agreed. Maybe after they talked she'd be in a better place to deal with the roller coaster of emotions keeping her awake every night. She shoved her work shoes into the bag at the bottom of her locker and yanked her purse off the shelf. Unfortunately, she hadn't closed the zipper all the way before stowing it, and the contents sprayed across the floor as she fumbled to keep it upright.

"Great. Just great." She sighed and bent down, gathering an array of items she didn't even recognize. Mascara, business cards, a few pens, old grocery lists. Then she saw the gala announcement that had arrived with the invitation, and she froze. As she reached for it the air vent overhead came on and blew it out of reach. Trinity collapsed in a heap on the floor. The significance wasn't lost on her. Had Blaze slipped from her reach? The look of relief in her eyes was unmistakable when Trinity had come into the room. Did that mean there was still a slim chance she hadn't totally blown it? She had no idea where they stood, except Blaze was still willing to talk. That was good. More than good. She'd thought their situation had become hopeless. She fought the stinging behind her eyes as the door opened and several of the ED staff for the next shift shuffled in, their jovial voices lifting the darkness surrounding her when all she could think of was losing Blaze.

"Hi, Trinity. How was last night?"

She picked up the last of her scattered items and stuffed them in her bag, glad for the extra minute to gather herself. "Kind of quiet for a Thursday night." She slammed her locker closed and spun the dial. "Have a good one." Trinity called over her shoulder, not wanting anyone to witness her emotional breakdown. Escaping through empty hallways and rarely used exits, she made it to her car before letting go of the fragile control she'd had on her tears. After the stream slowed, she had a conversation with herself. There was still hope. She had to take Blaze at her word and trust they'd talk.

As much as she wanted to air her feelings, anxiety clawed at her. She wasn't good at off-the-cuff stuff. She was used to standards of procedure. Steps to follow in an orderly method. Nothing was orderly in her thinking pattern these days. Kelly wasn't going to be home until much later, so she had the place to herself, which was good because she wasn't sure she could concentrate enough for a logical conversation. The only therapy for her current state would be a massive cleaning.

Trinity stripped down and pulled on an old T-shirt and shorts. She attacked the kitchen floor with a mop, and the water containing pine scented cleaner tickled her nose. While the floor dried, the dust bunnies under the furniture and hanging out behind knickknacks were next to go. Two hours later, she flopped onto the papasan chair and flipped the top of her soda can. The frenzy she'd lost herself in had been cathartic and she could begin to focus her energy on how to handle the situation with Blaze because no matter what she thought, or felt, or pretended, she wanted to see this through.

Trinity sighed, no closer to the answers she was looking for than she had been before she'd raced through the house declaring war on dirt. A shower would help her relax and she'd contact Blaze after she'd gotten some much needed sleep. Hopefully by then her head would be clearer and she'd be able to tell her how she was feeling. Sharing her innermost thoughts with anyone except Kelly wasn't something she did, but Blaze was the one person who deserved to know.

CHAPTER THIRTY-THREE

Blaze stared at the ceiling. She hadn't felt good about sending DJ away. Though lately DJ pushed her buttons more than she ever had. Still, Blaze couldn't fathom their friendship ending. No matter what, they would get through this situation. It wasn't the first one they'd had, and she was fairly certain it wouldn't be the last, but they were good at weathering the rough storms life threw at them.

She wasn't able to rationalize if the fixation on Trinity was good or bad, yet the yearning remained. Her arm throbbed, the feeling akin to how her heart hammered when Trinity was near, though the two were opposite types of pain.

Trinity's dreams came first, and Blaze could understand dreams. She had a few of her own. She hadn't expected Trinity to show up at the ED. Her heart had beat a little faster knowing she cared, and this time she was certain Trinity wasn't there out of a sense of duty. Her desire to talk gave Blaze a sliver of hope, and she planned on hanging on. Today was that day. All she had to do was keep busy until she was sure Trinity was awake.

The sinking sun shone through the big front window. Blaze sat on the couch with the phone cradled on her thigh, her palms sweaty. She hadn't been this nervous since high school, which wasn't typical since she'd been popular with both the boys and girls and had never been shy. Still, when she asked the first girl she'd ever crushed on out to a movie, she'd nearly peed her pants. That was a long time ago. She was an adult now, and she could handle the pressure of any situation. *Christ*. She sounded like her father, though that wasn't a bad thing.

Her finger hung in midair as she decided between her two options. Text or call. Both had pros and cons. Both were viable. A text would give Trinity an out if she was having second thoughts, but Blaze wasn't sure she wanted to give her one. No matter what the outcome, one way or another she needed to get on with her life. She hoped Trinity would be in it, but if not, maybe she'd actually use one of those dating services DJ had mentioned. The idea of putting her future in some random hit-or-miss website motivated her. She pushed a button and took a breath.

"Hi," Trinity said, picking up on the second ring.

That damn knot in her throat was back. All it took was hearing her voice and Blaze became a hot mess. "Hey, how are you?"

"I should be the one asking you. How's your arm?"

"Sore, but better."

"That's really good news." Trinity's voice was so soft it felt like a caress.

Blaze pushed on. "We should talk."

"How about now?"

She looked around the less than clean house. She'd been rather slack in her chores, her mind preoccupied by a million things. Trinity's voice brought her back.

"If you'd rather not…"

"No. I mean…" *Shit.* What did she mean? "I'd like to see you." She took another breath. "So we can talk."

"Only if you're sure."

"I'm sure." She hadn't been sure of much lately, but seeing Trinity was one thing she definitely wanted.

❖

Trinity's heart was racing as she jumped in the car to go to Blaze's place. Looking at her watch, she knew there was a good chance Blaze hadn't eaten and she stopped to pick up dinner. At the last minute, she grabbed a six-pack of beer, knowing she'd need a little something to calm her frayed nerves. The last time she'd been up the mountain, she and Blaze had made love. She had to keep telling her body to stay in check. They were going to talk, and there was no promise of more, but that was okay. It took some of the pressure off. Trinity traversed the mountain curves as cautiously as she had the first time. Blaze had offered to come to her place, but Kelly was home, and this needed to be a one-on-one conversation. The breathtaking sky above her displayed streaks of pink and purple that reflected in the clouds, and she slowed to take advantage of the view. Still a little way from the house, she dimmed her headlights and stopped. Birds twitted and peepers chirped. The light breeze lifted wisps of hair from her face. Leaves danced in the air as they fell, undulating back and forth like lovers waltzing to a silent orchestra. She could get used to life on the mountain and she understood why Blaze loved it here.

As darkness began to creep in around her, she flicked on her headlamps and crawled along, remembering Blaze telling her the woods were teeming with life. Blaze held a deep reverence for all living things, and she didn't want to disturb the balance of woman and nature. Parking between the house and the garage on the circular driveway, Trinity imagined Blaze standing on the wide porch with a cup of morning coffee and she wondered if she was naked when it was warm weather. Trinity hadn't seen another house in any direction.

From the passenger seat, she pulled out a shopping bag full of food and the six-pack, not caring that she'd brought enough to feed a small army. Nerves had gotten the best of her and she'd ordered everything that sounded good.

Breathing in through her nose and out through her mouth as she neared the door did nothing to help settle her. Only Blaze could do that. She set the bag down and rang the bell as she rolled her neck. She heard wind chimes and smiled. Leave it to Blaze to find a bell tone that wasn't annoying as hell. She told her feet to stop shuffling. The door opened and the breath she'd taken left her.

Blaze wore faded, form-fitting jeans. The boot-cut legs pooled at her bare feet. The black V-neck shirt hugged her torso, and she couldn't miss the fact she wasn't wearing a bra. Blaze's nipples poked the fabric as she continued to stare until Blaze cleared her throat. Trinity met her knowing gaze. Blaze looked so damn good her knees threatened to buckle. Somehow, she stayed upright.

"Hi," Blaze said.

"Uh…hi." Trinity felt foolish. She couldn't believe she'd been caught staring at Blaze's breasts.

Blaze opened the door wider and stepped back to make room. "Come in."

"Thanks."

Blaze smiled. "It was difficult for me to put a bra on for a while. I got used to not wearing one."

Trinity sighed. "I couldn't help noticing."

Blaze laughed.

"I brought food and beer." She reached into the bag. "I hope you haven't eaten yet." She hefted the food onto the counter. "Do you like Mexican? I don't know anyone who doesn't, but that's presumptuous. I should have checked with you…" The rambling had started already. Her hands shook.

"Trinity…" Blaze said as she moved closer.

She'd been avoiding looking up, afraid the anxiety was hers alone. She forced herself to find the slate-colored eyes she missed seeing. "Yes?" Her voice broke.

"It's really good to see you." Blaze reached for her hand. "I'm glad you're here," Blaze said before her gaze dropped from her eyes to her lips and back again. Blaze's lips brushed over hers.

"Me too." She glanced at their joined hands and gently squeezed, glancing at the scar and vivid bruise. "Do you want to tell me about how this happened?" She pointed to the spot.

Blaze trailed soft, trembling fingertips along her cheek. "Let's eat first. I don't want to bore you with tales of stupidity." Blaze's chest rose and fell quickly.

If she was trying to act nonchalant, Blaze wasn't succeeding. Trinity pulled her hand to her chest, knowing Blaze would feel her own pounding heart. "Seems we've been here before."

Blaze stared, appearing to be memorizing her features. "The question is why?"

"Yes, it is. That's why I wanted to see you."

"Before we delve deeper, I'd still like you to join me for Thanksgiving."

"Blaze, I—"

Blaze shook her head. "You don't have to decide now. A day or two before is fine." Blaze's gaze fell to the table as though not wanting to see if Trinity had already decided to turn down the invitation.

"Thank you." She knew what meeting someone's parents meant. Was she ready for a commitment with Blaze and to take the next step in their growing relationship? Everything pointed to yes, yet she couldn't get the words out. They sat at the table and stared at each other. Trinity's cell phone rang. Her forehead wrinkled. Work never called.

She stood. "I'm sorry. I have to take this." Trinity stepped near the front door. "Hello?"

"Trinity, it's Dr. Falcon. There's a level four trauma heading in. We need all hands on deck. ASAP." In the background she could hear staff calling out orders, directing others, carts moving. Their caster wheels squeaking in concert.

"ETA?" She grabbed her jacket and keys before turning for the kitchen. Blaze stood in the living room.

"Hard to say, but likely to start arriving in ten." He moved the phone from his mouth and mumbled a directive. "I'm sorry to ruin your night off. How soon can I expect you?"

She thought about the road below. "I can be there in twenty. Twenty-five, tops." It would take her a bit to get off the mountain, but once she hit the main road, she could make up time. She hoped. Blaze approached as she ended the call. "I have to go to the hospital. Serious casualties coming in and everyone is needed."

"Let me take you." Blaze grabbed a jacket from a peg by the door and shrugged it on as she stuck her feet into boots.

"You don't have to do that."

"I know these roads better than you. I'll have you there in fifteen." Blaze ushered her outside and jogged toward the garage. Her long strides quickly covered the distance, and Trinity ran to catch up. The garage door was open by the time she got there, and she jumped into the passenger seat and buckled in as Blaze turned the key.

"What about my car?" Not only was she about to leave it, but she was semi-blocking the driveway.

Blaze flashed a breath-stopping smile. "Four-wheeling has its merits."

They shot onto the driveway and Blaze swerved around Trinity's car, then roared down the road. She drove well, but Trinity worried about the stress on her arm. As tricky as the switchbacks were, they reached the main road in under five minutes, and her anxiety dropped a notch since she was no longer being jerked around as they hit curves at less than prudent speeds.

Blaze reached for her white-knuckled hand. "Relax. I told you I'd get you there."

She laughed. "You forgot to mention the word safely."

Blaze's face became serious. "I'd never put your life in jeopardy. Just because I was in a motorcycle accident doesn't mean I'm reckless."

Trinity pursed her lips. "I didn't mean to imply you were."

"It's okay."

A few minutes later, Blaze pulled up to the ED entrance.

"Call me when you want me to pick you up."

"I can get a ride home and Kelly can bring me to pick up my car," she said. Kelly would have a million questions since she didn't know she'd gone to see Blaze.

"I mean it. Call me whenever you're ready. We'll pick up where we left off, okay? Good luck."

Blaze's eyes were bottomless pools and she wanted to swim in them forever. But flashing lights and sirens interrupted the moment, and she focused on what she needed to do.

She opened her door, then leaned back in to give Blaze a quick kiss on the cheek. "Thank you." Words weren't nearly enough to express her gratitude, but it would have to do. She put Blaze out of her mind as much as she could and ran through the doors. She found her counterpart directing the stretcher into trauma room one.

"Where do you want me?"

Sally's harried expression relaxed a tad. "Thank God you made it. Can you check room two? I've got more ambulances heading in."

Trinity tossed her jacket over a chair and pulled on a lab coat. "You got it."

❖

The wall clock read two minutes after seven, and Trinity was beyond tired. For the first three hours after arriving, there'd been an endless stream of emergency vehicles and police cars transporting injured from the accident scene. She leaned against one of the few unoccupied walls.

Over the last ten hours, the team had treated twenty-three patients from the bus-tractor-trailer collision. Thankfully, more than half of those had only sustained minor injuries and had already been discharged. Of the remainder, four had ended up in surgery, three were in casts, and five more were admitted for observation. One person had died. Even though Trinity hadn't taken care of her, she felt the loss.

"Get out of here," Dr. Falcon said. "I've rearranged your schedule. Don't bother coming back until the afternoon shift on Tuesday. The only people on duty today are the nurses who were sleeping or on vacation when I called you in."

Trinity was grateful for the change and even more so that there were fresh nurses to take her place. She ran her hand over her face, fatigue stealing what little energy she had. "I won't argue with you." Her laugh was half-hearted. "Thanks for the time off."

He patted her shoulder. "Thank *you*."

She was standing in the parking lot before she remembered she didn't have her car. "Fuck." She glanced around to see if anyone had heard her curse. She had no choice but to call Blaze since Kelly would be one of the nurses coming on duty. The only thing she wanted was a shower and sleep. Not necessarily in that order. Her vision blurred. After random swipes and swearing under her breath, she finally found the phone icon.

"Hi." Blaze sounded out of breath.

"Uh, hey. Am I interrupting?" She heard a bang that made her jump.

"Sorry, I got bored and…never mind. Are you ready?"

"Yes." She pinched the bridge of her nose, willing the headache that threatened to go away.

"On my way. Give me twenty."

With time to wait, she spotted a bench and sat outside the ED. She got as comfortable as possible and soaked up the sunshine. With her arms crossed, she closed her eyes.

"Trinity."

The word drifted into her consciousness, recognizable with its warmth. A hand touched her shoulder, then slid to her wrist, giving a light tug. "Trin, it's Blaze."

"What…where?" She fought to open her eyes in the bright sunlight seeping through her slitted lids. A shadow blocked the strong rays and she could finally see. She couldn't make out the person's face, but she didn't have to. She knew the body well. "Sorry." Trinity tried to stand, but her legs weren't cooperating, and Blaze pulled her against her to steady her. She looked around at the people milling near the entrance. She was so tired.

"Let me give you a change of scenery." Blaze slid her hand into Trinity's.

Her back was stiff from the bench. Her eyes burned. She glanced at her watch, noting she'd been up nearly twenty-four hours. She considered herself lucky. She'd managed to grab a protein bar and a juice, but the cold cup of coffee had done little to energize her. Blaze helped her into the car, and she managed to buckle her seat belt. She was running on empty, especially once the adrenaline rush of the first critical hours had worn off.

"Thanks for the lift." Trinity stifled a yawn, covering her mouth with the back of her hand.

"I said I would. I keep my word." Blaze pulled out of the lot. "Why don't you relax. Traffic isn't bad, so we should be back soon."

She hated to admit she'd reached her limit, but she'd be a fool not to. Blaze had to know she was exhausted, so who was she trying to kid? "Okay. Just a few minutes," she said as her eyes grew heavy and the motion of the moving car lulled her back to sleep.

CHAPTER THIRTY-FOUR

B laze hated the idea of waking her. When she'd seen Trinity sound asleep on the bench, something deep inside her stirred to life, and all she wanted to do was take her in her arms and hold her. But that wasn't her place. They'd just begun to repair what little there was between them before Trinity had to leave, and she wished they'd had more time.

She left the Jeep running and trotted up the stairs to open the front door. As quietly as she could, Blaze unfastened the seat belt and slid her arms beneath her, praying she had enough strength to lift her. She waited, checking for pain, and when there was none, she carried Trinity from the car and slowly took the stairs into the house.

"Arm," Trinity mumbled against her neck.

"It's okay," she said, but Trinity was already asleep again. She laid her on the guest bed, then removed her shoes, wishing she could get her more comfortable, but afraid she'd wake her again. The room was cool, so she covered her with the quilt from the foot of the bed. She stared for several minutes. *So beautiful.* Before she left, she brushed wayward curls off her face and sighed, content knowing she'd done her best under the circumstances. She took care of the car and closed the front door, then got a bottle of water and placed it on the nightstand. Blaze couldn't help remembering Trinity turning down her previous overnight invitation and smiled. This wasn't quite what she'd hoped for the next time Trinity was in her bed. She closed the door behind her, knowing even though Baxter hadn't showed, she was naturally curious and sooner or later would jump up to check out who was on *her* bed.

Blaze started a small fire and poured another cup of coffee. Not knowing what else to do, she flipped through the channels without paying attention to what was on the screen. All she thought about was Trinity so close, yet worlds apart. She still longed to know her better. Still wondered if she were being a damn fool for wanting Trinity in her life. Still wondered if there'd ever be more than one-night stands or if they were all she was meant to have.

Blaze glanced down the hall. Just a quick peek. She told herself she was just being mindful of Trinity being in a strange environment as she cracked open the door and peered inside. Even with the blinds closed and the drapes pulled, there was enough light from the bathroom window to see Trinity sprawled on the bed sound asleep. A pile of clothes lay crumpled on the floor, and she chuckled at the image of Trinity sitting up and stripping, totally unaware of her surroundings. The next image was one of Trinity's body clad in only her bra and panties. Heat coursed through her and thoughts of how enticing it would be to run her palm over the curves and valleys of her body brought a groan to her lips. The closed door was the only barrier between Blaze and her runaway imagination. It was going to be a long day if she didn't get a handle on her libido.

Restless and aware of her body firing on all cylinders, Blaze decided physical activity would best serve her. She changed into running shorts and a tank top and got on the treadmill. An hour later, her legs were screaming and her lungs burned. Bent over and sucking wind, she wiped sweat from her face with the edge of her shirt. In recovery mode, she took a water from the small refrigerator tucked in the corner of the room. It had come in handy. Middle of the night thirst meant she wouldn't have to navigate stairs. Blaze looked over the railing and listened for movement. The only sound she heard came from Baxter purring on the foot of her bed, satisfied by a full belly and basking in the sun.

Cooled down, she stepped into the oversized master shower and let the hot needles pound away on her muscles. A sponge filled with her favorite gel slid over her tanned skin—the only perk to her weeks of rehab was the amount of time she got to spend outdoors. Thoroughly scrubbed, she slid her hands over her body to remove residual suds. She brushed over her mound and an electric current of need shot through her. So much for running off her sexual tension. She hesitated for a minute. She wasn't alone in the house. Knowing it wouldn't take her long, Blaze fingered her clit. She was so sensitive, her knees nearly buckled. She alternated her strokes with entering her throbbing center. Soon her belly tightened and the pressure inside grew with intensity until lights shattered behind her eyelids and her body convulsed. Blaze cried out softly.

Her breathing returned to normal. Even though she was physically satiated, the source of her unease had nothing to do with sex and everything to do with the ache in her soul.

She shook her head. Now wasn't the time for contemplation. Not with Trinity in the house. At some point she was going to wake up, and when she did, Blaze wanted to have a clear head, uncluttered by random ruminations. Dressed in worn carpenter pants and a three-quarter sleeve tee, she picked up the book she was reading and headed out the back door, leaving it open in case Trinity looked for her.

The afternoon had warmed from the morning's cool temperatures, and Blaze settled in her rocker to lose herself in the pages of her favorite author.

CHAPTER THIRTY-FIVE

Trinity inhaled the fresh scent of bedding and smiled at the memory of linens hanging on a sagging clothesline at the trailer. They hadn't had much, but soap had always been plentiful, and it was her sister's job to wash their sheets every week by hand and hang everything out to dry. Too bad there wasn't any place to hang them outside now.

Her eyes popped open when she realized she wasn't in her own bed. Her heart rate increased before she remembered where she was. Long night working. Exhaustion. *Blaze.* She wiped her face and sat up. Panic hit when she saw her clothes piled on the floor. She shook her head and relaxed. Blaze never would have left them a haphazard mess if she'd undressed her. She'd done it herself at some point. Trinity glanced under the covers to find her bra and panties still on.

She really needed to pee. The sun was midpoint in the sky when she looked out the bathroom window. At least she hadn't slept the whole day away. She took in the tastefully decorated bathroom of pale greens and soft browns. The sink held a new toothbrush, toothpaste, and a small bottle of mouthwash. She peeked in the shower to find sample size bottles of shampoo, conditioner, and bath gel. She smiled at the attention to detail that was so much Blaze. The simple task of brushing her teeth had never felt so good.

A hot shower was tempting, but she'd been in the same clothes for far too long and the thought of having to put them back on made her cringe. She had a change of clothes in a gym bag in her car. She tried not to think about it as she pulled on her crumpled shirt and pants and went to find Blaze.

When she reached the living room, she glanced out the open door and saw Blaze sitting on the covered porch where stripes of sunlight reached the edge of the outdoor rug. Blaze held an open book in her hand, though she didn't appear to be looking at it. She must have heard her approach because she turned in her direction and smiled. The warmth in her eyes slid over Trinity's skin.

"How did you sleep?" Blaze rose and came to where she stood against the doorway.

"Like the dead. I'm so sorry I passed out," she said.

Blaze cupped her cheek. "Don't apologize. You were exhausted." Blaze looked back and forth between her eyes and her lips. She took a step back. "Are you hungry?"

Her stomach rumbled. She grinned. "Starved." They laughed. "But I really need a shower. I'm a mess."

"I think you're beautiful." Blaze's gaze held hers, dropped again to her lips for a long beat before returning to her eyes. She loved the way her eyes held her captive. "If you don't mind leftovers, I'll heat up the Mexican you brought over last night while you shower." Blaze looked her up and down. "Everything I have will be too big, but I'll find something."

She tried to remain calm under Blaze's scrutiny. "Leftovers are great, and I have a gym bag in my trunk with clean clothes."

"Good planning. Your keys are on a hook by the door. Help yourself to whatever you need in the bathroom. I'll start..." Blaze glanced at the time. "Dinner?"

"Close enough."

Blaze started removing items from the fridge, but Trinity couldn't move. All she could do was imagine this was what living with Blaze would be like, and she wondered if anyone had lived here with her.

"Trinity?"

"Huh?"

"You okay?" Blaze asked.

She pushed away the thought, not really wanting to know. "Yeah. Guess I'm still tired." She swallowed the jealous streak of wanting Blaze's home to be someplace only she'd been. "I won't be long."

The hot water was glorious, and she played with the massaging showerhead, finding the perfect setting. Trinity squeezed bath gel onto a washcloth before she began to scrub the grime of the ED away, then used the lavender shampoo. The conditioner was a treat since she rarely bothered with. It made her long strands feather soft, and she imagined Blaze running her fingers through them like she had before. Their night together had morphed into so much more. If she let herself, she could still picture Blaze pressed against her. Tasting her. Filling her. A knock on the door jostled her back to the here and now.

"Trin, you all right in there?" Blaze asked.

She could see the bathroom door ajar as she wiped away the steam from a section of the glass. "Yes, I'm fine. I'm finishing up now."

"Just checking on you. Take your time."

The door closed and she let out a breath. Trinity dried quickly, then glanced at the clock on the shelf. No wonder Blaze had checked on her. She'd been in the bathroom for a good half an hour. Not wanting to delay the dinner that was probably getting cold by now, she wrapped her hair in another towel and pulled on clean clothes. The breakfast table was set, and Blaze was pulling dishes out of the oven.

"I'm so sorry. I totally lost track of time. You've got a great showerhead."

Blaze quirked a grin at her and removed the oven mitts she was wearing. "Glad you approve."

"Hope you don't mind the towel while we eat. My hair takes hours to dry."

Blaze stepped close and inhaled. Her fingers neared her face before Blaze pulled back. "I don't mind. What can I get you to drink?" She had a hard time deciding until she saw a small pitcher among the bowls of steaming food.

"Is that margaritas?"

"It is. I didn't feel like wine, and beer doesn't go all that well with the cuisine, so I took a chance."

"That's perfect." Trinity sipped the fruity drink appreciatively, glad to have something to take the edge off the tension rippling through her. They settled into their meal in silence. Blaze appeared preoccupied and she wanted to know what she was thinking. "A quarter," she said, making her look up in confusion.

"I'm sorry?"

"With inflation and all, it has to be a quarter for your thoughts by now, don't you think?"

Blaze chucked, but her smile was tight. "Sure. Makes sense."

"Out with it." Trinity waved her fork in the air.

"Why is it we have such a hard time with conversation?"

Trinity bit the inside of her mouth, not sure if she was ready for the talk they were about to have, but it had been too long coming, perched between them like the proverbial elephant in the room. "I'm not sure, but I'm listening now."

"I don't want to bore you into a sleep coma."

She laughed. "You could never bore me, but eating while it's still warm is a good idea."

"Thanks for the spread," Blaze said appreciatively. The silence grew between them.

They started talking at the same time and laughed.

Blaze stuck her fork into an enchilada and ate, rolling her eyes. "This is good." The tension dissipated.

Now that Trinity had her talking, she wanted to know more about the last time she'd seen her. "Are you ready to tell me why you were back in the ED?"

Blaze took a drink, grabbed a chip, and scooped guacamole. "I was thinking about…" She glanced down at her plate. "Stuff."

Trinity stared at her, waiting.

"Anyway. I was using the table saw. Pushing a piece of wood along the blade. When I got to the end, it kicked back."

"Oh my God, that sounds horrible."

Blaze shrugged. "It happens sometimes, but if I were paying attention, it wouldn't have hit my arm."

"What were you thinking about?"

Blaze glanced up then, holding her with her gaze for a long beat. "You. Us. Thanksgiving."

Trinity set her fork down. "Tell me."

"I couldn't help thinking if I'd said or done something differently, you would have given me a chance."

She swallowed hard. It was time to be totally honest and let the cards fall where they would. "It wasn't about you." She looked away, unwilling to see the hurt in Blaze's eyes any longer. "I was scared."

"Of me?" Worry creased Blaze's forehead.

Trinity shook her head, unsure where to start. "My parents…I think they loved each other, once. But they could never get ahead, never get above water. They both started drinking and it only got worse. My older sister died of an overdose, and my brother disappeared. I think he's living in New York somewhere, but I'm not really sure. My younger sister has a chance. I help her the best I can, but she's struggling in school." Trinity pressed the heels of her hands to her eyes to shove away the tears. "I promised myself I'd get out and stay out. I've worked so hard, for so long, to make sure I never have to go back to that life."

"Jesus. I'm so sorry." Blaze held her hand gently, her eyes never leaving Trinity's face.

"I always thought if I ended up in a relationship it would just turn out like my parents'. And I don't want that." She let the tears fall and felt the walls she'd built around her heart beginning to crumble. "But you make me think it doesn't have to be an either-or choice."

Blaze stroked Trinity's hand, her expression thoughtful. "I think for a while I was doing exactly the opposite. My mom and dad have something so special between them, I didn't think I'd ever be as lucky, and I didn't want to settle for less." She looked up, her eyes serious. "I don't want to let what we could be go. I won't turn away from what I believe is something real."

Trinity held Blaze's hand between hers. "I don't either. I should have reached out to you. Ever since that night, I've wanted nothing more than to have time with you." And there it was. The truth laid bare. Trinity's eyes shimmered, blurring Blaze's features. A sob escaped, and before she could do anything to stop it, she found herself in Blaze's arms.

"I've got you. You're okay."

Blaze rubbed her back, cradling her head to her chest. She made consoling sounds and spoke softly, though Trinity wasn't sure what she was saying. She trembled in Blaze's grasp. Regret coursed through her. Blaze hadn't done anything to warrant her mistrust. Then or now. She leaned back.

"But I managed to treat you like shit, and all because I convinced myself that success and stability were more important than a relationship."

Blaze unwrapped her hair, combing it with her fingers. Her touch was tender, calming. "Growing up is hard, isn't it?"

Trinity laughed, agreeing.

"Things happen. It's human nature to mess up shit on a regular basis." Blaze pulled her close for a moment, then held her away. "Shall we try to eat a meal without interruptions?"

"That would be a change." Trinity grinned and slid onto the seat.

They stuck with safe topics over the meal, but all the while Trinity knew there was more to say, and much more to let Blaze see. She didn't know where to pick up the discussion. Her childhood had been like so many shattered pieces of a broken mirror, and for a long time she never wanted to look at the reflection. When the conversation finally stalled, Trinity took a shaky breath. "I don't know what else to say."

Blaze slid her hand along her arm until their fingers entwined. "It's when the talking is truly over that you know there's no hope." Blaze pulled her closer. "I'll talk all night if it will keep you here."

"Oh, you will, will you?" she said into her chest, a place she could get used to being if she wasn't so damn stubborn, and she believed Blaze would always feel like a safe place. She squared her shoulders. She could take her time with Blaze. More importantly, she wanted to. To explore what they had and be okay with the outcome, whatever it might be.

Blaze smiled and nodded. "Let me clean up and we can go on the porch."

"Can I help?"

"I'm good. If you don't mind taking our drinks out, I'll join you in a minute."

Trinity was about to say she'd wait, but something in Blaze's demeanor told her she needed a minute. She couldn't blame her.

The screen whispered as it slid along the track and she set their drinks on the table. She leaned on the railing, looking up at the clear sky. Darkness had fallen, like the night she'd let her fears rise to the top, pushing Blaze away. Tonight, the stars shone in a blanket across the sky, and without city lights to dull their brightness, she could make out a few constellations. *So peaceful.* That's how she felt when Blaze was near. At peace. She settled down in a padded chair and inhaled the fresh air. Blaze had the right idea, submersing herself in the serene quiet that surrounded her. It was nothing like the trailer park of her childhood. Nor her apartment for that matter, which was less like a home and more like a place to sleep and eat between shifts.

Blaze nudged open the screen while balancing a tray.

Trinity jumped up. "I'll get it." She opened the screen all the way and Blaze set the tray on the table between the chairs. It held an array of lit candles in small and medium sized glass jars. The scent was familiar, but she couldn't name it. Blaze began placing the containers at various locations around them, including the wide railing, and a medium size one on the floor near their feet. When she was done, Blaze sat in the other chair and smiled at her.

"Sometimes the darkness is a little off-putting if you aren't used to it. I thought a little ambience was in order." She handed Trinity a glass of the margarita concoction, then picked up hers.

"This is nice."

"It is."

She sipped her drink and reviewed bits and pieces of her life. There were things she might have done differently, but she needed to focus on moving forward. She set her empty glass down. The night had turned cold and she shivered. Blaze seemed comfortable. She was probably used to the mountain chill.

After a few minutes, Blaze shifted to look at her. "No one may have told you, so I want to. There's no shame in where you start in life. It's where you go from there that counts. I think you're amazing, and after all you've been through, I think you should be really proud of yourself for all you've accomplished."

She thought about Blaze's words. "I'm not sure I'll ever really believe it."

Blaze was quiet for a long time. "No matter how you see your younger self or your parents, I'm grateful for them." She grasped her hand and held it, gently rubbing. "Without them, I wouldn't have met you."

Trinity couldn't respond because the lump in her throat threatened to choke her. Blaze's compassionate nature was one more reason to keep Blaze in her life. Blaze must have sensed she needed a break from reliving memories she'd tried to forget.

"Your hand is cold. Let's go inside and I'll fix us a cup of coffee."

She groaned. "You've discovered my weakness." Blaze gathered the candles and Trinity took care of the door as she carried the tray to the bay window seat and set it down.

"Can I help?" She liked the sound of Blaze's laugh.

"I might not be one hundred percent, but I can manage coffee, though I wouldn't mind the company."

"Where's Baxter? I haven't seen her at all."

"Who knows. Chasing down wildlife. Looking for a girlfriend."

"Do you leave her out all night?" Trinity didn't like the idea of Baxter having to fend for herself.

"She'd scream her head off if she couldn't get in. She has a cat door in the mud room." Blaze readied the coffee pot and set out mugs.

She wanted a better look at her arm. "Can I see?" She pointed.

Blaze nodded and pushed up her sleeve.

Trinity cradled her arm and assessed what she was seeing with a critical eye. The fresh bruise was a deep purple, with a hard center. Otherwise, the skin was pale, and the girth of Blaze's forearm was a bit smaller than her left one. She'd lost muscle mass, but not much. The scar ran from just below her wrist to just below the elbow. The incision was narrow and clean. The stitch marks were small and precise. She could see where the bone had poked through the skin. "The incision is well healed. Dr. Jonas did a good job minimizing the scarring. I have a cream that might help, if you'd like some." Trinity lightly ran her fingertip along the incision line. "Does it bother you?"

"Only if I can't do something I want to do." Blaze's gaze held hers and she had the distinct feeling it's what she *wasn't* saying that held meaning. "I still wear the sleeve when I work." The brewer beeped and she poured, then set out sugar and cream. They fixed their cups and moved to the living room.

"I didn't see your family at the hospital."

Blaze stared into her mug. "I didn't tell them. They live a few hours away and I didn't want them driving. My brother, Josh, wasn't with them. He's a bit of a wanderer and he lives in Vermont for the time being."

"He's younger?"

"Six years. Do I have competition?"

"Sorry, he's on the wrong team." Blaze smiled, and she sensed their sibling rivalry was just good-hearted ribbing.

"He followed me around all the time as a kid."

"Big sister idolizing?"

Blaze laughed. The sound filled the space, gently surrounding her. She liked it. She wondered if there'd been a shortage of laughter in Blaze's life since the accident.

"Something like that. When I was younger, I saw him as more of a pain in the ass, but we're close now. Have been since we were teenagers."

"Tell me more about your childhood. Where did you grow up?" she asked.

Blaze stood. "I'll start a fire."

Trinity could have used a little warmth of the human kind, but Blaze was being gracious and giving her space. She didn't want to seem ungrateful. Maybe they could find common ground after all.

She settled back on the couch and listened as Blaze began to talk.

CHAPTER THIRTY-SIX

Blaze studied the growing flames. She hadn't realized Trinity's childhood had been so difficult. There'd been nothing in her own childhood to compare it to, and Trinity's reluctance to rely on a partner became clearer under the circumstances. Her heart was what interested Blaze the most. She glanced at her huddled in a quilt as she leaned against the couch. After settling on the floor next to her, she handed her a fresh cup of coffee.

"Better?" she asked.

"Yes. Thank you." Trinity looked pensive as she sipped. She tossed the quilt aside and got on her knees, then set her mug down. "I've been wanting to kiss you since the last time you kissed me." Trinity glanced between her mouth and her eyes. "Can I?"

Blaze didn't bother to answer, but rather pulled her into her lap. The need she found in Trinity's eyes stirred her in a million ways. She snaked her hand beneath Trinity's long, wavy tresses and guided Trinity's head until their lips met. Softly and subtly, Blaze moved her mouth over Trinity's, searching for answers she hadn't dared to ask. Did Trinity want to be with her? Was she willing to take a chance on love? Trinity's tongue slipped between her lips, making her moan. Heat flared in her lower belly. She didn't want her physical craving to overcome her mental needs, but she was powerless against her body's reaction to Trinity's nearness. She pulled back, breaking contact and breathing hard.

"I want you," Blaze said as desire seeped from every pore.

Trinity shuddered before pressing a hand to her chest, creating distance. "It's not just physical. I've missed you. Talking to you. Laughing with you." Trinity caressed her face, then held it and pulled her in for a searing kiss. As the heat built between them, moisture pooled in her crotch. Out of breath, Trinity pulled away first this time.

"Wait here." Blaze got up, glad for the physical distance. She needed to slow down and take her time. There was no rush, and she wanted everything to be perfect.

She stoked the fire, then went to the hall closet and gathered a pile of blankets. She spread out a thick layer on the rug not far from the growing flames. At the last minute she added throw pillows from the couch, and she felt Trinity following her movements. When she was done, she held out her hand, hoping Trinity would accept her offer. She was asking for more than what was happening between them tonight. She was asking for tomorrow, too, and all the days to follow, but she didn't know if Trinity understood how much further Blaze wanted her to go. When Trinity slid her hand into hers, nothing else mattered. She had tonight, and if the accident had taught her anything, it was to take each moment as it came.

They stood at the edge of the makeshift bed. "I want to make love to you." The buttons of Trinity's top were proving more difficult than she'd thought.

"Let me help you." Trinity undid each one slowly.

She pushed the fabric aside, kissing her exposed flesh, taking in the scent of Trinity's warm skin. Blaze guided the fabric down her arms and thumbed open Trinity's bra, freeing her breasts. Her nipples were erect, but she resisted the urge to take one into her mouth. She ran her palm against her stomach and inside the edge of her underwear, sliding to the back and grasping her firm cheek.

"Do you want me naked?" Trinity asked.

Blaze didn't trust her voice and nodded. The slow unveiling left her breathless, then she knelt in front of Blaze and removed her clothes. Blaze stood over her, watching the flames reflect on her smooth, flushed skin. Her vision narrowed.

Trinity stretched out in the middle of the blankets. "Lie down with me."

Blaze traced each curve of Trinity's body before rolling one nipple, then the other, between her fingers and gently tugging. Trinity arched into her touch. She moved her hand lower, brushing along her thighs as she went in for another kiss. The minute their lips met she was lost, letting go of any lingering worry, vowing to enjoy the here and now.

Trinity pulled away out of breath and her chest heaving. "Touch me," she whispered against her mouth.

Wishing she could have lain on top of her, but unsure if she could support her weight for a length of time, she guided Trinity to straddle her hips. "We're going to have to make do for now."

Trinity leaned over and her hair created a veil around them. "I don't mind." After a quick kiss, Trinity cupped her breasts and massaged her into a frenzy. Her nipples puckered hard and tight.

She snaked her hand between them to find Trinity's center hot and wet, and she pressed two fingers inside, loving the way Trinity's body responded to her. With every stroke she rubbed her thumb against Trinity's swollen clit, eliciting a gasp.

"Yes." Trinity hissed, moving her hips, taking her deeper. She tightened around her. "Harder."

Blaze rolled them until Trinity was on her back, her thigh caught between Blaze's, and settled into a position that would give her more leverage.

Trinity's eyes opened. "But—"

With her weight evenly distributed, she wasn't worried. "Shhh, it's okay. Let me fuck you, baby." She pulled back and added another finger before entering her again. At first, she went slowly, watching Trinity's face, seeing the pleasure written there. Blaze moved a little faster, a little deeper, and Trinity's muscles clamped down, locking her inside as she cried out.

"Blaze." She arched up, driving her deeper still, and grabbed her wrist, holding her in place.

The spasms from Trinity's orgasm sent her own body to the brink of climax, but she held back. She wanted to enjoy every second as Trinity's skin flushed a deeper pink and her stomach muscles twitched. Finally, Trinity relaxed and let go of her. Her eyes slowly opened to display a post-orgasm haze.

Trinity smiled lazily. "What you do to me."

Blaze returned the smile. "Good things, I hope." She leaned down for a kiss, needing intimacy. Needing to know they weren't done yet.

"Very good things." Trinity ran her fingertips over her flexed arm where it rested between her thighs. "Is your arm okay?"

She wiggled the fingers of her left hand. "This one's a little tired, but it's okay."

Trinity slapped her. "Not that one."

"Just teasing. It's fine."

"Okay, but I have to see for myself."

She pushed on her shoulder until she was on her back and Trinity straddled her thigh. She couldn't help the groan that escaped when her soaked folds slid against Blaze's muscle. Trinity lifted her scarred arm and gently cradled her elbow in one hand, before she began to kiss the tip of each finger. Watching her swollen lips was driving her crazy. When she seemed satisfied, Trinity placed her hand on the floor and turned her attention to her other one.

"And how is this one?"

Blaze wiggled her fingers again, then made a fist. "You tell me."

Trinity repeated kissing each tip, then took her index finger into her mouth and sucked, repeating the motion until she'd cleaned all of them. Blaze forgot to breathe.

"Mmm…not bad, but I need a comparison."

As she bent over, Trinity traced her nipples with her tongue before moving farther down her body, placing small kisses along the way. She settled between her thighs and Blaze grabbed a pillow from the pile around her so she could watch.

"I think I need to start here." Trinity sucked on the cord of her inner thigh, then ran her tongue along the length. "Or here." She licked along the junction of her leg and hip, making her squirm. "Or here," she said just before she slid a finger into her slick opening and licked the length of her.

"Oh, God." Despite her best efforts, she wasn't going to last, and could already feel her orgasm approaching.

"You don't like that?" Trinity stopped and pulled out, waiting for her to respond, though by the look on her face, Blaze could tell she knew exactly what she was doing.

"Yes, but you're going to make me come." She gritted her teeth and hoped she could hold off long enough to enjoy Trinity's attention.

Trinity's eyebrow lifted and a smile played on her lips. "Unless I've got it terribly wrong, that's the point of what we're doing." Without breaking eye contact, Trinity slid all the way inside her.

Blaze's sex clenched. "Christ, woman, a little pity here." She took a deep breath, but when she glanced down Trinity was licking her lips, poised at the ready, and looking as though she were ready to eat her alive.

Flattening her hand on her abdomen, Trinity applied pressure. "You've got this, baby. Just enjoy it," she said, then her tongue outlined Blaze's swollen folds.

She fisted the bedding under her while a thousand fireworks went off inside her. As much as she wanted to hold off climaxing, her body craved release, begging for the imminent explosion that would catapult her into the blissful state she remembered from their first encounter. All things considered, Blaze thought she was doing fairly well until Trinity closed her lips around her clit and began to alternately suck and flick at the tip. Lost in the overwhelming pleasure Trinity's mouth provided, Blaze gave in to the hum building throughout every fiber of her, and when Trinity circled her, she exploded.

"I'm coming." Her body convulsed below Trinity's talented mouth, and Trinity moaned at her release, the contractions gripping her, clamping down around the finger buried inside.

"So good," Trinity murmured, licking at her juices.

After a few intense minutes, Blaze's body relaxed and she pulled air into her lungs. Her climax had been so strong, she hadn't been able to breathe. She was about to say something profound when Trinity curled two fingers inside her, rubbing the inner ridge, and sent her skyrocketing into another earth-shattering orgasm. Bucking beneath her, Blaze rode the waves coursing through the length of her body until she finally begged her to stop. Trinity's touch was like no other. Maybe that was because Blaze had fallen in love with her.

Trinity moved up her body until their wet centers met. "I love watching you lose control."

She couldn't help laughing and pulled Trinity to her, knowing she didn't have the strength to move. "Oh, you do, huh?" Blaze kissed her and tasted her own flavor on Trinity's lips. She pictured Trinity's folds below her mouth, and she wanted her again. Wanted this night together to last forever. All she had to do was convince Trinity to take a chance on the future, and on her.

CHAPTER THIRTY-SEVEN

Trinity lay snuggled against Blaze's long, firm body, enjoying the heat emanating from her and the flickering fireplace, adding another level of romance to the setting. She hadn't had any design on their evening together, but she thoroughly enjoyed not only the sexual part, but the parts that had been missing in her life, like when Blaze held her. Comforted her. Sensed her turmoil. She'd never understood when couples talked about feeling cared for without reservation. Now she did.

"You okay?" Blaze asked, her hand rubbing soothing strokes over her back.

"Very." She looked up into Blaze's soulful eyes. "You?"

"Absolutely okay."

Blaze traced lazy circles over her back. There was something Blaze was ruminating on. She could tell by the set of her jaw.

"What are you thinking about?"

"I have a question."

Trinity pushed up on her elbow. "What?"

"The gown you wore to the gala…"

"Yes?"

Blaze's hand moved lower. "Were you wearing anything underneath?"

She fought not to laugh at the anticipation on Blaze's face. "Not a stitch."

"Damn." Blaze took possession of her mouth, and Trinity's passion reawakened.

❖

Trinity dozed lightly before Blaze's stomach rumbled, then her face colored as she broke away. "I might be hungry after expending all that energy." Her stomach growled again.

"A little?" she asked, laughing.

"Okay, I may be starving. I'll waste away to nothing soon."

She ran her hand over Blaze's hard abdominal muscles, and they twitched beneath her palm. "I wouldn't want that to happen. Your body is perfect just like it is." Trinity kissed where her hand had been, and Blaze moaned.

"If you keep that up, you're going to have to endure more rumbling while I take you again."

Trinity glanced sideways. "Promise?"

"Oh yeah, right after I eat." Blaze rolled away and got up, searching for her discarded clothes and started dressing, minus undergarments.

She followed her into the kitchen, running her fingers along the high polished wood of the breakfast bar, then she stopped abruptly. Her smile faltered.

"Hey," Blaze said, and stepped closer. "What's wrong?"

Her cheeks heated. "I should probably wash my hands before I touch anything."

Blaze pulled her close. "I don't mind. I like how we taste."

The shiver that traveled through her had nothing to do with the fact she was only wearing her shirt and underwear. Even Blaze's voice set her body on high alert. Blaze kissed her neck and wrapped her arm around her waist, pulling her against her.

"Even after making love to you over and over, all I can think about is the next time."

Trinity loved how she felt in her embrace and wondered how it would feel to be there every day. She pictured a life together, just the two of them, in the house Blaze had built. Blaze nipped at her neck, sending another jolt of electricity coursing through her.

"Do you want something to eat?" Blaze asked. She stood in front of the open refrigerator and started pulling out packs of deli meat, cheese, and bread. She lifted the cover on a bowl and wrinkled her nose, then scraped the contents in the trash. "That definitely wasn't fit for human consumption."

"What are you offering?" She cocked an eyebrow and giggled when Blaze slumped against the counter and held her hand over her heart.

"Are you trying to kill me?"

"Hardly. You're the sturdy sort. I'm not in the least bit concerned about your stamina." Trinity opened the bag of chips, fully in the moment for probably the first time in her life.

Blaze set their plates down and Trinity brought bottles of Perrier to the table. "So," Blaze said. "I hate to press the issue, but…"

Trinity looked stricken. "But what?"

"I'd really like you to spend Thanksgiving with me."

Trinity rolled her eyes. "You're not going to give up on this, are you?"

She sat back. Maybe she should leave the topic alone. The only problem was, she didn't want to leave it alone. She wanted Trinity with her, especially since Trinity had no idea what happy holiday gatherings looked like. "No. I can't. I really want you to go." Trinity ran a hand over her face, and Blaze thought she was going to be disappointed by her refusal.

"Fine. I'll go with you."

She's coming home with me. Even though she hoped she could talk Trinity into the trip, she hadn't been at all sure she'd be able to.

"Earth to Blaze." Trinity waved a hand in front of her face.

She blinked, then focused. "Sorry. I expected you to turn me down."

"Well, if you'd prefer I not…" Trinity said, but the twinkle in her eyes gave her away.

Blaze jumped up and pulled Trinity into her arms for a crushing hug. "Oh my God. I'm so glad you said yes." Trinity chuckled then struggled in her embrace, and she loosened her hold.

"If that's how you show you're happy, I'm going to have to be careful. You could break a rib." Trinity rubbed her sides.

She felt her face heat. "Sorry. Sometimes I forget how strong these big arms are." Blaze smiled, remembering how Trinity had described them.

Trinity sat and took a drink. "Tell me what the plan is and when we leave."

Her heart soared. Of all the scenarios she'd played out in her head, she'd been resigned to feeling disappointment. This was the opposite. This was elation, and Blaze felt like shouting from the rooftops, though that was reserved for declarations of love, and they weren't there. Yet.

CHAPTER THIRTY-EIGHT

B laze raced outside, meeting Trinity at her car before she'd even turned off the engine. "Hi," she said as she pulled Trinity into her arms, remembering to be gentle, then brushing her lips over Trinity's.

"I could get used to this kind of a greeting."

Her pulse kicked up a notch. "I hope so." She had to tamp down her enthusiasm. While Trinity was going with her, neither had said the words dating or exclusive, though for her part she didn't have to. Blaze was already committed.

Trinity responded by opening her trunk and pulling out a rolling duffel bag. "I have a couple of things in the back seat, then I'll be ready."

Blaze stowed the bag in her Jeep, then went to help Trinity with the rest. "What all have you got here?" she asked as Trinity handed her a couple of bags and a wrapped box with a fancy ribbon.

Trinity shrugged. "I couldn't show up without bringing something."

"You didn't have to do that."

"I know. I wanted to. It's good manners."

Trinity's smile appeared tight, and she wanted to put her at ease. "There's no reason to be nervous, babe. You've already met my folks and Josh. They're ordinary people."

Trinity nodded, then stowed her backpack on the floor and got in. She took a deep breath as though to settle herself.

"All set?"

"I'm being silly, aren't I?" she said, looking across to her.

She took her hand and rubbed the knuckles against her cheek. "No, you aren't. I get that you're nervous. You're going to be fine."

❖

Seeing Blaze's parents again reminded Trinity how wonderful a real family could be. They welcomed her with open arms. Blaze had obviously prepared them for her arrival, and it was apparent they were thrilled Blaze had finally brought someone home to share in their celebration.

Trinity left Blaze and her father to hash out football statistics about tomorrow's game and went to the kitchen to see if she could lend a hand.

"Can I help, Mrs. Carter?"

"No need to be formal in our house. Anyone Blaze brings home is part of the family, like it or not. It's Millie from here on out." Her smile mirrored Blaze's, setting her at ease. "And that old coot will tell you the same thing." Millie chuckled, then pointed to the counter where salad ingredients were piled around a well-worn cutting board. "If you don't mind, those all need your knife skills."

"I'm glad to help." She washed her hands and began slicing, dicing, and tearing.

"Have I been replaced in the kitchen?" Blaze asked as she stole a chunk of cucumber.

"Maybe," Millie said. "She doesn't sass back."

Blaze put her hand to her heart. "I'm crushed," she said, winking.

"Now if I could just get your brother in line."

Blaze groaned. "No such luck. When is Josh heading in?" She popped a grape tomato in her mouth.

"Stop snitching food." Trinity didn't really care and didn't think Millie did either. It was nice to feel comfortable around the two of them.

"In case you haven't noticed, it's been hours since we ate. I'm starving."

"You're a bottomless pit," she said.

"Ha," Millie quipped. "It didn't take her long to peg you."

"Mom," Blaze whined, then laughed.

They sat down to a simple meal of chili, salad, and cornbread. When they were done, Millie and Blaze worked on homemade pies, and she got to play sous chef. It was after ten by the time the pies sat cooling on the counter. Blaze asked if she was tired and announced they were going to bed.

Her nerves returned. She shouldn't be embarrassed by sharing a bed with Blaze. They were both adults. But the thought of doing so in the Carters' home felt strange. As she said good night she felt heat in her face, and once they were in the bedroom she voiced her concern.

"Honey, they know I'm a lesbian, and I'm a grown up. They'd think it was odd if we didn't share a bed." Blaze held her shoulders and her eyes softened. "Even when you're shy, you're beautiful. It's okay."

It helped that Blaze had her own bathroom, and no one would see her moving about. Thankfully, Blaze's parents' bedroom was on the opposite side of the house. "I know, but…" Trinity glanced at the closed door.

Blaze took her hands and held them behind her back. "Relax." She captured her mouth and slowly pressed her tongue inside, probing and stroking. Before she could stop it, a moan escaped. When they broke apart, Blaze's eyes darkened, verging on black, and her muscles twitched beneath Trinity's fingers. Blaze kicked off her shoes and indicated she should do the same. Hands still entwined, Blaze led Trinity to the bathroom. Blaze stripped, then grabbed her toothbrush and paste.

Trinity tried not to look at Blaze's body, but when their eyes met in the mirror, Blaze grinned. She rummaged in her toiletry bag, needing a distraction from what she imagined Blaze was thinking. Not that she wasn't thinking it, too, but she couldn't have sex with Blaze here. She could wait a few days.

"Shower with me."

She chewed on her lip. "I don't think we should."

Blaze adjusted the water. "It's been a long day and I need one. If we take one together, we'll save water." Blaze appeared serious. Even though she knew better, she couldn't say no.

Blaze lathered up a washcloth and handed it to her before turning her back to Trinity. She ran the cloth over Blaze's wide shoulders, down her arms, and over her back. She hesitated at the cheeks of her ass. She was being ridiculous. Not trusting her wandering mind, she hurried to finish. Blaze moved under the showerhead, then faced her.

"Your turn." The glint in her eye told Trinity she had more in mind than just washing.

I can do this. She faced the wall and Blaze moved the washcloth over her shoulders and back before replacing it with her hand.

"So smooth."

Blaze whispered next to her ear, the hot breath scorching her sensitive skin. Blaze's hand moved lower.

"So sexy," she said as she cupped her ass and squeezed, making her tremble. A finger slipped into the crevasse between her cheeks, then followed the path forward until she was just below her opening. "I want you," Blaze growled.

She braced her hand on the shower wall, her legs barely holding her upright.

"Please?" Blaze nipped at her neck.

She was powerless to refuse her. Trinity started to turn, but Blaze slipped inside her, filling her. A few deep strokes had her on the verge of orgasm, but Blaze stilled her movement. Trinity turned her head to complain, but Blaze's lips covered hers, taking possession of her mouth while her knee nudged her legs farther apart and Blaze's other hand covered her mound until she found her distended clit. She fought for a breath, the onslaught of sensations stealing the air from her lungs. Finally, Blaze's mouth moved to her shoulder, nipping at her neck.

"Touch me."

Trinity found Blaze hard and swollen, and she pulled and squeezed in a rhythm that matched Blaze's. She felt her thick thighs tremble, then her stomach muscles tighten as Blaze pulled her tighter against her and groaned.

"Come with me, baby."

Blaze filled her again, stretching her and thumbing her clit while Trinity played her fingers over the knot beneath them. Faster, harder. Blaze cried out as her clit throbbed in Trinity's hand and her own orgasm tumbled through her, threatening to send them both to the floor. Somehow Blaze got to the ledge and sat with her in her lap, shaking as the last of her climax coursed through her.

"God, I love making love with you." Blaze's words were breathy as she recovered.

Trinity turned in her arms and held her face as the steam began to clear. "I'm so glad you do, because I feel the same way." She kissed Blaze's swollen lips.

Though the water had cooled, the bathroom was warm, and they tenderly dried each other. She spent a few minutes drying her hair, getting as much moisture out of it as she could before joining Blaze in bed. "So much for water conservation," she said. Blaze laughed. It was a sound she didn't think she'd ever grow tired of hearing.

"The mind was willing to wait, but the body won." Blaze kissed her forehead. "I hope you didn't mind."

She looked up into the questioning stormy gray eyes that were so much a mirror of Blaze's feelings. "Not for a second, though I'm not sure how I'll face your parents in the morning."

"Don't worry. I'm sure they knew what we were going to do tonight."

Trinity groaned and covered her face. "Oh no."

Blaze chuckled, moving her hands. "Babe, it's okay. They're well mannered. They'd never say anything."

"Even so…" All she could imagine was having a flashback of them in the shower and turning bright red. "If they do, I'm going to blame you."

"A blame I'll gladly take." Blaze pulled her closer and moved them lower in the bed. "Are you warm enough?"

"Perfect." The weather forecast threatened snow. Blaze had put a down comforter on the bed, telling her there was nothing like snuggling under covers, but Trinity knew she'd done it for her. She minded the cold more than Blaze as evident by her flannel shirt and down vest, though it was only in the twenties when they arrived.

Blaze rubbed her back and sighed contentedly. "Sleep well, darling."

"You too," she said. It wasn't long before Blaze's breathing evened. This was their first night of sleeping together and Blaze had acted as though they'd been doing so for a long time. She'd been anxious, but Blaze had a way of putting her at ease, no matter what the circumstances. Though she had nothing to compare it to, she was finding it harder and harder to resist Blaze's charm. She was thoughtful and caring and honest. Trinity knew without a doubt she was falling in love, and she had no idea how she was going to handle it.

The morning was a raucous affair. After a light breakfast, the turkey was put in the oven and later on the ham would follow. There were potatoes to peel and vegetables to cut, and of course, green bean casserole to prepare. The rest of the family would be arriving with all the accompaniments, including homemade cranberry sauce. Trinity was looking forward to trying a little of everything.

Josh arrived midmorning, surprising her with a smaller version of the bouquet he brought for his mother, and she saw the love reflected on Blaze's face for his gesture to make her feel like one of the family.

When there was a lull in the activity, she stepped outside and took a deep breath while she waited for someone to pick up the other end of the line.

"Yeah?"

The gruff voice of her father shocked her. He sounded older than the last time they'd spoken. Sadly, she couldn't remember how long ago it had been.

"Happy Thanksgiving, Dad."

"Who's this? Trinity?"

"Yes, Dad. It's me."

"What do you want?"

She cringed. After all this time, she'd never asked her parents for anything, and that wasn't about to change. "I don't want anything. I just wanted to wish you and Mom a happy Thanksgiving."

"Well, it's not gonna be very happy without a turkey and fixings is it?" He coughed into the phone, and she pulled it away from her ear until he was done.

"Is Mom there?"

"She's still asleep. I'll tell her you called." The line went dead.

"I love you, too, Dad." She shoved the phone in her pocket and swiped at the errant tears. She wasn't going to put herself through that again. She'd tried to reach out to her parents from time to time, but it was always the same. What do you want? Do you have any money? Can you cover this month's rent? They rarely asked how she was or if she was dating, not that any of it mattered to either of them. She'd call her sister later, and hoped she'd made plans to spend the day with a friend. She closed her eyes, wishing she didn't care what happened to her family, but she did. Being around Blaze's family reminded her just how different their backgrounds were.

"Trin, you okay?" Blaze hugged her from behind. She took a shaky breath and turned in her arms.

"I am now."

"You've been crying." Blaze's forehead creased with concern. "Do you want to talk about it?"

"Just family stuff. Nothing to worry about." She tipped her chin toward the house. "Let's not leave your parents alone with Josh. They've already got their hands full with getting that huge meal on the table."

Blaze laughed. "Don't worry about them. They've been doing this a long time." She kissed her lightly, then wrapped an arm around her. "Let's go in and discuss who you're rooting for in the first game, then I'll know where to look for your body."

She punched her in the stomach, not surprised when Blaze didn't even flinch. "I know what to do. I'm going to ask your father who *he's* rooting for, then you won't have to worry."

Blaze beamed at her. "I knew you were smart."

The smartest thing she'd done lately was open her heart to Blaze.

Chapter Thirty-nine

They'd left Blaze's family after the festivities had quieted down a bit, leaving a handful of relatives cheering the last quarter of the football game. Blaze wanted them to spend the night at her house and had gladly given up her room to her favorite aunt and uncle. Trinity could see why. Ellen and Bob were sweet and fun. They doted on Blaze, and Trinity could tell they were close.

After a leisurely morning in bed making love and talking about her family's antics, Blaze got up, insisting she stay in bed and enjoy her day off. She'd fallen back asleep only to wake to the scent of coffee coming from the mug on the nightstand. When she was awake enough to shower and dress, she went to find Blaze. They took a walk through the woods behind the house and when they returned, Blaze proclaimed being famished.

She watched Blaze move around the kitchen, making them a simple lunch. Trinity didn't know if now was the time to broach the subject, but she was still bothered by thoughts of DJ. She didn't want DJ to come between them, and she wanted to know where she stood.

Blaze tapped on the table to get her attention and Trinity glanced down at her plate.

"Trinity, talk to me. I know something's on your mind by the way you're making a meal out of your bottom lip."

"Fine. I was thinking we should have talked about this sooner."

Blaze tipped her head, clearly confused.

"The first time I met DJ, she had it out for me. And that night you were out with her, she wasn't very happy I had your attention. I get the feeling she doesn't like me, and I'm not sure why."

Blaze patted her sandwich. "She's overprotective and doesn't want to see me get hurt."

She could understand that kind of friendship, but that wasn't the vibe she got the last time she was around DJ. "I don't think that's it. When she said I had ulterior motives I think she knew it was an outright lie."

"We've talked this out, believe me. She was upset by what happened after our date. She thought you were only interested in sex, and she knew I was looking for a committed relationship and someday, a family."

Her food stuck in her throat. "What did you say?"

"That she thought you were only interested in sex?"

"Not that."

Blaze smiled. "A family?"

Trinity nodded, her skin cold.

"Oh yeah. I want kids. Definitely."

She blinked several times. "You've never said anything about children before."

"We've never had this kind of conversation before." Blaze's smile slowly faded.

"I don't want children." All she could picture was the small trailer shared by six people and no room to breathe. She hadn't worked and saved and studied just to throw her freedom away and spend all her time raising a family.

Blaze reached for her hand. "You'd make a great mom, and…"

Trinity jumped up, nearly toppling her chair. "No. My mother gave up what little she had to take care of us. She never got to do any of the things she'd dreamt of doing because she worked so much, and when she wasn't working, she was looking after the house, and my dad, and—" A sob wrenched from her throat. Everything she'd tried to escape as a child, Blaze wanted. Only this time it felt like a vise grip closing in on her. A relationship was one thing. The rest would drown her. "I'm sorry. I can't be what you want me to be."

She rushed out of the room and grabbed her bags as she ran to the front door.

"Trinity. Wait." Blaze was there in an instant, standing in front of her. "What just happened? Can't we talk about this?"

Tears streamed down her face. "There's nothing to talk about. I don't want to end up like my parents. I don't want kids. I don't want..." She grabbed her keys off the table. Her mind was a firestorm of conflicting emotions, and she grabbed onto the one that rose to the top. The one she'd constantly worried over. "Maybe DJ can give you what you want."

"What does she have to do with us?" Blaze asked.

In the time between her outburst and where they stood now, she stopped caring about treading lightly around the subject of DJ, and her biggest fear about moving forward in their relationship. "Don't you see it?"

"See what?" Blaze took a step closer.

"DJ's in love with you." Blaze looked shocked, and Trinity wished she could take it back, but it was too late. "I think she always has been," Trinity whispered before moving around Blaze to open the door. The cold air hit her in the face. Like Blaze's revelation, she didn't have any protection from it, and she hurried down the steps. There wasn't anything else to say. She had no leverage over the years DJ had with Blaze, and she definitely had no interest in raising children. She stumbled to the car. All she could think about was the way her heart felt, like it was being ripped open, knowing the future no longer held the possibility of a happy life with Blaze.

Chapter Forty

What the fuck just happened? Blaze stood rooted in the spot where Trinity had left her, speechless and confused. It was one thing to hear Trinity didn't want children, and really, they hadn't discussed having a family of their own. Hell, they hadn't discussed dating either, let alone a future like that. It was just conversation. She could even understand Trinity's reluctance given that their childhoods had been so vastly different. Her heart ached as she listened to Trinity talk about the struggles her family had faced. She'd been even more surprised to find out she still carried the shame of being poor when there wasn't any reason. Those were circumstances beyond her control.

She'd been encouraged by Trinity's visit home. When they made love, the fire that burned between them reignited, and she let it consume her. It had been perfect.

And now to find out Trinity believed DJ was in love with her? *Fuck.* The kitchen nook had the remnants of their unfinished meal, but she couldn't think about cleaning it up. Her stomach churned into knots of unease. Times like these she'd normally take her bike for a spin. but she was too upset and too confused to go out. She wasn't about to chance another injury. Fists on hips, she looked around until her gaze landed on the bottle of scotch she hadn't touched in weeks. Blaze took the bottle and a clean glass and headed for the back porch. She'd built this space specifically for the times she needed to do deep thinking.

She took a sip, then another. Baxter jumped up beside her and watched, sensing her unrest. Baxter blinked, then extended a paw to get her attention. Blaze ran her hand over the silky fur and Baxter purred in contentment. She closed her eyes and listened for the sounds that soothed *her*. Crickets chirped and owls hooted. The crunch of underbrush as animals foraged. And the steady rhythm of Baxter's purring against her.

Able to think clearer, she concentrated on recent conversations she and DJ had regarding Trinity and past loves. Blaze had been upset, naturally, and DJ had been there to help her through each and every time, telling her she deserved better. Telling her they'd never...she gasped. DJ had told her those women couldn't love her the way she needed. Blaze had never really studied her words, but now that she did, what had DJ meant? She began to pace the length of wood planking, cold under her feet.

"Wouldn't I have seen it?" she said into the brisk air, puffs of steam trailing from her mouth. The afternoon had turned frigid. But the cold kept her mind sharp, and the alcohol had no effect on her. The more she recalled, the more she wondered if Trinity had been able to see what she'd failed to. That DJ was *in* love with her. Was that the reason for DJ's former "going nowhere" relationships?

The last woman DJ had been with appeared to be a perfect fit, but it had ended less than a year after it had begun with DJ citing they had "little in common aside from sex." Blaze was left to question DJ's investment in her own relationships.

There was nothing she could do right now about Trinity. She didn't think she'd answer if she called. Especially not since she'd scared her by using the word family. But she could sure as hell get in touch with DJ and have an apparently long overdue heart-to-heart. Blaze winced at the cliché. How could she have been so blind for so long?

❖

An hour later, Blaze finally heard from her.

"Hi." DJ sounded upbeat. "Is everything all right? It's not like you to be calling instead of texting."

She battled for control of her rising anger. She'd called at least a dozen times, and by now all she wanted to do was yell at her. "We need to talk."

"Okay." DJ drew out the word as though she didn't have a clue what the topic was. Blaze doubted her naivety.

"In person." It came out harsher than needed and she took a moment to calm down. "It's important."

DJ sighed. "It must be if you want to see me. Give me a bit to change."

"Fine." She hung up and tossed the phone aside. The situation was a mess. She ran her hands over her face, startled when Baxter nosed her arm. "Where did you go?" Baxter let out a low whine and put her paws on Blaze's chest so she could rub against her. She buried her face in the soft fur as she scratched under her chin. "This is the only reason I have you, you know."

At least she had a game plan. Phase one: talk to DJ and either confirm or refute Trinity's suspicions. Phase two: talk to Trinity and rationally discuss what they both wanted out of life…and each other. All she could do in the meantime was wait for DJ's arrival. Waiting had never been her strong point.

"Is it true? Are you in love with me?" Blaze asked as she stared into DJ's eyes, wanting to see all the way to her soul.

"You know I love you."

"That's not what I asked."

DJ took her mug and headed for the kitchen. "Don't you have anything stronger than coffee? Like whiskey?"

She came up behind DJ and set a bottle of Tennessee bourbon on the counter. "One shot, then you tell me the truth. All of it." She pulled two shot glasses down from the cabinet and poured, handing DJ one while lifting the other. "To best friends."

"To best friends," DJ said, her hand shaking so much the liquid cascaded over the edge, staining her shirt before she got it to her mouth.

Arms crossed, Blaze locked her gaze and waited.

"Yes. I'm in love with you."

Her back stiffened. "When…" she began, then shook her head. "How long?"

DJ glanced away, then came back to her. "Forever."

She dropped onto a stool and poured another shot, downing it, then poured another. Anger rose again as past relationships played in her mind. "Amber. Remember her? We were good together. We wanted the same things and it seemed like we were getting in deeper, closer. Then all of a sudden, she was gone. I never knew why." Blaze threw back her third shot. "Do *you* know why?"

DJ blanched, and her eye contact became tentative and wavering. "I may have said something about you just being interested in a good time."

"A good time? For Christ's sake, DJ. I was falling in love with her."

"I know. But she wasn't good enough for you."

Blaze picked up the bottle and slammed it back down. She was surprised it didn't shatter. "I don't understand. What happened? I thought we came to an agreement that our friendship was more important than a physical entanglement."

"That was your decision, not mine." DJ's voice cracked. "All I ever wanted was to be the one you chose as your partner. You were everything I'd ever wanted in a woman. You're funny and intelligent and kind. When you cared for something…someone, you gave your everything. Every time you found a woman to take my place…" She hung her head.

Blaze couldn't see her eyes, but she didn't miss the tears that fell. "Don't you already know," Blaze said. The sorrow she was experiencing was so deep it stole her breath. "No one could ever take your place. Not then. Not now."

DJ sobbed and tears flowed down her cheeks when she looked up. "But it wasn't just your friendship I wanted. It's all of you. I tried not to love you. I knew you didn't want it. Didn't want *me*. And every time I thought I'd mastered my feelings they came back tenfold. My relationships failed because I couldn't let you go." DJ turned away and moved toward the door, her shoulders shaking.

Blaze grasped her hand. "DJ, I don't want you to go." She pulled her into a seat, so they were facing each other. "I love you. I'll always love you, but not in the way you want. I thought we were on the same page. I'm not going to say I'm not pissed about you interfering, but you're my best friend."

Another sob escaped from DJ and she swiped at her tears. "Where do we go from here?"

Blaze's anger dissipated in the face of DJ's obvious pain. She'd managed to break DJ's heart and she hadn't even noticed. She'd never taken the time to analyze things DJ said or did as meaning something else. "First, you promise me you'll leave decisions about who I choose to date or love to me." DJ quickly nodded. "I mean it, so don't forget it. I may not be so forgiving next time." She took a breath. "I want you to take a step back." DJ's eyes welled up and Blaze took her hand. "I need time to reconcile your feelings, and I think some space will help us both. You need to let go so you can find someone else. Someone you can be really happy with."

"Okay." DJ's voice was quiet, and she looked utterly defeated.

"Then you remember we're best friends and no matter what, that's not going to change."

"Even when I totally screw up?" DJ still looked stricken.

Blaze shared a small smile. "Especially when you screw up. And I expect the same from you."

"Done." DJ let out a breath.

Blaze poured two more shots and handed her one. "Finally, we toast to not hiding any more secrets from each other."

They tossed back the amber liquid. Blaze knew she couldn't let DJ leave even if she wanted to. The liquor would go straight to her head.

"What are you going to do about Trinity? Do you want me to—"

Blaze held up her hand. "You've done enough." She softened her gaze. "I'm going to have to handle this one on my own." She wiped her hands over her face and told DJ what had happened between them.

DJ stood. "You've probably had enough of me. I should head out." She swayed and reached for the counter.

"You aren't going anywhere," Blaze said. "I know what a lightweight you are when it comes to bourbon. You can spend the night in the guest room, but I'd lock the door because I'm still pretty pissed at you."

DJ's eyes got big and her mouth fell open.

"Only kidding, but it was worth the look on your face." She grinned.

"Very funny. Is that how you charm all your women?" DJ asked.

"Sometimes," she said, winking. "Get some sleep. I'll cook you breakfast in the morning."

CHAPTER FORTY-ONE

Trinity glanced at the clock and groaned. For the last two days she'd barely gotten more than a few hours of sleep here and there, and her lack of energy at work was a direct result. She'd spent the time reasoning the pros and cons, but no matter how much the idea of having children scared the shit out of her, a future without Blaze in it didn't sound at all inviting.

She stumbled out to the kitchen. Her last shift ended on time but had felt like a double. The aroma of coffee helped wake her sleepy body. Her mind was already in overdrive.

Blaze had left voice mails and sent numerous text messages since she'd run out without giving her a chance to elaborate, and Trinity ignored each one, unsure how to face what she really wanted.

The mug shook in her hand as her phone vibrated for what must have been the hundredth time, and Blaze's image flashed on her screen. It had been unfair to use DJ's behavior as a reason to run, but she knew Blaze would see beyond that, and Blaze's family had shown her a very different meaning of family. One where people loved and cared for and about each other. She hadn't given Blaze the opportunity to discuss her feelings either. Wasn't that what couples did? Talk things out. Weigh their options, their differences, and come to a mutual understanding, if not an agreement? Why couldn't she seem to get a grip on being rational? Or was she simply using her background as a safety mechanism to keep her distance and not take a chance on the outcome? Her life was already very different from her parents', and her future would be, too. Trinity hit the mute button, silencing the vibration. She couldn't think if she heard Blaze's voice, the one that spoke of things she'd never dreamt of having for herself, or a special someone to share them with. If she went back to Blaze, she needed to be sure she could be the person Blaze deserved.

She felt like screaming. She'd been so single-minded that she hadn't seen what was right in front of her. Life didn't have to be all or nothing. It wasn't black and white. She could be successful and have a relationship, too. It had been stupid on her part to think otherwise, and now she was alone. Every time they touched, her world spun out of control and she questioned why she'd ever doubted how much she wanted Blaze to be her special someone. She wasn't naive enough to consider years down the road. The future was never a given. She'd seen too much tragedy in her life to be fooled into thinking she'd be spared heartache at some point, but that didn't mean she couldn't be grateful for today or tomorrow. In her quest for independence she'd wasted precious time. It took her a minute to remember what Blaze had said.

She chewed the inside of her cheek. Kelly was still sleeping, but she needed her opinion. She crept into Kelly's bedroom and sat on the edge of the bed with a fresh cup of coffee. It wasn't long before she began to stir and stretch, blinking at the sunlight streaming into her room because Trinity had pulled the curtain back.

"Geez, what's with all the light?" Kelly groaned and rolled onto her side, shielding her eyes.

"It's better than me fumbling around in the dark and scaring you." Trinity grinned even though Kelly wasn't looking at her, and she moved the steaming mug closer.

Kelly rubbed her eyes, sat up, took a sip, and sighed. "What time is it?"

The guilt she was already experiencing over ignoring Blaze increased. "A little after nine."

"You do know I got home four hours ago, right?"

She nodded. "Yes. I promise I'll let you sleep all day if you want, but I need to talk and it can't wait." Trinity pulled her phone from her pocket and shoved it at Kelly, who squinted as she tried to focus.

"What am I looking at?" She set her drink down and reached for it, then scrolled through the list. "Oh, wow," Kelly said as she viewed the phone log of missed calls, then texts. "Blaze really wants to talk to you." She looked back up. "And there's voice mails. Have you listened to them?"

She hadn't had the courage to hear Blaze's voice, afraid of what she might hear. "I want to, but I can't."

Kelly sat up higher in bed, stuffing pillows behind her. "Why not?"

Trinity shook her head. "I don't think I can give her children, and I think that's what she wants most."

"Jumping to conclusions without facts isn't like you, and it's not fair for you to assume Blaze is sold on having children, even if she did mention it." Kelly pursed her lips and took her hand. "Do you want to listen to them together?"

Did she really want to hear the deep alto, sexy-as-hell voice she remembered so well when all she'd been trying to do was forget how wonderful it was when they were together? She glanced from the phone to Kelly. "I have to, don't I?"

"Only if you want to, but I think you need to. You haven't been the same since you stormed out of her place, and we both know it."

The first message was from the night when she'd left. Blaze asked her to call. The next was another request to talk and that they needed to "clarify some things." The last one was a plea, saying she was miserable without her and they couldn't resolve anything by staying away from each other. As much as she didn't want to admit it, she missed Blaze every minute of every hour. Maybe the only way she could have peace was by seeing her and telling her exactly how she felt.

"So, are you going to continue to bury your head—and your heart—in the sand, or are you going to do something about it?"

All too well, she knew the truth. It was time she took a step forward and stopped letting inertia rule her mind, and her heart, as Kelly so eloquently said. "I'm going to call her." It was the only sensible thing to do and she'd wasted enough time worrying about an outcome she couldn't predict.

"Cool." Kelly handed over the phone. "Now go away." Kelly snuggled down under the blankets. "And pull those damned drapes."

She stared at her phone, took a calming breath, and pressed Blaze's number as she closed the door softly behind her.

CHAPTER FORTY-TWO

B laze continued to squeeze the tennis ball. Cassie instructed her to continue with the exercise to decrease the muscle fatigue she occasionally still experienced. Trinity's name flashed on her screen. Maybe her persistence was paying off. *Finally.* She hadn't been patient. She couldn't let Trinity walk out of her life without some form of reconciliation.

"Hi."

"Uh…hi. How are you?" The nervous breathiness in Trinity's voice traveled over the distance between them.

"I'm okay. Good, even."

"Oh." Disappointment laced that single word.

"I'm good because I'm talking to you." Blaze knew if she didn't confess now, she might never be able to. "But I'm not okay about how things are between us. And I miss you terribly."

Trinity's voice sounded small and vulnerable. "Really?"

"Yes, really." She put down the ball, wanting to concentrate on every word between them. She would have taken notes if she thought it necessary, but she hung on Trinity's every word whenever they talked so there wasn't any reason to think this time would be any different. "Can I see you?" Blaze wasn't about to let this opportunity slip by. Nothing would be resolved over the phone. She needed to see Trinity's reaction to what she had to say.

"Now?"

"Yes. Unless you're going to work, I won't take no for an answer." The silence on the other end tightened her chest with dread.

Maybe Trinity had already made up her mind and only called to say nothing would change it.

"Can I bring anything?"

"All I want is you."

She hung up and began to pace. The argument in her head—the one she'd practiced so many times and all the while thinking she might not ever get a chance to say—didn't carry as much weight as it had when she'd started formulating it. It wasn't about who was right or wrong. Being apart proved it didn't matter. She couldn't go back, and she was sure Trinity couldn't either. The most important thing in her world was having Trinity in it. She'd do whatever she had to, even if it meant giving up her dream of having children. What would holding on to a dream matter if the woman she wanted to share it with wasn't there?

It wasn't like her to be nervous. Normally, she remained calm in trying situations without displaying outward signs of distress. But right now, Blaze felt like a caged animal, ready to spring. For the last few weeks she'd tried to deny the truth, but there it was, staring her in the face when she glanced in the mirror. She was in love with Trinity.

Thirty minutes later, the doorbell rang, and she gave herself a last-minute pep talk. *I can do this.* Trinity wore dark skinny jeans with a grass green sweater beneath her jacket. The color accentuated her stormy eyes. Her smile was tentative, reassuring Blaze they were both apprehensive.

"Hi," she said. As much as her fingers tingled to touch Trinity, she held back, unsure where they stood on the intimacy scale.

"Hey you." Trinity looked around. "Can I come in?"

She'd been so lost in Trinity's beauty, her manners suffered. "Sorry. I was…" She shook her head and stepped aside. Maybe Trinity didn't want to hear about her infatuation.

Trinity held up a wax-coated bag. "I wasn't sure what the meal for midmorning should be, so I opted for donuts."

Blaze smiled. "There's never a bad time for donuts. I put on a fresh pot of coffee if you'd like some." She opened the fridge, more for something to do to calm her racing heart than to take inventory.

She always knew what was inside, just like she knew what was in her heart. "I've also got milk, juice, seltzer, and beer."

From her perch on a stool, Trinity grimaced. "Definitely not beer. Milk is good."

Including beer as an option was meant to lighten the tension that hung between them, but since that failed, she stood a short distance away, though it felt like miles were between them. "Do you want to sit in the nook?"

Trinity glanced over. "Uh, do you mind not? Our last conversation there didn't end so well and I'm hoping we don't repeat it."

Her brain wasn't functioning. She should have remembered. "I've got the perfect place. Grab your jacket." She placed their drinks on a tray, along with napkins and the donuts, then pulled on a heavy flannel shirt from the hook by the back door. "Follow me." The sun shone brightly and would provide warmth, just like Trinity's gaze always did. They walked along the stone path, taking the left fork. When she reached her destination, Blaze set the tray down and sat.

"This is beautiful." Trinity slid onto the facing seat before running her hand over the smooth surfaces.

The double Amish glider with a wooden roof had been one of the first projects she'd completed after the house. It was where she often came with a sketch pad to design furniture. "Thank you. It's one of my favorite pieces." She glanced at the small pond thirty feet from where they sat, and the variety of the tall autumn flowers she planted in the rock garden. There'd been a few nights of frost, and the blooms appeared frozen in time. "I come out here to work sometimes. No electronics."

Trinity sat back. For the first time since arriving, she looked relaxed, and Blaze knew she'd picked the right place for their talk.

"If I lived here, I'd spend hours out here, too." Trinity looked off in the distance, as though lost in the moment. Or maybe she was thinking country life wasn't so bad after all.

"You can come out here any time you want. There's solar path lights to lead the way when it's dark." She opened the pastry bag to look at the selection and chose a glazed donut. When she looked up, Trinity was staring. "What?"

"Are you serious?"

She looked back in the bag. "There's another glazed. You can have this one." Trinity's hand touched hers, sending a familiar shock of electricity up her arm.

"Not that. About offering your home to me?"

Blaze wanted to pull her close and kiss her. Instead she shrugged, as though the gesture she'd made was no big deal. "Yeah. It's a big place with lots of room. Plenty more than one person needs." There was a lump in her throat. Blaze had spent a lot of time thinking since Trinity left. She'd built the house and areas throughout the property for herself and a partner to enjoy. It wasn't being utilized in the way she'd originally imagined, and as hard as it was to admit, she was lonelier than she ever thought she'd be. Every day she grew a little more so.

"You built everything with a family of your own in mind, didn't you?"

Tears stung her eyes. She wanted a family that included Trinity, but she still wasn't sure they could mend broken fences. "It's been a dream for a while now, and the older I get, the more I realize how much. I even left a downstairs wall structurally ready for an addition. You know, in case there's a need for more bedrooms." She broke off a piece of the donut and chewed, but when she tried to swallow, it stuck in her throat. She gulped milk. *It's now or never.* "You had a dream, too, and it drove your actions. It's part of who you are, right?"

Trinity reached into the bag and pulled out a frosted donut. She took a healthy bite then dropped it onto her napkin, washing it down with milk. "I don't want you to misunderstand what drove me to work so hard."

"And to run so fast at the mention of family?" Blaze shared a crooked smile. They'd beaten around the bush long enough. She had to focus on why she'd asked Trinity to come here.

"About that…" Trinity's cheeks colored. "It wasn't the thought of having a family with you. It was knowing how terribly wrong a situation can turn when people aren't paying attention."

She understood the logic, though in their case she didn't think it applied. She leaned forward, wanting Trinity's full attention. "I can only assume that your parents didn't have the best start in life, and it manifested itself with children and a whole host of other complications. You and I, we have what it takes to make *us* work. I know in my heart we'd be good together." When Trinity didn't look away, she went on. "Yes, I want a family. I want to leave a legacy. I want children to pass my knowledge on to. Just like my father and his father before him. I know you'd be an outstanding mother because you understand what it's like *not* to feel loved and cared for. And I'd do my damnedest to be one, too." Blaze took her hand, feeling the tremor in it, and knowing this was their turning point. "But I'd give up the notion of children if it meant not being with you. All I'm asking is for you to give us a chance."

A torrent of shades of green reflected in Trinity's eyes. Blaze could see the fear in them and wished she could find the words to make her see there wasn't anything to be afraid of. Even if she was wrong, not knowing—not being sure—would be worse than not trying at all. At least for her.

"Kids are a big leap from being single. Are you ready for the whole parenting thing?" Trinity bit her lip. "What happens if it goes south?"

Always the optimist, she replied, "What if it goes north and just keeps climbing?"

A small grin pulled at Trinity's lips. "Are you always so self-assured?" She nibbled on the edge of her donut.

"No. Not always. But when it comes to matters of the heart…" She shrugged again. "I prefer to think positively."

Trinity's mouth dropped open for a moment before she snapped it shut. "Your heart?" she asked, her voice barely loud enough to be heard, but Blaze heard her.

"That's the only plausible explanation for thinking of you day and night." She brushed a wayward curl from Trinity's face. "I want to see you as often as possible. If you want to date for a while, I can do that, too. But there's no question in my mind I want you beside me for as long as you'll be there."

Trinity caught her hand, held it to her cheek, then closed her eyes and took a breath. "I'm scared. What if we fail?"

"Relationships don't fail. Sometimes people aren't as compatible as they thought, or they have different goals in life, but that doesn't mean it was a failure. It just means you haven't found the right person." The fact that Trinity seemed to consider her words was encouraging. *At least she isn't bolting like last time.*

"I don't know if I want children. It's a big responsibility."

"So is the job you have, and the people whose lives you're in charge of. You face more than your share of responsibility there, but you've got a whole team to help you, so you don't have to do it alone."

"We aren't going to have a whole team to help *us*."

"Yes, we will. I'll be your number one, and then there's Kelly, and DJ, and my family. Your family, too, if you want them around. And I'll bet between us, we have a lot of friends. We'd have a village." Blaze swallowed hard. "There's so much we could give our children."

Trinity groaned and rolled her eyes. "You keep saying children. *If* the time comes, can we settle on one? At least for a while?"

She nodded her agreement. "Absolutely. We'll start there." She grinned.

"If I say I want to give this whole relationship thing a try, we'll need to go slow. Okay? And if we manage to not make each other too crazy as a couple, we can revisit the idea of a family."

Her excitement grew with each passing moment. The hum that had started running through her brain traveled to her toes. "Sure, sure." She took Trinity's hand and kissed her knuckles. "I think you're amazing, and beautiful, and so many more things I don't have words for right now. But are you sure you want to be with me?" She was putting her heart in Trinity's hands, but she had to know.

Trinity closed her eyes. "When I lie in bed, all I can see is you. Your expressive eyes let me know exactly what you're feeling even when you don't say the words. When I'm at work and struggling through my day, I can feel you touch my cheek and tell me how capable I am. When I'm in the shower, I feel your arms around me and think of the way you touch me, the way you make me feel beautiful and wanted in a way I never have." She opened her eyes and smiled softly. "I'm haunted by your laugh, your smile, the strength of your hands, and the way you seem to live your life trusting the world without giving room to negative thoughts. I want more of you, and as terrifying as it is, I can't imagine my days without you."

Blaze's chest felt like it would explode, and she pulled Trinity to her for a slow, sweet kiss full of potential and promises. Reluctantly, Blaze let go without the dread Trinity wouldn't be in her arms again.

Trinity finished the last bite of her donut and licked her lips before using her tongue to clean her fingers. Erotic thoughts ran amok, and Trinity knew what she was thinking because her grin became a seductive smile as she leaned across the table. "So, when do we have our next date?"

Oh my God. This is happening. "Now. Or tonight. You tell me."

Glancing down at her clothes, Trinity chuckled. "I'm not dressed for a date, so it will have to be later. How does six sound?"

The feeling was like the first time she'd asked a girl out. Tingling sensations shot through her limbs as she anticipated what lay ahead. "Perfect."

After finishing off her milk, Trinity became somber. "There's one more thing we need to discuss. Where does DJ fit into the equation?"

Blaze knew this was coming and she'd been prepared for the inevitable. "We...DJ and I...had a serious conversation." She took a steadying breath. "You were right. DJ confessed she's in love with me."

"And?" Trinity looked troubled.

"I told her she would always be in my life and always be my best friend, but that I never have and never will love her in any other way. I made my point very clear, and I can assure you there won't be any future problems." Blaze was confident DJ realized the fantasy of getting together would never happen, and she agreed Blaze needed to focus on building her relationship with Trinity, finally telling her how happy she was that Blaze had found someone to love. Blaze would miss her.

"I'm sure you can imagine why I'm cautiously optimistic, but I'm glad you spoke with her." Trinity wiped her mouth and stood. "I've got some things I need to do. How should I dress for tonight?"

She would have liked to have said "Don't wear anything at all," but that was her libido talking again. Lucky for her she'd already thought about what they would do on a date, if the time ever came. This time her planning hadn't been in vain. "Something you can comfortably couple dance in, but we won't be going to the club." Trinity's eyebrows rose but Blaze wouldn't tell her anything more.

They walked to the house holding hands. The earlier tension had dissipated, replaced by anticipation. Blaze was ready for the next chapter. Ready to find out if her instincts and her heart were working in concert when it came to Trinity. How had she fallen so hard? How did she know Trinity was *the one*? Trinity leaned against her car and Blaze held her face in her hands, running her thumbs along her bottom lip.

Then she kissed her. Gently. Tenderly. The soft lips under hers opened to her and she slowly pressed her tongue inside, savoring the flavor of her. When Trinity's hands ran up her arms, gooseflesh pimpled her skin and she stifled the groan threatening to escape. She took a half step back.

"I'll pick you up at six." The last thing she did was let go, knowing she never wanted to let go again.

CHAPTER FORTY-THREE

Trinity sat at the end of Blaze's driveway, her fingertips playing over her lips. Blaze had said her heart was involved but hadn't said the word love, so she couldn't be sure what that meant. She looked in the rearview mirror once more at the home Blaze had built before checking to be sure the main road was clear, smiling as she drove down the mountain. The thought of going on a "date" with Blaze, even though they'd slept together several times, seemed a bit out of order. She was okay with it.

Blaze picking her up meant either she would drop Trinity home at the end of the night, or they'd head back to the mountain. *I should pack an overnight bag.* Trinity shook her head. That would be presumptuous on her part. She'd make do if that happened. She needed to stop assuming sleeping together was a given, although, since she agreed to give their relationship a go, it wasn't off the table either, was it? They were going dancing, something she was comfortable with, though it sounded like there'd be no bump and grind involved. *Oh, God. What if it's ballroom again? Or the jitterbug?* She wasn't very good at traditional dances, though she managed to stumble through at weddings. If she didn't stop fixating, she'd be a hot mess by the time Blaze arrived.

She flew through the door to find Kelly at the table, open containers of leftover Chinese spread across the surface.

"Hey. Where were you?" Kelly burped, then giggled. "Sorry."

Trinity snagged a fried dumpling before she headed to her bedroom, intent on finding the perfect outfit. "I went to see Blaze," she called over her shoulder. She heard Kelly say something unintelligible. At the far end of her closet hung her meager selection of dresses. The gown she'd worn for the gala was too fancy for a date. Besides, Blaze had already seen her in it. She pulled out a royal blue crepe with accordion pleats, held it up against her, and looked in the mirror.

Kelly sauntered in and plopped on the bed. "What are you doing?" she asked, watching her.

"I have a date." She returned the blue one and pulled out a red summer dress. It was way too light for the weather.

"With Blaze?" Kelly perked up. Trinity nodded. "Back up and tell me what happened."

Once she'd recounted the morning's events, she brought out the last of her choices. A simple black dress she wore to funerals, and a deep purple one, the cut of which made her feel frumpy—the last thing she wanted to feel tonight. She chewed her lip. "Great. Our first official date and I'm stuck wearing a funeral dress." She collapsed on the bed next to Kelly.

"Wait here," Kelly said. She disappeared down the hall.

Left with the feeling she needed to start paying more attention to her wardrobe, she shoved the closet door closed and tossed the dress over the armchair before throwing herself back on the bed to think about shoes. At least black went with everything, so she could manage a decent pair of heels. Kelly came back in carrying a garment bag and hung it on the hook of her closet door.

"What's that?"

"Something I bought and never wore. It's a little snug on me, but I think it will be perfect for you. Now close your eyes."

"Really? We're not in high school, you know."

Kelly's hands went to her hips. "Yes, really."

Trinity covered her eyes. She heard the zipper and then rustling of the bag before the room got quiet.

"Okay. You can look."

She stared at the mid-calf, satin dress of the most beautiful shade of copper she'd ever seen. "Oh, Kelley, it's beautiful." She got up, needing to find out if the material was as luxurious as it looked. She wasn't disappointed.

"Try it on."

"I can't wear your dress. The tags are still on it." She let her hand fall away as she considered if it would work. Even though it was sleeveless, the fabric was weighty, and with her black pashmina and winter dress coat, she'd be fine.

"Don't be ridiculous. I obviously have no place to wear it. Besides, I know it will look much better on you than me."

Kelly's breasts were larger than hers, and the dress's halter top neckline with a deep plunge made her swallow her original excitement, but she had to try it on. "If you're sure you don't mind." Kelly motioned for her to continue. She pulled off her clothes and slipped the dress over her head. It glided over her body with ease. She turned to the mirror and smiled. The bra she was wearing would have to go. She was glad she'd bought a roll of wardrobe tape a while ago.

"I don't know." The thought of going out in public braless, again, let alone with Blaze, made her heart beat a little faster.

"Turn around. You need the full effect without a bra."

Trinity spun and Kelly unhooked her bra so she could pull it free. When she looked at her reflection she gasped. "I don't know if I can go out like this. It's even more revealing than the gown." A hint of the outer edge of her breasts peeked out of the material, and for once she was glad she was small enough to pull off a daring outfit, but she still wasn't sure if she wanted the whole world to see her side-boobs.

"Don't talk crazy. You look beautiful and sexy as hell," Kelly said.

"I'm afraid when I dance there'll be a wardrobe malfunction. I'd die of embarrassment." Kelly huffed then took her hand and led her to the living room.

"Alexa, play slow dance music." "Unchained Melody" began to play, and Kelly took the lead position. "I'm not as tall as Blaze, but we'll manage."

After a few steps, she remembered the way Blaze had slow danced and adjusted Kelly's hold to mirror Blaze's. When the song ended, she felt more confident she'd manage to stay covered, but that was one slow dance. "What if we do ballroom? Or salsa?"

"God, you're frustrating." Kelly smiled, letting her know she was poking fun.

A half hour later and after they'd tried songs of every imaginable genre for partner dancing, Kelly handed her a bottle of water and laughed.

"Are you convinced now?"

She took a long drink as she worked on getting her breath back. The salsa had been fast, and they'd worked up a little sweat. "Yes, but just to be sure, I'm going to wear wardrobe tape." She collapsed in a heap on the couch before remembering she was wearing tonight's dress. Trinity popped up and went to her bedroom to hang it up, then pulled on clothes.

"What are you going to do for the next two hours while you obsess over every detail for your date?" Kelly grinned.

"Smart-ass. I'm not going to obsess. All I have to do is shower, figure out my hair, and put on makeup." She thought about her long curls, wondering if her hair should be up, down, or braided. With no time to make an appointment with her stylist, she'd have to wear it down, but she didn't think Blaze would mind. And she'd keep her makeup simple. A little liner and mascara, lip gloss, and perfume. The clock on the mantle ticked at her. *I need to get moving.* Her stomach rumbled. She hadn't had anything since the donut. Blaze hadn't mentioned food, but since she loved to eat, it was a given.

"I'm going to grab a yogurt. Want anything?"

"I'm good. Aren't you going to have dinner?" Kelly asked as she curled up in the corner of the couch and faced her.

"I think so, but just in case." She shoved a spoonful in her mouth. It wasn't long before it was gone. "Okay. Off to get beautiful."

"You're already beautiful, but if I know you, you're going to need every second to get ready. I'll stall her if she shows up early."

"Thanks." She leaned over and hugged her. "This is why I love you." She meant it. Kelly was good for her soul *and* her ego. She hoped Blaze could give her the kind of supportive caring partners provided, but her biggest fear was that she wouldn't be able to do the same in return.

CHAPTER FORTY-FOUR

B laze smoothed her hands over her trousers, straightened her tie for the dozenth time, then rang the bell. Her afternoon had been filled with emotional ups and downs. The more she thought about the future, the more anxious she became. Those moments had been interspersed with visions of Trinity sitting across from her, her green eyes sometimes stormy, then becoming soft, sensual.

The door swung open and Kelly smiled at her.

"Hi, Blaze. Come in."

She cleared her throat as the nerves returned. "Kelly, it's nice to see you again." Her usual confidence had disappeared, and she found herself shifting her weight from one foot to the other.

"Why don't I get you something to drink? Trin could be a while yet."

Kelly headed toward the kitchen and she followed, grateful for something to do while she waited.

"What can I get you?"

"Water?"

"Huh. I would have pictured you as more of a beer woman." Kelly set a bottle of water on the counter.

Blaze relaxed a little. Kelly was easy to talk with. "Actually," she said. "I'm a scotch drinker, but since I'm driving, I'll start with this."

"You do that a lot. Drive I mean."

"I want Trinity to be safe when she's with me."

Settling across from her, Kelly rested her chin on her fists. "Me, too." She watched Blaze for a long beat. "So, what are you doing on your big date?" Her eyes held mischief.

"Dinner and dancing." She'd made reservations at her favorite midtown lounge. At eight o'clock, a local band would begin playing, and she and Trinity would have a chance to slow dance for as long as they liked. Thoughts of holding her close, feeling Trinity's body against hers, warmed her all the way to her toes.

"Sounds romantic."

"I hope so. Trinity deserves to be treated well." Blaze held Kelly's gaze.

"Yes, she does, and I'm glad you have respect for her, because if not, you and I would be having a different conversation," Kelly said. "Look who's finally decided to join us."

Blaze stood to face Trinity, and the sight of her once again took her breath away. "My God, you're stunning." She closed the distance between them, lifted Trinity's hand and pressed it to her lips as she brushed her other hand along Trinity's cheek. Trinity's cheeks turned a lovely shade of pink, and Blaze's heart twisted with the intensity of her beauty.

"I hope the dress is okay." Trinity looked up from beneath her thick lashes.

It took her a minute to find her voice, but she managed to sound more in control than she felt. "It's more than okay because you're wearing it." She meant every word. Trinity could be wearing rags, and no one would notice because her beauty commanded attention. But the just visible soft curve of her breasts took what little saliva Blaze had from her mouth. She couldn't help wondering if her own attire could hold up against Trinity's. She'd chosen a charcoal gray tailored shirt, black pleated dress pants, and black wing tipped shoes. As luck would have it, her paisley tie was vivid, with a copper, white, and black pattern. She'd left her jacket in the car. It would have to do. "We should go. We have a reservation."

"I'm ready."

Blaze faced Kelly. "I'll take good care of her."

Once they were in the car and on the road, Blaze stole another glance. Trinity seemed nervous. The radio played softly from the rear speaker, but the silence was deafening. "I hope you like French cuisine." She'd managed to get the perfect table at Chez Michele. It was a little-known place, tucked into a hillside cove with a view of Glen Lake. She'd stumbled upon it a long time ago when she was exploring the area.

"I've never been to a real French restaurant before, but I'm sure I'll like it." Trinity shared a tentative smile. "Tonight's more about the company."

Blaze took Trinity's hand in her larger one. "Are you all right? You seem anxious."

"No, it's just..." Trinity looked out the window. "I haven't dated anyone in a long time. I'm not sure I remember what it feels like."

She could sympathize. Of the women she'd been with over the last few years, she hadn't been serious about any of them, even though a few would have liked to pursue something deeper with her. She just hadn't been interested. Or maybe she hadn't found the right one to be interested in. "Well, that makes two of us, so we should be fine."

Trinity shook her head. "I find that hard to believe. Whenever I've seen you at the club, it didn't appear you were lonely."

Internally, she sighed. She didn't want to carry around the playgirl label anymore. "They were...acquaintances. Not dates."

"You mean hookups?"

Her jaw tightened. The last thing she wanted was for Trinity to think she was a player. She'd never taken advantage and always made her intentions clear. Trinity was far above a one-night stand. Then she caught the twinkle in Trinity's eye and relaxed.

Trinity laughed softly. "I've done much the same the last few years. I didn't want to become involved and complicate my already hectic life."

Blaze wanted to comment. Wanted to ask what had changed. Maybe nothing had, and Trinity was making an exception. She turned into the lot filled with a variety of vehicles and pulled up in front of the door. "I'll let you off here, so you don't have to walk over the gravel."

"It's fine. I don't mind walking as long as you hold me up."

She had the feeling Trinity was asking for more than physical support. "I'd never let you fall." Luckily, she found a spot not too far away. She opened Trinity's door and held out her hand until they were standing toe-to-toe with a sunset streaked sky above them. There were so many words she wanted to say, but they died on her tongue. Blaze was afraid she'd ruin the night before it began. She wrapped her arm around Trinity's waist and sensory memories flooded in. The firmness of her flesh. The scent of her skin. The softness of her breasts. She longed to hold her closer. Skin on skin. Trinity's voice startled her.

"Where did you go?"

They were standing at the entrance. She didn't remember walking. She needed to pay attention. Tonight was the first of what she hoped would be many dates. Even if they moved in together, she had every intention of treating Trinity as though every day was a first date. She opened the door and ushered her inside, her hand resting at the small of her back, her fingertips electrified even with Trinity's coat between them. The host knew her by name since she'd crafted most of their tables when they'd remodeled several years ago. After holding the chair for Trinity, she unbuttoned her jacket and sat across from her, watching her take in the decor. Large picture windows framed the lake in front of them.

"This place is beautiful. How did you find it?"

She ordered a bottle of wine, with Trinity's approval, and told her the story. Trinity listened with rapt attention, her eyes sparkling in the candlelight. *God, she's so beautiful.* Her heart pounded in her chest.

"It's really a shame." Trinity sipped from her glass, her lips twitching as though she were trying to keep a grin from forming.

"What is?" Blaze was almost afraid to ask. Afraid Trinity was having second thoughts about dating.

"The restaurant is nice, but you're much more appealing to look at." Trinity's eyebrow rose as she smiled seductively.

Blaze had never been comfortable with compliments directed at her rather than her work, and she tried to hide her embarrassment behind her goblet. "Maybe you need glasses." She drank deeply before putting on the brakes. She couldn't let her nerves make her do something as reckless as drink too much.

Trinity waved her hand in the air. "Oh, come on. We both know you dressed like that to get my attention, and you have."

"I could say the same for you." She let her gaze slide from Trinity's eyes, to her lips before continuing down the column of her neck to the daring opening of her dress. She wondered how she was keeping the material in place.

"I shouldn't have worn it. Kelly talked me into it," Trinity said. She began to tug at the material.

She reached to stop her. "Don't. It's perfect. Like you."

Trinity huffed. "I hate to disappoint you, but I'm nowhere near perfect."

"To me you are," she said, as she watched the fast rise and fall of Trinity's chest.

Trinity sat back. "Stop. Please. I…" She looked off, as though to gather her thoughts. "I don't know how to be when you look at me like that." She finished her wine in one gulp.

Blaze held up the bottle.

"Yes, a little."

The last thing she wanted was to make Trinity uncomfortable. She nodded to the waiter and he brought menus. "Let's order, I'm hungry." She was hungry for more than food, but she wasn't sure where the night would lead. Food would help her find her balance and tamp down her craving for Trinity. For now.

Chapter Forty-five

L aughter filled the air around them as Trinity got out of the car. So far, she'd had a magnificent time, and she wasn't ready for it to end. Blaze made sure their dinner included a variety of dishes and they shared everything. She'd had a bit more wine than she might otherwise because Blaze had refrained most of the night, telling her it was because she was a responsible driver, and Trinity respected her even more. While she finished her wine, Blaze had coffee, and a live band began to play. True to her promise of dancing, she'd been swept off her feet by the debonair Blaze Carter, who led her through a variety of slow dances and intricate moves.

She unlocked the door and held it open until Blaze stepped inside. "Do you want something to drink? A nightcap or more wine?"

Blaze shook her head. "I still have to drive home."

Trinity tossed her coat and slipped out of her shoes before placing her hand on Blaze's chest. She could feel the pounding of her heart. Heat emanated through her clothes, and Trinity wondered how she could be so warm and not sweat. She focused on Blaze. "I was hoping you'd spend the night."

"I'd love to, but do you want to sleep with me on our first real date?" Blaze brushed the back of her hand along the side of Trinity's face, and she caught it and brought it to her lips.

"I'm not usually that kind of girl, but tonight I'll make an exception." Her heart was already beating faster, and hot blood coursed through her. Her cautious side, the one that had ruled her actions for so long, had gone swimming in the wine.

"What about Kelly?"

She took a step back to calm down. Her heart was going to beat out of her chest if she didn't. "Working the night shift. She won't be home until morning." For once she was grateful to have the apartment to herself. Trinity never liked being alone, and she hoped she wouldn't be tonight.

"In that case…" Blaze backed her up against the wall and took possession of her mouth. Hungry. Insistent.

She arched into the kiss, desperate and yearning for more. She wanted Blaze to take her. To possess her. To let her know how much she was desired. Unable to breathe, she turned her face and Blaze's forehead leaned on hers.

"I want you so much I can already taste you." Blaze's hand cupped her breast and squeezed. "This dress…" Blaze said before snaking her thigh between Trinity's, "has taunted me all night."

Trinity moaned at the pressure against her sex and trembled. Desire made her limbs heavy, emboldening her. "Take me. Take me the way you want to."

Blaze growled and picked her up, carrying her to the living room where she bent her over the back of the couch. Teeth grazed along the back of her neck, nipping at the flesh and making her wetter than the last time they'd been together. Blaze lifted the hem of her dress and squeezed the cheeks of her ass.

"I'm going to fuck you," Blaze whispered in her ear as she yanked her panties down. She pushed her fingers inside and groaned. "You're so wet for me I wish I had my cock."

Trinity gasped at the picture that formed in her mind. It didn't take long for her body to speed toward an orgasm while Blaze firmly stroked in and out, hard and steady. Blaze continued whispering all the things she wanted to do to her while kissing her neck. When she moved her attention to Trinity's swollen clitoris and began alternately rubbing and squeezing, she stopped breathing. Convulsions of her climax sent lightning bolts through her. She collapsed against the couch, boneless.

Blaze turned her over, covering her face with kisses before finding her lips. Softly tracing her mouth with her tongue then sliding inside, and for the first time in her life, Trinity felt loved. Blaze's eyes swirled with more than desire alone.

"Where's your bedroom?" Blaze asked.

Still unable to find her voice, she pointed toward the hall. Blaze picked her up and carried her and she was grateful, unsure if she could have stood on her own. "Here," she managed when they got to her door. Blaze set her on the bed and helped her out of her dress. Some of her strength had returned and she leaned back on her hands, watching as Blaze undressed slowly. Trinity took time to appreciate the finely sculpted muscles and some of the details she'd missed before. Blaze's mound was trimmed close, and her light brown curls glistened. She scooted back until her head was on the pillows, and Blaze lay over her, supporting her weight on her forearms.

"Are you okay?"

She nodded, and Blaze kissed her gently.

"I'm not sorry for taking you so fast, but I want to make love to you. Take my time. Is that all right?"

"Yes. As long as I get to do the same for you."

A smile played on Blaze's lips. "Thank God, because I'm really wet and wanting."

She pressed her thigh between Blaze's. "I can tell."

Blaze kissed her again. Hungry, but controlled. The intensity built between them, making her whimper. Blaze lightly tugged on her lower lip with her teeth before moving off to the side, her hand fondling her breasts, tugging at her nipples. They tightened under her ministrations and she begged for more. After what seemed like an eternity, Blaze's mouth found her swollen, hot flesh. She licked and stroked and kissed her until she was shivering beneath her, then lapped up her juices until she had nothing more to give. Blaze climbed up beside her and kissed her, then rolled them over and pulled her close.

She laid her head on Blaze's chest, enjoying the closeness and luxuriating in the feeling of being cared for. Blaze spoke above her.

"Was that okay?" Blaze asked. Her hands smoothed over her back.

Trinity managed to raise her head. "More than okay. I'm…" She hesitated. What was she trying to say? She knew but was afraid. Afraid of the idea she'd be rejected if she confessed what she was really feeling. She moved her mouth to search out Blaze's, teased her lips and slipped her tongue inside to explore her. She rubbed her palm over Blaze's breast and the nipple tightened, the flesh pebbling beneath her hand. As much as she wanted to taste her, Trinity needed to be inside, and she ran her fingers through her wet heat, making her groan.

"Honey, I'm not going to last if you touch me," Blaze said, her voice strained.

"Yes, I know." Trinity slowly circled Blaze's rock-hard clit before pressing inside and Blaze's hips rose to meet her. She continued the torturous pace until Blaze tightened around her and she stopped moving. "Open your eyes, baby. I want to see you come." Blaze shuddered beneath her and Trinity knew she was barely hanging on, but her eyes opened, letting her see the storm raging there. She entered her hard and her thumb pressed against Blaze's clit. With a side to side motion, she flicked over it and her walls locked her inside. A low groan emanated from Blaze as her climax took over and she watched her eyes contract with the intensity. Blaze bucked beneath her and she wrapped her arm around her back, hanging on as she rode out the waves. Trinity saw everything she needed in that moment. Blaze was so trusting. So willing to show her vulnerability. She wanted to cry for ever doubting her.

When her body settled, Blaze pulled her down for a kiss, and she felt the shift between them. They moved onto their sides and stared into each other's eyes. Blaze held her face.

"I want you in my life, Trinity. We can have it all."

She wanted to believe her. Knew Blaze meant it, yet doubt crept in. "How can you be so sure?"

"Because I love you. I love you so damn much it hurts in a most exquisite way."

Her doubts faded away as she realized the thing that had scared her the most since meeting Blaze was the fear of never loving enough. Never giving enough in return. One look into Blaze's soul, into the depths of her eyes, reassured her she had nothing to be afraid of. Together they would face the future, and for once the future didn't scare her.

"I love you, Blaze Carter."

Blaze kissed her with all the passion she could have hoped for. The years ahead of them were looking bright. Blaze made love to her again while whispering words of adoration and love. She fell asleep with her head on Blaze's chest, her steady heartbeat reassuring her that their love was a bond that would endure whatever was to come.

EPILOGUE

A little more than two years later...

"Hey, babe, will you heat up a bottle?" Trinity called out the door. "I knew it was coming, so I'm already on it." Blaze ducked her head in the doorway, smiling like the happy mother she was. "You two okay?"

Her heart tightened a little, overflowing with the love Blaze showed her every hour of every day, just like she'd promised during their wedding vows more than a year ago. "We're perfect," she said. Blaze swaggered into the room, making Trinity smile more. If she thought Blaze strutted before, since the baby's arrival she'd turned into a peacock—all her feathers on display.

"You most certainly are." Blaze kissed her, then looked at their son. "As for this little guy..." Blaze rubbed Elijah's head. "It remains to be seen."

Trinity was taken aback. "What? What do you mean?"

"We'll have to see how he handles his first chisel."

Trinity laughed. That was how their life had been. Encouraging each other; reassuring each other that no matter what happened, they'd handle it together. The doorbell rang and she smiled again. She finished dressing the baby and picked him up.

"Hey..." DJ said. "Is it okay if I hang out with you guys for a little while?"

"Of course, it is. He was just going to have a bottle. Want to feed him?"

DJ's eyes lit up as she took the baby from her. "Seriously?" Trinity nodded. "So cool." She left the room talking baby talk.

She and DJ had made amends not long after Blaze announced their engagement. Trinity understood DJ would always be a part of Blaze's life and she wanted Blaze and DJ to remain solid in their friendship. So, when Blaze asked her permission to name DJ as a guardian, she'd agreed. DJ loved Blaze, and any person who loved Blaze would do everything in their power to do the best for Blaze's child. Trinity could live with that. She leaned against the archway watching Blaze and DJ with Elijah.

Blaze gave DJ instructions. "Keep him upright so he doesn't choke, and always test the temperature no matter what."

Her face was so serious, Trinity covered her mouth to stifle a giggle.

DJ rolled her eyes. "You do know I've done this like a million times with my nieces and nephews, right?"

"Yeah, but they weren't my son." Blaze glanced up. "Our son."

"All the more reason to trust me. Isn't that the reason Kelly and I are his guardians?"

Blaze stood though Trinity could tell she was hesitant. "Fine. Pay attention to what you're doing." DJ ignored her and offered the bottle to the baby. Blaze just shook her head and stood by her side.

"I'm going to have to keep my eye on those two."

Trinity placed her hand on her chest. "I had no idea life could be like this."

Blaze snaked her fingers in her hair and pulled her closer. "I love you."

Trinity didn't need convincing. Blaze often showed her how much by the things she did, like encouraging her to include her family in their lives. The only one she wanted was her younger sister, Jane, who lived close by and loved spending time with the three of them.

After a couple of minutes of staring into Blaze's beautiful eyes, she smiled again. She did that a lot. "I love you, too, Blaze. Even when I don't tell you, I love you."

It was here, with Blaze, that she'd found her future and it no longer frightened her. Blaze would never let her feel she had to do anything on her own again, and she looked forward to the years ahead, knowing Blaze would always be at her side, cheering her on.

About the Author

Renee Roman has lived in upstate New York her entire life and can't imagine living anywhere there isn't a change of seasons. She works at a local college and writes lesbian romance, intrigue, and erotica in her spare time.

Her first novel, *Epicurean Delights*, was followed by a second, *Stroke of Fate*. During a small break in writing and edits, she tried her hand at an erotic short, "Hard Body," before continuing on to her third novel, *Where the Lies Hide*.

You can follow Renee on Facebook, Twitter, and at www.reneeromanwrites.com, and she enjoys interacting with readers and fellow authors via email at reneeromanwrites@gmail.com

Books Available from Bold Strokes Books

All the Paths to You by Morgan Lee Miller. High school sweethearts Quinn Hughes and Kennedy Reed reconnect five years after they break up and realize that their chemistry is all but over. (978-1-63555-662-9)

Arrested Pleasures by Nanisi Barrett D'Arnuck. When charged with a crime she didn't commit Katherine Lowe faces the question: Which is harder, going to prison or falling in love? (978-1-63555-684-1)

Bonded Love by Renee Roman. Carpenter Blaze Carter suffers an injury that shatters her dreams, and ER nurse Trinity Greene hopes to show her that sometimes hope is worth fighting for. (978-1-63555-530-1)

Convergence by Jane C. Esther. With life as they know it on the line, can Aerin McLeary and Olivia Ando's love survive an otherworldly threat to humankind? (978-1-63555-488-5)

Coyote Blues by Karen F. Williams. Riley Dawson, psychotherapist and shape-shifter, has her world turned upside down when Fiona Bell, her one true love, returns. (978-1-63555-558-5)

Drawn by Carsen Taite. Will the clues lead Detective Claire Hanlon to the killer terrorizing Dallas, or will she merely lose her heart to person of interest, urban artist Riley Flynn? (978-1-63555-644-5)

Every Summer Day by Lee Patton. Meant to celebrate every summer day, Luke's journal instead chronicles a love affair as fast-moving and possibly as fatal as his brother's brain tumor. (978-1-63555-706-0)

Lucky by Kris Bryant. Was Serena Evans's luck really about winning the lottery, or is she about to get even luckier in love? (978-1-63555-510-3)

The Last Days of Autumn by Donna K. Ford. Autumn and Caroline question the fairness of life, the cruelty of loss, and what it means to love as they navigate the complicated minefield of relationships, grief, and life-altering illness. (978-1-63555-672-8)

Three Alarm Response by Erin Dutton. In the midst of tragedy, can these first responders find love and healing? Three stories of courage, bravery, and passion. (978-1-63555-592-9)

Veterinary Partner by Nancy Wheelton. Callie and Lauren are determined to keep their hearts safe but find that taking a chance on love is the safest option of all. (978-1-63555-666-7)

Everyday People by Louis Barr. When film star Diana Danning hires private eye Clint Steele to find her son, Clint turns to his former West Point barracks mate, and ex-buddy with benefits, Mars Hauser to lend his cyber espionage and digital black ops skills to the case. (978-1-63555-698-8)

Forging a Desire Line by Mary P. Burns. When Charley's ex-wife, Tricia, is diagnosed with inoperable cancer, the private duty nurse Tricia hires turns out to be the handsome and aloof Joanna, who ignites something inside Charley she isn't ready to face. (978-1-63555-665-0)

Love on the Night Shift by Radclyffe. Between ruling the night shift in the ER at the Rivers and raising her teenage daughter, Blaise Richilieu has all the drama she needs in her life, until a dashing young attending appears on the scene and relentlessly pursues her. (978-1-63555-668-1)

Olivia's Awakening by Ronica Black. When the daring and dangerously gorgeous Eve Monroe is hired to get Olivia Savage into shape, a fierce passion ignites, causing both to question everything they've ever known about love. (978-1-63555-613-1)

The Duchess and the Dreamer by Jenny Frame. Clementine Fitzroy has lost her faith and love of life. Can dreamer Evan Fox make her believe in life and dream again? (978-1-63555-601-8)

The Road Home by Erin Zak. Hollywood actress Gwendolyn Carter is about to discover that losing someone you love sometimes means gaining someone to fall for. (978-1-63555-633-9)

Waiting for You by Elle Spencer. When passionate past-life lovers meet again in the present day, one remembers it vividly and the other isn't so sure. (978-1-63555-635-3)

While My Heart Beats by Erin McKenzie. Can a love born amidst the horrors of the Great War survive? (978-1-63555-589-9)

Face the Music by Ali Vali. Sweet music is the last thing that happens when Nashville music producer Mason Liner, and daughter of country royalty Victoria Roddy are thrown together in an effort to save country star Sophie Roddy's career. (978-1-63555-532-5)

Flavor of the Month by Georgia Beers. What happens when baker Charlie and chef Emma realize their differing paths have led them right back to each other? (978-1-63555-616-2)

Mending Fences by Angie Williams. Rancher Bobbie Del Rey and veterinarian Grace Hammond are about to discover if heartbreaks of the past can ever truly be mended. (978-1-63555-708-4)

Silk and Leather: Lesbian Erotica with an Edge edited by Victoria Villasenor. This collection of stories by award winning authors offers fantasies as soft as silk and tough as leather. The only question is: How far will you go to make your deepest desires come true? (978-1-63555-587-5)

The Last Place You Look by Aurora Rey. Dumped by her wife and looking for anything but love, Julia Pierce retreats to her hometown, only to rediscover high school friend Taylor Winslow, who's secretly crushed on her for years. (978-1-63555-574-5)

The Mortician's Daughter by Nan Higgins. A singer on the verge of stardom discovers she must give up her dreams to live a life in service to ghosts. (978-1-63555-594-3)

The Real Thing by Laney Webber. When passion flares between actress Virginia Green and masseuse Allison McDonald, can they be sure it's the real thing? (978-1-63555-478-6)

What the Heart Remembers Most by M. Ullrich. For college sweethearts Jax Levine and Gretchen Mills, could an accident be the second chance neither knew they wanted? (978-1-63555-401-4)

White Horse Point by Andrews & Austin. Mystery writer Taylor James finds herself falling for the mysterious woman on White Horse Point who lives alone, protecting a secret she can't share about a murderer who walks among them. (978-1-63555-695-7)

Femme Tales by Anne Shade. Six women find themselves in their own real-life fairy tales when true love finds them in the most unexpected ways. (978-1-63555-657-5)

Jellicle Girl by Stevie Mikayne. One dark summer night, Beth and Jackie go out to the canoe dock. Two years later, Beth is still carrying the weight of what happened to Jackie. (978-1-63555-691-9)

Le Berceau by Julius Eks. If only Ben could tear his heart in two, then he wouldn't have to choose between the love of his life and the most beautiful boy he has ever seen. (978-1-63555-688-9)

My Date with a Wendigo by Genevieve McCluer. Elizabeth Rosseau finds her long lost love and the secret community of fiends she's now a part of. (978-1-63555-679-7)

On the Run by Charlotte Greene. Even when they're cute blondes, it's stupid to pick up hitchhikers, especially when they've just broken out of prison, but doing so is about to change Gwen's life forever. (978-1-63555-682-7)

Perfect Timing by Dena Blake. The choice between love and family has never been so difficult, and Lynn's and Maggie's different visions of the future may end their romance before it's begun. (978-1-63555-466-3)

The Mail Order Bride by R Kent. When a mail order bride is thrust on Austin, he must choose between the bride he never wanted or the dream he lives for. (978-1-63555-678-0)

Through Love's Eyes by C.A. Popovich. When fate reunites Brittany Yardin and Amy Jansons, can they move beyond the pain of their past to find love? (978-1-63555-629-2)

To the Moon and Back by Melissa Brayden. Film actress Carly Daniel thinks that stage work is boring and unexciting, but when she accepts a lead role in a new play, stage manager Lauren Prescott tests both her heart and her ability to share the limelight. (978-1-63555-618-6)

Tokyo Love by Diana Jean. When Kathleen Schmitt is given the opportunity to be on the cutting edge of AI technology, she never thought a failed robotic love companion would bring her closer to her neighbor, Yuriko Velucci, and finding love in unexpected places. (978-1-63555-681-0)

Brooklyn Summer by Maggie Cummings. When opposites attract, can a summer of passion and adventure lead to a lifetime of love? (978-1-63555-578-3)

City Kitty and Country Mouse by Alyssa Linn Palmer. Pulled in two different directions, can a city kitty and country mouse fall in love and make it work? (978-1-63555-553-0)

Elimination by Jackie D. When a dangerous homegrown terrorist seeks refuge with the Russian mafia, the team will be put to the ultimate test. (978-1-63555-570-7)

In the Shadow of Darkness by Nicole Stiling. Angeline Vallencourt is a reluctant vampire who must decide what she wants more—obscurity, revenge, or the woman who makes her feel alive. (978-1-63555-624-7)

On Second Thought by C. Spencer. Madisen is falling hard for Rae. Even single life and co-parenting are beginning to click. At least, that is, until her ex-wife begins to have second thoughts. (978-1-63555-415-1)

Out of Practice by Carsen Taite. When attorney Abby Keane discovers the wedding blogger tormenting her client is the woman she had a passionate, anonymous vacation fling with, sparks and subpoenas fly. Legal Affairs: one law firm, three best friends, three chances to fall in love. (978-1-63555-359-8)

Providence by Leigh Hays. With every click of the shutter, photographer Rebekiah Kearns finds it harder and harder to keep Lindsey Blackwell in focus without getting too close. (978-1-63555-620-9)

Taking a Shot at Love by KC Richardson. When academic and athletic worlds collide, will English professor Celeste Bouchard and basketball coach Lisa Tobias ignore their attraction to achieve their professional goals? (978-1-63555-549-3)